THE DREAM BUILDERS

AF730110

Celebrating
30 Years of Publishing
in India

Praise for *The Dream Builders*

"Oindrila Mukherjee's *The Dream Builders* is such an impressive feat of storytelling, a novel that examines the constraints of class, of gender, of history, while showcasing the sheer expansiveness of the endeavor, skillfully shifting the point of view amongst a group of characters who each demand a claim on the story. It's a marvel of a structure, built by a great talent."

—Kevin Wilson, bestselling author of *Nothing to See Here*

"*The Dream Builders* is a novel of epic proportions that follows Maneka Roy and those around her as they each ponder the power of forgiveness and learn none of them can wield that power without first forgiving the self. Oindrila Mukherjee allows full life for these characters who are often real enough to remind us of ourselves, even as they betray one another . . . even as they betray themselves. This is a lovely debut."

—Jericho Brown, Pulitzer Prize-winning author of *The Tradition*

"Mukherjee has written a funny, moving, and often deliciously cynical novel about the illusive ideal we sometimes call the New India. Written from almost every angle imaginable, the novel demonstrates how each of us might be a hero in our own narratives while being the potential villain in someone else's."

—Tiphanie Yanique, author of *Monster in the Middle*

"A multitude of voices and visions—arresting, wrenching, desiring—come together to create an astonishing, and astonishingly accurate, portrait of contemporary India. Oindrila Mukherjee has done a superb job."

—Chitra Banerjee Divakaruni, bestselling author of *The Mistress of Spices*

"*The Dream Builders* showcases a vibrant cast of characters whose complex lives are a testament to India's astonishing diversity. Oindrila Mukherjee has written a soulful novel that'll break your heart with its truth."

—Samrat Upadhyay, author of *Mad Country*

THE DREAM BUILDERS

A NOVEL

OINDRILA MUKHERJEE

HarperCollins *Publishers* India

First published in India by HarperCollins *Publishers* 2023
4th Floor, Tower A, Building No 10, DLF Cyber City,
DLF Phase II, Gurugram, Haryana – 122002
www.harpercollins.co.in

2 4 6 8 10 9 7 5 3 1

Copyright © Oindrila Mukherjee 2023

PISBN: 978-93-5699-291-7
EISBN: 978-93-5699-299-3

This is a work of fiction. All of the characters, organizations, and events portrayed in this novel are either products of the author's imagination or are used fictitiously.

Oindrila Mukherjee asserts the moral right
to be identified as the author of this work.

All rights reserved. No part of this publication may be reproduced, stored in a retrieval system, or transmitted, in any form or by any means, electronic, mechanical, photocopying, recording or otherwise, without the prior permission of the publishers.

Typeset in 11.5/15.2 Minion Pro at
Manipal Technologies Limited, Manipal

Printed and bound at
Manipal Technologies Limited, Manipal

MIX
Paper from
responsible sources
FSC® C043100

This book is produced from independently certified FSC® paper to ensure responsible forest management.

for my parents

Safe upon the solid rock the ugly houses stand:
Come and see my shining palace built upon the sand!

—"Second Fig", Edna St. Vincent Millay,
A Few Figs from Thistles

SUMMER 2018

From the sky, the buildings of Hrishipur look smaller and smaller, shrinking into shadows of themselves. Some corners of the city flicker with lights like stars fallen from heaven. Others lie in darkness, pools of quiet amid the surrounding noise. From up here, the city is a stranger, remote and foreign, not unlike herself a few months ago. The distinct shapes of the many lives and stories that coexist there have already begun to coalesce into a dream with blurred edges. The aircraft ascends gradually until clouds sweep beneath it in a dramatic fashion to obscure the view of the people she grew to love. What remains is the memory of a burning-hot summer, in a land that will always be hers, no matter how time transforms it, no matter how far she wanders. There will always be the possibility of return.

MANEKA

THE INVITATION ARRIVED IN HER INBOX JUST HOURS AFTER HER own arrival in Hrishipur. She was lying in bed, bruised from the long flight and slightly stunned by this return to a country she no longer recognized, a home without her mother, and the prospect of an endless summer, when the cell phone next to her lit up with the new text. As soon as she glanced at it and saw who it was from, Maneka knew she would accept. She would appear at this party, even if her reasons were all wrong.

She clutched the phone in a tight grip, afraid that if she let go the text might disappear like many other things in her life. The glow of the screen was the only glimmer of light at the end of the long, dark tunnel she had inhabited these past few months. The damp and trembling cloud she had been living inside had solidified only a few hours ago, with the proverbial return of the expatriate, the return they had always warned her would be the hardest.

The moment of landing at Indira Gandhi International Airport earlier that night had been one of confusion, when she couldn't quite tell if she was departing or arriving. This airport was nothing like the small, sedate one in Kolkata that she had used in the past. Inside the lounge, a bewildered Maneka had stared up at the wall where gleaming bronze hands twisted in various mudras of classical dance to welcome visitors to a land of ancient traditions. But just beyond the lobby, the luxurious duty-free shop made her feel like she was in an airport in another country, somewhere in the Western world, somewhere she was just passing through.

She had lingered for a while among the bottles of Scotch and cartons of expensive cigarettes before forcing herself to walk to the entrance and confront the sight of her father standing alone. His solitary figure looked unmoored without her mother's next to it. His hair had turned completely white since she had last seen him six years ago and he had acquired rolls of fat everywhere—under his chin, around his waist, over his previously slim shoulders. Her once handsome, athletic father looked old, almost as if he were someone else's father. Her throat had ached as she tried to smile for him. Six years was a long time to stay away from your country. Long enough to lose one parent and become a stranger to the other.

The familiar and unfamiliar had blended together as Maneka stepped out of the airport into the blast of dry, scalding air. What she had known all her life growing up was that heat, those chattering crowds, the cacophony of car horns, the sea of brown faces, the aunties in their salwar kameezes, and the scent of Old Spice on her father's body next to her. And then there was everything that had changed since the last time, since her parents had uprooted their lives and moved across the country to this new city just outside the capital, the city everyone in India talked about these days, the one she was about to finally discover for herself.

When they were leaving the airport, she had craned her neck to look back at it so she would remember this bittersweet homecoming for the essays she was supposed to write over the summer. What she saw was a billboard with a pertinent question: *Trump Has Arrived.*

Have You? The letters were scrawled across an outline of a building that stretched all the way to the top of the billboard, as if it were trying desperately to touch the sky. She had flown thousands of miles but the shadow of America had nonetheless preceded her here.

As their car sped along the broad expressway that led to Hrishipur, Maneka had moved her head from left to right as if she were at a tennis match. On either side, neon signs flashed the names of multinational corporations. Sony. Google. Microsoft. ESPN. Bank of America. Even in the dim light, she could discern the silhouettes of the buildings, glass and steel, rising like trees in a forest. Despite her grief at the gaping hole that was her mother's absence, Maneka had also felt something else. A little stirring inside as if something dormant was finally awakening. The bright lights and clusters of tall buildings reminded her that this was life in a big city, life among people. Her own people. Already, Heathersfield seemed very far away, and with it, Mike's face had begun to recede as well.

That night, before the text came, she lay awake in the room her mother had decorated with such apparent enthusiasm as she waited for her daughter to finally pay them a visit in their new home. Maneka had looked up at the old photographs on the wall, fragments from the life she had lived in their hometown of Kolkata before she first left for America twelve years ago. Photos of her winning prizes at high school debates, of her thirteenth birthday celebration surrounded by friends, of a vacation with her parents among the hills of Kalimpong. Her mother was only present in the last one, where she smiled indulgently at the camera, her eyes twinkling with mirth. But Maneka, gazing up at it from her bed, knew how that smile could shift, suddenly and without warning, into a thunderous rage. And she knew her mother was present everywhere.

The first night back in India was one she had always treasured in the past, when the memories had warmed her and made her feel safe. Now they mocked her. Had her mother known all along that her daughter would come back only after she was gone? Was this her idea of revenge, placing these souvenirs of the past strategically so they would stare down at Maneka as she lay in bed? Here in this rented flat, where her father now lived alone, with only a maid out in the servant's room, Maneka covered her face with her hands, still unable to weep, but overcome with exhaustion. What would happen to them without her mother? How would her father live by himself, without any income apart from the meagre interest from his modest savings? The future was an unknown void and this summer was the beginning.

That was when she had seen the phone flicker beside her pillow. The sender was also apparently unable to sleep at three in the morning, but in her case perhaps due to excitement.

Dearest Maneka, I hope you will come to our party this Saturday. My husband and I want to make a special announcement. There will be people, music, dancing, drinks. But the best part will be seeing you, after all these years. Oh, please, do come. Love, Ramona.

Nobody in America signed off casual messages with *love*, not even Maneka's friends from graduate school when they used to all get wasted together, not even the men she had dated briefly, not even Mike in the last year.

Salil and I want to celebrate our good news with friends.

Ramona had included her among those whom she called friends. She had said *please* and *love*. She had declared her eagerness to see her, Maneka, a girl she had never even spoken to back when they went to the same posh school eight hours a day, five days a week, year after year, for fifteen years. Maneka was surprised Ramona even remembered her name, but Facebook did that to people these days. It forced them to recollect obscure acquaintances from their pasts no matter how little they might have known of each other. It made them believe they were all friends. But was friendship even possible with someone from Ramona's set? Maneka did not think so. But the invitation had come, nonetheless, and she grasped at it as if it could save her.

Her father did not want her to go.

"You have only just come home, Mishti," he said. "Aren't you jet-lagged? Are you ready to go to a party? Perhaps you should wait."

Wait for what, Baba? she wanted to say. For Ma to come back and yell at us? For more deathly quiet nights in a town covered in snow? For a lifetime of loneliness?

The look on his face told her he wanted her at home with him so he wouldn't have to spend another evening alone.

"Maybe you should come with me," she suggested. "Maybe you should stop sacrificing everything for her."

He looked away into the distance outside the window, where the city skyline was incandescent in the light of the morning sun.

"You will need to forgive her," he said finally. "If you want to find any peace."

The sunlight was too strong in this place. It was only the beginning of summer but a drought had already been declared in the north. The monsoon would come late, if at all. Inside the flat, the air conditioner hummed without pause for her benefit. Maneka wondered what it would do to the electricity bill. She longed for rain, heavy, dark rain that would pour down in sheets and wash away their memories and her regrets.

It was difficult to forgive her mother. She was the one who had made the decision to move out of Kolkata. After years of being a housewife, just a month after her husband's mandatory retirement when he turned sixty, and within a few weeks of Maneka's return to the States following her last visit, she had wrenched them from everything beloved and familiar and brought them here so she could take a job at a new school that was looking for French teachers. It was Maneka's mother who persuaded her father to sell—yes, *sell*—their cosy flat in Jodhpur Park, the home where Maneka had grown up, and book a new condo in one of the many properties under construction in Hrishipur. Who knew the traditional woman from one of the oldest neighbourhoods in Kolkata had so much adventure in her? Who knew she could take such risks?

The risk had not paid off. The new property with the ironic name of Jannat, heaven, never materialized. *We made a mistake*, her mother had said on the phone a few months ago. It had been several years, by that point, since the first investors had made their down payments, and not a brick had been laid.

In India, Ma, you cannot afford to make mistakes, Maneka had shouted that night on WhatsApp from the other side of the world. Her voice had risen until it cracked. She had screamed and screamed, getting revenge for all the tantrums she had been subjected to in her childhood. She blamed her mother for ruining their lives. It was the last time they had spoken.

"Who is this Ramona?" her father asked her now, as he took a bite out of his toast and orange marmalade. Crumbs flew across the table. "I've never heard of her before. Was she a friend of yours?"

Maneka shrugged, eyeing the toast warily. Was his blood sugar under control? Was the marmalade sugar-free? She would have to take a look at his latest prescription.

"We went to school together," she said. "We were all friends." What she remembered of Ramona and her girls was that they were beautiful and rich. They were driven to Burton House in Daewoo Cielos and Mitsubishi Lancers. They knew all the popular boys in the school across the street. In the afternoons when classes ended, they went to the Saturday Club to play tennis and swim and eat chicken sandwiches and lemon tarts. They lived in leafy neighbourhoods like Alipore and visited relatives in London or New York every summer. They didn't excel at anything in school, but it didn't matter, for their lives were cocooned from any troubles. They looked through Maneka and her middle-class friends as if they were transparent. They never invited her to any of their parties.

"What do you think they will announce? A baby?" she asked her father.

"What else could it be? If they don't have children and she is your age, it's long overdue. Naturally they must want to celebrate."

Maneka felt sorry for him, for having let him down in so many ways. She had wanted to fly to India the day after he called her at four in the morning and said her pet name like a question. *Mishti?* She had known in that instant, from the sound of his voice, that this was the phone call immigrants were warned about. They were supposed to brace themselves, but she had not of course. Not yet. Not for the news of her mother's death, which came like the slamming of a door, sudden and loud and leaving the world closed behind it.

She had wanted to come. She really had. But the semester was in full swing and the flights were too expensive. The winter storm made it hard to drive to the nearest international airport three hours away, and she didn't want to ask Mike, whose teenage daughter was recovering from an opioid overdose. She could come only for a couple of weeks, and it would be too late to even see her mother's bloated body lying in the middle of the room wrapped in one of her favourite saris. It would be too late to accompany her father to the burning ghat where she might smell her mother's flesh as it caught fire. She had asked her father what she should do, knowing well what he would say. She had allowed him to make the decision for her. Of course she should wait, no point wasting money now that her mother's schoolteacher's salary was gone. She should come in the summer, the entire three-month-long summer, for that would be more meaningful for them both. She had agreed and told herself she was being a good daughter.

Maneka had stayed in Heathersfield for the rest of the spring semester. She had continued to drive to campus along the pretty, tree-lined lanes, walk between the red brick buildings named after rich Republican donors, and teach her creative writing classes to the undergraduates who found her intimidating no matter how hard she tried to smile for them. She had continued to grade their assignments in the small coffee shop behind the school where the music was loud enough to drown out her thoughts. In those weeks, she ate little and lay awake at night next to Mike, who remained preoccupied with his own family drama. She had listened to the deafening silence that always surrounded her in Heathersfield. The silence of winter that persisted all year long in the small towns of the American Midwest.

The party would have music, dancing, drinking. It would have Ramona, whose parties had been legendary.

"I should buy her a present," said Maneka. "For the baby."

It was an excuse to venture out to one of the malls Hrishipur was famous for. But Maneka couldn't drive a stick shift on the right side of the road in crazy Indian traffic, and her father didn't want her to call an Ola cab.

"It isn't safe," he said.

"Baba, I live alone in a foreign country and drive across states. I drive in the middle of the night in snowstorms. I'm thirty-five years old."

He shook his head. "This is not your little postcard town in America, Mishti. It's North India. It isn't safe here for women. Haven't you read all the reports about the rapes? And you've only just come back. How will you even find the mall? There are forty-five of them. What if the driver takes you to the wrong one?"

It was a predicament she had not considered. Heathersfield had just one mall on its periphery. It was where you went if you wanted to watch a movie, buy shoes, or see the giant Christmas tree around the holidays. It was located at the end of a single long street; you couldn't get lost on your way there even if you wanted to.

She finally accepted his offer to drive her, not because it was practical but because she knew he too wanted to get out of the flat.

The roads were crammed with traffic, chaotic and swirling, even worse than the jams she remembered from Kolkata. But it was the cars that caught her eye. Audis, Mercs, BMWs, even a Ferrari glinted in the light of the midday sun as they made their way past several malls until they arrived at Eternity, whose facade was plastered with billboards announcing shops, movies and restaurants such as Subway and Ruby Tuesday.

Their car was searched for explosives and weapons before being waved through to the basement parking lot. Then Maneka and her father were frisked at one of the entrances, where a bored security guard rifled through her purse with glazed eyes. She emerged on to the smooth, tiled floor inside feeling like she had accomplished something. But it was only when the blast of cold air touched her skin that she realized why there were so many people here in the middle of the day. The malls were oases of shade and respite from the heat outside and from the astronomical electricity bills that were a part of summer in India.

Maneka tried to imagine Mike with her now, walking through the mall with his tall, lanky frame, but the fantasy was too strange to sustain. Once again, she felt him slip away from her as if he belonged to another planet.

She bought a stuffed elephant, a gender-neutral purchase for an unborn baby in India, where determining a child's sex before birth was still illegal. The elephant was pink and grey and small enough to stuff inside her purse that evening. It made her feel like an adult. *Look Ma, I remembered to buy a present.* She stroked the faux fur as she threaded through the crowd after her father, and hoped that Ramona, who no doubt was stocking up on toys and clothes from the most upscale malls and designer stores, would find it endearing.

That evening, the gates of Magnolia Gardens parted to let the BMW in and immediately closed behind it, secluding the world she was entering from the one outside. The car that had been sent to fetch Maneka glided past a cascading waterfall, a row of shops, and a swimming pool whose turquoise waters sparkled in mockery of the drought that was driving farmers to suicide across the northern states. When it finally came to a stop at one of the towers surrounding the smooth lawn, Maneka thanked the driver just like she thanked all the cab and Uber drivers back in America, automatically, from habit, without giving it any thought. He glanced at her quizzically in the rearview mirror, surprised to be acknowledged. She stepped out into the warm air and looked up at the pale-pink buildings. Thousands of windows stared back accusingly. Why are you here? they seemed to ask.

She was here because seventeen years after they left high school, Ramona had finally invited her to a party. She was here because the last five days enclosed in the flat with her father, surrounded by her mother's things, had been unbearable. She was here because she and Mike had decided on a break to "reassess" how they felt. She was here because she had spent too many nights alone in the heartland of America. *Shut up*, she whispered to the windows that reflected the orange light of the setting sun back to her. *Let me have this night.* She wanted a night free of anger, regret, grief, or worry. If anyone could provide such a distraction, perhaps even amusement, it would surely be Ramona.

There were two elevators in the lobby. No, no, *lift*; she was back now, back *home*, remember, she told herself. Two girls with ribboned braids giggled and talked loudly in Hindi as they entered the service lift with manually collapsible gates. Maneka was debating whether to join them when the automatic steel doors of the lift next to it parted and an unseen force propelled her into its mirrored interior. Thankfully her left-leaning English department colleagues back in the States couldn't see her now. They couldn't see the silver BMW that had just dropped her off like Cinderella's coach, or the gathering upstairs to which she was headed.

The buttons inside went from twelve to fourteen. Maneka wondered if all the gated high-rise condominiums in Hrishipur, with names like Sunset Boulevard, Orchid Petals, Belvedere House, and Palm Springs, names that evoked faraway worlds and lifestyles, had eliminated the thirteenth floor in hopes of banishing ill luck to other, less fortunate, places. She wondered if Jannat, had it ever seen the light of day, would have had a thirteenth floor. She had never asked her parents on which level they had planned to live out the rest of their lives.

On the fourteenth floor, she stood outside Ramona's flat, listening to the music and shrieks of laughter coming through the door. The sounds reminded her of Ramona's friends back in high school. The beautiful girls. How carelessly they had all laughed. How coolly they had regarded her. She had hovered on the periphery of their lives, watching from a distance as they stood near the school gate after the final bell rang out, untying their hair and applying lip gloss for the boys.

And now here she was, at their door, suddenly more nervous than she'd been before. But no matter—she would use Ramona's guests for research. She would indulge in superficial chatter for a few hours to take her mind off the lingering ache. She would have a drink or two and pretend to have a good time until she forgot what was real and what was not. The lime-green plant climbing the wall next to the door already comforted her. Her mother, who had loved plants, would have wanted her to come tonight. She steadied herself and rang the bell.

The door swung open to reveal guests with drinks in hand scattered across a room that smelt of kababs. It was obvious at once that this was different from the gatherings hosted by her colleagues at Blue Lake College. There everyone stood around talking in low voices about the heirloom tomatoes they had planted and where they were going camping that summer with the children. While at the Indian potlucks she was occasionally invited to in America, the men and women sat in different rooms and the children watched movies in the basement. This, on the other hand, was clearly an adult event. No sign of children, and a lurking sense of danger.

How, Maneka wondered, would the arrival of a baby change this pristine environment with its carefully curated colour scheme? The white leather sofa and chairs and the glass tables were planted on a chessboard floor of black and white tiles. A black accent wall formed a stark contrast to the spotless white ones all around. Throws, rugs, and pillows in fluorescent colours had been flung all around the living room, like paint splashed carelessly on a canvas. It was like the beautiful girls themselves—artfully casual and impossibly sophisticated. Ramona's touch was unmistakable.

As Maneka stood by the entrance, unsure if Ramona would be able to recognize her from the photos on Facebook, a tall man with carefully tousled gelled hair walked up to her. His maroon rolled-up shirtsleeves revealed toned biceps; his goatee was just beginning to sprout some grey.

"Hello, you must be Maneka. Salil Singh," he said, extending his hand. So this was Ramona's husband, the aspiring liquor baron. He smelt of Davidoff Cool Water, a fragrance that transported her back to the teenage boys she and Ramona once knew. "What's your poison?" he asked, waving at the row of bottles on the bar. They were all labelled Black Diamond, which Maneka knew was the name of his start-up.

She was tempted to ask for something outrageous just to see if he would be able to concoct it.

"Can I have Scotch with white wine and a splash of liquor? And any tropical fruit juice would be lovely. With a little sugar to sweeten it?" Maneka smiled as if she drank that all the time.

Salil shot her a look before waving off the uniformed waiter. "I'll make Madam's drink myself." He scooped a generous portion of ice from a bucket and deposited it into a tall glass with a noisy flourish. "You Americans love ice," he said.

"I'm not American."

Salil ignored her and continued talking as he made the drink.

"I want to introduce you to my friends," he said. "My wife's been telling them all about her old classmate who's a professor in America. A lot of them have degrees from there of course. MBAs from Wharton and so on. But they returned home because this is now the happening place, not Europe or the States. And thank goodness. Look at what's going on over in your country these days. It must be very tough for immigrants like you."

Maneka wanted to tell him that the suffering of children in cages at the Mexican border and of the thousands of undocumented immigrants was far greater than her own. But he had already turned away to tap the shoulder of a guest.

"Meet a very old friend of my wife's. They went to Burton House together in Kolkata. Now she is a professor of English literature in the States."

Maneka glanced at Salil to see if he was being facetious, but he looked sincere. She did not expect him to know she taught creative writing—not English literature—but did he really think she and his wife had been friends once? What had he heard about her?

Salil handed her the glass with the dark-pink drink, the colour of which matched his shirt. It was stronger than Maneka had planned. Her head spun with the very first sip but she wasn't sure if it was the liquor or lingering jet lag.

The guests mingled as if they had known each other forever. Women in tight backless dresses and high heels and men in jeans and button-down shirts, all of whom threw their heads back and laughed at one another's jokes. Maneka envied their casual familiarity with each other and with this life. She glanced down at her own outfit—the dark-grey skirt, blue-and-white printed blouse, predictable black pumps. She felt as excluded here as she did at gatherings in Heathersfield. As if she were condemned to being an outsider everywhere, always looking in through a window at other people's brightly lit lives.

The sounds of the party blended together. The tinkling of champagne flutes. The chorus of voices. Spice Girls playing on invisible speakers. It was like being back at a dance social in the pillared hallways of their grand school founded by an errant British aristocrat nearly two hundred years ago. And yet, there was something different here. This felt too new, too glossy. Everyone was too groomed. Everyone except that one guy standing alone in the corner, slouching against the wall.

He was staring at Maneka with unapologetic curiosity. His attire—a green cotton kurta, jeans, and brown leather sandals—reminded her of activists at the college in Kolkata that she had attended before leaving for graduate school in America. His unkempt wavy hair covered one of his eyes. His stubble made him look a little scruffy—not enough to be uninvited to this event, but enough to be sexy. It was hard not to notice him in this crowd. Just as Maneka realized she was staring back and tried to look away, he raised his mug of frothy beer to her and began walking over.

"Hi, I'm Ashok," he said. "You look lost here. That's a good sign. I thought you might need rescuing."

How could he know? Somehow the sight of him, looking like someone who was determined to stage a rebellion, comforted her, as if an old friend had turned up. But before Maneka could respond, there she was. The apsara, the ice maiden, the one the boys had circled.

Ramona stood in the doorway, surveying the gathering with a slightly puzzled look on her face as if she couldn't quite remember what all these people were doing here. Light from one of the table lamps fell on the right half of her body, illuminating one silver stiletto pump, a slim calf, half a magenta dress, an arm hanging limp by her side. The other half of her stood in the shadows. She looked as ethereal as she had when she was a teenager, half present, half absent, both of this world and not.

Suddenly, she turned and saw the two of them across the crowd. The expression on her face flickered and the hand at her side clenched into a fist. She began to walk over to them with a familiar poised gait. She was as slender as a glass figurine, so fragile that if someone breathed in her presence she might shatter.

It was only when she was nearly next to them that her eyes widened in recognition. Her face broke into a broad smile that lit up the room even more than it already was.

"Maneka," Ramona cried, with her palm on her lips. She smelt of lilies.

"I can't believe it's you. I would never have recognized you if it weren't for Facebook. You look more—" Ramona paused and squinted, searching.

Maneka was tempted to help her. Sophisticated? Professional? American?

"Never mind," Ramona said. "You are still our Minka. And I'm so sorry about your mom." She reached out and touched her arm.

"Thank you," Maneka replied. They had all said that to her in Heathersfield. *We are sorry for your loss. Let me know if there's anything I can do.* But Ramona had touched her like an old friend. "I see you've already met our friendly vagabond Ashok." Ramona gave him a look of reproach. "Would it have killed you to dress a little more suitably?" She turned to Maneka. "Ashok is a wicked one. You can never tell if he's serious or joking. And he has the maturity of a fifteen-year-old."

"Well, if she wants to talk to mature men, there are plenty around," Ashok said. "Take your pick. In fact, here's one right now."

As Salil strode towards them, Maneka noted that he and Ramona were dressed in matching colours—two different shades of burgundy.

"Have you met my husband?" Ramona said. "I've told him all about you."

Maneka nodded. "He made my drink. It's very strong." She wondered again what Ramona might have told him. Maneka had once followed the details of their lives like a fan reading a gossip magazine. But she had always assumed that Ramona had known nothing about her.

"Isn't he handsome?" Ramona asked, linking her arm in Salil's.

"He would have to be to have married you."

Salil laughed with satisfaction. Ashok looked away. Ramona pulled her husband a little closer and leant against him, but Salil gently disentangled himself from her.

"I am glad you will be here for three months," Ramona said. "It will give us enough time to catch up."

Ashok raised his left eyebrow. "Three months in Hrishipur?" When he smiled, the left corner of his mouth turned upwards. He looked like he was mocking everyone around him.

"I am here with my father. He's alone now."

Salil leant forward. "I'm so sorry about your mother."

Maneka was surprised to find the same gentleness in his eyes as in Mike's. But unlike his eyes, the sound of Salil's voice, slightly affected and overly cheerful, grated on her nerves. Unlike Mike, who was so authentic she had begun to find him boring, Salil seemed determined to conceal his real self.

"Her mother passed away just a few months ago from a heart attack," Ramona explained to Ashok.

Ashok's eyes flickered away towards the french doors that led out to the terrace, where the sky, glimpsed from between the curtains, was now completely dark.

"Maybe you can show her around Hrishipur, dude." Salil thumped Ashok on the back so hard a little beer spilt from his mug. He turned to Maneka. "You see, Ashok needs something to do. Some structure in his life. He has too much freedom."

He could have been talking about her. Already the days seemed to stretch aimlessly ahead. Without structure, Maneka thought she might unspool like one of the old French cassette tapes she had found among her mother's things that afternoon.

"I would like to explore Hrishipur for my writing," she said. "I'm intrigued by this city. All the properties and development, the retail chains and shops, the cyber hub. I am curious about what it must be like to live here."

Ramona was nodding. "Hrishipur is very interesting," she said in that calm, low voice that defied anyone to contradict her. "It's much cleaner than Kolkata, as you would have no doubt noticed, and we have all the things we need. Shops that sell organic food and quinoa and avocados. You won't miss any of that here. And of course, we have these lovely flats. Don't just go by this one. It's a bit cramped, but we won't be living here forever."

Ramona exchanged a look with Salil. Her stomach, unlike the rest of her, was beginning to show the slightest curve. Maneka tried not to stare at it.

"What is the occasion for this gathering?" she asked. "The surprise you mentioned?" She groped inside her bag for the reassuring softness of the elephant, wishing she had thought of wrapping it first.

"You will find out very soon, I promise," said Ramona. Maneka took her hand out of the bag. She didn't want to ruin the suspense they were trying so hard to build up. It was rather sweet. Her father was right. Ramona had been one of the first girls in their class to get married. They must have waited a long time for this.

"I believe you need another drink, prof," said Salil, taking the empty glass from Maneka's hand.

"Maybe I should stick to one," she said.

"Rubbish," said Salil. "You Americans can drink us under the table. I'll be back in a jiffy." He snaked his way through the crowd.

"He's very chivalrous," Ashok said. He was still leaning against the wall as if standing up straight was too much of an effort. "So, how long have you lived in Aahmerrycah?" he asked, looking at Maneka, drawing out each syllable.

"Twelve years," Maneka said. "I went for graduate school, but one thing led to another as they always tell you it will. I just didn't think it would also happen to me."

"Dr Roy was a brilliant student back in school," Ramona said. "Always topped the English exams."

So, she had noticed her after all.

"You went to that same elitist school as her? The one whose name sounds like a snooty hotel and where you were all served caviar and champagne on the school's birthday?"

"Really?" Maneka asked. "I must have missed those events. I only remember chicken biryani and Fanta."

Ramona flicked his arm. "He's always making fun of me," she cried. Her voice, for a second, sounded like a young girl's, unguarded and wanton. It almost sounded like she was flirting with Ashok, but when Salil returned moments later with Maneka's drink, Ramona immediately intertwined her arm with his.

"Sal is such a good host. That's why everyone loves our parties."

"You're not so bad yourself, babe," Salil said. "She's the one who organizes every last detail. The flowers, the catering, even what we're going to wear. That's why we're always colour coordinated."

"Only Ashok never gets the memo," Ramona sighed.

One of the other guests shouted out from across the room that the suspense was becoming unbearable.

"To make you drink more of my booze, dude, so that you buy it for your hotel," Salil yelled back before turning to his wife.

"Ramona, we need to talk to them."

Ramona looked at Maneka. "Please excuse me for a bit, Minka. You see," she lowered her voice, "there is no use in throwing a party if we don't network."

She smiled at Salil, who did not smile back. Instead, he put an arm proprietorially around her waist and led her across the floor, the two of them together looking like an elegant bougainvillaea plant weaving through the crowd.

Maneka felt uncharacteristically reticent now that she was left alone with Ashok. They sipped their drinks in awkward silence until she finally forced herself to start a conversation.

"Are you enjoying this?" she asked, gesturing in the general direction of the guests.

"Now I am," he said. "Are you really planning to stay here for three months?"

"I'm here for my summer break. Though it's not really a break. I'm supposed to research my book."

"What is it about?" Seeing her hesitate, he waved his hand. "You don't have to answer that question if it annoys you. I bet everywhere you go for the next three months people will ask you that."

"And every time, I will have to come up with a new answer," she replied. "It's a book of essays on contemporary India."

The description sounded utterly vague to her ears. She felt like an impostor. How could she know anything about this country any more? It had changed so much, was changing even as they talked. Where would she start?

"Contemporary India," Ashok said, stroking his chin with fingers as brown as the branches of a tree. "You are in the right city. It doesn't get more contemporary than this. But I confess I'm a little fascinated by the hypocrisy of postcolonial scholars and writers in the diaspora. The elites who go abroad and eat organic food and drive hybrid cars and write papers about poor people back home."

"Well, I confess I am very fascinated by judgemental Indians who resent anyone who lives in the West."

"You're right. I am brimming with resentment," Ashok laughed.

His laugh replaced the smirk and made his eyes suddenly mischievous. He was probably younger than her by a few years. She thought of Mike's face at the airport as she was leaving and the gentle, serious blue eyes behind his glasses, not a blue as brilliant as the lake but a more subdued shade that matched his personality. She had asked him not to see her off, but he had insisted.

"This drink is strong," she said. "I don't even know what exactly he put in it."

"Shall we go outside for a little fresh air?" Ashok gestured towards the room. "This is too loud. Besides, the view out there is interesting. I think you might like it. It may come in useful for the book."

"What if they make their big announcement while we're gone?"

"It's too soon. Some of the important guests haven't even arrived yet. Salil Singh won't be making any announcements until everyone is drunk and the mystery has built to a crescendo."

Maneka followed him out to the terrace. Magnolia Gardens was located just a few blocks west of the entrance to the city, where neon signs flashed red, blue and green in the dark sky. Between Ikea and Siemens, a fluorescent sign spelt out the word *Atmosphere*. The most expensive of all the malls, located right next to the bright lights of the seven-star Monsoon Palace Hotel. The skyline was a mountain range of high-rises. Millennium city. Mall city.

Maneka felt conflicted as she looked out at the landscape.

Her father had talked about moving back to Kolkata. There was no reason to linger here now that her mother and her mother's job were gone.

But the lights on the horizon blinked like tiny flames. When she was growing up in that genteel, laid-back city full of old houses and colonial buildings, Maneka had dreamt of skylines and lights that shone all night long. She knew, as did all the other girls, that one day they would leave. For Delhi, Mumbai or Bengaluru, or farther, beyond the country's borders, anywhere but their hometown. Maneka looked at the headlights of the cars on the highway to the east and wondered if going backwards now was really wise. Wasn't that the wrong direction in which to travel? Wasn't that what her mother had once said when they were not arguing for a change?

In Kolkata, her father would not enjoy the same access to medical facilities or the resources of the capital that lay thirty miles away. Besides, the thought of visiting Kolkata triggered emotions in her that Maneka preferred to suppress. Everything she had loved there once was gone. Her mother. Their home. Her friends. Everything had changed too much. She couldn't even bring herself to call it by its Bengali name, a name revived by politicians in an attempt to wipe out its colonial history. But to Maneka, that name felt almost foreign, the renaming a betrayal of everything she had loved. And so she clung to its British name just like she clung to her childhood memories. Now, with her mother gone, it was more important than ever to preserve the impressions she carried with her. Impressions that might prove to be an illusion if she went back to that city. No, surely, they did not belong there any more.

Ashok leant over the ledge and lit a cigarette. His arm went up and down in easy, languid movements as he smoked it. They could no longer see the other guests from here, but the thumping of the bass reached them in a slow vibration, an almost imperceptible earthquake.

"You were right about the view. The skyline is pretty."

Ashok laughed. "Of course you think the skyline is pretty. That's what this place aspires to. To be some kind of desi New York. Your validation will be important to them. You should write to the prime minister and compliment him on his initiative to turn Hrishipur into a potent symbol of our collective development."

Maneka bristled. "I find a lot of things pretty. City skylines, mountains, oceans. Would you rather I gushed about the slums and shanties where the servants live? Or would that make me even more American?"

Infuriatingly, he laughed again. "You won't find slums and shanties here. If you want to see where poor people live, you'll have to take a long drive. To where they've been effectively shunted. Heaven forbid you should see a tin shack anywhere near the JW Marriott." He paused. "If you want, I can show you where they are. Where the real people live."

"We are all real people," she said, quietly.

"Heathersfield. Sounds like a village in a children's book. Like the Enid Blyton books we used to read. Remember? Cherry Tree Farm,

Mistletoe Farm. Whenever a place is named after a tree or flower, I have to wonder if it's real or just a figment of someone's imagination."

"And what about Magnolia Gardens?" asked Maneka. "Or the other properties here named after flowers that don't even grow in the tropics? Are these places real?"

Ashok shrugged. "They are real to the people who live their lives in them, just as Heathersfield, I suspect, is real to those who live there. Unless of course you happen to pay for a condo in one of the properties but never get possession because the construction is never completed."

One night when her mother as usual couldn't remember the time difference, she had sent Maneka a photo of a vast empty meadow. It was supposed to be the location of their future flat, nonexistent at the time but already assuming shape in her mother's dreams.

"The unfinished constructions," Maneka said. "What happened to them?"

"Unfortunately, the housing bubble in Hrishipur has burst. The developers kept taking money from people and kept buying land from farmers and kept promising new projects. They overstretched themselves. Hubris. Avarice. Lust."

She wasn't sure if the warmth she felt was from the summer night or from Ashok's body. Unlike Salil or the other men back inside, he wasn't wearing cologne. His smell was masculine, a mix of sweat and cigarettes.

She debated whether to mention her parents' flat. She had told Mike about it, and he had made sympathetic noises. But it was impossible for him to understand what this meant for an ageing middle-class couple in India. To have to pay rent on top of everything else, the medical expenses, the inflation. With no Social Security or pension or any other kind of help from the government. Maneka had decided that Mike would have been genuinely concerned had she had children and worried about them, but parents just didn't have the same sort of effect. One was not supposed to be responsible for them. But Ashok was here, from here, from this soil. Perhaps he would understand. Then again, who *was* he? A friend of Ramona's? Ramona, whose parents probably still spent their weekends playing golf and lunching at various clubs in Kolkata. Would he really understand why she stayed up at night worrying about the future?

Above them, the sky was luminous. No moon, no stars, just a hazy, silvery light that drifted everywhere, covering them like dust. "I've always found city skies to be pretty," she remarked, determined to defend her original position.

Ashok glanced at her with an indulgent smile. His face was hollow in the dim light, his cheeks almost concave. She longed for a puff of his cigarette but felt too shy to ask him.

"It's pollution," he said. "This is, after all, a suburb of the most polluted city in the world. I'm surprised you can breathe here, having just arrived."

"Where I live," she said, "you can see thousands of stars."

"Do you want to see a star? One that shows the way to paradise?" Ashok asked. "Come." He led her around the corner of the terrace. "Focus," he commanded. His shoulder lightly brushed hers, and Maneka stood still so he would not move either.

The skyline was behind them now, and it took her a minute to grow accustomed to the sudden darkness of the horizon. She gazed out in the direction he was pointing in. He stood so close to her she could feel his breath on her neck. She imagined making love to him on the terrace while the party was in full swing inside. The summer suddenly seemed filled with the possibility of passion. Maneka had missed that with Mike. She had missed it ever since she left graduate school and moved to the midwestern college town where everyone was unfailingly polite and no one ever raised their voices.

As she focused, a flicker of light came into view. It glowed like the tip of a fire, a beacon from a lighthouse. It was small and yet so distinct that it drew attention to the emptiness behind it.

A stretch of land with no hotels, malls, or offices.

"Why does all this look so naked?"

"It used to be farmland. Just like this place. Everything here was farm country thirty years ago, until real estate developers began to swoop in. Now that stretch you see in darkness is all that's left. But not for long. It is the site of the grandest residential project of them all. And I present to you, Madam, the one and only Trump Towers." Ashok bowed low when he finished and stood up with a flourish.

The light was in clear focus now. The golden glow of a sign that spelt out two words. They were hard to discern from this distance, but Maneka knew what they were.

"I saw the sign at the airport. So, they got their finger in the pie. Why should I be surprised?"

"Yes, your president is a powerful man. Especially in this city, where the only gods people really worship are made of concrete."

"He is not my president," she protested.

Ashok shrugged as if to say it hardly mattered whether she had voted for him or not. He was the president, and she lived in his country.

All her colleagues and graduate school friends took great pride in saying those same words as a show of resistance. But in her case, it was true. She had lived in America first on a student visa and now on a work visa, with a green card in process for an indeterminate amount of time. Everything took so long these days, and until she became an American citizen, she would have no voting rights. She had opinions of course, but the times being what they were, she had stopped tweeting anything political or posting updates on social media that went beyond food porn or literary quotes. Perhaps that was why she was compelled to write essays. She felt a perpetual longing to pin down with words the thoughts and ideas that floated about in her head but that she was too afraid to express in public.

She and Ashok stood side by side, their elbows on the wall, and gazed out at the distant sign. It seemed to beckon to desperate folks who longed for something more than what they already had. Even in this city of successful, corporate, polished professionals with their foreign degrees and brands, there was so much longing. Maneka thought she could reach out and touch it, thick in the humid night air.

"Can I get a drag from your cigarette?" she finally asked, unable to resist any longer.

He handed it to her, and she slipped it between her lips. Its red glow blew sparks between them as if it could set them afire. She took a long breath. No one she knew in Heathersfield smoked. Only a student here and there, standing alone outside Dekker Hall, looking like an outcast. They handed the rapidly shrinking stick back and forth in silence. It was the most erotic act she could remember performing since she became a professor. "My mother couldn't stand me smoking when I was in college. She would throw a fit if she saw it now." Maneka smiled to herself in the darkness. "I miss her fits."

In response, Ashok tossed the butt on the ground and crushed it with his heel. "You need a refill," he said, gently prizing the glass from her hand. "Do you really have no idea what he put in this?"

Maneka laughed, mainly to cover up her embarrassment at having shared something about her mother only to receive no response. It was too soon for that sort of thing. She might never even see Ashok again. No need to act like a foolish teenager, smoking and flirting as if she were really back in high school.

"I think it had whisky and wine. And something pink."

"Maybe I should get you some Pepsi," he said as he walked away. "That's the key to making sure Salil never invites you again to the House of Booze."

The terrace felt desolate once she was left alone. This city was less familiar to her than the small towns she often drove through in the States when she needed to think. She had been away too long.

A single row of planters with flowerpots ran around the entire length of the ledge. Maneka manoeuvred her way between two of them and leant over. Fourteen—or thirteen—floors below, a watchman in a khaki uniform walked by. He looked rather small from up here. If she gently nudged one of the flowerpots, it would drop on his head and crush him. And the pot would end up in a cloud of dust. From this height it stood no chance of survival.

It was a sultry night, but Maneka shivered. Suddenly, she couldn't wait to get away from the terrace. As she turned to go inside, she took a last lingering look towards the west. The starless sky was smooth except for that one gold sign in the distance, a steady gleam as seductive as Gatsby's green light, tempting and teasing those who glanced at it.

Back in the flat, the music was louder than before. A group of men near the entrance to the terrace were talking about money. "I am paying sixty thousand rupees a month EMI on top of my rent," one said. "They were supposed to hand over possession of the flat two years ago."

"Same here, dude," another man added. "Our flat is almost ready, so now I'm paying over a lakh. Need to move in soon so that we can stop paying both rent and monthly instalments at the same time."

"Sue the bastards," one of them slurred, slapping the wall next to him. "These builders need to be taught a lesson."

"In this country, that is of no use. Beating them all to a pulp may be the only answer."

Maneka had just placed a hand on the wall to stop her head from spinning when Ashok emerged around the corner with a woman and, as promised, a glass of what looked like Pepsi.

"Jess, this is Ramona's school friend Maneka, who lives in the States. Maneka, this is Jessica Pereira. She catered the delicious food."

Jessica smiled, flashing brilliant white teeth. She, too, was dressed incongruously for this event. Her eyes were thickly lined with kajal, and she wore a long, flowing skirt embroidered with mirrors and a loose blouse draped with a batik wrap. It resembled a costume, conspicuously ethnic, as if she were playing the part of a nomadic Banjara woman.

"It's lovely to finally meet you," Jessica said. Then she lowered her voice. "I don't usually attend these gatherings. I just started my catering thing on top of my regular job, *and* I am a single mother. Who has the time? Besides, these parties are mostly for the corporate crowd to schmooze at."

"How old is your child?" Maneka asked.

"She's eight. Here." Jessica showed her a photo on her cell phone in which a child stood to attention, staring straight at the camera. She was skinny and dark, and her hair was cut short like a boy's. Jessica continued to scroll through photos in which the little girl became younger and younger. In the last one, she was a toddler, clinging to Jessica's skirt with a thumb in her mouth.

Maneka tried to find Jessica's sharp features in her but could not.

As if guessing her thoughts, Jessica said, "I adopted her."

"What's her name?"

"Titli. Because she flutters about like a butterfly. Her name at the orphanage was Maya, but I wanted to invent a new life for her that is based on reality and not illusions."

"Beautiful name," Maneka said. "It must be hard to be a single mother in India, especially of an adoptee. I've heard they don't even like to approve the adoptions unless you're married."

"Yes, it was a fight, but film stars like Sushmita Sen have made it a little easier. And I wouldn't exchange the challenges for anything." Jessica's eyes lit up like her teeth when she talked about her daughter. "Listen, here's my contact information." She dug into her multicoloured, mirror-encrusted tote bag for a card.

"I'm having a little reception to celebrate the launch of Kalypso Kitchen next week. You must come along with Ramona. It's so rare to find someone with whom one can have an intellectual conversation around here. I love to read, you know. I go to all the book launches in Delhi. But whom can one discuss such things with, in this crowd?" She waved her hand around the room in a dismissive gesture.

Maneka was about to ask her what sort of books she read when the lights suddenly dimmed like the interior of a theatre.

Only a lamp at the far end of the room continued to shine. In its pool of light stood Ramona and Salil, looking like movie stars. Behind them, the wall formed a blank canvas for various artworks, including a distinctive Jamini Roy painting of horses captured in mid-gallop. Its dark-red shades bled into one another. Maneka realized that the hosts' outfits matched the backdrop. They had positioned themselves strategically against the wall. Ramona lifted her face to her husband's but he looked straight at the crowd and cleared his throat.

"Friends, we love having you here in our home," he waved at the room. "We all work very hard in this city. We do what we can to flourish and fulfil our dreams. But it means nothing without our friends old and new." Salil paused and took a sip of his drink.

The room was silent. All the guests had their faces turned towards the couple. From some other flat came the sound of bhangra disco. On a Saturday night in Hrishipur, it sounded like a lot of people were partying.

"Stop keeping us in suspense, Sal," someone shouted. "Just tell us."

Salil smiled and stroked his beard.

"We want to let you all know that we have made an investment."

Maneka shook her head. Surely, he was not going to call his unborn child an investment.

"We have bought a flat in Trump Towers. Yes, we know that all the flats had been sold. But I managed to find a broker who knew an investor who wanted to sell his. That fool got scared looking at all the unfinished projects and thought he would bail while he could. I had no hesitation." Salil finally looked at his wife. "To be fair, Ramona was the one who egged me on, gave me the courage. It was a big investment but I have little doubt that this particular property will not be stuck. Construction has already progressed quite rapidly in the last year, as we have all noticed, and we have been assured that it will continue to proceed at breakneck speed. The Americans don't mess around when it comes to deals."

His voice was overpowered by the cheers that had broken out in the room. Salil held up a hand to silence them. He began to list some of the amenities in their future home. Gold bathroom fittings, Italian marble floors, dishwasher, Jacuzzi.

But the rooms Maneka was thinking of were not in Trump Towers. The kitchen that got too hot in the summer. The smell of fish frying. Black-and-white photos of her grandparents on the walls. Curtains fluttering in the breeze. A narrow balcony overlooking the children's park down below. The neighbourhood Durga Puja celebrations in autumn. The cool moisture of rain.

Maneka sank down in the nearest chair, her exhaustion bone-deep. Their home in Kolkata had been the only life she had known, a life of stability, a life that had made her restless to explore the world. She missed it now with the same aching sense of loss she felt when she thought about her mother.

In the final year of her mother's life, her parents had visited the temple every Sunday, just to pray that if they didn't get the flat in Jannat, then at least they would get back their down payment. Then, gradually, her mother had started to give up, until one day she died from a heart attack in her sleep. But Maneka suspected that it was really from disappointment. Her mother had dreamt of a heaven right here on earth. But she had lost. Maneka's parents had lost.

And here were Salil and Ramona, engulfed by friends and well-wishers, for surely that was what they all were, or why else would they be here tonight? Maneka could not even see Ramona any longer from where she was sitting. But she did not need to, for she had viewed the image a thousand times when she was younger. Ramona surrounded by admirers. Ramona in the centre of the circle. Ramona, who always had everything. Why should things be different now?

"Which river will you be living in?" someone shouted out. "Danube, of course," Salil said, only to be greeted by more cheers.

Bewildered, she turned to Jessica, who leant in to explain.

The seven towers were named after seven rivers. Amazon, Mississippi, Indus, Danube, Murray, Nile, Onyx. Every continent was represented.

Maneka looked around the living room. The glasses in people's hands sparkled like jewels. Yes, it was true. After all these years, despite the PhD, the tenure-track job, the books lining her shelves, the opinions and unwritten essays, one emotion above all else washed over her tonight. She was jealous. She always had been. She wanted what they had. She didn't hate them. She wished she was one of them. At least for a few days, maybe a summer, just long enough to forget her own insipid life.

The lights remained dim and the music changed to a slow ballad. The hum of chatter and laughter grew louder. Things looked a little out of focus.

She wove her way through the guests, all of them strangers, searching for Ramona so she could say goodbye. When she passed one of the men who had been talking about monthly instalments a short while ago, she heard him whisper the words *professor in the States*. She had only dwelled on her own questionable motives for coming here tonight. But why had Ramona invited her? Was it because she had finally accrued value, like a good real estate investment?

It was inside a bedroom at the end of a carpeted hallway that she found Ramona standing alone in the darkness, looking out the window at the faint shimmer of a gold sign in the distance.

"Are you all right?" Maneka asked.

Ramona flicked a light on, and the world outside the window disappeared into a black square.

"Come in, come in, I wanted to talk to you. But these parties get so crazy. Too many people. I don't even know some of them." The bedroom was tasteful and classic, just as Maneka had expected. On one of the nightstands, next to a brass lamp, stood a photo in which

Ramona and Salil had their arms around each other in front of a pristine lake.

Ramona saw her staring at the photo. "Geneva. We went to Switzerland for our honeymoon. It was nearly ten years ago. Sometimes it seems like yesterday. And sometimes, like a very long time ago."

"I met your friend Jessica," Maneka said. "She seems interesting."

"Yes, she is. I wanted her to meet you. You two have a lot in common. Her friends are all activists and artists."

"Her little girl is cute. It's brave of her to adopt alone."

Ramona's smile disappeared. She placed the photo back and glanced out of the window with a hand on her stomach, the one Maneka had mistakenly assumed was pregnant with new life.

"This home is temporary," Ramona said in a flat voice. "It's too small. The woodwork is not great, as you may have noticed. The one in Trump Towers is a lot better. It has a view of the outdoor swimming pool and is surrounded on all sides by lawns. Much prettier than this."

"Ashok told me about it on the terrace."

"Ah." Ramona turned, her green eyes narrowed, which made them more catlike. "Ashok and you on the terrace? Did you talk a lot?"

"Yes, he showed me where Trump Towers is supposed to come up."

"It will be wonderful when it's ready. The interiors are being designed by an Indo-French decor company." She clasped her hands as if in prayer. "Trump Towers is unlike the rest. The developers have struck deals with people in the US. It will be ready in no time at all. It will be perfect."

Maneka wanted to tell her that her life and everything in it was already perfect. It always had been.

"I'm so glad you're spending the summer here, Minka," Ramona continued, in a tone infused with warmth. "I know it must be difficult after what happened. But we have so much time now to catch up. It will be just like old times."

She smiled at Maneka without any sense of irony. A genuine smile that made Maneka feel slightly ashamed of being so cynical. The silk bedspread in peacock blue looked inviting. A part of her wanted to lie down here tonight and go to sleep and wake up to Ramona's life.

"I should go home now. My dad is alone. But I'm glad I came this evening. I don't know anyone else here, and it's all a bit strange. I'm happy you're here at least." Maneka realized as she spoke that it was true.

Ramona clutched her hand. "Rajesh will drive you home." When they emerged back in the living room, Ashok slipped a piece of paper into her hand. "Welcome to Hrishipur."

Ramona glanced at the note, her face smooth and expressionless as always. Maneka couldn't tell if she approved or not. She wanted her to. She realized she had sought the approval of the beautiful girls for a very long time. She unzipped her bag.

"I bought you a present from one of the malls this morning. It's a very silly thing." Maneka held out the grey elephant.

Ramona let out a cry of delight as she clasped it to her breast. "Minka," she said and hugged her, engulfing her in floral perfume. "Thank you. I will cherish it." She cradled it in her arms as if it were a baby. Her eyes, Maneka was startled to find, filled up.

She wanted to hug Ramona back but was overcome by shyness. It felt like hugging a celebrity. Instead, she tapped her lightly on her arm and whispered, "Thank you for inviting me tonight. It brought back memories. It made me feel alive again."

Maneka stepped out of the flat and caressed a tendril that had come loose from the creeper on the wall. The coarse texture surprised her. It was plastic.

When she got home, her father had gone to bed. But he had left a note underneath the thermos of cold water on her nightstand. *Mike called to see how you were. Nice of him.*

The note irritated her. Why did Mike not leave her alone? Maneka thought she had been harsh enough with him that day, not long after her mother had died, when she told him they had nothing in common. Yet he had hung around, and until now she had let him, grateful for his reliable presence and reluctant to break things off entirely. But tonight, he reminded her of a pesky fly. And now her father, who had expressed dismay through her mother just a year ago at the thought of his daughter being involved with an older, divorced man, suddenly thought he was nice?

She lay in her bed after taking off all her clothes because it was just too damn hot despite the air-conditioning, and imagined herself and Ramona standing side by side on the terrace in the weeks to come, gazing out at the horizon. Despite their differences, they shared a common past. Three months in Hrishipur suddenly didn't seem so terrifying any more. Perhaps she would have a fling. Perhaps she would sift through her mother's things and be able to piece together the fragments of her life. Perhaps she and her father would finally be able to have a meaningful conversation. Perhaps here in this new city, she would at last get to experience the life that once only the beautiful girls had lived.

Somewhere below, as her eyes drew shut, Maneka heard the intermittent tapping of the darwan's stick as he made his rounds, ever alert and watchful in this city of buildings that burnt all day and night with their dazzling lights.

RAMONA

THE MOMENT SHE WOKE UP IN THE MORNING, RAMONA'S EYES went to the window facing west. From where she lay on her bed, wrapped in satin sheets, she saw only a sliver of the sky, still pale blue at this time before the sunlight bleached it of colour. What she couldn't see was the outline of the sign whose gold letters had glowed all night long. But she knew it was there, watching over the city, and that was enough. It made it a little easier to untangle herself from the sheets to face another day in the world.

But first, she lay in bed a few extra minutes, envisioning the gleaming granite structure of Trump Towers looming in the distance one day soon. Once they moved into their new flat inside a tower named after a river in Europe, everything would be easier, she told herself, even as she pressed the cologne-scented handkerchief to her forehead to dull the ache. The bottle of Chianti she had finished the night before while she waited for Salil to come home had, inevitably, led to another hangover. She had fallen asleep by herself again in her shorts and blouse. And this morning, it was clear that Salil had once again spent the night, or what was left of it by the time he came home, in the guest room.

Ramona got out of bed and walked to the door of the guest bathroom in the hallway, where she strained to listen as he talked on his cell phone inside. He kept his voice suspiciously low for someone who liked to yell at his employees and, lately, his wife. Then the tap ran—clever fellow—and drowned out his voice. She imagined him still speaking softly or perhaps texting. It used to be so easy to take a quick look at his phone, until he went and changed the code. The memory of that night led her to instinctively caress the tender flesh right above her left elbow. The bruise had faded, but the thought of someone's grip on her arm made her move away quickly before he emerged.

She flung open the wardrobe door in a gesture of defiance and stared at her clothes, determined to wear something beautiful that would make her feel in control. But it was not easy to find the right outfit on days of diverse outings like this one. Ramona would have preferred to go to the spa the day before, but the driver had failed to show up the previous morning. If only these people realized what kind of disorder they set in motion when they missed a day. Still, the thought of getting out of the flat for several hours, especially with Maneka, who had agreed, miraculously, to come along, made her smile. She had asked her shyly, feeling silly about the mani-pedi, and only marginally more confident about Jessica's reception afterwards, but to her surprise, Maneka had not needed much cajoling. This summer, it felt like everyone was lonely or searching for something.

Ramona decided to wear the sleeveless floral dress with buttons all the way down the front. It was perfect for a hot day, easy to slip off during a facial, feminine and elegant for an afternoon get-together. Besides, even though it was a Vandana Dutt original creation, it looked simple enough for Jessica's arty-farty crowd, who would be sure to exchange glances if she wore anything that looked like it had stepped out of the pages of *Vogue India*. Ramona wasn't about to make that mistake again. She was fastening her bra when Salil walked in with the scent of his musky shampoo, wrapped in a green towel, hair tousled from the shower. Ramona turned around so her breasts faced the other way. These days she felt self-conscious about him seeing her without clothes on. Since the incident three months ago, they had not been naked together. He had shown little interest in her body, making sure he looked only at her face when he spoke to her. Now he went to his side of the built-in wardrobe and began to move everything around. Ramona had spent a few hours the previous day trying to arrange his shirts neatly into piles. It had given her something to do with her restless hands, prevented them for a short while at least from involuntarily moving up to her stomach.

"Where the hell is my navy Burberry shirt?" he said. "I'm so late. My flight is in two hours. I can't afford to miss it; there's a client meeting an hour after I land in Dubai."

Shirts flew along the shelf like a flock of unruly birds, a blur of colours and designer labels. A few landed on the floor in a crumpled heap. They would all have to be ironed again, by one of the maids who already spent most of her time ironing their clothes. Ramona buttoned her dress quickly in case they had to summon her for assistance. But just then Salil walked over to the suitcase that lay open on the chair by the window.

"Here it is," he said, looking at it suspiciously, as if someone had surreptitiously put it there.

"You may as well keep all your clothes in there," she muttered. Ramona turned back to the dressing table to do her makeup.

In the mirror, she saw not only her own face as it began to gather colour and definition, but also, behind that, the reflection of her husband getting dressed. He was looking out of the window while buttoning his shirt, staring into the distance, not in the direction of Trump Towers but the other way. His back rippled underneath the fabric when he moved. His legs, uncovered except for their coarse hair, were sinewy and long, his body devoid of fat.

He was too busy to eat any meals with his wife, and yet he always found time to work out at Body Bazaar with the other executives and entrepreneurs in town.

A familiar wave of anxiety began to sweep over Ramona. Why would Salil, who was in better shape now than he had been when she married him, care so much about his appearance? She ran a palm slowly over her belly, which looked like it was beginning to swell a little, ironic given how empty it was nowadays. She sucked in her breath to see her face narrow and then let it out again. Yes, no doubt about it, her face was growing fuller despite her careful diet. She too needed to go to the gym. But it was hard to get the energy up these days. Most of the time she felt like a weightless balloon, not really standing on firm ground but floating just above it. She had not exercised since that night at the hospital. Perhaps that was the reason Salil was always checking out other women. And coming home later and later and travelling all the time.

He walked over to the mirror and stood next to her, carefully mussing his hair, which had begun to accumulate grey like sprinkles of sand. "I have to rush to catch that flight. What are your plans today?"

"I'm going to the spa and then to Jessica's thing," Ramona answered mechanically.

"What are you doing at the spa?"

"Facial and mani-pedi."

"Regular pedi or wax pedi?"

Ramona hesitated. Salil glanced down towards her feet through the mirror.

"It's okay, you can decide later. Just don't do it if it isn't necessary. Your feet look fine."

They finished getting dressed side by side. Salil sprayed Cool Water on his wrists and neck, while Ramona slipped on her earrings. She remembered how in the early days they would smile at one another in the mirror, their bodies fresh from the shower they had taken together. But when Salil's eyes shifted towards her now, she quickly averted her face and pretended to look for her lipstick.

"Is your American friend going with you?" he asked casually. Too casually, Ramona thought.

"Yes. And she isn't American, as you know very well."

Salil shrugged. "She seems sharp. And doesn't have an accent. People go there for six months and return with an accent. I like that about her."

"I'm sure you do," Ramona said. "I saw you the other night. The young girls weren't enough for you. Harry's wife wasn't enough for you. You had to also flirt with my friend."

"Hey," Salil said. His voice was a lot louder now than when he was having a secret phone conversation inside the bathroom, Ramona thought bitterly. "Don't start all that again. I need to focus on my meeting and not get distracted by this shit."

Ramona stormed out to the living room, where she spotted his phone lying on the end table. She picked it up and stared at it, trying to persuade it to yield its secrets. Then she dragged the slider to the right and tried the old code even though she knew it wouldn't work. She frantically entered numbers without thinking. Nothing happened. What kind of husband kept his phone's passcode a secret from his wife? He didn't even trust her. How could he not trust his own wife?

Sensing him behind her, she whipped around. He stood there glaring at her, but for once she didn't flinch.

"Seriously?" he asked softly. "You're still doing that?"

"Who were you talking to in the bathroom?" Ramona demanded, aware that her voice was sounding shrill. How she hated that. *Women from good families do not screech like banshees*, her mother had once said to her back in Kolkata after they had witnessed a maid in one of the neighbours' flats screaming at her husband's mistress. *That is the difference between them and us.*

"There's no reason I should tell you," said Salil. "But if you must know, it was Vikas Malhotra, who is supposed to meet me at the airport in," he paused and looked at his watch before continuing, "thirty fucking minutes."

"What if I need to use your phone?" she cried. "What if there's an emergency and I can't find my own phone or it … it … it, I don't know, falls into the toilet or something?" She tried to use logic, a language she thought he might understand.

Salil regarded her with a slight smile. "We have a landline," he said. His voice was gentler, as if he were speaking to a child. "Once upon a time, when we were kids, there were no cell phones. Even you must remember those days."

"You seriously won't give me your passcode?"

"No, because it's *my* phone and I am entitled to some privacy. I have very important work calls coming in, and messages through text and WhatsApp. I can't afford to lose any. And I can't afford to waste any more minutes right now talking to you about the same old thing. I do not have time for this, Ramona."

"You never have time." Her voice sounded whiny even to her. "You're always working." She wanted to ask specific questions. Why had he been smiling when he was looking at the laptop screen two nights ago in bed? Why did he close the browser so quickly when she climbed into bed next to him? Why did he carry his cologne to work every day and smell so strongly of it when he got home late at night, as if he'd sprayed it on recently?

Why was he wearing a dark shirt in the broad daylight instead of one of his pastels? Why did he insist on taking an Ola to the airport rather than have Rajesh drive him? But Ramona knew the maid was listening. She was washing dishes in the kitchen, but the servants always had one ear out for such conversations. By the end of the morning, the gossip would have travelled through the intricate domestic-help grapevine to all their neighbours at Magnolia

Gardens. So she took a deep breath and lowered her voice. "Is Harry's wife going?" Ramona asked the question in the sweetest voice she could manage. She knew she should stop, that she was going too far. He was already upset, and she wasn't helping the situation. But once the words began to come, they just poured out of her these days, a torrent she could only watch in horror.

Salil sighed and rubbed his fingers across his temple. "You're becoming a bit crazy, Ramona. And no," he raised a hand to stop her from protesting, "you do not need a therapist. It's a waste of money, especially since we have to pay for the new flat. But maybe now that your old friend is here, you will feel better."

He still believed everything she told him. Even the lie that Maneka had once been her friend. The foolish hope he had expressed a second ago brought tears to Ramona's eyes. But she didn't want Salil to see her cry. She had not cried in front of him even on that unseasonably warm evening in February when he had stood here in this same living room with a vacant look on his face as if he couldn't quite comprehend what had just happened.

But it was too late to hide it. He had seen the tears. He came closer and placed a hand on the back of her neck.

"Babe. I know you're still grieving," he said. "Everything will be all right. We will be all right. We will try again. We will do all the treatments you want. Just give it a little time. It's better for you to let your body recover first. And let me solidify our assets a little. You know the new place is costing us nearly as much as the rent here and the instalments will keep increasing as the construction progresses. I have a lot on my mind."

"It's not that," she said. The day-old roses in the silver vase had already wilted in the heat. They looked sad and pathetic, drooping as if there was nothing to look forward to. "It's not just that," she whispered.

"What else is wrong?"

Ramona found it incredulous that a man who was so sharp at work could be so obtuse in his marriage.

"It's not working any more, Sal," she said. "With us. I just don't know how long we can go on like this."

The stunned look on his face provided a little satisfaction. She couldn't bring herself to do something crass like slap him, but this was almost as rewarding.

"What do you want?" he asked. "What are you saying? You know there are no other women, don't you? I don't know how to convince you."

Ramona had no idea what to say next. She had neither anticipated this conversation nor thought this through. But now that she had said the words, she felt relief. She had been bottling up those sentiments for what felt like much longer than three months.

"What do you want me to do? How can I make things better?" Salil persisted.

His appeal surprised Ramona. She had expected anger, yelling, some form of violence. But here he was, looking vulnerable.

He even seemed to have forgotten about missing his flight. She didn't understand him at all any more.

Cancel your trip, she wanted to say. Spend the day with me. Let's talk.

They never talked like they used to. When was the last time they had had a proper conversation that was not about a real estate investment or about how much money she had spent that week? They didn't even talk about babies any more. Let's cry together. Let's hold each other.

"I don't know," she said.

"Ramona." Salil closed his eyes. "This is not a great time for this discussion. You know we have to close this deal in the Middle East. You know I'm under a lot of stress at work right now."

Ramona felt sorry for him. She had an inkling of the problems at work; Harry's wife shared some of the news with her even if Salil didn't. Several of the employees had been laid off recently, and Salil felt responsible. He was a popular guy. Everyone liked him, not just the women but the men as well. His kindness was one of the things that had drawn her to him nearly sixteen years ago when they first met on an old college campus in Delhi. He had been so full of fire, but also different from her father and the boys she used to know back in Kolkata. He possessed an innocence that the others didn't. Small-town Salil had brought a warmth into her life she had not known was missing. "I have a request," she said. "Let's go to Singapore together in July. Or anywhere. We could go anywhere. You pick." She tried to smile.

He shook his head. "I can't take leave this year. I simply can't. Things are too precarious. I have already offered to buy you a ticket to Singapore. You can spend some time with your sister and her family. It will be good for you after what's happened."

"The company won't fall apart without you here for ten days."

Ramona nearly blurted out her suspicion that he wanted to be alone with a woman while she was gone, perhaps even bring her home. She clenched her fists at the thought. "Will it?"

Salil ran a hand over his eyes. "Tell you what? Next summer, we'll go somewhere special. Greece, Turkey, Iceland. You choose. Anywhere. For two weeks. The most luxurious resort you can find. I promise. And you know I keep my promises. But now, baby, I have to go. My Ola is waiting."

"Why are you taking an Ola?"

Salil looked confused. "What?"

"What's wrong with Rajesh? Why can't he drive you?"

"Because you said you need him to take you to the spa in less than an hour."

He suddenly leant forward and kissed the top of her head, like he used to do when they first started dating. It surprised her so much that she took a step back. Salil looked disappointed, then picked up his suitcase and walked towards the door. Just before he left, he turned around. "What time do you think you'll get back today?" he asked.

"By six, I should think."

"There will be a nice surprise for you this evening." He winked at her. "Something to wipe the sadness away and make you laugh," he said. "It's been so long since I heard you laugh." And then he was gone.

Ramona felt the walls close in around her. Why couldn't she be the one to catch a flight overseas to meet with powerful men? Why was she the one always left behind in the silent flat? Then she remembered the look on Salil's face when she challenged their marriage, and it made her miss him. She had no life without him. Her entire existence was wrapped up around his. It had made her obsessed with what he was doing, who he was talking to, who he was, perhaps, sleeping with. And lately, she had been having trouble distinguishing between what was real and what was not. It was either the summer heat or the incident or the sugary pills from the homoeopath.

Ramona looked around the living room she had decorated with such care. It was a beautiful home, and her husband was still capable of surprising her. She wondered what he had in mind. What could he possibly want to surprise her with? She smiled. It was sweet of him to try. Maybe he did care after all. The thought of their marriage being in serious trouble appeared to have bothered him a lot more than she'd expected it to. Salil was right. Whatever else his flaws might be, he did not break his word. Ramona straightened her shoulders and picked up her grey Prada bag. Having someone like Maneka around was already changing her. She had looked her husband in the eye and told him that things needed to be different, and he had acquiesced. Hope surged through her as she walked out and shut the door behind her.

It seemed impossible to win Maneka's approval. Ramona couldn't even understand why she cared for it so, when they had little in common. But it had all started a long time ago. In a darkened auditorium where she was one of hundreds of girls in white school uniforms, staring up at the golden light of the stage where Maneka stood at the podium delivering her debate speech. Ramona had wondered what kind of confidence it took for someone to stand up there in the spotlight and talk to a roomful of strangers. Her voice had sounded low and steady over the microphone as she rattled off facts and figures and made wry jokes that elicited an explosion of spontaneous laughter from the audience. Everyone knew then that Maneka would go far. And where would Ramona go? Probably to the Saturday Club for high tea.

And now here they were, sitting side by side in the jasmine-scented spa with their feet immersed in bubbling lavender-coloured water. Young men dressed in black uniforms sat at their heels, clipping toenails and scrubbing soles.

Ramona stole a glance at Maneka. Her face wore that familiar look of scepticism, which made Ramona anxious. Surely, she could not find a flaw with this plush spa. As a regular patron of Diva, Ramona received VIP treatment, especially on this day when she had gently informed the manager, Mrs Khanna, that her friend from the States was with her. The staff fawned over them, refilling their glasses of nimbu paani. Mrs Khanna, who had tried unsuccessfully to sell Maneka several beauty packages for the summer, stuck her head in every few minutes to see if they needed anything.

Ramona wanted the staff to leave them alone so they could talk. She had little curiosity about life abroad—when she was growing up, her parents took her and her sister to London every summer to visit her cousins, and she and Salil had travelled to several Western countries together. She did not feel the need to ask Maneka how many varieties of cereal one might find in a supermarket, for instance, or what it smelt like inside a Bloomingdale's. Then again, was there a Bloomingdale's where Maneka lived? How could anyone live in such a small town by herself and not go out of her mind?

What Ramona really longed for was information about this American man Maneka was involved with. She had learnt that he was fourteen years older, which made him nearly fifty, and that he had been married until recently and had teenage children. Ramona wondered if Maneka was dating him just to be rebellious. Or did she, like Ramona, feel attracted to men who were nothing like herself?

She had tried to find a picture of Michael on Facebook, but there was no trace of his existence on Maneka's timeline, which had only sporadic posts about books and what she had eaten for lunch, or occasionally a news item that she later deleted. Unlike Ramona's own timeline, which was dominated by photos of Salil. Even her profile picture showed the two of them holding each other and laughing on the white sands of Mauritius, cheek to cheek, hand in hand, as if they would never let go.

"So," Ramona asked, trying her best not to sound overeager. "What's Mike like?"

Maneka wriggled her toes in the tub. "He's a nice man. A serious, responsible person." She was staring at the array of shades on the nail polish tray next to her. "He is very disciplined, unlike me. Wakes up at five every morning to work on his research. He's writing a book on suburban literature in America." She glanced at Ramona. "But you would be bored by all that. He's blond and has eyes that look grey or blue depending on what colour shirt he wears."

The suggestion that she would not find Mike's research interesting warmed Ramona's face. Was it always going to be like this, everyone assuming she was stupid and shallow, interested only in the colour of people's hair?

"Try the Mystic Mauve," she said, nodding towards the tray. Sometimes she felt like people gave her cues and all she had to do was read the lines.

Ramona wondered if she should ask about the book or Maneka's own writing, but the truth was, the thought of a lengthy conversation about that sort of thing did make her feel like she was back in a classroom listening to a teacher drone on about some dull subject. Maneka was right. That was not the topic she was curious about. The unasked question lingered in her throat. What was he like in bed?

She wanted to know if white men made love the same way Indian men did. She had unexpected fantasies sometimes. About servants, people who were much older or younger, anyone that might make her parents' ears burn with shame. Right now, Ajay the pedicurist was gently kneading her calves with the lavender scrub without looking up at her. The men never looked at the clients' faces as they worked. They maintained a respectful distance even as their fingers massaged oils and creams on to the limbs of the ladies who visited the spa. Ajay, like the others, was a rustic fellow, imported here from the hinterland. He spoke no English. His fingers pressed into her flesh just below her right knee. Ramona imagined them sliding upwards, into her thigh, and upwards still near her groin, and she let out a soft moan. If the man heard, he gave no sign but kept his head down and switched to the left leg.

Across the room, a stocky middle-aged woman was speaking loudly into a phone she held in her right hand while one of the men massaged her left arm vigorously. She spoke a mix of Hindi and English in that rough North Indian accent that grated on Ramona's nerves. Her words drifted towards them. "Really? Yaar, I'm telling you, I felt it the other night also. The way he looked at her. With his wife right there. Every other weekend, I believe, they are off somewhere. And she's just out of college, no? Looks like his daughter. These secretaries are the worst, I tell you. Cannot be trusted."

Ramona stared to see if she knew the woman, because if she did that might mean she was talking about Salil. Wouldn't that be something, if she learnt of her husband's indiscretions through spa gossip.

Maneka leant over to whisper in her ear. "Fascinating conversation, isn't it? I used to think that beauty salons and bars were the same all over the world, but in Heathersfield people don't talk about anything except the weather, even when they're getting their hair done. Everyone bottles everything inside. It's a wonder they don't implode."

Ramona didn't know what Maneka was going on about. The American Midwest sounded like a thoroughly dull place to her. But she wondered if Maneka could tell she was worried about her husband. She had a suspicion that Maneka might not be as sympathetic if she heard all her worries. Maneka was the type of person who might ask for evidence or suggest a therapy session, a session her husband had already refused to pay for.

"Salil is sending me a present tonight," she whispered back.

"What is it?"

"It's a surprise."

"Mike and I only gave each other books," Maneka said with a sigh.

Ramona studied her profile, wondering why Maneka had used the past tense when referring to Mike. This was new information, and for some reason, it made Ramona uneasy. She debated whether or not to probe, but something in Maneka's expression made her decide against it. It was too soon for such conversations.

Ajay and three other guys were now painting the nails on their toes and fingers.

"You cut your nails all the way," Ramona remarked.

"Yes, I can't type with anything longer."

There wasn't much point coming to the spa for that, Ramona thought. But she had no intention of giving Maneka style tips today. It was far more effective to quietly take someone to a boutique or book them an appointment with a hairdresser. Little gestures of friendship that slowly, subtly, began to create change. Ramona had learnt these things when she was very young. That was what had made her the centre of the coolest group of friends at school. They had a secret nickname: the beautiful girls. She glanced sideways at

Maneka now. What would she say if she knew the nickname they had bestowed upon themselves?

When their nails had dried, they went upstairs to adjoining rooms for their facials. Maneka wanted a fresh-fruit facial, the cheapest one.

"You're putting actual pearls on your face?" she asked Ramona.

"Ma'am," Pinky the facialist interjected. "The pearl facial gives your face a wonderful glow. The scrub, cream, and mask all contain pearl powder."

"Real crushed pearls? The kind you wear around your neck?" Maneka asked again. "How much does it cost?"

Ramona thought it tacky to talk about money, especially in front of the help. The pearl facials, which were one more thing Salil did not know about, were a birthday present from her mother. She glanced at Pinky, who was radiating with her own glow, explaining things to the visitor from America. Ramona almost regretted her decision to loan Pinky for the day. She felt a twinge of envy now, for Pinky gave the best massages, always kneading the muscles on her shoulders a few minutes longer than expected. And as she lay there with her eyes shut in the darkened chamber, wearing nothing but the thin cotton gown, Ramona found herself telling Pinky the things she could disclose to no one else. The tension eased away from her when she was there, until she felt light enough to fly. She would miss that feeling today, for there was no way she could confide in anyone new. Still, a facial with Pinky would probably go a long way towards converting Maneka. She had faith in her girl.

Afterwards, when Maneka and Pinky emerged from their room, she watched them closely, trying to gauge whether Pinky had divulged her secrets to her new client. But no, Pinky was talking about Bengali fish curry.

"This spa is quite fun," Maneka said, looking around. "I feel like I'm ready to take on the world." She laughed, flexing her arms.

It had worked then. Ramona was relieved. How could it not? After these three months with her here in Hrishipur, Maneka would never want to go back to Heathersfield. The good life ultimately suited pretty much everyone. Even the pretentious pseudo-intellectual activists at the gathering they were headed to next, who were really, if you thought about it, a bunch of hypocrites. At least Maneka had never been like that.

A wave of affection washed over Ramona. She hooked arms with her old friend. It was good to have Maneka around. She was a part of Ramona's past, a past wrapped in shiny, coloured paper, a treasured ornament to cherish forever.

Jessica lived in the oldest neighbourhood in Hrishipur, one from three decades ago when retired army officers, senior doctors, and veteran lawyers decided to leave the capital's politics and real estate prices and move west about sixty kilometres to a new place rumoured to be full of land ripe for development.

The pretty pastel houses on either side of the streets of Sunder Bagh were shielded from the afternoon sun by a canopy of yellow amaltas trees overhead.

"Is this Jessica's house?" Maneka asked as the car pulled up to a gate where a brick-red sign, still smelling of paint, spelt out *Kalypso Kitchen* in cursive letters. The small house had a little garden in the front and walls draped with purple bougainvillaea shrubs.

"Yes. She rents it."

Ramona didn't know why she felt compelled to add that information. She was surprised at herself. Jealousy and resentment were not emotions she had ever felt when she was younger.

But these days, every visit to Jessica's home had become complicated. She felt wistful at the sight of the plants growing wild in the garden and the slow creaking of the small gate that led them in. But the real reason she felt a twisting inside as they stood on the porch and rang the doorbell had nothing to do with houses or gardens, or at least not by themselves. Not without the laughter of a little girl ringing out among the shrubs or the whisper of little footsteps on the house's tile floors. Even though it was too early for the child to be home from school, Ramona found herself wishing she would be the one to open the front door instead of this whirlwind that was suddenly thrust upon them.

"Hellooooo," Jessica said in her low, sexy voice, as she hugged them. Her smile—white and even, like American smiles—set off the colour of her skin, which the matrimonial columns still called 'wheatish'.

Entering Jessica's home was like visiting the Cottage Emporium to look for gifts for people who lived abroad. Hand-woven rugs, batik cushion covers, silk tapestries, Kathakali masks. It was all a bit too much really, like Jessica herself with the phulkari dupatta from Punjab and the long skirt adorned with blinking mirrors from Gujarat. Nearly all the states seemed to be represented. Ramona felt crowded. She glanced around quickly to see if the little girl might somehow be home but saw no sign of her. She was both disappointed and relieved.

In the centre of the room, on the dining table, lay the bowls of food, the reason they were there.

"Everything is from Goa. I made my favourite dishes, my mummy's recipes. Shrimp recheado, minced lamb croquettes, masala fish fry, pork balchao." Jessica pointed at the different platters. "There's rice and toasted pav. Help yourselves from this table. The food over there is for Ashok's photo shoot." She waved at a small table by the corner set perfectly for one.

"Everything looks delicious. And it smells so good too. I have not eaten a proper meal in years," Maneka said.

"Well, we must fatten you up," cried Jessica. "Or at least I will try to fatten you up. I don't think Ramona even knows what that means."

Ramona watched Maneka ladle heaps of food on to her plate and wondered if she really had not eaten in a while. She herself took tiny portions, ignored the bread, and began to pour herself a glass of Goan port. It was sweet, like syrup. She could drink the entire bottle in five minutes. Then she remembered the headache from earlier that morning and stopped herself from filling up the glass.

Quick, catchy Portuguese music played in the background. The room was packed with people.

"Come, let me tell you who they are," Ramona whispered to Maneka. It would give her something to do besides trying once more to have conversations with this crowd, which inevitably left her feeling drained. "That woman there with the sari pallu flung carelessly across her shoulder is Sakshi Mehta, a Supreme Court advocate who is on the news on Capital TV nearly every night as an expert on anything that happens in the country. The gentleman she's talking to is Jayant Kumar, a retired diplomat who now writes fiction. You can tell from his last name that he belongs to a scheduled caste. Many of them join the foreign service through the quotas. His third novel was published a few weeks ago. His son, Monty, is an accomplished golfer who travels across Asia to participate in tournaments. The woman in that corner with the grey streaks in her hair is Jayant's wife. Her hair is actually rumoured to be black. But she colours it salt and pepper so she can look like Indira Gandhi. There's Anika, the editor of *Newsworthy*, a new notoriously anti-Party online magazine. It has become the favourite magazine of this crowd. Oh, wait, she's looking at you. I bet she will ask you to write for them. They need contributors. Can't pay though. The investors have quit because they're afraid the government will come after them."

Anika was next to them before Ramona had finished speaking. She nodded at her before turning to Maneka. "Jess tells me you're a creative writing professor in the States. It's wonderful to meet you." Soon she was showing Maneka the magazine on her phone. "Will you promise to write something for us? About Indians in America. Any aspect from a progressive angle."

"I'm not sure I'm qualified," Maneka replied. "I don't know much about Indians in America. I'm a bit of a misfit there really. They all have families and very different lives and think I'm strange."

"Perfect," Anika squeezed her arm reassuringly. "You'll fit right in with us. We are the Misfits of Hrishipur."

Their names rhymed, Ramona thought idly. She listened half-heartedly to the chatter of the Misfits as she picked at her food daintily to avoid soiling her dress.

Maneka was approached now by the children's book illustrator from Kerala, a short man with suspiciously black hair who, as always, was wearing his state's traditional white mundu wrapped around his legs.

"Are you writing a novel?" he asked her.

"No, essays comparing India to the US. I write creative nonfiction."

"*Creative* nonfiction? Isn't that what journalists do?" he said, laughing at his own joke.

Ramona thought Maneka's topic had changed since the last time she had heard her talk about her book, but she couldn't be sure. It was likely that she misunderstood these things.

The first time Ramona had attended one of these gatherings, everyone had turned to glance at her. They didn't stare of course. They were not servants or construction workers. But it was even worse. Ramona felt their eyes on her even when they were not looking. And they rarely spoke to her unless it was to politely mutter something about the food. Over the last couple of years, it had become more bearable thanks to the efforts of Jessica and Ashok to include her. They invited her to everything and sometimes walked in with her, treating her like a good friend in front of everybody, for which she was immensely grateful. Of course, they owed her gratitude too. For hadn't she helped them, supported their careers, introduced them to people in the corporate sector, in Salil's world, even to her parents' friends in Delhi and Hrishipur?

Which was why, when Ashok walked towards them with that perpetual smirk of his, Ramona smiled at him as usual before realizing that today he wasn't even looking at her.

"Hello ladies," he said, looking only at Maneka. "I see you have now also met the intelligentsia of Hrishipur."

Maneka giggled in response. "Seriously, though, is this all you people do? Go to parties?"

"Madam, speak for yourself. I am on assignment," he said, stretching to his full height.

Ramona had not thought Maneka capable of giggling. She was glad to see her happy, or at least less careworn than she had appeared a week ago. She herself was responsible for this too, was she not? Spa treatment, chauffeured car, Goan cuisine, new friends. It was almost like being a mother. But when Ashok leant closer to Maneka and whispered in her ear, something pulled at Ramona. It was nothing like her insides melting when she saw Salil smile at his cell phone in bed, but still. Betrayal could come in many forms.

Ramona watched from a distance as Ashok took pictures from various angles, once again admiring how devoted he was to his profession. Like Jessica in the kitchen, where she was giving instructions to a ponytailed young cook from Goa. Like Salil in his eighteenth-floor glass office. Like Maneka, no doubt, with her students in the States. They were all busy and led interesting lives. Even her own mother, who didn't seem to have time to talk to her these days and only sent her hurried texts between meetings at the Horticulture Society of Bengal. Ramona had often fantasized about running a little boutique like many of her high school friends now did. A short summer course in fashion design from Paris or Milan would give her the necessary credentials. But Salil had dismissed the idea when she brought it up. She didn't understand what it involved, he had told her. He could barely manage his own start-up with four partners.

Ramona stood sipping her third glass of port, feeling invisible. As the wine warmed her, a familiar melancholy began to overtake her until she almost couldn't keep her eyes open. She was only half awake when the voice rang out through the house.

"Mamma, mamma."

A jolt went through her body.

In the middle of the room stood Jessica's daughter. Her mother scooped her up, showering her with kisses all over her thin arms and legs and her little face. Ramona felt a familiar longing. She had never imagined that Titli, of all the children, would have this effect on her.

When she first met her five years ago, right after Jessica brought her home from the orphanage, Titli was a shy little girl, hiding behind her mother's skirt with a thumb stuck in her mouth. And she spoke no English. Ramona had come away shaking her head at Jessica's decision. Adopting an underprivileged kid sounded very romantic, but did you really want to raise the help's children as your own? But now Titli was wearing the blue-and-white school uniform of the only convent school in Hrishipur, an old-fashioned school Jessica insisted on sending her to so she could 'learn values'. Now, the child spoke English like other eight-year-olds in the city, and her hair looked less dull and unwashed. Her complexion was still dark, but then so was Jessica's. In fact, when she leant over and wrapped her arms around the child, Jessica could almost pass for her biological mother. Or perhaps Ramona had simply grown accustomed to seeing the two of them together, mother and daughter.

She pressed her hand to her empty stomach.

The guests were asking Titli questions about school and homework. Jessica began to explain how she had started a WhatsApp group for single adoptee mothers across the nation.

"The women belong to all communities and regions. You'd be surprised. Maneka, you must talk to them for your book. They have so many stories to tell. You know the struggles of living in a patriarchal society."

Maneka and the others sat in a circle on the floor, avoiding the chairs. Someone brought up a new photography exhibition by an Australian that attempted to capture the lives of homeless people around the country.

"It is total objectification and nothing else," said the Malayali illustrator.

"But it's also art," said a young woman.

An indignant chorus rose around the stranger, who put her hands up in the air in a conciliatory gesture. Ramona felt sorry for her. She looked young, in her twenties, maybe straight out of college. The others closed in on her, attacking the motives of the foreign photographer.

Ramona tuned them out until they became white noise. She found it difficult to keep up with their debates. Not that the topics were of no interest to her, but because they flitted from one to the next with such speed it was impossible to think about anything deeply. And even if she did think, what was the point? What did her views matter? No one was going to publish what she said or ask her to appear on their TV show to discuss issues of national importance.

She tried to look at the room objectively, as if it were a scene in a play. Maneka was surrounded by people, people Ramona had introduced her to, and here she was, alone. Years ago, when they all lived in Kolkata, when Hrishipur was a cluster of villages none of them had heard of, it had been Ramona who sat in the middle, surrounded by admirers; it was she they had all wanted to talk to, especially the boys. And now not even her own husband would look at her with any real interest.

She looked around for the child, who had wandered off to a corner with the bar of Toblerone Maneka had brought for her. By the time Ramona walked across the room, slowly so as not to startle her, Titli had torn off the wrapper. She grabbed the bar with both hands, opened her mouth wide, and began to eat with large, messy bites as if she had been starving for months. Like a little beggar child off the streets. There was something wild about her that perhaps no amount of elite schooling would ever cure. Watching her eat sickened Ramona a little. She did not think herself capable of doing what Jessica had done. She did not possess that kind of selflessness. When she tried to imagine a child like Titli sitting with her parents on the veranda of the Saturday Club in Kolkata, she felt despair. She would have to find a natural way of having her own child, one she could carry to term, one that looked like her or Salil and behaved like her parents, and before them, her grandparents. Or she would have to die childless with this ache in her heart.

"Would you like to see what I brought for you?" She showed Titli the large colouring book with drawings of cottages and gardens inside. "Would you like to paint these together now?"

"I have to go get my paints," Titli said, momentarily taking a sticky hand off the chocolate bar to flip through the pages.

"No, you don't. All you need is water and a brush. For now, we can even use our fingers." Ramona poured a glass of water from the jug on the table and sat down on the floor next to Titli. "Here, look."

Titli put the bar down entirely and gazed with her mouth open as Ramona traced the drawing of a unicorn with her finger moistened in water. Pale colours began to appear on the page.

"Look, it's magic," Ramona whispered. "Colours appear as if they were always there. We just couldn't see them before. Do you want to try?" She took Titli's hand, which was soft and still sticky. It fit easily into her own fist. She dipped one chubby little finger in the glass of water and then guided it over the drawing in slow motions, willing the colours to show up. She and her sister had spent hours with the magic painting books as children. Out of all the expensive toys, the bone china tea sets and Barbies her parents brought back from their shopping trips to Bangkok and Dubai, those books were the ones that she remembered now.

Titli laughed and pressed against her, and once again Ramona felt the longing envelop her like a warm cloud.

"What a lovely gift Ramona aunty brought you. Did you say thank you?" Jessica came up and hovered over them, reminding Ramona not only that the child was not hers, but that she too had been promised a present that evening.

When she suggested to Maneka that they leave, as she had to get home before six, a chorus of goodbyes rang out. The diplomat promised to send Maneka a copy of his second book, a novel in verse that had apparently not sold well.

"But you will like it, my dear," he told Maneka. "Not too many understand it."

The illustrator in the mundu scribbled something on a piece of paper. "Watch the documentary and let me know what you think. It's inspirational for independent artists."

And there were goodbyes for her too.

"Bye Ramona, lovely to see you again. What a beautiful dress as always," said Anika, kissing her on both cheeks.

"Ramona makes us all look like villagers," laughed someone else.

Ashok escorted them to the car. "Don't forget, Sunday," he said to Maneka. He glanced up at Ramona, sounding almost apologetic. "We are going to see the sights of Hrishipur, which means as many of the malls as we can fit in. I will serve as the native guide to the foreign tourist."

"That's nice," she said, refusing to meet his glance. "I hope you both have a wonderful time."

The driver was fast asleep in the car with his seat reclined all the way back. Ramona tapped his window sharply with her cell phone. Rajesh awoke with a start. His seat shot upright and the locks clicked open. They climbed inside the furnace of a car and groaned.

"How were you sleeping in this heat?" Maneka asked Rajesh.

"They can sleep anywhere. They're used to all sorts of conditions," Ramona explained patiently.

Rajesh adjusted the rearview mirror, and for a second, Ramona thought he exchanged a glance with Maneka. But she must have been wrong. The heat—thirty-eight degrees Celsius inside the car even at this time of day—did strange things to the brain.

They drove through the neighbourhood past ice-cream trolleys and carts heaped with fresh flowers.

"Tell me something," Maneka said. "Jessica works in PR, right?"

"Yes, that's her day job."

"How much do PR companies in India pay nowadays? How does she afford to rent that house? And the capital for the business? I saw all the art there too. It must cost her a fortune to keep up this life."

Ramona was quiet. Salil had wondered the same thing several times. He had come up with a few theories, claiming to be worried about her. Ramona suspected that he found her attractive. In any case, she was reluctant to share those theories with Maneka.

If people began to talk about each other's private lives, who knew what they would discover? It was nobody's business. On top of which, she had just dined at Jessica's home. Whatever the differences between them, they were friends. It was one thing to gossip about strangers, but she did not feel comfortable talking behind a friend's back.

"Maybe she has family money. I don't really know," she replied finally. "And who cares? So long as she's happy." Ramona thought of Jessica holding her daughter and swaying to calypso music. How could someone like that not be happy?

They turned on to the main road and into a different world.

Cars rushed past, honking wildly. On either side, buildings rose to the sky. The tinted windows of the BMW made the city outside appear discoloured as they drove past malls and offices.

Ramona gathered up her hair, which had begun to turn just a little frizzy, and piled it on top of her head. The air-conditioning wasn't very effective in the summers, even in this powerful car.

She took out a white handkerchief from her bag and began to fan herself with it before remembering that Maneka, no longer used to this heat, might need it more. She held out the hanky so the curly *R* embroidered in crimson faced Maneka.

But Maneka apparently misunderstood its function and wiped her face with it. Then, suddenly, she gasped. “What the fuck?” She was staring out at something to her left. It was the familiar black sign with the gold letters. “How is this construction progressing so quickly?”

Ramona was surprised too. A wall surrounded the property now. On the other side of it, workers carried loads of bricks and bags of cement on their heads. The buzz of activity signalled ongoing construction. A year ago, that had been typical all over this city. Now, most of the other sites lay still and waiting. But not this one. Not Trump Towers. Here, things were moving.

“I don’t know that I could live somewhere that shared his name, let alone somewhere that helps him make a profit,” muttered Maneka.

Not politics again, please. Ramona knew the president was a weird, creepy guy, but she didn’t live in America and Trump’s policies did not impact her. Besides, people everywhere used a lot of things whose origins were suspect.

“What’s Heathersfield like?” she asked, partly to change the subject.

Maneka talked about the city where she now lived almost as if she were delivering a promotional lecture on it. It was a quiet place where people liked to go hiking in the woods or swimming in the lake. In the summer they picked cherries and blueberries in orchards, and in the fall they picked apples. Then they made jams and jellies from the picked fruit for the cold months ahead.

“It sounds like a charming life.”

“It’s pretty. But I miss big cities. I run away to Chicago whenever I get too lonely.”

“You are so independent,” said Ramona.

"It's not easy. Sometimes I get tired of making all the decisions myself. What car to buy, what neighbourhood to live in, what airlines to fly."

On the horizon, the last rays of the sun were shining on the tops of buildings, making their glass windows shimmer.

"It must be nice," Ramona said. "To make decisions."

An advertisement started to play on the radio that Rajesh had apparently turned on. *Are you still childless after marriage? Text Baby 113 Fertility Clinic.*

Her hand went to her stomach again. The food she had eaten a short while ago had vanished just like the baby had. All that remained was an empty crater. She had carried the emptiness around like a ghost since the miscarriage. She had not been able to talk about it with anyone. But Maneka was someone she had known a long time ago, when they were both children. Surely that meant something. Here was someone who had seen her when her life really had been flawless, someone from the old days. So what if they now lived on opposite sides of the globe? So what if Maneka read books Ramona had never heard of? So what if she wouldn't be caught dead with a designer handbag? An image of their school with its lush green lawns and prize-winning dahlias flashed before her. And all the girls were there in the snapshot, whether they were in her circle or not, all of them who had been members of a charming, blessed time.

She turned to Maneka and put a hand on her arm.

"I must tell you something," she said. "Once we are alone."

"Is it another party you want to take me to?" Maneka laughed.

She may as well have struck her across the face. Ramona shrank back at her words until she was curled up like a newborn baby herself. How could she have expected her to understand?

Maneka, the clever one, who lived by herself, who did not visit her parents for six years, the last six years of her mother's life, the one who had no apparent desire to have babies or settle down. The one whose eyes had not teared up even once when she spoke about her dead mother. She pressed her hands between her knees so Maneka would not see how they trembled.

It was just after six when she finally got home. The maid brought a glass of ice water on a tray as soon as Ramona had kicked off her shoes. She sipped it slowly, allowing the cold water to trickle back into her throat, when she suddenly remembered.

"Did anything come for me?" she asked.

The maid nodded and pointed towards the coffee table, upon which sat a gift-wrapped box with a pink bow around it. Ramona's fingers quivered as she opened it. It had been so long since the last surprise. It couldn't be a dress; the box was too small.

Shoes? Her fingers moved faster now, tearing bits of white wrapping paper to shreds. Lingerie? Or a crystal figurine? Her mother used to collect those when she was younger. Salil had seen them at her parents' home in Kolkata. He had broken one on his very first visit. Maybe he remembered after all.

The paper finally came off to reveal a brown box. Shorn of the wrapping, it looked rather mundane. She used her long, freshly painted nails to claw at the cardboard. Then it was open. Ramona stared at it. Inside was another box, this one from the store. There was no mystery any more. It was the iPhone X. Ramona picked up the little gift card. It said, *Now you don't have to worry about using my phone in case of an emergency*. He had included a smiley face.

Ramona got up and walked to the bar, where she moved aside the Black Diamond bottles that her husband was trying desperately to sell to a client in the UAE until she reached the row at the back. She poured herself a shot of Smirnoff and went out to the terrace.

It was a still night. She leant against the wall and looked at her nails. The paint was chipped from the unwrapping, her manicure now ruined. She caressed her fingers one by one as if to comfort them. Something hurt, but she wasn't sure what. The vodka burnt her throat. She took large gulps until the glass was empty. For a second, she was tempted to fling it down the fourteen floors and hear it crash on the concrete below. But what if someone walked into its path? What if it was a little child?

Ramona took out her old cell phone, her Samsung Galaxy A5, and looked at it fondly—this was a treasured thing she would not replace. Then she made a call and pressed the phone to her ear until she heard the voice on the other side.

"Can I come over?"

"I'm really tired tonight and I have so much work to finish. Rain check?"

"Please?"

"Ramona," he sighed. "The landlady's having a family gathering. May not be wise. Someone might see you."

She started to sob softly.

"Oh, God, please don't cry." His voice grew gentler. "Okay, come over, but give me a little time. How about a couple of hours?" He hung up.

She stood looking out from the terrace at the speck of gold in the night sky and wondered how it felt to be all alone up there, exalted beyond measure, the stuff of dreams and songs, so high above everyone else that you were destined to forever remain a distant star, beautiful, luminous, unreachable.

PINKY

HER CLIENTS CARRIED SECRETS INSIDE THEM LIKE TINY WINGED termites. The women brought them to the spa along with their naked limbs and touseled hair. The termites trembled and whispered inside the women, trapped and desperate, until she released them. Yes, it was she, Pinky, who was responsible for letting them out. She could almost see them emerging as her clients spoke, dark spots against the white walls of her little beauty room on the second floor. Then they turned into a cloud, floating over the starched sheets and the cart full of sweet-smelling cosmetics imported from Europe. When the women left, shutting the door behind them, feeling infinitely lighter than they had when they arrived, Pinky was left alone with the murmur of miniature wings around her. Not knowing what to do with the creatures she had helped bring forth, she swallowed them all.

The secrets she knew could fill the pages of all the glossy magazines that lay scattered on tables throughout Diva. Her clients' trust in her was both a responsibility and a burden. As she grew older, she imagined the insects accumulating inside her until various parts of her body ached from their weight.

That summer, by noon each day, Pinky felt a dull throbbing pain in her right shoulder. But this was no imaginary pain. The doctor had warned her to be careful. But what did doctors know of her life? What did doctors, who sat in their sanitized chambers and listened to people's hearts through instruments, know about living in a cramped two-room apartment in a tenement building with three children who depended on their mother?

What her doctor did know, alas, was that a couple of vigorous massages on a day like this were enough to set the shoulder off. And the day had only just begun.

Actually, this particular day had begun earlier with some unexpected drama.

When Pinky had arrived at Diva, an hour before the spa opened, she saw Khanna Ma'am, the manager, berating Ajay, the pedicurist, who stood with his head lowered at the reception desk. He was slightly built, about twenty years younger than herself, and Pinky felt a tenderness for him that she always told herself was maternal. After all, he was only a couple of years older than her son. And unlike Jeevan, who was teetering on the edge of respectability these days, Ajay still retained the simplicity of a rural upbringing.

"We have a reputation to protect," Khanna Ma'am was saying. Her voluptuous lips were painted a dark red as usual. Her kajal-rimmed eyes glittered with anger. "You have been taught the rules. One more error like this, and you will be out on the streets. We are only giving you a final chance because you came here through Madam and because your father is ill," she said. "Do you understand?"

Ajay nodded quietly. He walked slowly towards the inner rooms with his shoulders hunched like those of an old man.

Pinky learnt what had happened once she got upstairs. All the girls were talking about it. Apparently, one of the clients who'd come in for a pedicure the day before had complained that Ajay's hand had reached farther up her leg than it needed to. No details were necessary. The very suggestion that he might have touched her inappropriately had elicited profuse apologies from Khanna Ma'am and a promise to fire him. But after Ajay literally fell on his knees and begged for another chance, the manager had placed him on probation. However, he was only to do manicures now, no pedicures. Sitting next to clients was deemed marginally safer—and less tempting—than crouching down at their feet. Also, whenever the client he'd offended visited the spa, he was to retire inside the staff room and not emerge until she had departed.

Pinky sighed and leant against the wall in between clients. She dared not sit for fear of not wanting to get up again. Mrs Lalwani was late. Every minute wasted meant a minute deducted from her large, round, acne-ridden face. The weekly facials Khanna Ma'am had coerced her—or rather, her husband—into paying a bomb for were helping calm down the acne scars, but unfortunately, they could not turn the middle-aged Mrs Lalwani into a beauty she had never been. Besides, she was Sindhi and gave no tip. Not a single rupee. And she talked incessantly about her children's accomplishments, which only made Pinky worry about her own son more. If she didn't show up for some reason today, Pinky wouldn't mind terribly. It would give her a chance to rest her shoulder, go see if Ajay was all right, and maybe even squeeze in a few minutes for lunch.

She went downstairs to the reception desk to find out if Mrs Lalwani had called to cancel, but of course she had not bothered to do that.

"Too late now. Forget Lalwani. You have the client from America next, much more important," Khanna Ma'am said.

Pinky's shoulders slouched as she recalled Ramona's friend from America, who had left her a measly fifty-rupee tip the week before. And she had made Pinky talk, which was not how things were supposed to go. She shook her head at the recollection, though Pinky had learnt, from the handful of expat wives she had tended to, that this was the Western way. They all tried to show an unusual amount of interest in her life, as if she were their equal and she and they were going to be great friends. Maneka had asked Pinky to call her by her name and not Ma'am. Then she had gone further and asked her where she was from, whether she enjoyed working at the spa, and so on.

At first, Pinky had been slightly wary of this woman who lived in another country. But when she discovered that Maneka was Bengali and that her hometown was Kolkata, Pinky had disclosed that she too grew up in West Bengal, in the foggy hill station of Darjeeling, far from these arid plains. She had had an unexpected vision of her childhood home, where she would walk to school before daybreak and watch the mist roll in over the mountains and cloud the tips of the Kanchenjunga before it shifted suddenly, dramatically, to reveal caps of glittering snow. The memory had opened something deep inside her. She had thought she sensed a smell, and it was not the rose or lavender that floated around these rooms. It was the pungent aroma of mustard oil. She had found herself telling Maneka a little story. How every Saturday, a Bengali cook would come to their house armed with a small bottle of the oil. She would use it to cook for the week. Cauliflower and peas, poppy seed paste with potatoes, leftover rice with raw onions and green chillies, and the pièce de résistance—rui fish in mustard sauce. Her mouth had watered at the recollection. Of course she rarely bought fish now because it was so expensive.

Maneka had asked if she could eat fish that had a lot of bones and Pinky had laughed. What point was there to eating fish if you didn't pick the bones out individually with your fingers? Maneka had asked how many children she had. Three. Did they like to eat fish too? Why, they loved it, especially her son. Hmm, Maneka had said contemplatively. Pinky had dismissed the lady's interest in her as bored chatter.

Now she found herself wishing it was someone else who was coming, someone like Ramona who would tip her more generously and do all the talking and leave Pinky alone.

On her way back up, she poked her head into the mani-pedi room. Poor Ajay. He was cautiously caressing the toned right arm of a young woman who was talking on a cell phone with her left. Pinky gave him a look of sympathy before heading back upstairs.

While she waited for Maneka, Pinky opened the common fridge in the small kitchen. She found her tiffin box crowded among all the others and took it to the small staff room, which was empty. Everyone was inside one of the beauty rooms, as Madam had christened them, where they were tending to the stay-at-home mothers who came in on weekdays to get their legs waxed or their faces scrubbed or their bodies massaged. Lunch had to be taken hurriedly, between appointments.

Pinky sat down to eat her slice of bread and chole without bothering to heat it up. The chickpeas were left over from last night's dinner. Her husband had taken a couple of bites and pushed his plate away so hard that it had spun and hit the wall.

"Is this food?" he'd said, slurring his words as he always did in the evenings.

Pinky had quietly cleaned up the mess, refusing to look at Dilip, while her daughters cowered and the apartment filled up with the odour of cheap liquor. She had gone to bed without eating and stared at the wall for a long time before sleeping. But this morning, the memory of the scene made Pinky feel sorry for her husband. He worked hard all day looking for odd jobs. Laying bricks here, carrying bags of cement there, knocking down a wall somewhere else. It was always difficult for daily-wage earners like him to find work. But lately, since all the real estate construction in Hrishipur had stalled, it had become even more of a challenge.

Dilip came home famished and despondent every evening and spent the rest of it in front of the TV, drinking straight from the bottle. What else could a man like him do?

Pinky listened to the piano piping out of the spa's speakers and sighed. Yes, it was her fault, for she had burnt the chole in her hurry to cook the food before he came home. Now, she wrapped pieces of bread around it to eat it, and it didn't taste so bad. And really, what did she care about taste? So long as her stomach didn't growl when she was standing behind the bed, looking over her clients' faces, pressing her fingers into their perfume-scented skin.

After she had eaten, she went back to her beauty room to remove the anti-acne products for Mrs Lalwani and prepare for Maneka's fruit facial. She soaked the gauze mask in cucumber juice to keep it cool and fragrant. Then she arranged the creams and scrubs on the cart, plugged in the galvanizer, placed two rolled-up white towels on the bed, and scattered pink rose petals on the bedsheet. The instant clients walked in, they felt like they needed a nap. And in the dark, deliciously chilled, sweet-smelling room, as they lay on the soft bed getting their faces massaged, they tended to doze off, which was convenient, for it left Pinky with peace and quiet in which to muddle over her own worries.

But usually, right before they fell asleep, the women talked. Pinky had heard of doctors who charged patients large sums of money just to talk about their problems while they sat in chairs and took notes. But how could any of them possibly compete with this, she wondered? Did they play gentle, instrumental versions of love songs in the background? Did they spray the room with delicate fragrances before the patients arrived? Did they dim the lights and use their fingers to rub away all the tension from their muscles? That was key. Pinky was known for giving the best massages during facials, longer and more intense than required.

While the other girls left the clients alone in the room with their masks on, to use the bathroom or get a bite to eat, Pinky stayed with them, kneaded their backs and arms, and listened.

Afterwards, she swallowed a couple of pills for the throbbing pain.

Now she walked into the bathroom and nearly gagged. Fifteen years here, and she still had not grown accustomed to the smell. Air fresheners were plugged into every socket in every bathroom so they could release generous doses of their sweet, oily floral perfumes. Pinky washed her hands with the jasmine-scented soap to make sure they smelt fresh for Maneka. In the mirror, she saw a reflection of the jagged skyline of the city through the window on the opposite wall, forming a blurry backdrop to her face with its sunken eyes and permanently etched frown.

When she emerged from the bathroom, Maneka was already in the lounge, anxiously studying her watch. The foreign-returned ones seemed to have forgotten about Indian Stretchable Time. However, instead of a scolding, Pinky received a smile.

Maneka held out a Tupperware container. "For me?" Pinky asked, surprised.

Maneka nodded.

Pinky opened the box and let out a little gasp. Several pieces of fish lay covered in yellow mustard sauce, in which shreds of green cilantro floated like seaweed. She closed the box quickly before the smell could escape and mingle with the various floral fragrances, but luckily the waiting area was empty. When she went to the kitchen, Maneka, inexplicably, followed her there. Pinky's hands shook as she put the container away in the fridge.

"I'm sure it's not as good as your childhood cook's. If my mother was alive, she would have made it much better."

Pinky brushed away tears with the back of her hand. She turned around and laughed.

"The mustard oil is making me cry. Sorry."

After Maneka lay down on the bed, Pinky wiped her face with freshly squeezed orange juice. It was gratifying to hear her make sounds of contentment. Sometimes, the clients moaned with pleasure while she was slowly rubbing their temples or making circles with her fingers over their eyelids. It always astonished Pinky to see how starved these women were for physical affection of any kind, even the touch of a hand. Her fingers, she had learnt, could perform magic.

Ever since Diva opened fifteen years ago, she had been coming to work ten hours a day, six days a week. During that time, many clients had come and gone. Locked in the small room with her, the regulars relaxed within a few minutes of lying down. Then their tongues loosened and just a casual question from Pinky, such as *How was your week?* or *How is everything?* was enough to let the secrets begin streaming out.

In the beginning, their confidences had shocked her. On the surface, they seemed so conventional. They fretted about their children not doing well at school or their grown-up daughters not getting married. They complained about how their mothers-in-law nagged them, or how their maids had gone home to their villages and not returned on time, thus throwing their households into disarray. But then, she turned the light off, covered their bodies with soft cotton sheets, and began massaging their faces. Pinky's presence behind the bed became so familiar, so comforting, that they almost forgot she was there. They felt only the gentle pressure of her fingers and succumbed to the luxurious serenity of their surroundings. What they disclosed to her in those two hours were things they could tell no one else. Not the women in their kitty parties with whom they lunched and played rummy each week. Not the sisters with whom they were forever competing over the size of their condo or their children's grades. Not even the best friends with whom they shared gossip about other people and shopped in the malls for branded clothes and accessories. And certainly not the husbands, whom they rarely saw anyway. No, the only person in the world whom they entrusted with their secrets was Pinky.

And she had learnt to be there for them. For the one who had never consummated her much-publicized marriage with her husband, the scion of a prominent business family. The one whose husband hit her during sex in order to come, not just with his hands, but with his belt, ropes, and sometimes her own highheeled pumps. The one whose cousin had shoved her into the bathroom during a family gathering and kissed her, after which she could not stop thinking about him. The one who sneaked out of her flat every night after her family went to sleep and went to her maid's little room to lie with her for a few hours.

Then there was Ramona, the porcelain doll whose makeup was always so impeccable when she arrived that Pinky hated having to scrub it off. Ramona, whose smile never wavered when she spoke to any of the girls. Ramona, whose gestures seemed to have been as carefully constructed as her body and face. But Pinky knew it was a disguise. She knew that underneath it all lay a trembling, vulnerable, insecure woman.

The last time Ramona had come, with Maneka, she had requested that Pinky do her friend's facial instead of her own. It was her gift to her, she had said. Maneka was too busy working all the time in America to take care of herself. But when Pinky had been about to usher her new client into the room, Ramona had caught her eye and given her a pleading, desperate look. Pinky had tried to reassure her with a smile.

Pinky listened to all of them in silence, without judgement. The women just wanted to talk, often rambling for a while before abruptly falling asleep, exhausted from the exertion or perhaps simply relieved from letting it all out. Every now and then, Pinky made comments like *And then?* or *Really?* Certain of her enrapt attention and undivided interest, the women felt encouraged to continue. They never asked for her perspective or advice, which was just as well. For Pinky did not know how to solve their problems—especially their relationship problems, which seemed to her as deeply rooted as the tradition of marriage itself. She knew only how to soothe their troubles for a couple of hours.

Today, Maneka seemed quieter than on her previous visit. All she said after she slipped off her blouse and lay down on the bed was, "You don't seem that busy this morning."

Pinky, who had steeled herself for a barrage of questions, waited for them to arrive as she began her work. Then the thought of the home-cooked fish curry, now stored in the fridge, slackened her resolve to the point where she blurted out a question herself. "Are you married?"

Maneka hesitated, making Pinky wonder if she too was unhappy with her husband like all the others. "No, but everyone always asks me that when I come to India."

"You live all alone in America?" she asked.

"Yes."

"I could never do that. You must be so brave."

"It's brave to be married," said Maneka. "To not be free."

In the darkness, Pinky whispered some advice about lightening her skin with homemade yoghurt mixed with chickpea flour. "Leave it on for ten minutes before your shower," she said. "It will get the tan off."

Maneka laughed. "I don't share the Indian obsession with fair skin."

She was definitely odd. The spa was full of women who came in for skin-lightening treatments. But Maneka had said "Indian" with a slight sneer. As if she were different somehow. Maybe life in a foreign country made you like that, always separate, never able to quite blend in. Pinky noticed the clear tan line on her skin, a sign that she had only recently been out in such relentless sunlight.

"Is it very cold there?" she asked.

"Snows for five or six months," Maneka said. "I have to drive my car in the snow, and when I'm walking I have to be very careful not to fall and break a leg. The snow swirls all around and the wind blows hard. And unlike the hot Loo here, over there the wind is freezing."

"You drive yourself? There's no driver?"

Maneka laughed again. "No driver, no servants. I do my own laundry, cook my own food, buy my own groceries."

Pinky felt sorry for her. Her life seemed more frightening to her than those of the other women who came in here and confessed to infidelity, the ones who lied to their husbands and children all day long. And even though Maneka laughed every now and then, her laugh sounded a little bitter, like the taste of orange zest when it accidentally went inside a client's mouth.

The smell of ripe papaya filled the room as Pinky smoothed the mask on to Maneka's face and covered it with the cucumber-soaked gauze. She placed two slices of cucumber on her eyelids, hoping they would add some extra coolness on what was yet another sweltering day outside, and then began to massage her arms. But every time she pressed down on Maneka's skin, a stab of pain shot through her shoulder. She had to grit her teeth to keep from crying out.

In the comfortable, air-conditioned silence, Maneka went on talking, as if it had been a long time since she had talked to anyone.

She worried about her father. She wished she had visited her parents sooner, but she had kept putting it off, summer after summer, until it was too late. Now she was discovering Hrishipur for the first time. She was surprised by the number of malls and was planning to write a book about them for people in America.

Pinky was surprised by Maneka's reaction to Hrishipur. Why, everyone always said that now India was becoming more like America. "Are there no malls where you live?" she asked.

The place Maneka described sounded nothing like the America she had caught a glimpse of in Hindi movies. It was a small, sleepy town, surrounded by farms and lakes. The people who lived there grew their own vegetables. Some even kept bees and made their own honey. Their idea of a vacation was to go camping and sleep under the stars just like they did back in the villages, where many of Diva's staff came from. Most of Maneka's friends in Heathersfield did not even have cable TV.

"What?" said Pinky, shocked. Maneka laughed. "No, no, don't laugh," Pinky said hastily. "The mask will crack." Despite the pain in her shoulder, she was doing her best, and clearly, it was working. A few minutes into the massage, Maneka said she had a secret.

"Can I tell you something?" she said. "I haven't really shared this with anyone yet."

Pinky nodded even though she knew Maneka couldn't see her. But she was suddenly struck with genuine curiosity about her client, something she had not felt in a long time. She wondered what revelation was coming and braced herself for the whirring creatures that would soon fill up the room.

She had met someone here. He was escorting her around the city as she did her research. A witty photographer who made fun of Hrishipur and its residents. For some reason, Maneka found this charming.

Pinky did not understand why this was a secret.

"You are both single, no?" she asked.

Maneka wasn't sure. She had someone in America. His name was Michael and he was a nice man but a lot older than her. He had a daughter, fifteen, who had a lot of problems. Here Maneka paused, as if she were debating how much to share.

"Is he married?" Pinky asked. In the secrets women shared with her, someone or the other was always married.

"Divorced. But he has a lot of things to worry about. Over the past few months, we grew distant. Especially when my mother died. I suddenly wanted to tell him all these things about my childhood, but I could not."

"A little rose water for your face." Pinky sprinkled drops of the scented astringent on her freshly scrubbed skin.

"I am leaving in a couple of months. Who knows when I'll be back here. My life is there now, for better or worse. But this guy here is so sensitive and sweet. He asks me questions about my life and work, and actually listens to the answers. What if he gets serious? What will happen at the end of the summer? And also, Mike depends on me, even if things have not been going well between us. He would be hurt. Of course, he doesn't have to know . . ." Her voice trailed off as if she were considering this option for the first time. "The guy here—his name is Ashok. I met him at Ramona's. He's quite young. In his twenties. But we connected instantly. It was so simple."

"Ashok?" Pinky repeated. "A photographer called Ashok?"

"Yes. Takes beautiful photos. Has promised to take me around Hrishipur while I am here. Pinky, am I stupid?"

"What? No? How can you be stupid? You are a professor in America. You live alone and drive a car in the snow."

"Yes, but what's the point? I am here only for a few months and my mother just died and there is a nice man over there who cares for me and … oh, what a mess I am. I can't seem to think clearly about anything these days."

Pinky remained quiet. This might be a large city, but people here were tied to each other by invisible threads. In a few months Maneka would leave, unlike her regular clients who would remain. She thought it best to say nothing. She touched Maneka's face gingerly to see if the clay had hardened. She wanted to give her neck a few extra minutes of massage. She had not forgotten the fish curry in the fridge. Pinky would not be able to make up for last night's dinner with her husband, but her children would have a feast they would savour. The thought made her want to sob with gratitude. But instead, she let out an involuntary cry.

"What's wrong?" Maneka asked.

Pinky closed her eyes to prevent the tears from spilling. She bit her bottom lip until she tasted blood. It distracted her from the shooting pain in her shoulder. "It's nothing. Something bit me, that's all."

"Pinky, what do you think I should do?"

Pinky froze, with her arms poised to attempt another squeeze.

"Me?"

"Yes, you are older than me and you live here and you meet so many people. Hairdressers, beauticians, they are always the wisest people. I want to know what you would do."

Maneka lay with her face covered in clay, her eyes shut beneath the slices of cucumber. She looked like any other client on that bed, just a body under the sheet and a face that wore no distinct marks of identity. Then Pinky thought of the fish again, and the fact that Maneka's mother had just died.

"Maybe," she said, a little hesitantly at first, then growing surer of herself and her words as she spoke. "Maybe this one summer, you should not think so much. Just do whatever makes you happy." The advice seemed too simple, but it was all Pinky could think of.

Beneath the thin crust of clay, she saw Maneka's lips curl up in a smile. Relieved, Pinky began to gently wipe the mask off her face.

Before leaving, Maneka opened her purse and took out fifty rupees. "I will be back in a couple of weeks," she said. "I can never afford a facial in America. I may as well get some here," she said.

Later that afternoon, when Pinky went downstairs and told Ajay how much Maneka had tipped her, he thought it was rather cheap for someone who lived in America.

"But she brought me fish curry," she said. "She cooked it herself, though apparently she can barely cook. She eats only sandwiches and salads." They were standing just outside the side entrance, which allowed them to look out on to the street. "And she asks me all kinds of questions and is genuinely interested in my life."

Ajay did not look impressed. He was a dour fellow, and today, obviously, he was in a particularly unhappy mood. He told her his version of what had happened the day before. The woman who had complained about him had been on her phone the whole time while barking orders at them as if they were waiters. She wanted tea, followed by lemonade, then an extra pillow, and finally someone to fan her while she sat with her limbs splayed.

"Fat spoilt cow," he scowled now as he rolled his beedi. He took a long drag before speaking. "Husband probably refused to buy her more diamonds. Takes out her bad mood on me."

A storm was brewing, and not just in Ajay's heart. The clouds rolled in from the south and the wind picked up pace, blowing dust from all the construction sites around the city. Pinky glanced up at the sky, worried. Her small apartment did not do well with storms. She hoped her younger daughter had come back from school without lingering to talk to boys on the street and that she had had the sense to shut the windows. She would have messaged her on WhatsApp but Namu had lost her cell phone last week, and there was no money for a new one.

The rich sweet smell of the beedi brought her back to the present. The wind and clouds had brought at least temporary relief from the oppressive heat. Ajay was no longer scowling. Instead, he stared into the distance with a wistful expression.

"I did the best I could. I thought I was giving her a good massage. I am always so careful. I cannot lose my job. Babuji's medicines cost so much. Then there is my sister. I have to save up for her dowry."

Pinky heard thunder overhead, instantly changing the afternoon. The sound, an accompaniment to Ajay's story, nearly broke her heart. The spa employed men exclusively to administer pedicures and manicures, although most of the clients were women. Pinky did not know the reasons for this decision, except perhaps that there were more unemployed men out there looking for jobs, willing to do anything.

The men who were hired were trained for weeks. They had to take courses just like the women upstairs did. Part of the training involved drilling into them the proper etiquette when dealing with their well-heeled—no pun intended—clients. Offer a beverage, be excruciatingly polite, never look up at their faces directly, speak only when spoken to, never let your eyes stray to any part of their body except the one you are tending to. The men disembodied their clients' limbs from the rest of them and pretended they were servicing artificial ones. Their job was to remove corns from feet, scrub and polish skin until it was soft and smooth, paint nails to make them look glossy and pretty, and give massages that made clients want to return again and again.

But tending to these women was a risky business. You never knew what might happen when you were oiling and moisturizing the arms and legs of entitled ladies married to influential men. One wrong move, a slip of the hand here or there, and before you knew it, your job was gone, to one of the many young men in the area who needed it, and you were out on the street where it was forty degrees Celsius, feeling dazed and disoriented.

"Don't worry," Pinky said gently, patting Ajay's arm. "You are still here. Now just be more careful. Ask Raju or someone else to keep an eye so they can bear witness."

"What good will their word do against a client's?"

Pinky was silent. They knew so many private details about these people's lives—she because they directly confided in her, and he because he couldn't help but overhear their phone conversations. They had enough material for a good old blackmail like in the movies. And yet, they all chose to keep their mouths shut out of some perverse sense of loyalty and an unwritten code they all seemed to share.

"Do you want me to go with you to the doctor?" he asked her suddenly.

It made Pinky wish she had not touched him. She tended to forget that even though he caressed and held women's hands all day long, he was seldom touched, even by accident. She took a slight step backwards, so that they now stood on either side of a large flowerpot. The red zinnias were wilting in the heat.

"No, I will go on my way home. It's the same old thing. Half an hour of physiotherapy, and maybe he will change the painkillers."

The wind kept blowing the dust around, knocking things over. The dark clouds brought respite from the harsh sun. But, as expected, it was just sound and fury. Not a drop of rain fell. That was the way in this part of the country. Just a hundred kilometres east of the Thar Desert, the air here remained arid and the landscape brown through most of the year. People looked up with parched lips and throats on days like this, yearning for rain the way farmers did in the villages so that their crops might flourish.

The sky teased them, splitting apart with streaks of lightning and even cooling down the air in anticipation. But the rain stayed away and, disappointed, everyone resumed their lives as usual.

For a second, Pinky thought of the rain in Darjeeling, how it fell in a steady drizzle all through the summer and turned the whole world green. She blinked, and it was gone.

Dr Prakash pressed her shoulder with his fingers, gently squeezing them almost like she did with her clients. Except in her case, the sharp pain shot through her arm again, forcing her to cry out. Dr Prakash looked grim. He had suggested an MRI but, at a cost of seven thousand rupees, it was out of the question. The X-rays had been bad enough at nearly a thousand rupees. Pinky felt terribly guilty for having to spend so much on herself.

Dr Prakash's thin grey hair barely covered the top of his head, and he kept running his palm over it as if to remind himself it was still there. He frowned as he looked at the X-rays. "No dislocations, but there is a slight tear in the rotator cuff."

"Can you give me more painkillers?" she asked anxiously. He shook his head.

"At this rate you will have kidney failure in a few years. You need to stop popping the pills."

"But I have to give massages." She stopped and looked at him, pleading silently to make the pain go away.

He put down the films and peered at her over the rim of his reading glasses.

"You cannot give any more massages for a few months. You have to stop. If you don't, you'll lose the arm. It will become inert and you won't be able to ever use it again. Is that what you want?" She stared at him, feeling miserable. The spa counted on her to give massages.

"I could cut them down slightly," she offered, trying not to think about how Khanna Ma'am would react to that suggestion.

"I am telling you that you should not use your right arm for any lifting or pushing down for about three months. Then, once it heals completely, you can resume. But if you don't rest it now . . ." He stopped ominously and looked at her like a schoolteacher issuing a warning.

Pinky gathered her things and got up to leave. The doctor stood too. His expression had softened.

"In three months, it should be fine."

She nodded.

"How's Dilip?"

"OK."

"Has he stopped drinking?"

"Do you think that's possible?"

"Ask him to come and see me again," he said. "For a checkup of his liver."

Pinky sighed. She had already reminded her husband several times, but he'd refused, saying there was nothing wrong with him.

When she walked outside the clinic, the surrounding market was crowded and lights flickered inside little shops. She groped for the fish curry in her bag, hoping it hadn't spoiled in the heat, and sent her older daughter Smriti a message, asking her to put some rice on the stove to boil, before starting her walk home.

In the aftermath of the storm, the world had become quiet and still, as if it regretted its outburst. Since no rain had fallen, the roads were left drier than before from all the dust that had blown around. The temperature was already beginning to rise again, and this time, it would be even hotter. Overhead, the moon was full and coppery above the roofs of the high-rises. On the horizon, to the far right, the gold letters spelt out the words *Trump Towers.*

All through the day the sign stood there, high above the others, a constant reminder of the construction that was ongoing beneath it. But once the sun set, it became a carnivalesque billboard, flashing its presence across the city and even on the highway that led away from Hrishipur, towards Delhi in the east and Rajasthan in the west. Like the neon signs that announced the presence of malls or the luminescent logos of five-star hotel chains, this one signalled an opulence that to Pinky was beyond the realm of dreams. Her fantasies were spun from simpler cloths. That her husband would stop drinking, that her son would get a job, any job, that her daughter would pass her exams, that her shoulder would stop hurting. She stared at the sign absent-mindedly while waiting to cross the thoroughfare, but could not wrap her head around what the finished construction would look like or what kind of interiors the builders were designing. The property was located just two kolimetres away, but to her it may as well have been on a distant planet. One that could be sighted every evening across the skies, alien and out of reach.

Pinky walked home along the crowded lane where stray dogs jostled with rickshaws and honking scooters. A drunk man yelled inside one of the tenements. She hoped he wasn't yelling at his wife, and if he was, that she wasn't alone.

She arrived at the chawl, the long two-storied building her family shared with twenty other families, and fumbled with the key. It was nearly ten. A cloud of insects hovered around the yellow light in the common courtyard, reminding Pinky of the secrets whirling inside her.

She approached her apartment with some trepidation, half expecting to hear a glass shattering, or a voice yelling foul curses or, worst of all, sobs.

But when she opened the door, all she heard were the sounds of a cricket match. On the old TV that stood in a corner of the room, Pinky recognized the jerseys of the two Indian Premier League teams—the Chennai Super Kings and the Delhi Capitals. Jeevan leant forward on the divan, his fists poised to pump in the air. Pinky felt a familiar sense of frustration when she saw him. He was twenty-four, old enough to start supporting his family, but all he wanted to do was play cricket. The coach at his academy had given him a part-time job helping train young kids, but it didn't pay enough. There was no future in sport for someone like him. He needed to give up that dream and find a new job. Instead, he had lately taken up with langda Gopal, the electrician who limped about from building to building fixing fuses and setting up appliances with that leery smile of his. Pinky didn't trust him one bit. Every time she saw her son with him, it sent a shiver down her spine.

Jeevan's father sat next to him on the bed. He wore a vest that had once been white but had now become cream with use, and a green-and-black plaid lungi wrapped loosely around his legs. On a small table next to him sat a bottle of Royal Stag whisky and an empty glass. But he didn't seem to be in a foul mood tonight. On the contrary, he stretched his hand out as Pinky walked past him and pulled her in.

"Rani," he said, slurring his words only slightly, "come sit with us. Delhi is about to win, and the weather is beautiful."

"The weather is terrible. You're crazy," she said.

"Rani," he said again, in a singsong voice. When he called her by an endearment like that, he was not too drunk, just pleased about something.

"Why are you so happy?" she asked.

In response, Dilip felt around the divan for something and then held up a five-hundred rupee note. Pinky's eyes widened.

"Construction. The new one, on Omega Road. The American one. They need a lot of labour and I was in the right place at the right time today."

"What did you have to do?"

"Helped to dig the swimming pool. There will be an outdoor one and an indoor one. Lots of work ahead." He grinned and rubbed a hand across his belly.

"Be careful. Don't strain your back too much. You remember what happened the last time? They stop the constructions suddenly and you are left with nothing."

"Arre, those Indian builders are useless. This is an American project. The person who owns the whole thing is the president of the United States. Do you think someone who can run such a big country will not be able to finish a construction like our losers?"

Dilip's eyes gleamed as he reached for his glass. Pinky noticed the small hole in his vest just below his underarm and resolved to darn it on Monday, her day off from work.

"Gopal has also started making a lot of money," Jeevan announced without looking up from the TV. "I think it has something to do with Trump Towers. He has promised to help me too."

Her eyes immediately went to the short, unkempt beard Jeevan had recently started sprouting. It made him look older. Pinky had tried to persuade him to shave it. She was worried that people might mistake him for a Muslim. There were rumours of men dressed in saffron clothes walking about these days, spying for the government, trying to find Muslims to harass. But Jeevan didn't care. He stroked his beard now, and grinned at her, challenging her to nag him.

Pinky sighed and looked at her younger daughter for comfort. Namita sat cross-legged on the floor, making dolls out of fabric. Scissors, wool, and pieces of cloth were spread on a sheet of newspaper. She'd made nearly everything that was pretty in their home. But she did it at the expense of her homework.

"Did you study, Namu?" Pinky asked.

"Hmm," Namita said, her brows furrowed in concentration.

Every time the crowd roared on TV, Namita looked up and asked her brother what had happened. He always patiently explained things to her. "That was not out." "He missed a catch."

"Don't think they can make it, just three overs to go." His tone changed when he talked to Namita.

Pinky entered the bedroom she shared with her daughters, where Smriti sat on the bed, studying for the accounting course she had been taking for the past year.

"Did Papa eat?" Pinky asked softly, reluctant to disrupt her concentration.

"Yes," Smriti replied. "He liked the food."

They looked at each other and smiled in relief.

Pinky quickly heated up the fish curry, which, she was glad to find, had not spoiled. There were five pieces, one for each of them. But since Dilip did not eat fish and had finished his dinner, that left an extra piece. Pinky wanted very much to give it to Smriti. Fish sharpened the brain, and her accounting exams were approaching fast. Besides, she was a responsible girl. She tutored the children in the neighbourhood, for very little money, but still it filled Pinky's heart with pride.

Jeevan took the plate of food she held out and started to eat it while still watching the cricket match.

"Come to the table, beta," she said. "You will make a mess." He ignored her, his eyes glued to the TV.

"Yes!" he yelled as another batsman got out.

Her husband peered at the plate in disgust. The smell of fish repulsed him. Even if it had been more affordable, Pinky would not have dared cook it at home.

"Eh, take the plate away," he ordered his son, who reluctantly got up and sat at the table.

The rui was delicious, fleshy and sweet. The sauce was spicy from the mustard seeds and green chillies. They mixed a little sauce with a lot of rice to make it last longer and ate it with their hands. Jeevan kept staring at the TV, but the girls wanted to hear about the client from America. Did she speak with an accent? Not at all, which was strange. Did she eat beef? Who knew, Pinky hadn't asked her that. How old was she? Thirty-five, she had asked her *that*. Was she married to a gora? She was not married at all.

"Hai," said Namita, shocked. "She lives *alone* in America?"

This threw Smriti into a pensive mood, so that she stopped asking questions and chewed in silence.

When Jeevan had finished eating quickly, taking large bites as always, he stared hungrily at the last piece of rui. Pinky tried to ignore him, but his thin body, sitting hunched there in the chair that was too large for him, suddenly looked so vulnerable that her heart melted. He was her firstborn, her only son. And he was a good boy. He didn't get into fights or harass women on the streets or carry a knife around. Yet. He didn't drink, which was a miracle. At least she had never smelt alcohol on him. But lately, he had begun to come home later and later. She knew that Gopal was responsible for it somehow. If he continued to go about with that good-for-nothing loafer, who knew what might happen. She wanted to envelop him in her arms and keep him safe. Before she could stop herself, Pinky took the piece of fish and put it on his plate. His face cracked into a grin.

"Me, what about me?" Namita wailed.

"Here, you can have half," her brother said, breaking off a piece—not quite half, Pinky noticed—for her.

In that moment, with her entire family safely around her and the sounds of celebration playing on the TV, Pinky felt perfectly content. She didn't think it necessary to mention her shoulder right then. The next morning would be a new day. A day to tackle problems one by one.

Before going to bed, she performed the nightly ritual that gave her more pleasure than any number of spa massages could. She bathed with the cold water stored in a clay pot in the corner of the bathroom. She poured it over her body with the plastic mug, letting it wash over every part of her. In this way, she tried to cleanse herself of the scent of other women's bodies, and of the sickly sweet jasmine oil she inhaled every day in the bathrooms at Diva.

~

The following day, Khanna Ma'am's lips pursed together tightly, making her mouth look like a single red line. Without looking at Pinky, she offered terse instructions to her new assistant, who kept saying "Yes, Ma'am" and "No, Ma'am." Pinky stood waiting in silence. With every passing second, her sense of dread increased. Behind her, she was vaguely aware of staff walking in and signing the ledger on the white marble table. One of them paused, and she knew instinctively that it was Ajay. She imagined him looking at the back of her head where her black hair, now mixed with some grey strands, was tied up in a bun. But she felt no urge to turn around. There seemed to be no point, and any movement felt like a futile effort.

Finally, after what seemed like hours, even though the wall clock above the reception desk showed that it was only ten past nine, Khanna Ma'am looked up at her, closed her eyes for a second, and took a deep breath. Her frustration almost made her seem human.

"If you can't do massages, you can't do facials," she said simply.

"I can," Pinky cried out without thinking. The look on Khanna Ma'am's face stopped her. Embarrassed, she spoke in a lower voice. "I can do everything else and maybe someone different can come in for the massage part. That's only five minutes. I can ask them myself. Jaya or Kim or Baby. They won't mind. I'll return the favour when I'm better, I promise."

Khanna Ma'am shook her head and spoke slowly, as if trying to explain to a child. "You don't understand, Pinky. Not only will that throw our entire schedule out of joint, because the girls will have their own appointments to keep and we can't have people running between rooms, leaving clients alone, but also … the massage. That's your signature thing. Every time we ask one of your clients for feedback, they say you give the best massages. That's why they want you and no one else. If we tell them you won't be doing that part, they won't want to get facials from you."

"But—"

"No." She waved, cutting short whatever it was Pinky was about to say. "I'm sorry. There's no other way. I am not firing you, Pinky. You are one of our oldest and you're very valuable. And I, *we*, are not inhumane. You need rest, fine. Get rest. Take three months off and come back when your shoulder is healed. With a doctor's note."

Pinky clutched the desk with both her hands. The room blurred.

"I can do something else. Haircuts. Waxing."

"You are not trained. We don't have the time or resources to train you now. No, you're our most valuable facialist, and that's what you will be when you come back."

Three months without a salary. Fifteen thousand rupees lost each month. Without that her family would be solely dependent on Smriti's tutorial money and Dilip's daily wages, which, despite his optimism of the previous night, were never going to be stable.

How would the children react? How would Jeevan react? What if it finally drove him over the edge to drugs or alcohol or even worse? Pinky felt sobs welling up inside her, threatening to burst forth. She looked at Khanna Ma'am with pleading eyes.

"Three months' salary gone, Ma'am," she whispered. "I have a family to look after." Her voice trailed off.

The young assistant looked up at Pinky, who felt ashamed of having shown such vulnerability.

Khanna Ma'am was busy thumbing through the family-discount cards she had persuaded clients to get for their husbands and children to ensure they never went to any spa or salon but Diva.

Pinky assumed she'd been forgotten and turned to leave. Just as she reached the foot of the stairs, she heard Khanna Ma'am's voice.

"Pinky," Khanna Ma'am said gently, without looking up from the stack of cards. "Don't worry, your job will be here. We won't replace you. Only three months. It will pass quickly. Why don't you use this period to relax a bit? Read some books, go to the cinema, spend time with your children. Think of it as a nice little vacation." She looked up and smiled indulgently, pleased with herself for having offered comfort. Then the phone rang, and she answered it and her voice changed completely. "Yes, Madam. Yes, of course, Madam. No problem, Madam. I'm so sorry, Madam, it was our mistake. It will be ready when you come in, Madam." Her hands trembled as she replaced the phone in its cradle, and she stood there for a moment without speaking to anyone. All Pinky could see was her back, heaving as she inhaled and exhaled. Her hair was brownish gold, a colour that did not suit Indian skin. Pinky watched her gather the strands up and drop them again, with still-trembling hands. Despite her own worries, Pinky felt curious. What could rattle Khanna Ma'am this way? Was she worried about her own job? Then Pinky remembered that she had just advised her to enjoy her 'vacation'. She stifled a bitter laugh as she walked out through the side door, making sure she would not see Ajay on her way out. She couldn't endure his pity.

Pinky felt almost renewed as she emerged from the chilled spa into the furnace outside. Something about the world seemed more real to her now. It occurred to her that she had just joined forces with the millions of people all over the country who were wandering around without a job or a steady income to rely on. But it was impossible to dwell on the world's problems when she was reminded of her own.

Of her daughters who would need dowries, and a son whose eyes already burnt with hatred for the world. How would they react that night when she disclosed the news? Pinky's legs suddenly gave way, forcing her on to a ledge on the sidewalk. A sprawling banyan tree dropped its roots around her, offering a little shade, but the relentless heat scalded her face.

Feeling dizzy, she looked up at the burning sky and saw right through it into another world, decades ago, when she ran about in the hills, calling out to the furry dogs and goats that ran with her. It was after school, and she was waiting outside the cottage where she lived for her father to come home from work. The air smelt of pine trees and rain.

On the road in front of her, fancy cars went by at great speed. Her clients rode in cars like that, driven around Hrishipur by their chauffeurs. She wondered what Maneka would think if she drove by now and saw her sitting there. How long would it take her to learn that this city, with its shiny buildings and glamorous people, was all fake, just like the plants inside Diva?

Pinky wondered if her regular clients would miss her. Would they just slip off their clothes when they went for their facials, lie in a different bed in a different room, and begin to spill their secrets to someone new? Or would they wonder about her and hope she was being loyal to them? Would they be afraid that she might divulge their secrets to someone?

From her conversations with clients over the years, it seemed that everyone wanted to either get married or stay married. Even the unhappy ones. They would have affairs, chat with strangers online, hook up with their exes. But they would not leave their husbands. It occurred to Pinky now that perhaps they couldn't leave even if they wanted to. They didn't have the means to make it out there on their own. You could never count on Indian courts to enforce settlements and long-term alimony. The children would be dismayed. The elderly parents would be mortified. In the end, they were all trapped.

Pinky laughed. She had a vision of the termites she'd pictured in her beauty room over the years. She imagined opening her mouth really wide to let them all out. How wonderful it would be not to hold anything inside. Perhaps they were not termites. If she breathed out all the women's secrets she'd kept within, perhaps they would turn into butterflies, not sordid after all but beautiful creatures with kaleidoscopic wings. They would fly in different directions, covering the horizon with their many colours. This barren, harsh city would be transformed into the garden of her childhood, into a green meadow that swam with butterflies and smelt not of jasmine oil but mustard oil.

The seeds of a plan were beginning to implant themselves in her heat-addled brain. She, Pinky, would be doing the women an enormous favour, she told herself. Setting them free. She would no longer be only their confidante, but also their saviour. And suddenly, as the Loo wind whipped her cheeks, she knew exactly who she would begin with. She imagined the look on that haughty face when she realized what Pinky had in mind. The idea made her giddy. Her body shook as the laughter began to pour out of her. Slow and unsure at first, then growing into an implosion of snorting and cackling, the laughter of a woman who couldn't tell if she was totally helpless or powerful beyond measure.

SAMIRAN

SAMIRAN WALKED SLOWLY UP THE STAIRS OF THE COURTHOUSE, his knees creaking as he went, one painful step at a time, until he finally arrived on the fourth floor. He leant against the bannister and took a few deep breaths. No lift. Did they assume all litigators would be young and sprightly? When he looked around at the packed waiting room, once again the answer was obvious. He was always the oldest person here.

He took out a handkerchief from his pocket and mopped his brow. One could not expect air-conditioning in a government building of course, but even the fan resembled an artefact from a black-and-white Bengali movie as it rotated feebly overhead. He let out a dramatic sigh. People his age were supposed to be relaxing in their rocking chairs with a newspaper splayed across their knees. They were supposed to be at home, their own home, preferably in their hometown where everyone spoke the same language and stood up immediately to offer their seats to senior citizens.

He looked for his group among the many people who had gathered there for the same reason. To sign papers, plead with the judge and his minions, and lament their fates with other litigators.

Every month for the past year and a half, Samiran had driven for ninety minutes—plus the delays from rush hour traffic—to get from Hrishipur to the Consumer Disputes Redressal Forum in central Delhi, to attend yet another hearing in the Jannat case. In his mid-sixties, he had found himself in the middle of a convoluted, archaic, corrupt judicial system whose inner workings boggled his mind. And for the past four months, he had tried to navigate this labyrinth of paperwork and legalese without the person who had gotten him into this mess in the first place. It didn't seem fair that his wife had abandoned him to these hearings in dusty courtrooms as if her genteel upbringing in the old parts of Kolkata was above all this.

"Mr Roy?"

He turned, confused. What did they want with him? He was usually just "Uncle," the foolish old man who, unlike the young and savvy investors, had sold off his only property to invest in a new one. Unlike them, he was no longer working and now had no income to fall back on. Samiran, ever conscious of his pitiable state, faced the man who had called out to him. It was Mr Mishra, an executive in his forties who diligently took time out of his hectic work schedule every month to come here.

"Where is your daughter? I thought she was coming too."

Mishra looked over Samiran's shoulder as if she might be hiding there.

"I told her not to come. She is not used to this kind of weather any more. She lives in a place where it is always cold. Anyway, what would be the point of coming today when nothing concrete will happen?"

It was a lie. Maneka and he had argued about moving back to Kolkata that morning. In the last few weeks, since she had started socializing with that girl from her high school, she had somehow decided that Hrishipur was the future. Their future. The argument had ended with her retiring to her room and shutting him out, a gesture that had sent an icy wind through him. But now he was glad she wasn't here. It was not right that she become embroiled in bureaucracy on her summer break. This dreary building, where not a single woman was in sight apart from the secretaries working in the office, was no place for Maneka. Besides, he was quite capable of handling his financial matters himself. He didn't need his daughter's help with everything. Not yet.

Mishra was still thinking about Maneka. "How long will she be here?"

"Two more months."

"Oh, good, then perhaps she could come with you for the next hearing. No doubt we will have several more before anything is resolved." He rolled his eyes. "I was looking forward to meeting her. My wife and I want to send both our sons to the States for college. Would love to ask her some questions."

"Both sons?" Samiran asked mildly.

He tried to do the math in his head. That would be in the vicinity of three or four hundred thousand dollars, a few crores in rupees. And this family, like him, had lost their down payment. The payment they had all been trying desperately to retrieve for the past year since it had become increasingly evident that Jannat would not see the light of day, at least not in his lifetime. But he wondered now if the Mishras even needed the money.

The Jannat investors stood in a huddle, muttering to each other in low voices as if they were the ones who had committed a crime. Samiran tried desperately to concentrate, but, as was often the case these days, the words sounded like a foreign language to him. Fund diversion, lack of regulatory oversight, instalment-based land-buying terms, credit crunch, collapsing returns. Only six years ago, he had been a senior manager at a multinational footwear firm in Kolkata. He had crunched his fair share of numbers and signed countless documents. But somehow, these post-retirement years and the loss of his wife had fogged up his brain.

He recalled once again the original centre-spread ads published in all the English-language newspapers. The towers rising like mountain peaks across the airbrushed blue sky, the heading screaming out *Jannat* in decorative font. He surveyed the paan stain on the wall, the grimy blades of the fan overhead, and the familiar look of despair on people's faces, and fought an impulse to laugh out loud lest everyone think he was senile.

The developers had named the property Jannat because it would be a paradise on earth. It had sounded too good to be true, not an aspiration for middle-class, retired folks like them. But Sandhya had insisted. *The world is changing*, she had said. *If we don't change too, we will get left behind*. Her motives had not been selfish. She had wanted to leave the flat behind for their daughter.

When they first moved to Hrishipur, it was known as much for its real estate boom as for its malls. All the young people appeared to be investing in a flat in one of the numerous complexes that were coming up. Upon completion, the flats would cost five times more than what they paid. The promoters promised possession within three years. Samiran and Sandhya had done the calculations. Or, rather, with her newfound confidence, she had done them, and he, a little bewildered, had been swept along. If they sold their place in Kolkata, they could afford the down payment and the estimated monthly instalments, or EMIs, that would increase only gradually as the construction progressed. With her income in US dollars, Maneka could pitch in later, for after all, the flat would belong to her one day. It would be a safety net for her own old age, a future Samiran and Sandhya couldn't quite envision but wanted to somehow be a part of.

But a year went by and another and another, with no signs of any activity on the construction site. Then one day, all the directors of Bhatia Developers resigned. Investigations revealed that the money collected from buyers in the form of various development fees had never been deposited with the government. Bhatia, the owner of the company, was said to have diverted the funds to other projects. And on the morning when Samiran and Sandhya had tried to go to his office to plead with him as an old, retired couple, they discovered that the office had moved. By the end, the company had shifted its office so many times that none of the buyers knew what the formal address was any more.

And then, the script fit for a movie, which Samiran had recounted the night before to Maneka, who had listened in disbelief. The freak accident that had resulted in Bhatia's death, leaving his estate and unfinished projects to his young wife, who had, until recently, been his secretary. When the news flashed on the TV screen, for one whole day before it was swiftly replaced by other stories, Sandhya had sat down in a chair, looked calmly at the photograph of the three of them in their old home in Kolkata that hung on their dining room wall, and declared that the dream was over.

When the judge finally sauntered into the courtroom, nearly three hours late, twirling his steel-grey moustache to make sure everyone noticed his presence, the investors followed him inside without a word of complaint. He sat behind the bench next to a young associate dressed in a brown sari who looked at him adoringly every time he spoke. The judge placed a hand on her shoulder and whispered something in her ear. It all looked completely official, even paternal. But Samiran, who had seen many such gestures himself when he was part of the corporate world, wondered if they were having some sort of inappropriate relationship.

Mishra suddenly flicked an eyebrow up and down briskly to indicate that Bhatia's widow had arrived at the door. Once again, Samiran was struck by how incongruous she looked in these surroundings, with the reddish-gold highlights in her hair and an expensive-looking steel watch on one of her handcuffed wrists. The pink lipstick glistened on her mouth, perhaps reapplied in the police car. This woman was more stylishly dressed than anyone else in the building. How did the Indian prison system enable a criminal to be so put together before a court appearance? Samiran didn't have to look out the window at the parking lot to know that her sons, who were now entering the courtroom behind her, had driven there in an Audi. How did she expect them all to believe that her family was bankrupt?

There was only one sign of disruption in her appearance. When she turned her head to speak to her lawyer, an intricate web of scars, like a lace pattern, appeared on her face, extending from her neck all the way up to her cheekbone. Then she faced them again and it was gone. Samiran felt an indecent urge, for which he berated himself, to walk up to her and peer at her face closely just to make sure the markings were real and not produced with makeup.

Someone began the usual rant about the woman and her conniving, lying cronies.

"No, no, no." The judge wagged a finger at him and frowned. "Do not speak like that about her. She is a lady. Would you speak in that manner to your wife or sister or mother?"

The associate was nodding briskly. Both of them shot the woman sympathetic glances from time to time. Mrs Bhatia stood demurely, gazing at the grimy mosaic floor, flanked by policewomen who looked utterly bored.

"The poor woman is not to blame. She's a victim. Think of what she's been through since the accident. Do you all know?" he continued. "How much she has suffered? Not only did she lose her husband and get disfigured, but her mother is gravely ill. She is bedridden. And this lady is in jail. She cannot even go to see her mother in her last days."

At this last bit, the woman let out a sob and tried to muffle it with her dupatta.

"If you all sign a release form, she can be allowed to get bail and go see her mother," the judge finished.

A commotion ensued. The men started waving their fists and yelling.

"Bail?" Mishra yelled. "That will be the end of it."

Everyone agreed. Nobody had any illusions about what would happen if bail was granted. Once out of jail, the accused and her Audis would vanish into the thick Indian air. The only money she would pay would be the bribes to various government officials.

Samiran well understood their frustration but dared not join in. Even if he shouted, his voice would probably be inaudible here.

Sandhya had always scolded him for not speaking up. *Be a man*, she would say. *You're too gentle. Everyone takes advantage of you.*

The rest of the people in the courtroom sat stony faced in their hard seats, unmoved by the drama at the front of the room, their spirits sapped not just by the humidity. The case of yet another unconstructed, undelivered property in Hrishipur was par for the course. After all, it was not Trump Towers.

"Order," the judge barked, and brought the gavel down on the desk. Immediately, the courtroom became silent.

The counsel of the accused stepped forward to tell the court that in case the bail was not granted, the investors would suffer as Mrs Bhatia would not be able to sell her lands to acquire the funds with which to repay them.

Samiran wondered if the woman, who stared at the ground in front of her, was really thinking about her mother. The thought passed through his mind that perhaps she had indeed been an innocent victim, ensnared in the machinations staged by her late husband.

Then he remembered the first time he and Sandhya had driven out to the construction site. She had taken pictures with her cell phone to send to her daughter, even though there had been no construction yet. Just an open meadow with yellowing grass, staring up at the white summer sky, awaiting its destiny. Now the dream was dead, and so was his wife. Her heart, he was convinced, had collapsed from shock. Samiran blinked away that memory. No, he could not feel much sympathy for this woman or for the dozens of developers in Hrishipur who had gambled with people's lives so carelessly.

Their group trickled out of the courtroom to the dank hallway outside. Their shoulders drooped as if they were wilting in the heat, resigned to sign the papers, not for bail, their lawyer assured them, but to forfeit their claims to any interest. Just the down payment. That was all they were asking for now.

Samiran's hand shook a little as he signed. Even this money was not likely to appear anytime soon. His only hope was that someday, perhaps when she least expected it, Maneka, for whom he would leave behind no property, not even a small flat in their hometown, would get a modest sum that would help her forgive her parents.

Loud voices spilt out from inside the judge's room, which was ensconced in a corner of the main office. Just as Samiran handed the document with the clipboard to a secretary who did not even look up as she took it from him, the door to the judge's room swung open. The man who strode out resembled a mafia don in one of the new slick Hindi movies about gangsters that Samiran enjoyed watching. He wore a black shirt with the top buttons undone to reveal a hairy chest and a thick gold chain. No, there was definitely more than one chain. Maybe two or three. He also wore rings with large stones on every finger. Samiran recognized the yellow sapphire, the cat's eye, and that flash of red from the coral. Moonga, the stone of vitality and ambition. It seemed to be working. The man stood in a corner of the room and turned his head to look in every direction with the deliberate gesture of someone used to being in command. And yet, he was neither good looking nor very sophisticated. In fact, there was something a little uncouth about him. His curling moustache and large girth overpowered the room even though he had not said a word.

"Mr Tripathy, please try to calm down," said the judge, who was standing up next to his desk. "This is a courthouse," he said. It sounded like a plea.

The well-built stranger positioned himself right in the middle of the office. He looked around at the crowd that had gathered in the hallway and wagged his finger at them.

"You all think everything is our fault," he said. "You think the developers are all crooks. But you don't know the truth. That we are not allowed to do our work. Our licences are not approved. These people," he snorted. "These people wield the power. The ministers, the judges, all in it together. To get bribes. And now that Trump Towers, how do you think that is coming up so fast? Huh? For the Americans, everything is waived. Everything is expedited. Ask him why." Tripathy pointed at the judge.

The judge straightened his collar to try and impose his own authority on the room before speaking.

"You all start your projects without acquiring the approvals and permissions necessary. You take money from these poor people, lie to them, and then buy more land and start more projects. All without even getting the proper titles. The Americans do one property at a time and have cleared everything before beginning."

"Of course they have! Who are the Indian partners? Which party are they in cahoots with? How much have they paid? Desh drohi." He spat out the last two words, whose sound echoed through the entire fourth floor.

Murmurs rose around Samiran. People were nodding in agreement, as if this thought had occurred to all of them already but until now had been bottled inside. *Traitors to the nation.* That was what they were. The government officials who licked the boots of the Americans, the brokers and business owners who sold American products to the people, and maybe even those among them who consumed it all. This was a new kind of colonization. Samiran felt a little nervous. It did not seem improbable to him that a protest would break out in that corridor. He imagined processions of flag-bearing Indians clamouring for liberation once more. But who was holding them hostage this time? Was it really a foreign power, or one of their own?

He turned to leave. There was no use in tarrying here. He would be back next month to do it all over again. He began the slow climb down the stairs, resting his knees on every flight. The last thing he heard was Tripathy's voice threatening to get justice one way or another. "You don't know me," he was shouting. "You don't know who you are dealing with."

Inside his old Hyundai Santro, which he had transported all the way from Kolkata, the temperature was forty-one degrees Celsius. It felt like an oven. The car had stood out in the glaring sun for hours and its air-conditioning was not as strong as it used to be. Samiran glanced at the odometer. Two hundred and nine kilometres. He wondered how many miles that was. He didn't want to ask Maneka because she would nag him about buying a new car. And when she noticed his hesitation, she would insist on paying for it.

He drove along the wide, tree-lined streets of South Delhi, past the foreign embassies and state houses that stood behind tall walls on either side, beneath the canopy of gulmohar and flame trees, without shifting gears. The traffic here was civilized compared to Hrishipur. No vendors allowed on these sidewalks. You couldn't even find a single ice-cream cart from which to get a little respite in the heat. Sandhya and he had often looked for one on their way back from the hearings, but with no success.

His heart ached for Kolkata. He missed the hawkers peddling their wares on the streets and the sight of homeless people washing pots and cooking meals on sidewalks. He even missed the open drains of water. All the things young people like Maneka hated about the old city. What they failed to see was the crumbling beauty of the buildings, the history in those narrow lanes where the only mode of transportation that could fit was the hand-pulled rickshaw, and the aroma of snacks deep-fried in open woks. And what they didn't appreciate was the warmth of the people, the only thing that mattered in the end.

They had moved to the north shortly after Maneka's last visit to India, when Sandhya suddenly managed to find a job at one of the many new schools sprouting up in Hrishipur. The years of French classes she had taken at the Alliance Française when her husband and daughter were away at work and school had paid off in a way no one could have imagined. *You're crazy*, the relatives had cried, when they heard of their plans. *Stay here where you belong. At your age you should not be seeking adventures in strange places.* But Sandhya had insisted, and the prospect of growing old without any income except the interest trickling in from their fixed deposits had been persuasive.

And there had been another reason.

The cross-country relocation had allowed Sandhya to finally dress up and go to work every morning. Even now, the memory of his ageing wife applying lipstick carefully in front of the mirror made Samiran smile. In all their thirty-nine years of marriage, he had never seen her more self-assured. How much it had all meant to her in that half decade that went by in a whirl. If only the flat had been delivered to them as promised. If only Maneka had come home once to see her mother in her new life, where she had students, colleagues, and the identity she had craved for years.

He wondered what he would say to his daughter when he got home and she asked what had happened at the court. When she was a little girl, he would often take things for her from his office at the end of the day. Balloons with the company logo, pretty pens someone had gifted him, and later, when he had risen in the ranks, sample pairs of shoes that were not quite ready for the market. But these days, it was she who bought him presents. When was the last time he had given her something?

He swung the car around for a U-turn. Instead of heading straight home, he would make a detour to the Bengali neighbourhood he had avoided since Sandhya's death. It was time. It was what Sandhya would have wanted.

The instant he entered Chittaranjan Park, his spirits lifted. Red petals fell from the flame trees overhead and floated gently to the ground, where they lay in crushed heaps. Samiran glanced up and caught sight of a man, even older than himself, standing on one of the balconies wearing a white undershirt and lungi. He stared placidly at the world below. A bolt of envy surged through Samiran. He had forgotten what it felt like to stand in one's own home and feel the ground so steady beneath one's feet.

Inside the market, some of his old confidence returned. This was a mini version of Kolkata, developed for nostalgic expats in the capital. The signs in Bengali, advertising chilli chicken and chow mein alongside mutton rolls and fish chops, and the snatches of conversation in his native language, made him feel at home in a way the malls and breweries of Hrishipur never would.

In the fish section, the rows of scaly creatures stared up at him with their beady eyes from the slabs of ice as if they had known him forever.

"Aashoon, dada," Kallol the seller called out to him.

Samiran used to come here regularly just to hear the shopkeepers speak to him in Bangla. Sandhya would shake her head in resignation when he got home, his arms loaded with smelly bags full of fish. She would complain, and then set about to cook it all. The truth was that if a week went by without any fish on the table, he began to crave it. You could take a man out of Bengal and so on.

The past four months he had not thought much about food. Chaya cooked North Indian vegetarian staples. An assortment of pulses, legumes, lentils and beans appeared on the dining table night after night. The only indulgence Samiran had allowed himself was his evening glass of Scotch and soda in front of the TV, accompanied by a bowl of fried peanuts or masala chips or some other equally unhealthy snack to munch on. The fact that his wife was not around to scold him and remove the bowl while muttering about cholesterol made it bittersweet. But tonight, he would sit with Maneka, and they would watch another Hitchcock movie together. It had been his idea to go through all the films before she left at the end of the summer. It was one of the few things they used to both enjoy when she lived in India. They had already watched *Vertigo* and *Notorious*. He might not be able to remember all the facts of the Jannat case, but he could rattle off the names of the lead actors in each of Hitchcock's films. And if he tried hard enough, surely, he could still connect with his only child.

Now, confronted with a variety of freshwater fish caught in the rivers of Bengal spread across two countries, Samiran visualized the dishes that would adorn the table the next few days. Parshe in pungent mustard sauce sprinkled with cilantro leaves. Fried ilish served with ghee and green chillies, rui cooked with yoghurt, bhetki mashed up and stuffed inside potato chops, prawns in sweet coconut milk. His mouth began to water.

"Have not seen you in a long time, dada," Kallol said. Samiran felt guilty. How could he think of such a feast without Sandhya? He imagined all the men in the crowd behind him boring their eyes into his back in disapproval. Then he remembered the reason he had stopped here.

"My daughter is visiting from America," he explained. "She never gets to eat all this fish." He waved at the beady eyes. "I have come to take some for her."

Kallol dove into the ice and emerged with a whole fish in each hand, his knuckles covered in scales.

"The freshest ilish for Didi," he said, holding up his right hand in triumph as if he had just caught the fish in the river himself.

Samiran eyed it with suspicion. "How much?" he finally asked.

"Two thousand rupees for one kilo."

"What?" he said "This pathetic-looking fish? It looks like it has no oil inside."

"This is prime quality, dada. Straight from the Padma River in Bangladesh."

Samiran inspected the ilish, still hoisted in the air like a flag.

"This doesn't look fresh. Tell me the truth, when was it caught?"

"I'm telling you, it's a fresh catch."

You could never really trust these Bengali chaps in Delhi.

Now if he had been standing in the middle of Lake Market in Kolkata, it would have been a different story. Still, Kallol had never cheated him. He wanted to surprise Maneka with the ilish.

It was the only fish she would eat when she was growing up. And she surely hadn't had any in the past five years. She ate canned tuna and fillets of salmon with no spice or oil.

But two thousand was a lot for just one kilo of fish. He debated what to do. Should he get several other varieties now and wait for a little rain, when the quality of the ilish would improve dramatically? Or should he splurge on this mediocre thing right here? Then he remembered what his in-laws used to always say. Those snooty folks over in that rambling old family home back on Girish Chandra Avenue did know their fish. And they insisted that a bad ilish could cause worse food poisoning than anything else. No, he wouldn't risk it. Maneka would be here until August. It was bound to rain, even in Delhi and Hrishipur. She wouldn't mind waiting. Meanwhile he'd get her other things, equally elusive in America.

"I will take the rui," he said, pointing to Kallol's other hand. "And I want parshe stuffed with roe that is silky as bone marrow, tangra, and bhetki."

Kallol crouched down and placed the plump rui against the upright blade of the boti knife. With his foot set on the instrument's platform, he cut the fish into large pieces.

"I hope the rui is not too ripe," Samiran said as he watched.

"If it is, you bring it back," Kallol assured him with the confidence of a man who knew how long it took to drive from interior Hrishipur to South Delhi on any given day.

The market was full of local residents and Bengali flowed freely. Samiran allowed himself a little twinge of resentment.

These people, or their parents, had received free land here in CR Park when they came over from Bangladesh in the seventies after the war with Pakistan. Once refugees, now they owned three-story houses in the capital. The morning's scene from the stuffy courtroom and that woman's painted face came back to haunt him. He tried to visualize his daughter's face instead. The poor child. How hard she tried to be brave and cheerful for his sake. She had talked incessantly on the way back from the airport, pointing at the neon lights and tall buildings, asking dozens of questions, appearing curious and interested. But he was her father. He had felt in his bones her sense of loss as she walked out of the chaotic terminal with her cart piled with luggage, her face searching in the crowd for her one surviving parent. And when they got home that night, she had taken out that bottle of single malt, purchased dutifully at duty-free. She had not forgotten that part, not even this time. He tightened his grip on the bag of fish.

~

An hour later, he entered his flat, his *rented* flat, with the smelly bags, and shouted for Chaya. The sweet girl came running with a glass of ice-cold water.

"Where's Didi?" he asked in a low, conspiratorial voice.

In response, Chaya pointed at the second bedroom, whose door was still shut.

"Has she been there all day?" he asked, surprised.

"Yes, Uncle," whispered Chaya. "I have not disturbed her."

Samiran knocked once and entered Maneka's room only to find her sitting cross-legged on the floor, surrounded by photos, French textbooks with illustrations, and notebooks in which he recognized his wife's beautiful cursive handwriting.

"Going through Ma's things again?"

"I keep learning new things," she said, looking a little perplexed. "I'm trying to understand what her life was like here, as a teacher." Then she remembered where he had been. "How did it go at the court? Any progress?"

He shook his head.

"It will take years. Maybe long after I am dead, you may get the money if you're lucky."

Maneka's shoulders drooped as she turned back to the album sprawled on her lap. "Don't worry about the money, Baba," she said. "Once I get tenure, I can take care of all your needs."

"You will not need to do that," he said, straightening his back.

"Come and see what I've got for you," he added in a cheery voice, eager to show her he was still able to buy things for her, still able to put food on their table.

They went together to the kitchen, which was so hot it made them both gasp. The air-conditioning from the other rooms didn't reach here. You couldn't even turn on the exhaust fan or it would blow out the flame on the stove. And the tiny window in the corner had to be kept shut after sunset to keep the mosquitoes from flying in.

The sink slowly filled up with fish. Chaya emptied the last bag, allowing the odour to float through the rooms. Whatever daylight remained outside drifted in through the open window.

"Baba, this is a lot of fish," Maneka remarked.

"It's for you," he said. "For us," he added. "I haven't eaten fish since ..." He paused before continuing. "I thought you would enjoy some old recipes, some dishes maybe you've not had in a long time." He listed the names of the fish, counting them off on his fingers. "I tried to get ilish but it's not very good yet. What's the matter? I thought you liked fish now. Don't you eat canned tuna and all that over there? Weren't you telling me the other day that you've come to appreciate Bengali cuisine because you don't get it now?"

Maneka nodded.

"Then why so glum?"

"Who will cook all this, Baba?" Maneka looked at him helplessly.

He stared at her. He didn't understand. She was an adult, a grown woman, she had lovers now, she was a professor. She cooked all her own meals over there, didn't she? "I thought you said you liked cooking. Ma would always tell me what you were cooking in America."

She shook her head. "I don't know how to cook all this. I make pasta. Meatloaf. Maybe some chicken curry. The only fish I cook is fillets, which I usually stick in the oven." She pointed at the sink. "That's a full fish head, with eyes and everything. Those recipes you're thinking of? Ma's recipes? I don't know any of them. I never learnt." She cleared her throat. "The only fish thing I can make, and not very well, is the mustard sauce. I made some for the woman in the spa the other day. But it was so watery. For her I thought it would be okay. But not for you, Baba."

Samiran felt the ground move beneath his feet. What would they do, he wanted to ask her. With the fish? With the photos? With the unlearnt recipes? He wanted to say it was not a problem. They could just throw it all away. But they couldn't. He had spent three thousand rupees on them. He, a retired man with no income now that his wife, the breadwinner in the last few years, was dead. What had he been thinking? You were *not* thinking, Sandhya would have said. He braced himself for a snide remark from his daughter. But none came. She was still staring at the fish with a look of helplessness on her face.

"Maybe Chaya can do something," he suggested tentatively. "She used to help Ma." He looked at the maid with hope.

Chaya put a fist into her mouth and stared at the fish as if she were afraid of it.

"I can only fry fish, Uncle," she said through her fingers. "But others, Aunty never taught me."

He had a sudden urge to hurl the stinking fish out of the kitchen window. Such urges were unlike him. He had never been the volatile one in the family. "Put it in the freezer," he told Chaya. "It will not all fit, Uncle," she said, looking down at the floor. "What will not fit I will give away to the watchman. There are many poor people here who will be happy to eat the fish. They don't wait around for fillets."

As soon as the words were out, he was overcome with exhaustion. It had been a stifling, fruitless day. He longed for some cold water to run down his back.

Maneka's eyes widened in surprise. She was not used to her father being angry, only her mother. Then they softened, and she looked at him with pity.

"I was planning to make dinner tonight. Spaghetti and a marinara sauce. I thought you might like a change."

"Is that the red sauce or the white sauce?"

"Red. The white is not good for your cholesterol."

"Fine," he said, mopping his brow and trying not to think about the tart taste of all the tomatoes in the sauce she would make. "Yes, I would like it."

"Good." She brightened. "Chaya will help me, right, Chaya?"

"Yes, Didi."

He was out of the kitchen when he remembered what he had wanted to say all afternoon to someone. "Fish is so overpriced here. It will be much cheaper when I am back in Kolkata."

He walked to the bathroom for his shower without waiting to see Maneka's reaction.

~

She brought up the topic when he least expected it, just like her mother used to do. They were watching *The Man Who Knew Too Much*, Sandhya's favourite Hitchcock film because of the song that would inevitably arrive just when she had had enough drama and suspense.

Samiran sipped his single malt, feeling lighter than he had in months. He thought he might be able to bear the vast emptiness left behind by Sandhya's death if his daughter were around. He tried not to think about the day, two months from now, when she would leave again and return to that faraway world that he couldn't even begin to fathom. Heathersfield sounded bizarre, unlike any notions he had ever harboured about Western countries. Deserted streets, snowstorms, silence. Listening to her speak about her life there made him afraid for her.

Just as the McKennas received news of their son's kidnapping, she blurted out what must have been on her mind all day.

"You are not seriously thinking of returning to Kolkata, are you?"

"It's called Kolkata now, Mishti. That is its original name. And it is my original hometown. We moved here for Ma's job. It makes no sense for me to live here alone."

What he didn't reveal was how much better Sandhya had adapted to life in this new city than he had. She would push forward in lines while he waited his turn, and argue with drivers and salesmen while he stood meekly by. On one occasion when they were on the busiest thoroughfare in the city, he remembered stalling the engine to wait for the traffic light to turn green. Around them, vehicles had roared past, ignoring the red light. *Why are you waiting?* Sandhya had asked incredulously. *This is Hrishipur, not your slow and steady Kolkata. You can't stop; you have to keep going.* Without her around, he felt inadequate to the challenge.

"I am getting old, Mishti. I should go home," he said.

"The hospitals and medical facilities are terrible in Kolkata," Maneka protested. "What will happen if you are ill? I know you're getting old. That's why I worry. You need good doctors. I am so far away. I can't help you if something happens. I couldn't help Ma."

Her voice hardened. He could not remember the last time he had heard her cry. Probably when she was a child. Even in the privacy of her bedroom this summer, he knew she had not cried because he had stood waiting outside her door with his ear pressed to it. Her refusal or inability to shed tears alarmed him, and he didn't understand this edginess in her voice. His wife's mood swings, he knew, had arisen from years of pent-up desires, released like pressure through a safety valve. Little storms that blew through their lives without causing long-term damage. His daughter's cold anger, on the other hand, was like a knife through the air, slashing whatever it touched.

Samiran wanted to tell Maneka that her mother had died here, in Hrishipur, despite the fancy hospitals and doctors it boasted. And when that happened, he had no old friends or relatives by his side. Only a couple of teachers from Sandhya's school came to the shraddha. Then they left, and he was alone with the young maid, both of them mute with shock.

"I need friends and neighbours who will talk to me and relatives who will drop in once in a while. I need people my age. And I need to live in a city where I can feel a living pulse. Not here."

Maneka leant forward. "But Baba, if you go to Kolkata, I will have to visit you there."

"It is your hometown too, Mishti."

"But it's not the same. Everything is different now. You won't live in the same neighbourhood. My friends have all moved out. What will we do there? There's nothing to do. It's so peripheral. All my life I wanted to leave and go somewhere where things happened, and now you want to go back?" There was a hint of desperation in her voice.

"What happens in Heathersfield?" Samiran asked. "How many people does it have?"

"Sixty thousand," Maneka muttered.

"Kolkata has fourteen million."

In response, Maneka took a sip of her drink.

Samiran found her attitude puzzling. She had been so happy in the city where she was born. Sandhya and he had made countless sacrifices when they were younger just to ensure that she could attend the most prestigious school. What was it about the city that now haunted her so? She wouldn't even be the one living there. She would just have to drop by once in a while to see him, if she wanted.

"You do not have to visit," he said, popping a fistful of chanachur into his mouth. "After all, you did not visit Ma for six years."

On the screen, Doris Day sat down at the piano and began to play 'Que Sera Sera'. Sandhya would have turned the volume up. Samiran waited to see if Maneka would do the same, but she just sat there like a stone staring at the TV where, from somewhere deep inside the building in the movie, a little boy began to whistle the tune back to his mother. The parents would soon be reunited with their child. Despite what the song said about the unknowable future, the McKennas' lives would go according to script, unlike his and Sandhya's.

When Sandhya had complained about their daughter's procrastination, it was Samiran who had tried to reason with her. First, she needed to complete her doctoral studies, then she had to get a tenure track job, and then she had to settle in a new place. He heard snatches about her life from his wife, who was the one who talked to her at length. They would sit on their balcony early in the morning, drinking their cups of tea, looking out over the abandoned construction sites to the right of their building, and talk about their daughter. She had a boyfriend who had been married for over twenty years, she was going on road trips across the country by herself, driving home late at night in the middle of blizzards, and joining protests against police brutality even though she did not yet have a green card. When Sandhya worried herself sick about Maneka, Samiran would gently remind her that they had let her go so she could be her own person. She would come, next year, or the year after, she would come eventually, and then the wait would have been worthwhile.

"I'm sorry," he said to Maneka. "Ma understood. And so do I. I am only trying to say that I will be happier in Kolkata. Here I feel as numb as if I were living inside a refrigerator."

"How will you continue to fight the Jannat case in Kolkata? You will never get the money if you leave now and fail to make the court appearances."

That was true. He wouldn't. He could hire a lawyer and give him power of attorney, but that would cost more than the lawyer he now shared with the rest of the group. Eventually, Samiran knew he would have to turn to his daughter for help, but he was trying desperately to postpone that moment.

"Think of how much I will save in Kolkata," he said. He did not mention the complaints he had been receiving from his cousins of late about inflation in Bengal. He refused to believe that it could be as bad as in Hrishipur. Everyone still shopped in open markets after all, not in malls. "Everything is cheaper there," he said with as much confidence as he could muster. "Labour too." He nodded towards the kitchen.

"Wait, what? You're going to let her go?"

"It's a waste of money," he said. "I pay her ten thousand rupees a month besides paying for her groceries, clothes, medical expenses. If I were not retired it would be okay, but I cannot afford a full-time live-in servant any more. Besides, she has hardly any work when you are not here. I can manage with a part-timer."

"You cannot live alone. What if you need some help in the middle of the night? You must keep her. I will pay her fees. I can afford to send you some money every month. Everyone does it."

"No one does it."

"The daughters do it."

"But how much do you earn? You are just an English professor. You don't even have tenure yet. You need to save. Buy a house."

"The exchange rate is going up. My dollars will go further here now. You have no choice, Baba. You have to accept my help. You can't let go of Chaya."

He put his fingers to his lips, but it was too late. Chaya's silhouette hovered behind the curtain at the kitchen door. He switched to English.

"You have to accept that I will make my own decisions, Mishti."

"Why suddenly now, when you let Ma make all the decisions for the past five years? Why didn't you protest then?"

The credits began to go up on the screen. As if on cue, the lights in the flat went out, plunging it into darkness. They waited in silence for the generator to kick in. Somehow, the loss of power softened the mood.

"Remember how we used to have power cuts in Kolkata when you were a child? We would sit in the dark and play cards by the light of a kerosene lantern."

"I can't understand how a city like this has such a bad power situation." Her voice was still rough, but less shrill now.

"Think of how much electricity is being used up. The malls and call centres burn with lights all day and night. Can you imagine how many ACs are on in every household this evening?"

"But if they are so keen on developing this city, why haven't they planned properly for the infrastructure?"

Samiran did not bother to answer the question. The lights should have come back by now. Chaya's figure glided across the living room to the balcony, looking like a ghost.

"Kya hua, Chaya?" he asked after her. "Can you see if the power has gone out all over the neighbourhood or just our building? Why isn't the damn generator working?"

"Uncle," Chaya shouted back. "Only our flat."

"What? Impossible." He strode to the balcony to take a look and sure enough, every other flat window was bathed in light.

"Bloody hell, is it a fuse?"

He stepped into the narrow hallway and peered into the electric metre with a flashlight, but all the switches seemed to be turned up the right way.

"Can we call someone?" Maneka asked, standing behind him and looking over his shoulder. "An electrician?"

"It's so late. Who will come now? Let me try."

He called the security watchman on the intercom. The regular electricians were unavailable. "Arrey bhai, just to take a quick look. Send anyone. Please. I bought so much fish today. It's in the fridge, will get spoiled." Then he added. "My daughter has come from America. She cannot sleep in this heat."

It worked. Someone knew someone whose friend was an electrician. Gopal was his name.

"Is that the fellow with the bad leg?" Samiran asked. He had seen him loitering downstairs once or twice, ogling the maids. He had not liked the look of him at all. But right now, there was little choice. "Fine, send him."

Chaya lit a few candles. One of them stood flickering on the coffee table. Samiran asked her to open the windows to let in a little air. Outside, the sky rumbled.

"Will it rain at all do you think?" Maneka asked. "I so wanted to hear and smell the monsoon."

"Maybe," he said. "All we can do is wait and hope."

He wanted to add that it was already raining in Bengal, that the monsoon never failed to arrive on time on the eastern coast. But he didn't want to return to that subject right now. He was reluctant to disturb the peace in the candlelit room. Maneka's face looked pensive in the semidarkness. When she spoke, her tone was subdued. She sounded less judgemental and more curious.

"I don't know, Baba, sometimes I wish my life were different too. You know how you said Hrishipur feels like a fridge to you where you are numb? Heathersfield is like that too. Literally. It is a fridge in the winter. Everything is frozen. The plants, the soil, the air. And me. I feel like a block of ice sometimes. As soon as I landed at the airport here, I felt like I was beginning to thaw."

If Maneka were still a little girl, maybe he would have known what advice to give her. But her world seemed outside his grasp. What did he know about academics in American universities or blond American men or retirement accounts or automatic transmission cars for that matter? Every time Maneka had brought up an aspect of her life she was not content with or seemed confused about, he had changed the subject, intimidated by the foreignness of it all. Now he wondered if she might be better off here in her own teeming country after all.

Lately, he had been thinking of his youth. The memories were sharper than he had expected. Sandhya had never wanted to be a housewife, even though that was what was expected of her. Her parents married her off at twenty, straight out of college. They didn't want her to work. He hadn't wanted her to work. In fact, he had specifically told her then to stay home and take care of her family. To be a wife and mother. And she had done exactly that. After the doctors had warned them against more babies on account of Sandhya's hypertension, she had funnelled all her energy into the one child and their home. Even though it had meant that for years she had been unhappy, restless, taut like a violin string bound to snap. He felt a tremendous need to confess. "When I was your age," he said suddenly, "there was so much I did not understand. How your mother was not meant to stay at home, for instance. Maybe that's why she was angry all the time."

"I have decided to focus my essays on the lives of women in India," Maneka said. "So much has changed and yet nothing has changed at all."

Her book idea seemed to constantly morph into something different. Samiran wondered why each of the essays couldn't simply be about something else. Wasn't India itself a good enough topic to tie it all together? But he was just a corporate guy. Sandhya, with her intellectual proclivities, might have been better able to grasp their daughter's literary visions. He would read whatever she wrote and tell all his friends about it, but he thought it best not to offer any insights on this subject.

"Baba," Maneka said. "Do you think the judge is having an affair with Mrs Bhatia?"

It was not something he'd suspected. Why, he'd assumed the judge was probably involved with his adoring assistant. But the accused who lived in jail?

"I suppose that in this country anything is possible."

The doorbell rang, interrupting the peace, breaking the spell. When Chaya opened the door, the figure of the electrician appeared in the doorway.

"Where is the fuse box?" he asked her in a gruff voice.

Samiran stood up abruptly, spilling some of the whisky in his glass.

"Bring him a glass of water, Chaya," he ordered, rushing to the hallway. "I will show him."

She scuttled away like a frightened insect. If Sandhya had been around, she would not have allowed Chaya to open the door to a stranger this late at night. He chided himself for not remembering sooner her mistrust of unfamiliar men and the trauma she still carried despite five safe years in his home.

Samiran held the flashlight aloft for the electrician as he peered at the fuse box. The light revealed the man's gaunt profile, now beaded in sweat, half of a pencil-thin moustache, and a rather large ear. Gopal was built slightly like all the others of his class. But it was his fingers that intrigued Samiran. They were long and delicate and moved swiftly like fluttering wings among the tangle of wires. Samiran watched him work with envy. Even he had a job to do, a profession he still belonged to, a purpose, really, in life. Unlike Samiran, now rendered useless to society, with no aim other than watching yet another movie or cricket match on TV.

"It is too hot," Samiran said, apologetically. "My daughter is here from America. She will find it difficult to sleep without power. That's why I needed someone to come this late at night. Glad you were around." He immediately regretted mentioning America. Now Gopal would demand more money from him.

Gopal chuckled, with his head half inside the box.

"Amreeka? Does she have contacts with the Tarrump people?"

"I don't think so. She is a professor there," Samiran said, as if that might explain everything, including why he could not pay too much. Professors in the humanities in America earned less than most of the people who lived in Hrishipur, Samiran had discovered, much to his horror.

"Ask her to get me a job there."

"In America?" Trust them to think it was so easy.

"Saab, I am not going to Amreeka. I want to live here in my own country. But I would not mind a job in that new building."

Gopal's back stiffened, and when he spoke again his tone had changed. It was no longer jovial. "The other day, I heard they needed electricians. But when I went, the manager looked me up and down and asked me for my papers. For my licence. He thinks this is Amreeka or what? Just a Sardarji from Chandigarh and showing me his colours. I turned around and left. Why would I want to fix their short circuits anyway?" His fingers moved faster now, twisting and turning in a frenzy.

"Maybe the residents will call you when there is a power cut," Samiran said. "Like I did tonight. When the central air-conditioning is not working in someone's flat at the height of summer, they won't care if you have a licence or not."

Gopal turned and wiped his brow with a sleeve. In that brief second, Samiran saw something on the man's face that made him take an involuntary step back. A look of pure contempt.

"Saab, there will not be any power cuts over there. Haven't you heard? It's a no-power-cut zone. Along with the hospitals and the five-star hotels. Even the malls have power cuts, but not Tarrump Towers. They will suck the power from everywhere else in Hrishipur."

One final twist of the hand and just as abruptly as they had gone, the lights came back on. Gopal slammed the metre door shut and scowled at the hundred-rupee note Samiran was holding out before putting it in his pocket.

"Water?" Samiran offered, and Chaya stepped forward, a little reluctantly, with a glass of water on a saucer.

"For me?" Gopal asked, looking confused.

Samiran nodded.

Gopal drank the water in a long, slow gulp, his Adam's apple bobbing up and down. Samiran felt a bit sorry for him as he hobbled down the stairs afterwards, not bothering to wait for the lift.

"Very bad man," Chaya said as soon as he was out of sight. "Always looking for trouble."

"But he helped us just now," Samiran reminded her as he shut the door.

And yet, Gopal's body odour lingered in their home, a sour smell of sweat reminding Samiran of the malevolence he had glimpsed on his face. He hoped that in the dim light, he had only imagined it.

CHAYA

CHAYA COULD NOT IMAGINE WHAT AMREEKA WAS LIKE. SO DISTANT that it took Maneka didi two days to travel even by plane, which was supposed to be a thousand times faster than a train. So vast that three Indias could fit inside it. So cold that Didi had to wear a heavy coat for half the year. Leaving her own small village and moving to Hrishipur had been overwhelming. How Didi managed to live all the way on the other side of the world by herself puzzled her. And why? Why would someone give up the comforts of a home with an air-conditioned bedroom, a maid, a TV, a mother who cooked all her favourite meals, a father who never shouted at her, and people she had known her whole life? Where Didi lived, there was no servant, no husband, no parents. Aunty had even complained to Chaya about the fact that her daughter seemed to have no friends. Why, then, would anyone want to go there?

Chaya had many questions. What did snow feel like? If you touched it, did it melt instantly? Was it like the ice in the freezer? Just how cold was it? And what about the food? There was no one to cook for Maneka, Aunty had said. It was difficult to find Indian food. You had to drive through winter storms to the one Indian grocery store in the town just to get frozen, stale paneer. Some days, her daughter sustained herself all day on coffee, fruit, and raw vegetables, because there was no time to cook. Chaya had glanced at the TV screen occasionally when Aunty watched a foreign cooking show. Some of the things people ate in other countries seemed odd.

Every now and then that summer, Chaya glimpsed something of Aunty in Maneka. When she insisted Chaya share whatever food she and her father brought back from restaurants, for instance. Or when she offered to help her wash the dishes after meals.

Chaya had grown accustomed to kindness in the last five years that she had lived here. She had come to this flat on edge, anxious like a wounded puppy after the way her previous employment had ended. Despite the fact that the watchman, Sunil, who was the son of the friend of a neighbour back in the village, had personally escorted her to meet the Roys, talking to her gently all the way about how these were elderly Bengalis from Kolkata and therefore unlike other people in the city, Chaya had not expected any affection. But that was precisely what she had received. Uncle and Aunty, after insisting she address them that way instead of Sir and Madam—*We are not your boss*, Uncle had said, laughing—had drawn her into their lives until she learnt to forget that terrible beginning in Hrishipur.

And yet, somehow, Maneka remained a mystery. With Aunty, Chaya had felt like she was with her own relatives back in the village. As they worked side by side in the kitchen, Aunty would tell stories about her childhood in an old house in North Kolkata. In return, Chaya would tell her about her widowed mother and four younger siblings back in the village by the river.

But Maneka was often distant that summer, as if her mind was far away. Sometimes, she sat silently with a book but forgot to turn the page. Every now and then, when Uncle spoke to her, she stared into space without responding until he repeated his question, first gently, and then louder. *Mishti*, he would say, and she would spring to attention as if someone had summoned her from another world.

Despite all of Aunty's yelling and slamming of doors, Chaya had never been unsettled by her in the way that she was by her daughter. No one would deny that Aunty had been volatile. Chaya couldn't imagine her own mother speaking to her father the way Aunty would speak to Uncle sometimes. Why, even at her former employers' home, she had never heard Kanwar madam speak roughly to her husband. Not even the night she had found him with Chaya, when her wrath had been unleashed only on the maid. As Kanwar madam had beaten her with her husband's belt, it had seemed to Chaya that she was beating her husband. She kept calling her names that were usually meant for men. Dog, bastard, sisterfucker. She had not thought the submissive wife to be capable of such cursing. But in this home, the wife had raised her voice often at the docile husband. And yet, to Chaya's amazement, just a few minutes later, Uncle was asking for another helping of peanut chaat and Aunty was laughing at something on the TV. She had learnt quite quickly what Uncle had probably known for years. That Aunty's temper tantrums were like a thunderstorm in North India. A lot of roaring and blowing around, quick to rise and quick to fall, with no traces left behind afterwards.

Now that Aunty was gone, Chaya missed the outbursts. In their place, Maneka had arrived with a kind of suppressed rage. It reminded Chaya of very hot afternoons in Hrishipur when not a leaf stirred outside, not a crow called out. The stuffy heat and brooding silence made her feel as if the whole world was waiting for something terrible to happen. It made her a little afraid.

Besides, a week ago, she had overheard the argument between father and daughter. They had spoken in Bengali, which she understood most of the time, before switching to English, but it was enough for her to realize that they were arguing about her continued presence in their lives. The knowledge had unsettled her. Unsure of her status in the household, she had avoided looking them in the eye since then.

That was why, on this morning, she stood uncertainly in the doorway to Maneka's room, holding in her arms the last present Aunty had given her, on a day when none of them had known that she would be in this world for just another month.

Until today, the salwar kameez had languished in a drawer in Chaya's small room, an annex with a separate entrance just next to the flat. The mere glimpse of the pink fabric beneath the other clothes was usually enough to make her burst into tears. The thought of actually wearing it had never occurred to her. But today, her friend Hillary, who worked in flat 8-C, had reminded her about the annual fair at Chikki Bazaar. The vision of its twinkling lights had compelled Chaya, almost as if in a trance, to take out the salwar kameez, smooth it with her calloused fingers, and bring it to Maneka didi. Somehow its tangible presence, a substitute for Aunty herself, gave her the courage she needed to ask for permission to go to the fair.

"What a beautiful colour," Maneka said, examining the chiffon tunic. "Ma always had such an eye for colours. I would never be able to carry off this pink." She glanced up at Chaya, a wistful look on her face. "But on you, it will look lovely."

Then her expression changed. "Put it on!"

"Right now?"

"Yes, let's see."

The cloth, light as air, floated about her like a cloud. Chaya draped the long dupatta around her neck and reappeared shyly before Maneka. The cup of tea Chaya had already warmed for her three times stood on the table next to her, looking like it had not been touched.

"Didi, will you mind if I go to the mela with my friend Hillary for a short while? I will come back before dinner to make the chapatis."

"Mind?" Maneka laughed. "Of course not. Baba and I will watch a movie. We won't eat until late. No, no, you should go out and have fun with your friend. You're always stuck here in someone else's home. It must be so difficult." She paused with slightly parted lips, as if she wanted to ask her something. But she seemed to change her mind and returned to her laptop.

Chaya wondered what she had been about to ask. Perhaps the same question that was on all her friends' minds. When would she get married? Did she have someone in the building, a driver or a friend's brother, someone who was perhaps going to the mela today too? Chaya almost wished Didi had asked her these questions so that they might have grown a little closer. Of course, she would have disappointed her for she had nothing interesting to divulge.

She had almost left the room when Maneka called her back. "Chaya?"

She turned around.

"If Baba goes back to Kolkata, I mean Kalkatta, will you want to go with him?"

When Maneka spoke to her in Hindi, she said the name of her hometown the way everyone in North India did, but on her lips it sounded unnatural. When she spoke to her father or to her friends on the phone, she said it the English way, making it sound alien to Chaya. If cities could have so many names, like these Bengali people, how could you ever know which version you belonged to, Chaya often wondered. Her own village had one name. Chamrauli. Everyone said it the same way, and no one fought about whether or not they should return there. They would, if only they could.

Chaya looked down at her feet. She had known nothing about that city until she met Aunty and Uncle. It sounded like the sort of place where neighbours might drop in at any minute and everyone ate lunch for hours, staying at the dining table to talk long after the food was all gone.

"If you all want me to, Didi," she said. "I don't mind."

"You will have to learn a new language and you might miss your friends."

Chaya didn't know what to say or even how to feel. If Aunty had been here, and wanted her to go back with them, it would have been easier. Didi's words made her nervous. A new beginning, yet again, in a different part of this vast country. Once more, she wondered how Maneka did it, living alone, far from everything familiar.

"Think about it carefully," Maneka said. "It's a big decision. Of course, we would like you to go. I will feel much better knowing you are there with him." She sighed. "I don't think he should move back. But he insists, and I don't really know what's right any more." She looked at Chaya as if she might have an answer.

Chaya was flattered by this new intimacy between her and Maneka didi. But she could not forget the words she had overheard the other night.

"Didi, does Uncle want me to go with him?"

Maneka smiled.

"Of course. My parents have always thought of you as a member of the family. It's just that Baba thinks it's not necessary any more to have someone all the time." Her eyes shifted to the balcony attached to her room, where her underwear and other clothes were hung out to dry.

Chaya followed her gaze. Maneka had warned her to be gentle with the bras that, she had learnt on Maneka's very first morning here, were more expensive than any clothes she owned.

She had been startled by their stiffness. They were almost conical and enlarged Maneka's breasts when she wore them. Unlike Kanwar madam's bras, which had been a lot softer, like little cushions. But she had never told Chaya to be careful with them. She bought new ones often and threw away the old ones.

American bras, Chaya thought to herself in wonder once again, as the black bra fluttered in the slight breeze. Four thousand rupees for one. It was nearly half a month's salary. If she had four thousand rupees to spare, she wouldn't spend it on a bra.

"Don't worry, Chaya, I can afford it," Maneka said, as if she had read her thoughts.

"Oh, Didi, I know," said Chaya, embarrassed.

"I will send the money for your salary every month if you decide to go with him. He won't admit, it but it will make him very happy."

"Oh."

Chaya thought of her old mother in Chamrauli, fanning chapatis over the kerosene stove at night, waiting for the beginning of each month when she would receive the money from Chaya through wire transfer. Maybe she and Maneka didi were not so different after all. Maybe Maneka too stayed up at night in that beautiful, cold place far away and thought about home.

Maneka took a wad of notes from her handbag and held it out.

"For me?"

"Yes, to spend at the mela."

Chaya tried to look calm as she accepted the notes, but already the thought of the foods she would eat that evening was beginning to moisten her mouth. Spicy pani puri, chaat, maybe even chicken biryani.

"And Chaya?"

"Yes, Didi?"

"Can you please warm up that tea once more?"

"Of course, Didi," she said.

She carried the cup of tea carefully with both hands, trying not to spill any on the salwar kameez, tearing up at the thought of how much this family depended on her, especially now that Aunty was gone.

The young man had been watching her for a while. At first, she hadn't been sure, but now, about half an hour since she and Hillary had arrived at the fair, Chaya began to feel certain of it. Perhaps the reason she didn't find it disturbing for a change was that he didn't stare at her. Instead, he glanced over every now and then, very casually. When he caught her looking back at him, he turned his face away quickly. Chaya thought it sweet. She even allowed herself a slight smile as she looked in his direction. But the next instant, her smile disappeared.

He had another man with him. It was langda Gopal, the electrician. She and the other girls hated the way he shuffled around, fixing people's fuses and wires, leering at them all, smelling of liquor. He reminded Chaya of why she did not trust men. Seeing him with the stranger now sent a jolt of fear through her. Gopal recognized her and offered a mock salute. She ignored him and turned her attention back to the cart, whose shining contents provided a heady distraction.

Hillary exclaimed in delight as she fingered the stone necklaces, dangly metal earrings, and chunky copper rings. Chaya picked up a thick rope necklace with a round blue-green locket the colour of a peacock's feathers. It was the same colour as the peacocks that would appear suddenly in her village in the monsoon, fanning their tails to prophesy impending thunderstorms. She ran her thumb over the locket's smooth surface and glanced at the sky, but it remained still and cloudless.

"Wear it and see, it will look really lovely on you."

The boy selling the locket could not have been older than fourteen or fifteen. He sported the beginnings of a wispy moustache on his upper lip. But he had already learnt how to charm women. It was necessary for his trade.

"Shall I put it on for you?" he asked eagerly.

Chaya shook her head from side to side. But as he put the necklace away, she looked at it longingly. Next to her, Hillary bought a silver anklet and allowed the boy to slip it around her ankle. Chaya held her breath and waited to see if he would brush Hillary's foot carelessly or press her leg before releasing it. But, to her surprise, he did nothing like that. He clipped the anklet on briskly and then waved his hand with a practised flourish.

"See how beautiful. Now as you walk around the mela, everyone will hear you," he said, beaming with pride.

Hillary giggled and stamped her foot on the ground to hear the tinkling of her new purchase. "Come along," she cried to Chaya, impatient to resume their stroll along the street where the lights were now coming on.

The bazaar was coming to life. Vendors stood at their carts filled with the most unexpected objects. The girls walked by each one, exclaiming and pointing. Sandals with sequined straps.

Bunches of bananas and grapes. Panties in every colour. Overhead, the sky was a roof of loosely strung festoons in red, green and yellow. Horns blared from autos and taxis on the main road.

Children cried out as they ran around the narrow street that had been transformed for this festival. Chaya imagined this was what it felt like to be drunk.

She paused at a cart on which rows of glass bangles stood expertly arranged. Midnight blue, baby pink, blood red, bottle green. Some had gold streaks on them like the brocade on one of Aunty's saris.

"Try one," said the woman at the cart, smiling. Before Chaya could protest, she had slipped a few on her narrow wrist.

Chaya stared down at her hand as if it belonged to someone else. The bangles alternated in colour. Some were turquoise with gold patterns and the others were dark pink.

"It matches your dress," said the woman with a sly smile.

The woman was right. The salwar kameez glimmered in the pale evening light. The dupatta floated out behind her. The weather was too hot for such fabric, but Chaya didn't care. It made her feel like a princess. And now, with the bangles, it was almost too much.

"Look at your friend," the woman cried out to Hillary. "See how beautiful she is." Then she slipped another identical set around Chaya's left wrist.

Someone whistled. Chaya glanced in the direction the sound came from. Not surprisingly, it was Gopal. She found herself looking beyond his shoulder to the young man with him. He seemed to be staring at her bangled arms. Her thin brown arms that to her seemed so rough after all the dishwashing and laundry she did, the arms that her former employer had once told her were delectably soft. Next to him, langda Gopal flashed a grin at Hillary, who fluttered her heavily coated eyelashes in response.

His eyes narrowed into slits. Even though he was looking at Chaya's friend and not at her, a familiar feeling rose in her throat, one she had almost rid herself of but that threatened to choke her on occasions such as this. She began to slip off the bangles one by one. It was harder than she had imagined. The woman had appeared to encircle her wrists with them quite effortlessly, but now that she was trying to free herself of them, she found her wrists too big. She had to twist the bangles off with some force.

"Careful, careful," yelled the woman.

But it was too late. As she wrenched the last two from her left hand, they slipped and fell on the floor, where they shattered in a tiny heap of blue and pink glass.

"Twenty rupees each," cried the woman.

Forty rupees for two broken bangles that she would never wear. She could have eaten a plate of biryani with raita for that amount. Silently, Chaya took out two of the crisp notes that Didi had given her earlier and handed them over to the woman, who was now muttering about girls going wild once they were at the mela.

"No shame any more," she said, grabbing the money from Chaya's hand.

Chaya squatted on the ground and carefully picked up the small, jagged pieces of glass, then wrapped them in her white cotton handkerchief. There they lay like little jewels, useless but still beautiful. She put them in her purse, wondering if she could somehow repair them. She felt as though she had betrayed Aunty by breaking bangles and wasting her daughter's money. The evening felt rotten to her now, tainted by her clumsiness.

Hillary had walked on, and the drama of a broken bangle or two was too commonplace to bother anyone else. Chaya blinked the tears from her eyes and forced herself to move onward as well. The lights flickered overhead. Lanterns hung over the carts.

Despite her mood, the bazaar looked magical. The crowd seemed to be growing by the minute. The rising hum of voices soon made Chaya feel like she was under a hypnotic spell. In a few minutes, her thoughts started to drift away from the broken bangles. Then, her resolve to remain sad out of loyalty to Aunty weakened and before she realized what was happening, she was swept up in a current along with everyone else, moving in the same direction, a stream of people flowing between rows of carts and makeshift stalls.

A little hill of plump brown dates stood on one of them.

"Straight from Medina," shouted the man. His long grey beard and skull cap offered proof of his claim. "Perfect for Iftar," he said, even though the beginning of Ramzan was a week away.

"Take one," he held out his hand.

Hillary grabbed it and put the whole thing into her mouth. "Mmm," she said, chewing heartily as the others looked on. When she spoke, with her mouth full, Chaya smelt the sweetness of the date. "Sweet like honey," Hillary said. She reached out her hand to grab another from the heap, but just as her fingers touched one, the man slapped it away.

"First, buy," he said.

"I want to taste one more, that's all," Hillary cried out. "Mean old mullah."

Someone behind them took up the cry. "Bloody mullah, won't give a few dates to the girl."

Before they knew it, a ripple of cries began to echo through the crowd. In response, another bearded man appeared to stand next to the cart, and then another. They looked identical with sharp black beards and skull caps. One of them shook his fist at the person who had yelled out. The energy around them shifted abruptly. Chaya was suddenly aware of just how humid it was.

Her underarms felt clammy and sweat trickled down her back.

"Let's get out of here," she whispered.

Hillary nodded. Chaya hastened her steps until they had left the narrow path and emerged on the other side. The men were still quarrelling behind them, but here, at the other end of the bazaar, the small square covered with grass, where people normally let their cows graze, had been transformed into a place that smelt like heaven.

Chaya's mouth filled with saliva. She watched the cooks, all men, chopping and stirring briskly as families, couples, and children waited hungrily for their food. One fried green peppers and onion with noodles in a large wok to make chow mein. Another toasted thick chunks of bread in a pan for pav bhaji.

"I want kababs," said Hillary, clapping her hands with glee.

She headed in the direction the smell was coming from, where skewers of red pieces of chicken roasted on an open coal fire.

Chaya was tempted to follow her. But she had already spent forty rupees and chicken was bound to be expensive. She decided to walk in the direction opposite to the bhel puri stand, where a young boy, about ten years old, was deftly tossing puffed rice with peanuts and slivers of onion and green chilli. She stood next to him, watching, along with the young children eagerly waiting.

The bhel puri came sprinkled with chutneys and sauces. A crisp fried papdi was perched on top to serve as a spoon. Feeling ravenous, she put a generous portion of the tangy, sweet stuff into her mouth, closed her eyes, and chewed slowly.

When she opened her eyes again, she saw him standing in a corner of the park, leaning against a lamppost.

It had been a long time since Chaya had felt shy with a man. When she was younger, seven or eight years ago, she had felt that way about a boy who lived in the neighbouring hut in their village. Chaya didn't know exactly how old she was of course, none of them did. But it was the year after she got her first period. Her father had started talking about sending her to the city to work in someone's house. It was around then that she had begun to notice the boy. Everyone knew he had been born deaf and mute. He herded buffalo in the field behind their hut. She would see him from a distance when she walked to school early in the morning. He never looked at her, which piqued her curiosity even more. He had been taken out of the school and sent to the fields to work. Chaya often overheard her mother and the other women gossiping about his family and how hard it was for them. There was something beautiful about the boy, about the way he moved, alone and without making a sound, through the tall sugarcane grass. His face was narrow and sharp, and his black hair was slightly long at the back, almost like a girl's. Once she had called out to him, boldly, as she was walking. "Hey, Anil," she had said, before remembering he couldn't hear her. But to her surprise, he had turned, and she had caught a glimpse of his startling eyes.

They were a light brown, a colour Chaya had never seen before, and completely still and calm, as if he never worried about anything. When she smiled at him, he turned back to his cattle with no response. But when she looked back a little later from the pathway, he was gazing in her direction, a slender figure in the middle of the field, as brown as the buffalo next to him. Chaya had wondered if not being able to hear made you not worry about anything. If you could not hear your little brothers and sisters cry from hunger or your father yell in a drunken voice all night, or your mother scream when he beat her, then what would you worry about?

When she was first brought here to Hrishipur by the neighbour who had promised to look after her, after she started working at the Kanwars' home, she would lie awake on the thin mattress in her room next to the kitchen after the evening's chores were done, and think about the boy out in the field, and wonder if he was still herding buffalo or if he had moved on to something else. That first year in this bewildering city, the memory of that silent boy had given her something to think about at night when her body was aching but tender. Something inside her would cry out for company, and she would fall asleep with soft moans and her fingers buried deep between her legs until they moistened.

Later, she would blame herself for those transgressions as if she had somehow willed whatever had happened with Kanwar saab, as if she deserved what came next. For, when Kanwar's wife took the belt out of the cupboard and whipped her with it, as her husband stood in the doorway and watched, Chaya understood that everything that was happening to her had to be her own fault. The employers were never to blame.

It had been years since she had felt any longing for a man's touch. But now, this stranger smiled shyly at her from behind the kabab stand. He did not look like a filmi hero. Not the type that Hillary found attractive. He had short hair combed neatly, as if his mother had parted it for him. His face was not sharp but slightly puffy and round. He had thick, pink lips. He looked sweet and gentle. He was slender and, unlike most of the people in the bazaar, quite light-skinned.

"Firang," Hillary whispered in her ear, when she caught him looking at them.

Maybe she was right. Even if he was not an actual foreigner, there was something of the outsider in him.

He came forward, not with the confident stride of the whistling men around him, but slow and unsure, and stopped before them.

"What were you looking at?" Hillary said in a teasing voice that Chaya found annoying.

Hillary was a nice girl. She had grown up with no parents in an orphanage where every baby was forced to become a Christian. She had never known a mother or her own real name. But her colourful clothes and singsong voice, aimed at drawing attention to herself nearly all the time when they were in the company of men, made an hour with her quite exhausting. Her relentless performance made Chaya feel more than ever like the embodiment of her name. She was no more than a shadow that silently followed her gregarious and popular friend. There Hillary stood, under the flickering lights, with eyes that shone like the gold zari on her dress, challenging every man in that place, however young or old, attached or not, to turn and look at her. No doubt this light-skinned stranger would succumb too.

Chaya turned away and tossed her newspaper cone into the rubbish bin, determined not to watch Hillary capture yet another young man's heart only to forget about him by the end of the evening. Chaya thought the men were fools. And sometimes she wondered what would have happened if it had been Hillary instead of her in Kanwar's flat that night, the night that his wife was supposed to not return with her two young children from her sister's. Would Hillary have willingly gone along with Kanwar, without trying to draw away or push his hands off her body? Would she have embraced the hairy man despite the stench of liquor on his breath? Would she have played with the gold chain around his neck and perhaps even slipped it off when he was too intoxicated to notice? How would the consequences have been any different? Chaya had not acted that way, and yet, she had been beaten until she lay on the floor in a crumpled heap, sobbing for her mother.

"You dropped this," someone said in a voice that was surprisingly low.

Chaya turned around. The stranger held out his hand. It was her white handkerchief, the one that held the broken pieces of bangle.

"Oh," she cried out, grabbing the handkerchief from him and shoving it inside her purse.

"Don't drop it again," he smiled at her. His teeth were very white. No paan stains. But his front tooth was chipped and impossible to look away from. "Or I will have to keep following you to return it."

Chaya felt a warmth creep up her neck.

"You have been following us all along," exclaimed Hillary in an aggrieved voice. "Better behave yourself. Don't try any nonsense." Then she linked her arm in Chaya's. "Come on, let's go."

Chaya smiled back at the man. "Thank you," she said.

She felt his eyes rest on her back as she walked away.

But they didn't walk far before the electrician came limping along. "Hillary," he whined in his nasal voice. He whispered something in her ear. Then they both turned to look at Chaya.

"We are getting a ride home," Hillary announced.

Chaya stood still. "We can just take a tuk-tuk back," she said.

"The drivers are not safe this late," said Hillary. "But his friend Jeevan, the firang, drives one." She gestured towards an autorickshaw that was now sputtering next to them. "They will drop us. It's safer," she said, and giggled as if she didn't really believe this was true.

Before Chaya could think, Hillary had slid on to the back seat of the auto, next to Gopal.

"Aaja Chaya, sit," she shouted.

There was not an inch of room next to the two of them that she could squeeze into. In the front, Jeevan sat erect with his hands on the levers, ready to push off into the night. He looked at her patiently without saying a word. Slowly, she crept to the rickshaw and, with a final look around as if someone might come to rescue them, climbed inside, making sure she was far enough not to touch him.

Jeevan revved the motor and took off, still without speaking.

Somehow, his demeanour reassured Chaya. She sensed how stiffly he sat. From time to time, she glanced at his profile. He kept his eyes on the road ahead. He was nervous, she realized. She loosened her limbs and sank back into the vinyl seat. Soon, they had pulled away from the human traffic filing out of the narrow alleyways of the bazaar. Now, in the quiet of the night, Gopal's voice sounded too loud.

"Jeevan, play a song," he called. His words came out slurred.

Chaya took a quick look back and immediately regretted it. He held a bottle in his left hand. His right arm was wrapped around Hillary's shoulder. Chaya felt apprehensive. But just then, the music began. It was Kishore Kumar's gentle voice singing an old Hindi film song, 'Mere Sapno Ki Rani'. It wasn't even a remix but the original from *Aradhana*. It was a song full of longing that Chaya's father used to sing on nights when he was only slightly tipsy, the nights he was in a good mood and not about to beat anybody up.

The music made Chaya feel a little giddy. She tapped Jeevan on the shoulder. "How did your tooth break?" she asked shyly.

He turned to her and smiled, showing the full effect of the chipped tooth. Chaya wanted to reach out and touch it.

"Cricket," he said simply. Then he lapsed into silence again, but his lips remained curled in a smile.

In the back seat, Gopal began to sing, loudly and off-key. Hillary giggled. Chaya resisted the urge to look back this time. Instead, she glanced at Jeevan. Quietly, he began to sing too. He had a nice, deep voice. The air smelt of earth, as if it was going to rain. Chaya looked wistfully up at the black sky. If only it rained now, with this music, and the young man sitting so close to her, the world would be so romantic. Chaya imagined herself with her hair piled high on top of her head, dancing in the rain as someone—young and handsome, like Rajesh Khanna from the movie—chased after her.

They drove past the squares of cordoned-off land that dotted the outskirts of Hrishipur. These were constructions that had never taken off. As they headed towards the heart of the city, the properties began to appear in various stages of completion. A few floors here, a block of towers there, piles of bricks and cement in random spots. In the darkness they stood like spectres, rugged and unfinished. And then, as they went around the corner, Gopal yelled out again from the back.

"There it is, the Amreekan building. Look how it winks in the moonlight. Bloody Indian Sarkar and its slogan, *Shine, India, Shine.*

Only thing that shines here is the foreign building and the foreign offices."

Chaya's body stiffened at the sound of his voice. She didn't turn to look at the building. She knew where it was and she knew what it looked like. She had seen it on the way to the fair. But she had no interest in it. It would be completed, rich people would move in, folks like the four of them would drive their cars, clean their toilets, and cook their meals. The luckiest ones among them might get to sleep in a little room somewhere on the property. To her, it didn't seem any different from the other high-rises.

The stench of alcohol now filled the car.

Slowly, she forced herself to crane her neck and look back.

Gopal was taking a long sip from the bottle. Hillary sat crushed up against him. His right hand cupped her breast. He passed the bottle on to Hillary and forced her to take a sip before she pushed it away, giggling.

"Bitter," she cried.

Gopal laughed and leant forward to share the bottle with Jeevan, who shook his head.

"What's happened to you, sitting next to a girl and lost your balls?" Gopal asked him.

"The cops have become really strict. If they see me drinking, they will confiscate my friend's rickshaw. He will not let me drive it. I will have to pay the fines and also find another job. My mother is not working any more." His voice trailed off. He shot a quick glance at Chaya to see if she was listening. He looked ashamed.

Chaya wanted to comfort him. Nothing to be embarrassed about, she wanted to say. It was his lecherous friend who ought to be embarrassed.

But Gopal was feeling generous. He wanted to share his bottle of cheap country liquor with someone. He shoved the bottle forward until Chaya felt its cold glass against her neck. She knew that odour well. She had spent her entire childhood trying to scrub that smell out of the little hut in which they lived.

"Drink a little, gudiya," he burped. "You will have more fun."

She pushed the bottle away, but he pressed it against her neck again. Suddenly, the autorickshaw went over a bump in the road, and some of the liquor spilt on to her salwar kameez. Chaya cried out in dismay. Country liquor left stains.

Gopal cursed her in a language she did not even understand.

She shook her head and kept her gaze straight ahead at the black road.

But the peace had been shattered. In the back seat, Gopal grunted. At first, Hillary made little sounds of delight. Chaya glanced at Jeevan, who continued to drive. His face was expressionless. She wondered what he was thinking. She wondered if he wanted to do the same things to her. She felt aroused at the thought. It made her want to weep with shame.

They had almost arrived at their street when Hillary began shrieking. "Stop, stop," she said.

Chaya whipped around. "Leave her alone," she said intuitively.

Gopal was splayed on top of Hillary. His pants were unzipped. He held his penis in his hand. Chaya half rose from her seat and tried to pull him off Hillary, who lay there whimpering.

"Help her," she whispered, looking at Jeevan.

He kept on driving, his face impassive. But Chaya noticed, even in her state of panic, how his right eye, the one nearest to her, twitched.

In the back seat, Hillary shrieked again.

"Tease," Gopal yelled. "All this time you flirt and make eyes and sway your body like you want it and now suddenly you're Sati Savitri? Whore." He slapped her.

Startled by the sound, Chaya twisted her body and tried to reach Gopal. She leant in between the two front seats and stretched until her hand touched his bony shoulder. He turned to look at her. His eyes were bloodshot and large with lust.

"You?" he sneered. "You had your way with the old employer over on Golf Course Road, and got kicked out when the wife found you. Now you're living alone with that stupid old man. But you don't want your friend to have any fun, eh? Wah wah, what a good friend. Tell me, are you jealous? Jeevan, I cannot handle both. Why don't you take this one? You've been eyeing her all evening. The quiet ones are the best, let me tell you."

Gopal spat at Chaya.

Disgusted, she recoiled, and wiped her face with the end of her dupatta. His words did not seem important. She knew what the servants said about her. All she wanted was to get out of the auto.

As if on cue, Jeevan finally spoke. "Let them go, Gopal," he said quietly. "We will get into trouble. There are cops here at night. I do not want trouble right now." He slowed the auto down until it came to a stop.

Before Hillary could react, Gopal pushed her out through the open door. Chaya followed suit. She turned to look at Jeevan one last time, but he had already taken off. She stood on the side of the dusty road for a moment and watched the black and yellow vehicle rumble off into the night, old Hindi film music still blaring from its speakers.

Then she remembered Hillary.

Next to her, the girl was still whimpering. Chaya saw that she wore only her kameez now. The salwar was missing. Even though it was a sultry night, Chaya took her dupatta and wrapped it around her friend's shoulders.

"Are you okay?" she asked, more sharply than she had intended. She was annoyed with Hillary, whom she blamed partly for the situation she had put them in. Hillary nodded, sniffing. She wiped her nose on the dupatta.

"Chal," Chaya said.

They walked down the street. The streetlamps were all unlit.

But overhead, the moon still shone. Somehow, Chaya felt quite brave. After the adventure of the night, the open road seemed safer. She looked around. It was a short walk to the back entrance.

She hoped they wouldn't run into Sunil, the watchman, who would be sure to deliver a lecture about wandering around alone at night.

Next to her, Hillary reached for her hand, but Chaya pulled hers away.

"Why flirt with someone like that? You know he's nothing but trouble. Must you have attention from every man?"

"At least he has the balls to take what he wants. What about the loser you were staring at all night? Did he come to my rescue? Did he try to stop him? Bloody coward."

"He did in the end."

Hillary let out a chortle.

"Only because he was scared of the cops. Idiot. The cops would have helped Gopal finish the job he started. He must not be very experienced." She laughed at her own joke and kept laughing.

Chaya was secretly happy to see her friend relax. But she couldn't laugh. Her heart felt heavy as they turned into the lane behind their complex. She kept thinking about the man who had smiled at her so gently back at the fair. Was Hillary right about him? Was life nothing but a series of disappointments? But he had looked at her with such tenderness. Would he forget all about her after tonight or would he know how to find her?

By the time she got home, Chaya's clothes clung to her. The heat was almost unbearable. Gopal's voice, sneering and insulting, rang in her ears. She could still see the lights shining in the bazaar. Part of her wanted nothing more than to go to bed, but another part wanted to return to the scene. She had felt alive in that crowd for the first time in so long.

When Chaya entered the flat, father and daughter were sitting on the couch and watching yet another movie in English. A flock of birds gathered on the screen until they covered the sky like a dark cloud. They looked like the crows that perched on the roofs of all the buildings of Hrishipur during the day. But on the TV screen they were frightening, as if they wanted to warn them all of some impending doom. Chaya shivered and looked away.

"How was it?" Didi asked from the sofa, where she sat crosslegged in a pair of shorts and a T-shirt that Chaya had washed and ironed that morning. Her eyes had not shifted from the TV.

Chaya was self-conscious in her sweaty clothes. "Great fun, Didi, but it was too hot. I smell bad," she said, unwilling to go any closer.

"What did you eat?" Didi asked.

Chaya paused for a second. The question reminded her so much of Aunty. That was what she had wanted to know every time Chaya went somewhere. What did she eat?

"Bhel puri, Didi."

"Bas?" Didi sounded disappointed.

"Yes, I was not very hungry."

"Okay, then you will have to have dinner."

"Didi, do you want dinner just now?"

"After this movie. Maybe in one hour."

"Then do you mind if I take a shower?"

Maneka laughed. "Why will I mind? Do whatever you want."

As she was leaving the flat to go to her own room, Chaya heard Maneka didi tell Uncle that she reminded her of those students in America who asked for permission before going to the bathroom. Chaya thought she was sweet. And yet, Maneka had not noticed that her dupatta was missing.

That night, after everyone had gone to bed and she had put away the dishes and retired to her room, Chaya took out the wrapped handkerchief from her bag and unfolded it carefully, as if it held within it a tiny living creature. Inside lay the shards of glass, broken like the evening. Pink and blue fragments of life, like memories. Of a mute boy standing alone in a field, a kind and loving aunty who used to spend hours in the kitchen with her, a friend who needed men to want her so much they would hurt her, a stranger who was capable of unexpected kindness but lacked the courage to do the right thing.

As she was tying the ends of the kerchief back together, she noticed the untidy scrawl on it. The name Jeevan spelled out in

Hindi, followed by a phone number—*2571927*. She recalled the shy smile in the darkness of the auto, the way he refused to look at her and sat all tensed up, as acutely aware of her presence next to him as she had been of his. Despite Hillary's misgivings, Chaya felt a thread connecting her to this stranger as if she had known him for a long time.

She placed the little bundle next to her pillow and lay down on the narrow bed. She gazed through the window in the wall at the smoky sky outside and fantasized about a man lying next to her, a man with a chipped tooth who held her hand and begged her not to go anywhere else but to stay right here with him in Hrishipur. And as she closed her eyes that night, hovering between slumber and wakefulness, Chaya promised him she would.

JESSICA

A PLAQUE ON THE WALL NEXT TO THE PRINCIPAL'S DESK READ *Hail the Cross, Our Only Hope.* Mary held baby Jesus in the corner, watching over all who entered, while from the four walls photographs of priests and nuns stared down at Jessica as she sat stiffly in her chair and waited for the principal.

It was difficult for her to not cross her legs at the ankles and fold her hands in her lap, or to not think about her own childhood spent in a convent school back in Goa. The same narrow, whitewashed hallways inside, the same pillars propping up smooth stone verandahs outside, the same melancholy strains of music, and of course the same principal's office to which she had, on countless occasions, been summoned. The memory of the swift raps of a wooden ruler on her soft young palm made her flinch now as she sat there, waiting to hear what her daughter's principal would complain about this time.

"Miss Pereira."

Jessica sat up straight at the sound of Sister Matthews's voice, hoping her lipstick wasn't too bright. She had chosen her lightest shade, which was not really very light, and applied only one coat.

She had also dressed in a black skirt as if she were attending a funeral. A skirt that went down all the way to her knees. No one could say she didn't make an effort for her little girl.

Sister Matthews walked to her desk, dressed in her trademark white sari and long-sleeve white blouse even in this heat. Jessica wondered if she changed into something more comfortable when she retired to her bedroom at night or if she slept with her limbs completely covered.

The principal wasted no time.

"She is failing everything, Miss Pereira."

Jessica found herself staring into a pair of small eyes beneath the glasses. Eyes narrowed in disapproval, making them appear smaller still. She wondered what Sister Matthews had heard about her.

"I go by Ms," Jessica said.

"Your daughter needs to stay back in Standard Three for a year. I cannot send her forward. It would set a bad precedent."

"Is there something you could do to help her? Maybe provide after-school coaching? Or offer an alternative to taking the exams? She simply does not do well with the traditional setup."

The principal took off her glasses to wipe them with a piece of flannel. She continued to gaze at Jessica as she spoke. "I think she has a more serious problem."

The ceiling fan murmured overhead but did little to cool the stifling office. St. Anthony's insisted that children did not need air-conditioning at school. Their parents and grandparents had studied without it, and they could survive the Indian summers as well. Jessica used to think this was not such a bad idea. Now, wiping her neck with a piece of tissue from her purse, she wasn't so sure. From her corner, Mary smiled beatifically.

"Exactly what do you mean, Sister?"

The principal's face hardened in anticipation of a struggle. "I think she would be better off at a vernacular language school."

"And why is that?"

"This school is not for everyone. The children here are middle class. At least."

Jessica raised a fist to protest but the principal held up a finger for silence. "We do not know, Miss Pereira, where she has come from, do we? I admire your intentions and efforts, and we are all fond of the child. But she does not fit in here."

"Are you by any chance expelling my daughter from your school?" Jessica tried to keep her voice even. If only she could have yelled, she might have felt better. But this school, with its ordinance of silence and prim, bespectacled nuns, did not allow for yelling. Twenty years ago, in Panjim, too, Jessica had wanted to yell but could not. She had had to find other outlets to let off steam. Outlets that, in turn, got her summoned to the principal's office. She chuckled at the irony.

"Miss Pereira," the principal said. "This is not funny. And I have no reason to expel your daughter. Do I?" The next moment, her eyes softened. "I am merely suggesting that she won't do well here. That this is not the school for that kind of child."

The words stabbed Jessica with the sharpness of a blade.

The mischievous little girl who had brought such joy to her life was the "kind of child" the school didn't want and wouldn't help.

"Titli has not even been diagnosed with anything. She is simply headstrong and passionate. What do you do to help children on the autism spectrum? I'm curious. Or those with learning disabilities. Do you just suggest to their parents that they take them elsewhere?"

Sister Matthews leant forward. "Miss Pereira, your tone is hostile. Our school has a specific mission and certain resources. We are not able to do everything for everybody. There are other places for different abilities."

Jessica stood up. She wished she had worn a shorter skirt so her knees would show. She wished she had worn mascara, maybe even a little eye shadow.

The principal gripped her hand with both of hers as if to sympathize. Jessica debated whether to say more. The temptation to be nasty to this woman was acute. But the wrinkles on Sister Matthews's face made her look older at close range. She wore no makeup of course. But her sharp features and enviable cheekbones made Jessica wonder. Did she ever wish she had a normal life, beyond the school's austere premises? Did she ever envy her girls or their mothers, who would step outside these walls to a world of shopping and movies and family intrigues? What kind of inner life could a nun have in this hedonistic city?

The principal was at least twenty years older than her. Jessica was reminded of her mother and her slow, laboured breathing on the phone that morning. Without another word, she turned away.

"Miss Pereira," called the woman behind her. Jessica paused at the doorway.

"You are doing a good thing by loving this unwanted child. We are all God's creatures."

Jessica nodded before leaving the office. As she walked down the long corridor, a chorus of voices rose in hymn. The familiar lyrics of "Make Me a Channel of Your Peace" soon echoed through the silent hallway, reminding Jessica of her own schoolgirl days, singing this song at morning assembly. She had followed the requests in the song and tried doing the right things, or so she had imagined. The strains of the organ faded behind her as she walked outside and blinked away tears.

Out in the harsh sunlight, while waiting for her Ola next to a sign that said *All girls must speak to teachers in a low voice*, she caught a glimpse of a student in a white salwar kameez and a red vest. In Jessica's time, girls in convent schools wore dresses or skirts and blouses. None of this ethnic shit. This was the influence of the saffron brigade, The Party's concerted effort to force everyone to return to their Hindu roots, even those who had none. An absurd attempt at Indianizing students in a missionary school run by Jesuit nuns inside an uber-Westernized town. The girl walked past her and entered a building with a sign overhead that said *Cell phones will be confiscated*.

Jessica made up her mind. Titli would not stay here. These schools belonged to the past. The principal was right. This was not the sort of place for her kind of child. Jessica would send her to one of the newfangled international schools that all her progressive friends in Delhi were talking about nowadays. They focused on extracurriculars and holistic well-being rather than homework and exams. Sakshi Mehta, the advocate, sent her autistic son to one of those schools that had a lyrical-sounding French name. But those new schools did not come cheap. The monthly fees alone were forty thousand rupees. And this did not include the cost of uniforms, iPads, air-conditioned school buses, customized meal plans, exchange programmes overseas …

Jessica tossed her head back as the Ola came into view. It was a new world, dammit. And she was Jess Pereira. She did things her own way, and so would her daughter. They were not meant to follow the beaten path.

~

On Saturday evening, lights burnt through the windows of the Monsoon Palace. It was just another night in an endless summer when the rain promised to wash away everyone's troubles but proved to be a trickster, just like the politicians and the numerous buildings that lay unfinished across the city. Unlike those skeletal buildings, however, the seven-star hotel was bursting with life tonight as it waited like a bride dressed up for a big, fat Indian wedding.

America had sent its prince to Hrishipur for the weekend. The news had been all over for days. That morning there had been a palpable buzz around town, at the spa Jessica had visited to get her legs waxed and at the health food store where she had stopped on her way back to buy chia seeds and soy milk at exorbitant prices to bake a cake ordered by a customer. A large billboard at the intersection in front of the hotel showed the American guest's face as he grinned down at the traffic, his eyes bulbous and his dark hair slicked back. His teeth sparkled diabolically on the billboard where he posed next to the Bollywood superstar whose last name, Khan, would likely arouse suspicion at immigration counters in airports across America. But here in Hrishipur, fifty kilometres away from the nation's capital, nobody cared about politics.

Leave all your troubles behind when you come home. The slogan for the Trump Towers property on Omega Road reassured any potential resident that the ordinary troubles plaguing millions of Indians every day—pollution, misogyny, communal violence and, of course, poverty—would be banned from its premises. The US president's son had flown nearly twelve thousand kilometres on Dad's private jet to remind investors of this fact.

That was why the celebration had to be held nowhere else but at the Monsoon Palace. Perched on an artificial hilltop, removed from the concrete jungle that was Hrishipur, it glittered in all its bejewelled glory on this scorching, bone-dry night.

Jessica climbed out of the plush, chilled interior of the gold Mercedes that Mukesh Tripathy had sent for her. A uniformed valet held open the door of the car. As she stretched her legs and tossed her long, curly hair back, Jessica offered him a slight, almost imperceptible, smile. She knew them all, and they knew her. But the valet merely saluted her smartly in response, clinging to the position assigned to him, unwilling to acknowledge her. So, it was going to be like this then. A night of performances.

The electric buzz of the lobby enveloped her in its embrace, but she felt like she was carrying the streets inside with her. The streets from which she had brought home her little wild daughter, the streets whose food she loved to eat more than any of the fancy cuisines served at hotels like this one. Giant white vases full of silk flowers stood on the marble floors of the lobby. Classical music piped softly through the air. Oil paintings in gilded frames hung on the walls.

Jessica took the lift all the way up to the penthouse suite that Tripathy used when he was in town. Her heels sank into the thick carpet lining the mirrored hallway. She refused to look at the walls where she might see her own reflection. She was aware of how she looked tonight. No one could complain.

"Deviji," Tripathy said as he opened the door, bowing his head subtly to let her know he had company.

She was glad. He never touched her when there were people around. His exaggerated regard for her in public, which included the divine epithet he had used to address her, always annoyed Jessica. She preferred the blatant flirting of other men, men who didn't pretend to respect her.

"MT," she responded, knowing how much her nickname irked him.

His smile flickered for a second like a candle that was about to die. Then he changed his mind and it broadened instead as he held the door wide open and waved her in. In the living room behind him, two men in black suits reclined on the leather couches. They rose as soon as they saw her.

"Meet Venkatesh, and of course you already know Bobby." Bobby, the shorter of the two, wore a black shirt and a thick gold chain around his neck. A toupee perched on his head. He looked like a villain from a seventies Hindi movie. One phone call, and he might summon up assassins or smugglers to do his bidding.

"Madam, namaste. How is your child?"

That was the thing about Tripathy's men. Unfailingly polite to women like her in front of the boss, no matter what they might actually think. Jessica didn't want to dwell on the kind of things they said about her when Tripathy wasn't around. She nodded at the men without smiling and walked to the bar. It had been a long week. She deserved a few drinks.

"Let me do that for you. You make yourself comfortable," said Tripathy, rushing to the bar. "We will be done soon, and then we can head down just a little fashionably late but not too much. We don't want to miss the fun. What do you two say?"

Bobby burst into laughter on cue, slapping his stomach and the other man's back in exaggerated glee. Venkatesh looked a little dazed.

"Are you joining us?" Jessica asked them.

"Oh, no, no, Madam, we are not invited," Bobby said. "This is a most exclusive event."

"Too bad, you will miss the tamasha," said Tripathy.

He handed Jessica a glass of rum and Coke. She knew even before she took the first sip that he had poured her too little of the Captain Morgan's. She rolled her eyes at him. In response, his twinkled like those of a good-humoured uncle. In the second before he turned away, Jessica noted that the grey in his temples had streaked farther back into his hair since the last time she had seen him, a few weeks ago.

"Why don't you rest a little while we finish up here?" he said gently.

She took the hint. He didn't want her around while they talked shop. Thank goodness. There was nothing about his work that interested her. He was a real estate developer, dashing between cities, barking on his cell phone, meeting with clients and promoters like these two. Their conversations, when she caught snatches of them, bored her to bits. When he was alone with her, Tripathy was a different man. The rest of the time she was an escort, a hostess, a trophy. Whatever he needed her to be.

She went into the bedroom and kicked off her heels before she stretched out on the black silk sheets of the bed and gazed out of the window that covered an entire wall. Streaks of pink and orange ran across the sky. The sun was setting over Hrishipur, preparing it for the night, when all the grown-up children would come out to play.

The luckiest ones among them would be here tonight, at this hotel. But if she had had a choice, she would have stayed home, tucked up on her sofa with her wild child.

She hoped Titli would not suddenly wake up in the middle of the night and call her on her cell phone like she had done two months ago when Jessica had gone out with Vivek—the very last time she had seen him. Unlike Tripathy, Viv had made Jessica realize that she still had a breakable heart. Titli's call had come in the middle of their argument about the woman Viv was seeing. Jessica cringed at her recollection of that evening and how vulnerable she had allowed herself to be. And then Titli's voice, *Mamma, mamma, please come home*, ringing on the speakerphone. Viv had turned away in exhaustion.

The sheets here were slippery and cool. Jessica sighed and closed her eyes. It had been a week of decisions and worry about her mother and her daughter, the two people whose care rested on her shoulders. She let herself drift off.

When she awoke, the last light had disappeared from the sky, leaving the room in complete darkness. She sat up feeling confused, wondering for a moment where she was. She was accustomed to waking up in other people's beds, but the sense of disorientation always left her a little dizzy.

Then she heard the voices rise in the other room. It was unusual. She strained to listen. Tripathy was yelling. Was it possible that they were fighting? Jessica got up and walked to the door and opened it just a little. No one noticed her.

Tripathy slammed his fist on the glass coffee table. "They have paid the government ten million dollars," Tripathy said to the men. "Which of us can afford to do that? I have paid too, but not that much."

"It's not just money," said Bobby. "I hear there's a hotline at the very top level. Prime minister to president."

"It is time to act. Bobby, are you sure these boys are reliable?"
"Very sincere, Sir. I told you. You shall see for yourself. I am trying to fix a meeting."

"I know about the older one. He has managed things before. I have heard he's a wily fellow. But this new chamcha of his. Can we really trust him? I cannot afford any mistakes, Bobby."

"Sir, I am telling you he needs money. He's a good boy."

"That's what I'm worried about. Is this the time to try someone new?"

"Leave it to me, Sir. Now let me show you the map." Bobby reached under the table and pulled out a rolled parchment. He spread it out on the table. "Venky, you are the engineer. Explain to Sir."

The men drew closer. Venkatesh, who had not said a word so far, began to speak softly. It was hard from where Jessica stood to hear what he was saying. The conversation turned apparently to machines and circuit breakers. The sort of mundane construction-related jargon that made her eyes glaze. But the men seemed engrossed. Their drinks lay unfinished next to them.

The clock on the wall said it was 9:30. Jessica suddenly felt impatient. This was not what she had dressed up for. The reception downstairs at least promised some music and the kind of smoky darkness one could get lost in on a Saturday night. She opened the door wider, hoping they would remember her.

Venky looked younger than the rest even though he was completely bald. His head gleamed every time light fell on it from one of the lamps overhead. His voice suddenly quivered as he spoke. "What if there's trouble, Sir?" he asked.

"What? Do you know who this is?" said Bobby, gesturing towards Tripathy. "He is an expert beta. Not to worry."

Tripathy sat straight in his chair, stroking his moustache thoughtfully.

"Don't mind, Sir. Venky is new here, Sir. Just came from Chennai. Thinks he will get into trouble." Bobby laughed and slapped Venky on his shoulder indulgently.

"Lost my position there, Sir," Venky offered. Tripathy stared at him without speaking.

Venky nodded reassuringly. "It's okay, Sir. I know you know everyone. And Bobby has already explained to me."

"Arrey this sort of thing happens here all the time," said Bobby. "Watch the fun. Diwali dhamaka in August only. What do you say, Sir?'

The two looked at Tripathy. He waved at them dismissively. "Not to worry. People lose their jobs and come here. This is the place to begin again. The place where people will take care of you if you take care of them."

Venkatesh looked uncomfortable. He picked up his glass of Scotch and swallowed it in a single gulp.

Jessica coughed.

"Baby."

Tripathy, startled, had reverted to his private term of endearment. Jessica grimaced. Ridiculous though it sounded to be called Devi, she preferred it in front of these people. At least it made her feel a little less like a vamp in Tripathy's B-grade movie.

"Is there going to be trouble?" she asked.

"Nothing important." He waved his hand. "Just usual business."

Jessica felt her interest wane. Men in their suits.

"Chalo." Tripathy had sensed her boredom. He was attuned to her needs, more than most husbands in this city were to those of their wives. More than Tripathy no doubt was to his own wife.

He got up. Immediately, the others rose like his shadows.

"Okay, let us head out." He clapped his hands. "Time for me to check out this motherfucker who thinks he and his family can ruin their country and then come over here and take ours. We got rid of the British, didn't we?"

But they had kept their buildings, Jessica thought, as she followed them down the hallway.

As the lift slid downwards, Tripathy turned to the men. "Jessicaji has started a home cooking business."

"Wonderful, wonderful." Bobby nodded in admiration.

"If you can spread the word. She is a terrific cook. The food is first class."

"Absolutely, Sir. We will tell everyone."

"Madam, do you have a card?" Venky asked her politely.

She tried to make eye contact, but he wouldn't look at her. She wanted to reassure him that it was all right. He would survive. Tripathy did take care of people. There was no one more loyal than him in Hrishipur. And many people lost their jobs now. Or their husbands. Or their kidney function. Somehow, in this strange, cruel world, if you could find your way to the right people, you could resurrect.

Jessica wanted to convey all this to the man. But he kept his eyes lowered on her hand as he took the proffered business card. She felt sorry for him. He lacked the sense of inflated self-confidence that most men who were not servants in Hrishipur displayed. Soon he would learn, however, that it was a necessary armour.

The beats of bhangra disco reverberated through the walls of the nightclub to their right as Jessica and Tripathy stepped out of the lift and walked down the carpeted hallway that was glowing with blue light from the room at its far end. Tripathy paused at the entrance to the Sapphire Room so they could walk in together, ever chivalrous, unlike the younger men she went with. She ran a hand down her floor-length gold dress with the demure slit at the back and smiled at him. His striped grey and purple shirt strained over his belly.

"Let's try to have fun," he whispered.

Jessica nodded. She would. But she was less sure about him.

Nothing about Trump Towers gave him any pleasure. The last time Tripathy had visited Hrishipur, they had driven around in one of his rented cars while he pointed out his various properties and cursed the government for withholding licences that would enable him to continue construction. And then they had stopped at the condos that seemed to grow by a floor every day, as if they were being fed some sort of real estate power drink. She remembered clearly the volley of curses.

Security was tight. Guests were being frisked. A uniformed security guard with an AK-47 attached to his torso like an extra limb clicked Jessica's beaded purse open and shut and waved them through to the door where the hotel's manager stood. He had taken it upon himself tonight to check the guests' credentials.

They could take no chances.

Tripathy did not need any credentials. "Hello, Sampat," he said, patting the manager on his shoulder.

"Mr Tripathy," Sampat cried out. "Good to see you back, Sir.

How are things in Mumbai?"

"It is raining there, unlike here," Tripathy said.

"Yes, Sir, seen all the flooding photos on the news. Ms Pereira." He turned to her and bowed his head.

"Is he here?" she asked him.

"Not yet, Ma'am. They are on their way from Delhi. He has been in meetings all day with various ministers and diplomats."

The instant they entered the room with the blue haze, Tripathy was surrounded by a group of men in suits and ties. Jessica wandered away, relieved to be on her own.

The ceiling overhead was a navy sky embedded with luminous stars. The chairs and sofas ranged from teal to cerulean. The wall behind the bar was one rectangular aquarium. A large strobe light at the far end cast its turquoise flashes across the dance floor, which, for now, was bare. But next to it, Celestial Cobras, the local jazz band that always played here on Saturday nights, was in full flow.

The last time Jessica had been here was with Vivek, for his friend's fortieth birthday celebration. It had been a far less elegant affair. There was yelling and dancing and tequila. And she and Vivek had held each other close when the music had slowed at the end of the night, almost as if they were a couple. Almost as if she could form an attachment to one of them.

In the dim lighting everyone looked like spirits, especially when reflected in the mirrors all around. There was that blond cricketer from South Africa or New Zealand or wherever who played for the Indian Premier League, with Bulbul Ahuja, the middle-aged writer of chick lit. Dressed in a ruby-red satin dress, she slithered across the floor with her boy, casting glances here and there to ensure she was recognized. There was a group of lithe girls dressed in identical tight black dresses tottering on their heels with martini glasses in their hands, apparently under the illusion that they were having fun.

Then, across the floor, Jessica spotted an ethereal figure draped in white chiffon. Even before the woman turned towards her, she knew it was Ramona. Her willowy form floated towards her like a nymph. They embraced in a cloud of J'adore, Ramona's favourite perfume.

"I didn't realize you would be here," said Jessica.

"Salil and his partner were invited. I seldom go out these days. I thought it might be fun to see the son. Maneka speaks of him with such scorn. But who has an opportunity to actually see any of them up close like this?"

"Where is he?"

"On his way from Delhi with his entourage, I believe."

"No, I don't mean the Americans. Where is Salil?" Jessica raised her voice to be audible over the strains of the clarinet as the band started up again.

"Somewhere in there," Ramona waved at the crowd behind her, sounding overly casual. "I am glad to see you. I don't know anyone here. Everyone is suddenly so . . . young."

"So are we!" Jessica cried. "It's a party. We will have fun. Come, let's drink." She dragged Ramona by the hand and led the way to the bar, where she ordered a lychee martini for herself.

"A G&T for me, please," said Ramona.

"Why not something more interesting?" Jessica pleaded.

Ramona shook her head. "I don't feel well when I drink these days."

Jessica took a closer look at her here, where the light from the bar was brighter. Ramona's eyes had circles under them and her face was more angular than usual.

"Have you not been eating, Ramona?" she asked. "Are you trying to lose more weight or what?"

"No, no, I eat. I'm fine." Ramona ran her fingers along her fine brown hair. "Just having trouble sleeping. I've been taking some tablets. I'm sure they will work soon."

They took their drinks and walked over to a side of the room that seemed a little less crowded.

"Has all of Hrishipur landed here tonight?" Jessica whispered.

"It's been so long since I've seen people." Ramona craned her neck and looked around.

"I wish I were at home," Jessica sighed.

"It's different for you. You are busy all day, like Salil. You see so many people. I am on my own with nothing to do but scroll through Facebook and see other people and their—" She paused. "Jobs and stuff."

"It's not that. I wish I were home because Titli is there."

Ramona looked away. A streak of aquamarine light fell on her profile. "I know," she said quietly.

"You should try again," Jessica clutched her arm. "There are so many new ways now. I know a doctor in case you're interested."

Ramona angled her body away and stared out at the crowd.

Jessica felt rebuffed. She understood what it was like to want a child. But Ramona and Salil were well off; they could spend lakhs on fertility treatments or surrogates or whatever else they needed.

People had bigger problems than them. She wanted to suggest that Ramona think about adoption. But the thought of Her Elegance with a brown, skinny child from an orphanage made her laugh out loud.

"What?" Ramona asked, startled.

"Nothing. Just laughing at all of us, waiting around for this American heir to show up for a few minutes. Who are these people?"

"Salil said all the investors were invited, along with all the well-known developers."

"They hate the whole thing. They were just invited to burn with jealousy. Tripathy is furious. And helpless of course. I mean, what can he do?"

Ramona pursed her lips and looked straight ahead.

"Oh, come on, I can't mention Tripathy? You're becoming such a prude. Is it Maneka's influence?" Jessica snorted.

Ramona frowned. "I wanted her to come along. Salil said he would try to wrangle an invitation for her as well. But she said no."

"Of course she would say no. She hates Trump." Jessica rolled her eyes. "She's one of the American liberals who wouldn't be caught dead at an event like this. Besides, she seems too busy with our adorable friend Ashok. I ran into them the other day at Atmos of all places. They were coming out of the movie theatre. There's one more good deed you have done."

Ramona straightened her back and looked away. The warmth of the last few minutes evaporated. Jessica had forgotten how possessive Ramona was. She wanted everyone to herself. Poor Salil. To live with someone like that couldn't be easy. She decided it would be wisest not to disclose her own lunch date with Maneka the day before, during which Maneka had asked many questions about her catering. For a book she was thinking about writing, about money in urban India and its impact on people's lives.

"Tell me something," she said. "Were you two ever really close? You seem so different."

"Do you mean I'm not bright enough?"

"No, of course not. I just think she's a little pretentious sometimes. Like she's better than us. When she is really not, if you think about it. She teaches at some obscure college no one has heard of. How many thousands of colleges do they have in America? And she's trying to write this book about India for her white American colleagues."

"Well, I would not get a job in any one of those obscure colleges, nor would I ever be able to finish writing a book for anyone," said Ramona. "Besides, her mother just died."

Jessica felt chastised. Her own mother's weary voice on the phone that morning, describing her first dialysis experience, returned to haunt her.

"Who is that guy?" she said, to change the subject.

The short, stocky man with a ponytail and glasses looked familiar. His fingers, encircling a glass of liquor, were adorned with rings, and he wore a black-and-white printed shirt tucked into jeans that seemed way too casual for this event. Next to him stood a slip of a girl, no older than twenty-two, whose silver dress ended just below her butt. She looked around disinterestedly until she met Jessica's eye. Jessica thought she felt some empathy radiating from the girl. An understanding of mutual boredom and resignation. It was cut short when the man put a proprietorial arm around her to whisper into her ear.

"Who?" Ramona swiveled like a fine chair, until she caught sight of the ponytailed man with the woman towering over him like a majestic statue. "You don't know him?" she said. "That's Rocky Venugopal. The guy who directed *Mumbai Vibes* and *Love Aur Revenge*. The girl with him is Varsha Vakil, who did that hot item number in his last film. Rocky is married, of course," she went on. "He sleeps with all the actresses before they make it big. Then they stop sleeping with him and date their co-stars."

"How do you know all this?" Jessica was impressed.

"When you don't have children or a career, you have time to do research."

Now Jessica recognized them. The film producer from Chennai made slick movies about cool young Indians and their complicated relationships. But Jessica was intrigued by the girl who looked at him with slight disdain. She wondered how she could bear to have this oily, pimpled stub of a man touch her.

Then she remembered what she was doing here and laughed out loud once again, startling Ramona.

"I need another drink," Jessica said, glancing down at her glass.

"Already?" said a voice behind her. It was Salil. "Maybe you should slow down a little."

"Don't tell her what to do," said Ramona softly. "She's not your wife."

Salil's face tightened. He continued to look at Jessica, but she felt awkward, as if he really wanted to look somewhere else.

"I just wanted to say, be careful with the drinks. The night is still young."

"Thanks, Sal," she said. "I can take care of myself." She gave him a wink and walked away, leaving him alone with his wife, which seemed like penalty enough.

At the bar, she checked her phone to see if her brother had replied to the text she had sent that morning. All she had asked of him was that he accompany their mother to the hospital three times a week. Jessica lived far away, not because she didn't care but because she had no choice. Someone had to make a living and take care of the family. Throughout their childhood it had been her mother, struggling to pay bills on an office receptionist's salary. And now it was Jessica.

When she turned from the bar, there he was. Vivek. About six feet away, the length of his body when he lay next to her. He was with a petite woman with a chic short haircut whom Jessica knew well from her social media pictures. She had stalked her online for weeks.

She walked directly into Vivek's line of vision and tried to catch his eye. But he ignored her and gazed pointedly in the opposite direction.

Jessica turned away, her face stinging just as it had in the lobby when the valet had ignored her. But this was Viv. How could he?

She needed to get out of this room. It made her feel like she was underwater. The guard held the side door open and let her into the surprisingly quiet hallway. The golden light and tan carpeting provided respite from the blues inside. Jessica leant against the wall with the drink in her hand and wished she had a cigarette.

Behind her she heard the door open and shut, but she didn't turn around. Not even when she heard Vivek's voice call out her name.

"Jess."

"Viv," she replied. The bastard. So, he had seen her after all.

How could he not have?

"Hey, got a cig?" she asked in her breeziest voice as she turned around.

He grimaced. "We're indoors, Jess," he said softly. "You can't smoke in here."

"Well, let's step outside for a minute then."

It was only after she had uttered those words that Jessica realized how badly she wanted that. Had wanted it since she saw Viv in the crowded blue aquarium. To walk on the hotel's lush lawns in the sultry summer night, away from the shrill music and ostentatious clothes in there. To walk with him.

But he shook his head. "I can't. I have to go back inside. Anjali is waiting for me."

"Anjali? Your betrothed? How sweet."

"I think we should get back. He's about to get here."

"Tripathy?" Jessica laughed bitterly. "He's not going to notice I'm gone. He's busy wheeling and dealing. Besides, he doesn't care. He knows I'm a free bird. He pays me to do this. It's just . . . company." She stared at Vivek in defiance, willing him to say something hurtful, to insult her again like he had the last time they'd been together.

Vivek looked at her with a puzzled expression in his eyes. As if he was trying to understand something. Finally, he spoke. "I wasn't talking about Tripathy."

"Then who?" she demanded.

"That guy. The son. He's almost here, I believe. To inaugurate the damn building."

"Oh, him. I had forgotten about him."

"Isn't that why we are all here?"

"I just go wherever I'm summoned."

He started to walk away. She knew she had to say something to make him stay or at least pause, something to remind him of who they used to be.

"How's your brother?" she asked. "Did he take his GMAT?"

"Yes. He's going to Wharton."

"Oh, that's great."

Vivek nodded. "He wanted to come tonight to see the son. They all went there too, you know. Dhruv is excited about everything in America nowadays. He almost has an accent." He flashed an indulgent smile that touched her. Vivek's brother was ten years younger than him, and unlike her baby brother, he was ambitious and determined to be rich.

"Why didn't you bring him?" she asked. "It would have been nice to see him."

"I only had one guest pass. I had to choose between him and Anjali. She really wanted to come too. I guess everyone wants to see the American president's son. Even if he's an idiot."

"You chose well," Jessica said.

He shifted his gaze and cleared his throat. "Well, I'm going back inside to see the fanfare. You stay here if you want."

She watched him leave and felt a familiar disappointment.

If only he had asked her about her family too. At least about the little one who had adored him. Her favourite uncle, she had called him. More handsome than all the others. He could have just pretended to care.

Suddenly, the security guard with the AK-47 came towards her with resolute steps. "Madam, Madam, inside please."

He almost pushed her into the Sapphire Room and closed the door behind her. She stumbled while her eyes tried to adjust once again to the dim lighting. The crowd near the front of the room had thickened as guests gathered to get a good view of the proceedings. Someone was making announcements on the stage.

"Jessica, where were you? I've been looking for you all night," said Tripathy, walking up to her. He frowned and rubbed a hand over his forehead.

"Is something wrong?"

"I have a headache. Too many problems with work."

"Do you have to think about work now, here?" she asked in her most soothing voice.

He sighed. "Jessica, why are we here? This is all work. Do you think I want to see these fools for my entertainment? But now that I have found you, I feel better." He smiled at her with genuine pleasure.

She squeezed his hand, but he looked around nervously and snatched it away.

"They are in the hotel," someone whispered behind them.

She turned. It was Salil.

"Hey," she said, smiling in relief. With Tripathy and Salil next to her, suddenly Jessica felt like she was with old friends.

"Where's Ramona?"

"She went home," he said.

"Why? Is she not feeling well?"

"She never feels well these days," Salil said. "I don't know what to do any more."

"Mukesh, will you get me another drink, please? Lychee martini." Jessica used her baby voice, knowing Tripathy would not refuse.

"Of course, Devi."

The moment Tripathy was gone, Jessica turned to Salil. "Have you considered seeing someone? For her, I mean? There are some good therapists in Hrishipur now."

"I don't believe in that crap. They're just going to charge me large sums of money to talk bullshit."

Jessica was about to ask since when had money been a problem for people like them when the lights flashed. The crowd broke into applause. For a moment, Jessica thought she had been abducted by aliens. Everywhere she looked she saw faces concealed by phones and tablets. The new iPad had been launched just last weekend and the line outside the Apple store in Pizzazz, the mall closest to her home, had snaked all the way down from the third floor to the first. She wondered whether the American guests who had apparently just entered the room would be disappointed to learn that a launch of the latest gadgets in Hrishipur was hailed with even more fanfare than that of a luxury residence.

Here they came now, towards the platform, through the crowd, pausing to shake hands. Jessica stood on tiptoe to see more clearly. Leading the way was Aditya Jain, the scion of the industrialist family who had partnered with the Trumps to enable this deal. And right behind him walked the son. He towered over everyone else, even the tall North Indian men.

He looked less sinister in person. In fact, Jessica admitted reluctantly to herself, there was something almost attractive about him. He had an olive tint to his complexion, and his features were gentler than they appeared in pictures. The only thing that was identical to the posters of him was his smile: his teeth were so dazzling, it was as if he'd painted them with whitener before the event. Jessica wished he wouldn't smile. Didn't any of his advisors think to tell him that?

Behind him came a white woman with blond hair in an updo. The daughter-in-law. She wore a lilac salwar kameez with a flowing dupatta. She walked stiffly, as if she were made of wood, and looked bleached next to the warm colours of the Indian women. "You're the only one wearing Indian clothes here, you fool," Jessica whispered to herself. She was surprised at how sorry she felt for the woman, destined to walk a foot behind her husband all her life, decorated in local ethnic garb, forced to shake hands with strangers she probably thought were giving her a terrible contagious disease.

"Do you know her name?" Salil asked, breaking her reverie. Jessica shrugged.

"I don't think anyone knows her name," Salil replied to his own question. "Nobody cares about these people in their own country. They are just the kids of you-know-who. But here everyone seems to care."

"They care about the flat they are going to live in a year from now," Jessica said. But was that really all? Didn't the last name help sell the flats? Wasn't that why Tripathy and his buddies were so outraged?

She looked for him. It worried her that he might be so busy at the bar trying to get her a drink that he'd miss this event. But no, there was his greying head bobbing in the crowd. She was relieved. She hoped that whatever he wanted to get from this evening would work out for him.

The VIPs had moved on to the stage. They walked over to a side that had been unlit until this instant. Now cheers rang out as the table came into view. A structure lay on it, covered in gold fabric. The claps became a staccato rhythm, slowly building anticipation. The woman stepped up to the table with the two men on either side of her as if she were a prisoner and pulled the cover off with as much of a flourish as she could muster. The gold fabric flew in the air. It matched the colour of her hair. She laughed with pleasure as she gazed into the dark blur of the crowd. For a moment her face lit up, also golden in the spotlight.

And there, in all its glory, sat the model for a flat in Trump Towers. Jain began to point out the various rooms. The servant's quarters, the study, the five balconies, the living room, the kitchen. The crowd pushed closer. Cameras flashed. A TV camera recorded everything for the national news.

Jain gave a speech about how excited they all were to be developing this marvellous property that would help transform Hrishipur into the most happening city in the continent, and how honoured they were to welcome this great man.

Jessica turned to her left and caught her breath. Right next to her stood the statuesque movie star with the alliterative name. What was it again? Vakil. Varsha Vakil.

The crowd broke into applause. The son was embracing Jain. Now he stood behind the podium and waited patiently as the manager rushed to it to adjust the height.

"I am a bit tall, sorry," he drawled. Everyone laughed.

His voice was a little nasal. Jessica realized she hadn't heard it until now. No one had. Why would they? He had nothing to say. But tonight, he unrolled a piece of paper from his pocket and began to read from it. "India is a great country."

Varsha Vakil was very thin and tall, and her hair, piled on top of her head, made her look even longer. Jessica stared at her sharp profile and then down to the swell of her breasts above the dress.

"India is a beautiful country. So many oceans, forests, rivers, mountains. And this wonderful city with its numerous investment opportunities. This is progress. This is the future. You are the future. You are no longer a developing country. This government's vision will take you forward. And we are so pleased to be part of this journey."

If she were to just move her hand, she would touch Varsha. If she lifted a finger, she would feel the heaving breast tucked inside the tight silvery dress. Jessica felt a warmth between her legs.

When she was a teenager, all the girls held each other. At sleepovers, they lay with their heads in each other's laps, stroking backs and legs. They sat entwined like that as they watched movies and talked about boys. Always boys. They spoke cattily about the lesbos and the ones who had 'tendencies'. Their touches and hugs were completely asexual. Or so they thought, or so they told themselves. Jessica had wanted to climb on top of Miriam, the sports captain who could run faster than all the boys. She had wanted to tear off the clothes of the glamorous cousin from Australia, the one with the short boyish hair who smoked a pack of cigarettes a day when she visited them one summer. It was Goa after all. Everyone visited them.

"I have observed the most remarkable thing here in your country. Even the poor people, who have nothing, and are starving, are so happy. They are always smiling."

What the fuck?

The applause was a little less enthusiastic this time, as people looked at each other, trying to decide whether the words that had just been uttered by the American were insulting or not. Up on the stage, with the spotlight on him, the guest beamed, trying no doubt to match the eternally positive energy he had perceived in the impoverished population of this nation. But where could he have sighted them, Jessica wondered. The streets of Delhi had been cleared of any signs of poverty in preparation for his visit. The government wanted to highlight that India was a shining sun. Could the visitor have somehow spotted an itinerant beggar through the car window as he was being chauffeured from one five-star hotel to another? Or did he imagine it from all the documentaries he had been advised to watch about India prior to his trip?

The ceremony had been concluded. The VIPs were being led out of the door. On the way, the Americans paused again to shake hands with some of the VIPs. There was Tripathy, standing on tiptoe, attempting to insert his arm through the bodies. The sight of his face, bobbing and gasping like a fish trying to survive on land, filled Jessica with revulsion. Hypocrites, every single one of them.

Varsha was looking around like another lost creature in this sea. Her face was so heavily made up, it was difficult to tell what she really looked like. At thirty-nine, Jessica was beginning to set herself apart from these members of a new generation who had been born into a liberalized Indian economy with malls and German cars and holidays to foreign destinations that were as much a part of their reality as Facebook.

She bottomed her drink and approached Varsha to ask if she was having a good time.

The girl stared at her with a blank expression. Probably stoned, Jessica thought. The girl reminded her of David. She hoped that if her brother was high on some beach full of Russian tourists, confused and lost, a stranger would be kind to him—and not just because he wanted cheap drugs.

"Are you having fun?" she asked.

"Yeah," Varsha replied.

"Do you know Hrishipur well?'

"No, I live in Mumbai."

"Want to see something?"

"What?"

"Come."

She led her to the bay window in the far wall that looked out at the night sky. "Magical, isn't it?"

Beneath the sky, at the foot of the hill, lay Leisure Valley. A string of bars formed the perimeter of the square. Lights flashed from each of them. Red and blue strobe lights from the rooftop club, golden lights hanging across doorways, neon signs on walls. The music that played too loudly to allow any conversation down there was inaudible from up here. It looked almost peaceful from the top of the hill although up close the reality was quite different. Leisure Valley on a Saturday night was a jungle of sweaty bodies gyrating against each other. It was, Jessica had thought on the few occasions she'd been there, the epitome of everything awful about Hrishipur. Vulgar displays of wealth by a generation that had come into it suddenly and found it overwhelming.

Varsha was gazing at the lights down below. What did she see there with her vacant stare? A life of hedonism that awaited her back in Mumbai? Or an illusion created by the lights, a fantasy that was more exciting when viewed at a distance?

"Pretty," she finally whispered.

"Not as pretty as Goa, where I grew up," Jessica replied.

"You grew up in Goa!" Varsha clapped her hands. She was not drinking, apparently. "How wonderful. That's my favourite place in the whole world."

"Would you like a drink?" Jessica asked.

"I don't drink," Varsha said, shaking her head. A few tendrils loosened from her hair and fell carelessly around her face.

Jessica marvelled at this young girl who wasn't even holding a drink to act sophisticated. She reached out and clutched her hand.

Varsha's eyes shifted warily behind her. Before Jessica could turn around, she heard the deep bass voice of Rocky the producer.

"I don't like my friends being spirited away by strangers," he said. He gripped Varsha's elbow and shot her a look.

The lounge had resumed its usual Saturday-night buzz, as if the American couple had never been there at all. The people of Hrishipur had memories as ephemeral as air.

Apparently, Rocky did not bear grudges. "I'm buying everyone shots," he declared to Jessica. "Come, please, join us."

A small group gathered around to participate. Jessica threw her head back for the shot, and then another and another. The liquor burnt her throat and sent the blood to her ears. The room swirled with phantasmagoric shapes. The mirrors reflected back the figures that crowded the lounge now, multiplying the number of people who were actually there. In the background, a woman's smoky voice crooned. Jessica longed yet again for the heady inhale of a cigarette.

She didn't know how she had ended up next to Vivek and his girlfriend, but suddenly, there they were.

"Hey, hey," she said, reaching out to Vivek.

He took a step back. Next to him, Anjali smiled at her, the innocent fool. She was thin as a twig up close, with boyish pixie hair. Jessica had a sudden vision of the three of them together, limbs entwined.

"I didn't notice you were wearing this one," Jessica said, tugging at Vivek's maroon silk tie. "Remember when we went to buy it together?"

He moved farther back and straightened the tie without speaking. His eyes were dark holes.

Next to them, Anjali smiled again. She fucking smiled. Because why wouldn't a strange woman fondle a man's tie at a place like this? Everyone was a friend from somewhere. Everyone was drinking. This was Hrishipur, and everyone was cool.

"Aren't you going to introduce me to her?" Jessica jerked a thumb towards the pixie.

"I'm Anjali," she volunteered, extending her hand.

"How lovely. Wonderful to meet you, darling." Jessica gripped Anjali's wrist and shook it vigorously.

"Let's go, Anju. It's getting late." Vivek put an arm around her protectively.

"But what's your name? How do you two know each other?" Anjali asked.

Jessica laughed. How could Anjali not have stalked her online also? Who did not do that these days?

"I'm Jessica," she said, straightening her back and tossing her head slightly to add some flair to the announcement.

"Hi. Nice to meet you," said Anjali. Her smile broadened. "Do you work for Citibank too?"

The music had changed to slow ballads. Couples were moving to the dance floor. Jessica swayed a little, feeling light-headed. This woman had no idea who she was. He hadn't told her anything.

Why would he? He'd called Jessica a slut the last time she had seen him. He had said his parents wouldn't approve. But this woman who looked so Westernized and hip—surely, she wouldn't disapprove. Surely, he would have mentioned his exes to her. All his exes.

"You asshole," Jessica screamed, flinging the remnants of her drink at Vivek's face.

Anjali screamed too.

Vivek stood there spluttering, wiping his face with his sleeve.

"Here, use the tie, you bastard. The tie I bought you with my hard-earned money." Jessica grabbed his tie and tried to rub his face with it.

"What is going on here?" A voice bellowed through the bodies on the dance floor that were now twisted to look in their direction.

It was Tripathy.

"Nothing, just catching up with some old friends," Jessica tried to say in a chirpy voice. But it came out slurred, as if she were talking in her sleep.

Tripathy stared at her and then at Vivek. Vivek looked away.

"What are you all looking at?" Tripathy demanded of the crowd. Reluctantly, they began to disperse.

Anjali was wiping Vivek's face with a napkin. They stood close to one another like that, whispering. Then they turned swiftly around and made their escape.

"Come, time for us to leave too," said Tripathy. "The show we came for is over. We saw the goras cut their ribbons. I want a drink in the peace of my room now. You can walk?" he asked.

Jessica nodded, though her head throbbed.

They stepped outside with others who were filing out.

"Stay in the lobby for a while," Tripathy said quietly. "Go to the shops. See if you like anything. I have to take care of some business."

Jessica shook her head at his receding back. The shops had shut down for the night like they were wont to do. She stood outside the Kashmir emporium where a multicoloured carpet hung from ceiling to floor like a tapestry. It had to cost a few lakhs.

Her own home was decorated with handicrafts too. But she had purchased those from the makeshift stalls at Dilli Haat or from bazaars and craft fairs around the capital, at a fraction of the cost.

She closed her eyes and pretended she was in Goa, in the yellow house she had lived in as a child with her parents and brother, before her father died. The short walk to the beach, flanked by palm trees, coconuts hanging overhead, the salty breeze, calypso beats at night, bebinca and wine on Sundays. If she died just now, would the last thing she thought of be her childhood home? A vision of a little girl with snot in her nose crept out of nowhere, and she opened her eyes with a start and began to rummage furiously in her bag for her phone to see if Titli had woken up in the middle of the night and called her. She had not.

She walked out to the long hallway that stretched from one wing to another. One of its walls was all glass, through which you could see the tropical courtyard outside during the day, with its palm trees and heart-shaped swimming pool. Now, she peered out and saw only shadows.

One of those shadows was Tripathy. Jessica blinked and pressed her face against the cold glass. Was it really him? Yes, it was. There was no mistaking that hulking body, that round stomach, that fleshy bottom. She knew that body well.

He looked around him somewhat furtively. It might seem to a stranger as if this were a hotel guest taking in some night air after drinking too much. No one would think anything of it. But something about him tonight bothered Jessica. He had been on edge, and clearly annoyed by the launch.

A couple of other shadows soon joined Tripathy. Why were they hanging out in the poorly lit courtyard? One of the men had a pronounced limp. He walked awkwardly, dragging his right leg behind him. Jessica could not see any of their faces. They stood in a circle, talking. Tripathy waved his arms in the air, then drew them close in a huddle. After what seemed like hours to Jessica, the huddle broke. Tripathy headed inside the hotel and disappeared from view. The two strangers remained. The shorter one shook his fist and gesticulated wildly at the other. Then they walked off in opposite directions. Jessica watched as the man with the limp went, slowly, clumsily, along the path, until he was out of sight. His gait lingered in her mind as she turned away to find Tripathy. She felt sorry for the stranger. Who was this disabled man who lived in this city that hadn't been built for people like him? How did he survive? Whose favours kept him alive?

Out in the hallway, Tripathy was taking deep breaths. His face was a little flushed.

"Where were you?" she asked softly.

"At the bar," he pointed towards it. "Talking to my associates about something." Then he seemed to see her properly for the first time that evening. He held her gaze. "I am free now. Let's go upstairs." His tone altered as it often did when he found himself alone with her.

In the lift, where there was no one else but them, he finally touched her. Rubbing his large, soft hand down her back, he spoke reproachfully. "You should not drink so much. You should just nurse one drink for a long time. I think you become a different person when you drink. You have to think of your reputation for the sake of the child."

Jessica looked straight ahead at the steel doors that parted to let them out on the twenty-seventh floor. Inside the suite, it was a relief to get out of that ridiculous dress and sit down in a bathrobe. Somehow, after the last couple of hours downstairs, she felt safer up here with no one but Tripathy. He unbuttoned his shirt, let out a sigh as he unzipped his trousers, and sat down on the bed with a heave.

"Are you all right?" she asked, as she stroked his protruding stomach with her hand.

"Yes, just an exhausting day at work. And what about you? Did you see the new school?" He always asked about Titli.

She told him about Lyceé des Etoiles, the school she had visited the day before. She had taken Maneka with her because she was an educator. They had both been fascinated by the concept of the new school but for different reasons. Maneka had looked sceptical. *Sounds interesting, but can these kids get into a good college? Will they get a solid foundation?* she had asked.

Maybe not a college here in India, but I would like to send Titli to the States anyway. She would do much better there, where it's all so inclusive, wouldn't she? Jessica had replied.

Maneka had laughed hysterically, and Jessica had assumed she was mocking her aspirations. Perhaps she thought Titli wouldn't get an offer from a university in America, or that she, a single mother, would not be able to afford it.

Now Jessica turned to Tripathy. "They focus on an all-round experience rather than a traditional education. Extracurriculars, sport, social skills. There's no homework or exams. And they tailor the curriculum to each individual student's needs."

"Do whatever you think best."

"It's expensive."

"How much?"

"Forty thousand a month. Plus extras."

When it came to her daughter, Jessica had decided it was best to be direct. There were no illusions left for either party here. Tripathy did not think she loved him, and he had not professed love for her. And yet, if there were some who might consider their arrangement entirely transactional, they would probably be wrong.

"Try the new school. See if the child likes it. Poor thing, she has had a tough start." His eyes misted over with compassion. "And your mother?"

"Started dialysis this week."

"Jaan," he said. "Come here. You've had so many troubles lately. Don't worry. Things will turn out okay. We are all here."

The truth was that only he was here. But his use of the royal we was meant to reassure. He was more powerful that way, and more reliable. She knelt by the bed and allowed him to ruffle her damp hair. Once again, his touch felt paternal.

"You relax now," she said. "You're tired tonight." She ran a hand over his arm tenderly. She felt grateful. She wanted to do something for him. She slipped the robe off her shoulders, exposing her naked body so that he could get an erection. He moaned and lay back against the numerous silken pillows on the bed. She carefully pulled his trousers down and folded them. She gathered up her long hair and piled it into a knot on top of her head, as meticulously as she did while baking. Then she stripped him of his jockeys and collected his penis in her hand. He smelt sour. He should have showered. She focused on the TV. It was monstrous; how big was it, seventy inches? There was one in the bathroom too, which you could watch from the Jacuzzi. She stroked his balls slowly, the way he liked it, but instead of the usual soft moans, all she heard were little snores. He had fallen asleep.

Jessica rose, naked, and went to the window. Down below, the bars were closing in Leisure Valley. One by one, the neon signs overhead went dark, as if they were exiting the party. The lights inside the bars dimmed and began to go out too. Soon, the area that had been so full of life just an hour ago would be reduced to a black square, an empty playground.

ASHOK

THE STORM BREWING IN THE SKY THAT MORNING WOULD NOT bring rain. Ashok knew this like he knew many other things in his bones. He knew the owner of this roadside dhaba he was sitting in would never send his nephew to school no matter how hard Ashok tried to persuade him. He knew most of the properties he had spent the morning trying to photograph for a business magazine in Mumbai would never be handed over to their owners. He knew he was not going to get the money to buy the waterproof, shockproof, freezeproof Nikon 1 AW1 he needed for his monsoon assignment. He knew that in a few weeks Maneka was going to return to her fairy-tale town in the American Midwest where she would resume her idyllic life, completely divorced from the reality of people in this country.

They sat on a cot woven from jute, whose strands stuck out at weird angles and pricked Ashok's legs through his dark jeans. Overhead, a fan rotated apologetically, hapless against the rising temperature. Through the open entranceway, sunlight streamed in, hazy and full of dust particles. There was a pleasant, lethargic vibe to this midmorning, as if it were a long and languid Sunday, even though it was, in fact, the middle of the week.

Across from him on the charpoy sat Maneka, scrutinizing the oily plastic menu with the expression of a child in an ice-cream shop. He barely recognized her from that first meeting at Ramona and Salil's nearly two months ago. The wariness had faded from her eyes. He wondered how much of her newfound sense of calm was because of the time the two of them had spent together these past few weeks. The thought both pleased and worried him.

Behind the cash counter, on a plastic chair, sat the dhaba's owner, Satinder Paaji, a large Sardarji with a white beard and green turban. Ashok ignored the knowing gleam in his eyes as he glanced at Maneka and then at him. He ignored the vibration of the cell phone in his pocket and waved Satinder's nephew over. Jaggu, whose twiglike arms and legs made him look younger than his fourteen years, appeared with a cloth flung over his back to take their orders.

Maneka read the names of some of the dishes out loud. She sounded excited, almost as if she were a white tourist. But she said the names—maa ki dal, kaleja fry, methi paratha—with no hint of an American accent, and not even a clipped Indian one. Her words had already borrowed some of the roughness of North Indian speech. That was one of the things Ashok liked about her, this apparent ability to mould herself to situations. Unlike women like Ramona, she did not stand out everywhere she went, drawing the glances of other patrons despite her best efforts to fade. Unlike women like Jessica, she made no attempt to attract attention to herself.

He had texted her that morning mainly out of spite. The desire to hurt did not come naturally to Ashok. For all his flaws, he was not a vindictive or cruel guy. But the thought of the camera languishing in his Amazon cart had dismayed him more than anything else. He could still hear the desperation in his voice from the night before as he pleaded for the loan. Sixty thousand rupees was a significant sum of money for him, but not for everyone. Not for the person he had turned to yet again. But the response to his pleas had been swift and decisive. *No.* Contrary to what some people might think, Ashok did not like to ask for things. The memory of last night's conversation stung his ears with shame.

Jaggu brought them frothy lassis in tall steel tumblers. He should have been in school. Ashok watched him amble off to the next cot, where a group of truck drivers sat cross-legged, their strong bodies heaving against the midmorning heat. There Jaggu stood and repeated their orders, counting each one off on his fingers, not bothering to carry paper and pen with him since he couldn't read or write. But there was never any doubt in anyone's mind that he would remember every order correctly.

"Mmm," said Maneka. Froth and cream formed a moustache on her upper lip. She didn't look so intellectual now.

The women he brought here, charmed by the dhaba's authentic rusticity, inevitably began to reminisce about some place they had visited once as a child, before tearing pieces of roti delicately with their fingers, making sure not to soil their long, manicured nails. But Maneka's nails were short and chipped. She sat with one of her legs tucked under her and looked up at the darkening sky beyond the awning that covered the shack.

"It won't rain, will it?" she said. "Just another aandhi?" She looked at Ashok for confirmation.

He nodded. The storm would blow windows apart, shatter glass, and uproot trees without a drop of rain. The aandhi in this region did nothing to relieve frustration; it only escalated it. It was a perfect metaphor for the expectations of everyone who lived in this city.

Paaji's Dhaba, off the highway that continued on to the neighbouring state of Rajasthan, was Ashok's favourite. Named to sound like it could belong to any friendly Sardarji neighbour or relative, it was devoid of frills, its menu far more limited than those at the air-conditioned joints they had driven past to get here, which served beer and, even more sacrilegiously, Chinese food. In a landscape increasingly dotted with McDonald's arches and KFC signs, this dhaba was an anachronism designed to accomplish a single objective: to remind people of a simpler time.

Apparently, Maneka had bought into the fantasy too. "There are parts of Hrishipur that are still unspoiled. Who knew?" she said.

"Or, as some would say, underdeveloped," he said.

He told her the story of the seven villages named after sages mentioned in the ancient Hindu scriptures. Where farmers once lived in relative peace outside the precincts of the capital, ploughing land for crops that could thrive in the dry climate. Wheat, maize, mustard. Until the 1970s when the seven villages were united into a single city. The city of rishis.

"Why is it named Hrishipur with an *H*?" Maneka asked.

"Like Hrithik Roshan's parents, whoever named it followed the advice of an astrologer. The addition of the extra letter was meant to bring the new city and its residents good fortune and prosperity."

"It must have looked very different then. I imagine they had trees."

"Yes, they had to cut all those old-fashioned forests down to make way for the concrete one."

They gazed out at the highway, where the cement platform that split the road in two was covered in bougainvillaea shrubs, the only flowers sturdy enough to flourish in the heat. Their dark pink colour stood out today against an overcast sky.

"This place is like a foil to Heathersfield. Being around Ramona reminds me of high school and the dreams we all used to have back then. How certain we were that America and other Western countries were more exciting, more *happening* as we loved to say," Maneka said. "And here I am now, living in a town where the height of excitement is the wrong political sign in someone's yard or a foreclosure on a home." She rolled her eyes. "Is there such a thing as too many daffodils and duck ponds? What was it Madame Bovary said? *She could not think that the calm in which she lived was the happiness she had dreamed.*"

Ashok could only imagine fragments of her life back in the States. He had left his own childhood home and friends in Indore and moved to Hrishipur because it offered him a job with a print magazine. It was supposed to be a stepping stone, an experience that would bring him closer to his dream of one day photographing wildlife for *National Geographic*. He had lasted ten months at *Zindagi Vibes*. During that time, the editors had had him substitute for the senior photographers when they were unable to go on an assignment, but for the most part he'd sat at his PC in the windowless room and typed away, editing other people's copy. He even made tea a few times for the reporters. In the end, what he had learnt above all else was that a cubicle and desktop computer were not for him. He didn't need anyone to tell him what to do in this new land of opportunity. He was young and free; he could take off in whatever direction he chose.

But first, he needed the fucking camera to complete his assignment.

His hand went instinctively to the pocket of his dark-green T-shirt, an old gift from someone he used to know—a lonely middle-aged assistant editor at the magazine who had invited him to her place for a home-cooked dinner one evening. He caressed the hard outline of his cell phone absently, hoping against hope that the cash would somehow materialize alongside it. This time, he knew it wouldn't. Things were changing, even for those who seemed to have it all.

He wondered what Maneka would say if he suddenly asked her for a favour. Lunch at this authentic dhaba in exchange for a little loan. Or gift. Surely, she could afford a few hundred dollars? The thought made him snort with laughter, not at anyone else for once but at himself. Maneka looked up at him, intrigued.

He was still chuckling when Jaggu brought them steel plates heaped with hot rotis fresh from the tandoor, black Punjabi dal with a dollop of butter, and a homely salad of sliced onions and green chillies. Ashok was pleased to see Maneka wipe her plate clean, first with her roti and then her fingers, which she then stuck in her mouth and licked one by one.

"I have missed this food. In Heathersfield, there's only one Indian restaurant called Taj Mahal that serves several curries with pink sauces that all taste the same. And saag paneer with little flecks of paneer and no spices. All the white people drink mango lassi with their tikka masala and say it's the best food they've ever tasted."

"It sounds unbearable," he said, and waited for her to contradict him.

"It's not," she said. "Heathersfield has other wonderful food that comes straight from the farms to the tables. Asparagus in different colours, heirloom tomatoes, fruit you can pick yourself. At the farmers' market you can get unusual produce you have never even heard of. Like purple potatoes, all kinds of peppers, hundreds of varieties of fresh herbs. And the cute little shops lining the lake sell homemade ice cream in strange flavours like avocado coconut and nectarine rosemary. Besides, I think I miss a juicy burger almost as much here as I miss goat biryani when I'm there."

"We should have gone to McDonald's then."

"I should have clarified that I miss a juicy *beef* burger."

"So, if you had an opportunity to stay on here, you would not?"

Ashok regretted the question as soon as he had asked it. It was the sort of thing people asked when they didn't want someone to leave. That was not what he had meant, but it was too late to clarify. Maneka averted her face to look down at her empty plate, but he saw the smile on her lips. She was pleased.

"I couldn't get a job here now if I wanted to come back, so this is an entirely hypothetical question."

Ashok shrugged. "You might. At one of the new universities that have sprung up. But you might not be able to keep it for long. Not unless you're willing to stop sharing your opinions, especially if they're about The Party. I have a feeling that would be hard for you to do."

Maneka nodded. "The prospect of a fixed retirement age with no help from the government afterwards doesn't seem so appealing now. It seemed just fine when I was an only child growing up in South Kolkata. The future was so far away and anything seemed possible then."

"It sounds to me like your life in Heathersfield is safe and sweet. I'm sure there's plenty there to keep you occupied."

Maneka glanced at him as he had known she would. He was curious about the boyfriend or whatever he was. He had tried a half-hearted search on Google for Michael Peterson but it had not revealed much beyond the basic bio and a thumbnail photo on the university's website. It was the foreignness, the contrast with his own life, that intrigued him. This man, this *gentleman*, for he was twenty years older than Ashok, sounded like a character in a novel. Pale-white complexion, the sort that turned red under the sun, hair the colour of straw, small eyes behind foggy glasses, a smile that signalled a lack of decisiveness. Michael, as Ashok called him in his head, seemed to publish scholarly papers on novels by writers who had all lived in small towns like Heathersfield. He had found the abstract for one of them. *In the fiction of Richard Ford, the characters choose to resign themselves to their collective destinies.* Michael sounded like a boring, pompous ass.

A slow growl came from one of the mangy stray dogs that sat about the dhaba. Ashok followed its gaze to the sidewalk across the highway where a speck of saffron was gradually growing in length. Within minutes, the speck had transformed into an orange ribbon, unravelling down the road from end to end. Dozens of men walked in pairs, balancing poles straddled across their shoulders.

"Who are they? What are they carrying on their backs?" Maneka asked.

"They are the Kanwariyas. Peaceful devotees of Shiva walking to Haridwar to fetch water from the Ganga with which they can wash the Lord's cock," said Ashok. "You will see them walking the other way in a few weeks, on their return journey back to their villages in Bihar."

"It's a long way to walk in this weather."

"Don't feel sorry for them. They are Hindu fanatics egged on by The Party. If they discover you don't like temples and gods, you never know what they might have to do to persuade you."

Ashok had seen them go back and forth every summer he had lived in Hrishipur. The Kanwariyas, like the cattle on the road, were a part of the landscape here. Maneka, who had apparently not encountered them in the sheltered neighbourhoods of Kolkata where she had grown up, was watching the men walk with their peculiar yet graceful gait, two by two, their steps as coordinated as those of soldiers in the Indian army. Their voices rose in a chant. *Bam Bol. Bam Bol.* They looked like a slithering flame that might, if ignited by a spark on this hot, dry day, erupt into a ball of fire at any moment.

"There's another reason for you," he said quietly. "To not return to this country."

"Eerie," said Maneka. "Just like the born-again evangelicals in the heartland of America. But I am envious of their sense of purpose and focus. What degree of commitment does it take to make this journey every year in temperatures this high just for water with which to bathe the penis of a stone god? What benediction do they receive from it beyond the satisfaction of a task completed?"

The satisfaction Ashok would not get this year with the monsoon photos from western India that an editor had commissioned from him. The satisfaction that eluded the builders and construction workers in Hrishipur these days. But it was the hope, he wanted to say. The hope of satisfaction that, even if briefly, made you feel alive. Without that, there would be nothing at all.

"Do you find teaching satisfying?" he asked.

She looked surprised. He understood that she was not used to people, perhaps men in particular, asking her such things. He was not performing, but genuinely interested in what she did over there and what kept her going in those deathly quiet surroundings.

She told him about the young undergraduates who worked two or three jobs to pay their way through college. Most of them came from even smaller, one-stoplight towns in the surrounding areas. For them, the opportunity to get a college degree and to live in a proper city like Heathersfield was an adventure. And when they saw someone like her for the first time in their lives, they were intimidated.

"The immigrants sound more worldly," Ashok remarked. "Isn't it odd how we all assume that it's the other way around, that Americans must be more sophisticated and cooler? Just because they use cutlery every time they eat." He held up his hand, caked with the dal that had dried on his fingers.

"Expectations will be the death of us."

Her smile twisted through Ashok's heart. He had forgotten he had one. He did not want to disappoint her or anyone else, but that was what he was destined to do. He just hoped, on this morning, to put it off a little longer.

"Your turn now. What about you? When did you first want to be a photographer?"

Ashok seldom talked about his childhood with women. His old life back home was his own untold story and he liked to keep it that way. But the knowledge that Maneka was going to leave in just over a month and the likelihood that he would never see her again made him loosen up. She was not from his circle and would not share this story. And so he told her about the red kite.

One afternoon, he and his father had stood on the roof of their ancestral house in Indore. His father, once a champion kite flyer, wanted to teach him the art of keeping the patang, the fighter kite, up in the air as long as possible, soaring freely in the sky, defying all other kites to challenge it. He saw his father's face now, with its twitching muscles and inflamed eyes as he yelled at Ashok to *pull*

pull pull. Their kite was a sunny yellow, a friend to the sun, dipping and rising cheerfully in the cloudy sky.

Ashok remembered how his soft young hands had bled as he clutched the glass-spangled kite strings. His father had grabbed the spool with a cry of exasperation, so that for a while they each held on to it together, and steered wildly. Ashok had spent most of his childhood trying to get his father to pay a little attention to him. Most of the time, he had been either absent or withdrawn. But on that day, they had been united in their mission. The other kite, whose unseen owner fought valiantly from somewhere across the neighbourhood, was fated to snap and collapse on the ground. He heard once again the sound of his father's triumphant laughter. But the image that stood out most prominently now was of the other red kite fluttering against the sky. Ashok had not wanted that kite to fall. He had wanted it to stay up there, trapped in its wooden frame.

When he finished the story, Maneka was looking at him with the same compassion in her eyes that she had when speaking about her father. Strands of her hair were plastered to her neck with sweat. He wanted to remove them with his fingers.

The phone vibrated again in his pocket. He imagined the texts there. *Please. Sorry. Try to understand.*

He ought not to have begged. Nor to have loaned langda Gopal twenty thousand rupees last week. But the man had sounded so desperate. His grandmother in the village needed to make repairs to her house. Ashok had had a weak moment and dug into his savings. Gopal had promised to repay him. Apparently, he was involved in a partnership with some powerful men in the city. Yeah, right. He was no longer even sure that Gopal had a grandmother at all.

"Do you still want to see it?" he asked Maneka, steering their conversation away from himself. "If other people's undelivered flats saddened you this morning, is this a good idea?"

"Yes. Like the Kanwariyas, I need to do this. It's my own pilgrimage."

"All right, then, let's wash our hands," Ashok said, pointing to the sink in the corner. "Time to head to the boondocks."

On his way out, he handed Jaggu a hundred-rupee tip he could not afford. Maneka took out another hundred and slipped the note into Jaggu's pocket, which made his smile expand like a rubber band.

When she had walked on towards the car, Ashok felt a tug on his sleeve.

"Bring her again, Ashok bhai. This one is nice," he said. Ashok slapped him on the back. "We shall see."

~

The unpaved lanes off the highway led to a smattering of small villages nestled against the distant backdrop of the craggy brown Aravalli hills. He drove through them until he reached a clearing with no more signs of life, just a row of makeshift shops with signs advertising electrical goods, bathroom tiles, plumbing supplies, paint, light fixtures, and other hardware. All the shops were shuttered.

When they climbed out of the car, the sky rumbled and dark clouds rolled over it. The construction site, which looked like a large meadow whose grass was overdue for a trim, had been separated from the street by a wall of hay.

Ashok swung his leg over and beckoned to Maneka.

"Are we allowed?" She looked around, as if a cop might come by any time.

"It's a piece of abandoned land, not fucking Trump Towers. Come on."

"But people own this. They have paid for it. People like my father," she said as she walked over to him.

Ashok led her to the tall white sign that stood in the middle of the overgrown grass like a scarecrow. They craned their necks to read what it said. *Jannat. Bhatia Developers. 01223 2584613.*

The ambiguity lay in the fact that Jannat could be this grassy field itself, a paradise by virtue of its distance from the madding crowds, or it could be something you could access by calling the phone number provided. Just like numbers scrawled on bathroom walls of bars in Hollywood movies or those listed at the back of men's magazines, this one implied that untold pleasures were just a phone call away.

"Does this look like heaven or hell to you?" Ashok asked.

Maneka looked around, searching for the answer in the landscape. "It's earth, isn't it?" she said, finally. "Neither heaven nor hell."

"That's one way of looking at it." He narrowed his eyes. "Such a sensible, unromantic thought."

"I'm a realist." She shrugged.

"Not really," he said. "You still believe in many things. Far more than most people who live in this town. It's unfortunate."

"Why?" she asked.

"You are going to keep getting disappointed."

She began to walk across the grass. "Well, I'll only be here another month. What new, disappointing things could I possibly discover in Hrishipur?"

Ashok felt an emotion he had thought was buried deep inside. Not love or sorrow or anything that intense, but a quiet, low rumble of guilt.

"It's actually quite pleasant here," she shouted as she walked away from him. "A lot more pleasant than the property itself might have been. Can you imagine this place converted into high-rises with lifts and shops and cars, and generators pumping electricity, and a gym and indoor swimming pools and restaurants serving chow mein and chilli chicken?"

"Don't forget Ruby Tuesday and Subway."

They laughed together. Maneka collapsed on to the ground.

"I can't believe I am laughing. I have stayed awake nights thinking about this place." She waved her hand around. "And my parents, my poor parents." She turned her face away from his. "My father did a foolish thing. For the past few years, my parents have not owned a home. It's so strange to think of them that way, as homeless. We were comfortable when I was growing up. Not rich like Ramona and her friends, not that posh, but we were genteel and respectable. Many people in this country must have thought of us as extremely privileged. And then they moved here, to this place, and just like that they lost their home. It used to really bother my mother. She even sent me photos of this site where their new flat would come up. It was a blank slate, a clearing filled with potential. It breaks my heart to think of the couples and families who imagined their lives in Jannat."

Ashok pointed vaguely in the direction of the shuttered stores. "Think of those guys. They are losing money too. Their income depends on these constructions. And they don't have offspring earning dollars in the States who might be able to help them out."

Her face looked like that of a child's, crestfallen and a little puzzled by her family's changed circumstances. Ashok wanted to wrap his arms around her, but instead he reached out with a blade of grass between his fingers and casually caressed the skin on her right arm. "If it's any consolation, nearly all the developers here are several years behind schedule."

"But why?" she cried out.

"They sell land without acquiring the licences they need.

Sometimes that land is purchased illegally from farmers. The previous government allowed the developers to do whatever they wanted. In exchange for cash of course. And now The Party wants revenge and wants to demonstrate how active they are in stopping corruption, so they have stopped the malpractices, cancelled licences, and aborted construction. Some of the developers are in jail."

"And yet, I see signs for new developments all the time."

"Yes, well, I guess we can safely say that India is still a developing country."

"Everyone in America wants to own a home too. They move somewhere for a year, they buy a house. They want their own home so they can do their own repairs and grow their own vegetables and so on. But here, right now, I feel like it's an infectious disease. It wasn't this bad when I was a kid. This clamouring for more property, for a condo in the swankiest building, for a certain address . . ."

Ashok knew what she was talking about. But it was not a virus he had been infected with. He hoped she knew that about him.

He couldn't care less about property. His grandfather's house in Indore would be parcelled off when the old man died and divided between all the cousins. They had already begun fighting over it. Ashok ignored them. All he wanted was his camera and the freedom to do whatever he desired without having to ask anyone for favours.

"What about Trump Towers?" asked Maneka. "How is that coming up so fast!"

"The Party is hardly going to stop them, is it? How many trade deals do you think depend on it? In fact, they have cleared licences for them at record speed I hear, and it's enraged the local builders. But there's nothing they can do. They can only stand idly by and watch."

Maneka didn't respond. She lay with her eyes shut. Her breasts heaved up and down, but Ashok looked away from them, to her face, small and half concealed by the grass.

"It's not all doom and gloom," he said, standing over her with his legs on either side of her body. Her hair was spread out around her head like a fan. "Everyone has a different perspective, you know. A lot of people are benefiting from the progress you see around you. Think of how happy those people will be who will soon move into Trump Towers and start their glamorous new lives there."

"You always sound so wise. How old are you?" she asked. Ashok grinned. "Worried I'm too young?"

"Too young for what?"

"I'm twenty-nine," he said.

"I'm thirty-five."

"I know."

"You know?"

"Let me see." He paused dramatically, finger on chin, pretending to strain to recall something. "You went somewhere with Ramona. Oh, I know. Your snooty school."

Maneka laughed. "And I thought I'd scare you."

Ashok crouched down so he was almost sitting on her legs but not touching them. "Scare me? By being six years older than me? Do you know anything about men at all? Or are you just worried that Indian men are too old fashioned? We're not, you know. We've changed. We've become Americanized." He lowered himself on to her knees, hoping he wouldn't hurt her. Women wanted him to hurt them. He had spent many nights in this town doing things to them he would have considered unspeakable. But unlike other men, he only did it because they wanted him to. "So, this Michael. Is he real or just someone you made up?"

"He's as real as anyone could be. More real than you or me. But right now, he's my ex."

"Ex?" Ashok was genuinely surprised.

"Yes, I broke up with him this weekend."

He hovered over her with his arms pinned on either side like an aeroplane about to take off. Her face was very close to his. Unlike Ramona, she wore no makeup.

"Are you all right?" he finally said, unsure if that was the right response.

She nodded.

"It was coming for a long time. We had grown apart. We had decided to take a break when I was leaving. I just realized I haven't missed him at all. I had no urge to call him or hear his voice or anything. He felt so distant to me here. Another world, another life."

A world and life she would nonetheless return to in just a few weeks. A world with Social Security and no Kanwariyas chanting mantras on the road.

"I'm officially single now," she said.

He lowered himself until her face became a blur of flesh. She grasped his collar and pulled him towards her. Somehow, in this moment, he thought it really might rain.

And for a few delicious seconds, it did. He felt the moisture in the breeze even before the first drops fell on his face and arms. It was warm rain, the kind that filled the air with the scent of earth, the scent that reminded him of his childhood. If he opened his eyes now, he might find himself in the narrow lanes outside the old ancestral home, the lanes where the boys from the slum floated tiny newspaper boats in the potholes. And there was Yasmin, the neighbour's daughter, hurrying home with newspapers on her head. In her scarlet dress she looked like the red kite.

But when he did open his eyes, the drops had already stopped falling and Maneka was wriggling out from beneath him. She was standing with her face turned up to the sky, which had grown dark as evening.

"Get up! It's beautiful. Look," Maneka said.

"There's no rain," he said quietly. Only a hint of it, a possibility. But her joy moved him. He felt a piece of himself being dislodged. As he stood up, he heard the crash of thunder. Then, a second later, lightning streaked across the sky.

"Can't you take some pictures?" she shouted.

He shook his head.

Maneka reached into her handbag for her cell phone.

"Be careful," he said.

Ashok considered running to his car to fetch his old DSLR.

There were sure to be a few plastic bags lying around on the floor that he could use to wrap around the lens. Then the likelihood of damage presented itself just in case it did rain again, and he decided it was not worth the risk.

Maneka pointed her phone in various directions. It was an iPhone 5s with a weak camera. It struck him as ridiculous that she had brought this old-fashioned phone with her from America while everyone in Hrishipur had the latest releases. Even Gopal the electrician had a newer iPhone.

"It's going to get wet, Maneka."

"But I just want to capture the lightning."

These pictures wouldn't be much good. He watched her without saying anything, as if she were a child whose illusions he didn't want to shatter.

Maneka clicked, again and again. Each time, she let out a cry of frustration. "I can't catch it," she said, looking at him in despair. Ashok took out his own phone, a Samsung Galaxy S9 with the variable aperture and the dual-pixel sensor. It had a better shot at catching what Maneka was after. He aimed it at the sky that was now beginning to look like a bruise, greyish purple, hovering between dawn and dusk. He couldn't afford a new phone either. But he wanted to do this so badly. It felt like the only thing worth capturing.

They ran around the field in opposite directions, their sneakers sticking to the damp ground, with their camera phones held up high. Ashok rather enjoyed this rare attempt at pointing and shooting with his cell phone for a change. Here he was, a professional photographer in the middle of this vast stretch of nothing but potential, with this woman from two countries, running about trying to photograph the lightning.

He pressed the white button but it was too late. The lightning had come and gone, lighting up the world for a second before it was once again plunged into darkness.

"There were a few drops," she cried. "I felt them on my skin." Maneka looked at him beseechingly, begging him to reassure her that it had indeed rained for a minute. Ashok pulled her towards him and kissed her lips, which were a little cracked from the heat just like his. They drank from each other's mouths as if they had been thirsty a long time.

Afterwards, they walked back towards the car without speaking. He caressed the cobweb of scratches on the old Maruti Alto, the loyal hatchback that had taken him across thousands of kilometres, before opening the door. The air inside was clammy. He rolled the window down to let in a little breeze.

"Open it all the way and turn off the air-conditioning," Maneka instructed him.

Her tone of authority comforted him. He was used to this. The women he knew in Hrishipur told him what to do. They texted him when they wanted, gave him directions, introduced him to people. He did as he was told on autopilot. At this moment, he felt like doing things for Maneka, but, he suddenly realized with a shock, he wanted to gain nothing from it at all. He drove out to the highway, aware that he was grinning, past hawkers selling various types of beverages from carts. Sugarcane juice, lassi, lemonade. Finally, Ashok pulled over where a bare-chested man crouched in his loincloth in front of a pyramid of green coconuts. Behind him, on the horizon, a familiar sign rose up higher than all the other buildings. Its letters were only half-visible against the fading daylight, but soon, after the sun had set completely, its gold light would command attention from all directions like a giant halo in the sky.

"Two coconuts, please. Make sure they have a lot of water inside," Ashok said.

The man lopped off a section of the shells with his curved, sharp knife, inserted straws in them, and brought them over. Maneka took a coconut from him and held it like a baby.

Ashok sipped his slowly. The water was sweet. Flecks of tender coconut floated up through the straw. Despite the lukewarm temperature, it soothed him.

"Is it true?" she pointed at the sign in the distance. "That Trump Towers has named its buildings after rivers?"

"Yes. In this desert, they want residents to imagine they are surrounded by water."

"I wonder what the inside will look like."

"Like a swank hotel combined with a country club and a golf course and Atmos. I find it harder to imagine Heathersfield than I do Trump Towers."

He beckoned to the man who was waiting patiently on the sidewalk to collect their empty coconuts.

"Who drives by here?"

"Babus on their way back and forth between Delhi and Jaipur. Developers and investors for the properties along the road. And poor construction workers. All equally thirsty."

"When do you think that building will be ready?" Ashok gestured towards the cordoned-off construction site behind him.

The man threw his hands up in the air. "Who knows, Saab. Now, they are all late."

"When it's ready, this road will change, no? Will you still be allowed to sell coconuts here?"

"Will not need to, Saab. My brother's father-in-law's neighbour has a shop on the street across from Tarrump Towers where he sells granite and marble. Once the builders start doing the countertops, he has promised me a job helping there. So, it is good that it is coming up every day, bit by bit. We are all waiting."

"So are the investors," Ashok said.

"But they have money, Saab. They are not selling coconuts by the road."

The man suddenly yelled to someone in the distance and ran off. The subject of his wrath was a monkey perched on top of the coconut heap. It took off, pursued by the man. When he came back to take the empty coconuts from them, he was panting.

"Saaley monkeys, can't take your eye off for a minute."

"Buildings," Maneka muttered next to him. "My book has to be about property and constructions. It's been staring me in the face all the time."

Ahead of them, a white Mercedes pulled up and one of its dark-tinted rear windows rolled down. A woman's toned arm reached out and waved a bunch of rupees at the man, who went running to the car. A couple of monkeys watched from a few feet away.

They climbed the narrow, steep stairs all the way to his barsati on the fourth and top floor, where he stood fumbling for his keys by the crooked sign on his door that said *Ashok Sharma Photographer*.

"How charming," said Maneka.

He hadn't even inserted the key in the lock before Alexander began to bark.

"You have a dog?" Maneka asked.

In response, Ashok opened the door an inch. In an instant, the black puppy was all over them, jumping up and down, wagging his curly tail, covering the tips of their fingers with his little kisses. Ashok heard Maneka laugh in the dark as he groped for the light switch. The room still smelt of the leftover egg curry he had cooked the night before. He hoped she wouldn't mind.

"Down, Alex," he yelled. "Leave her alone."

"It's fine," Maneka cried as the dog reached up to lick her face. "He's so tiny and squirming."

"Someone found him on the streets and gave him to me to take care of. It was a gift."

"From a woman?" Maneka said, trying to sound like she was joking.

Ashok shook his head. "From an electrician who lives nearby. We smoke beedis together sometimes. He brings me all the gossip, who's screwing whom, both in bed and otherwise. He thought I needed company."

Alex was the one good thing that had come out of helping Gopal, who was always rescuing little kittens and puppies on the streets. This one he had given to Ashok as a thank-you gesture for the loan, his temporary gift until he cut the deal with whichever rich guy had apparently promised to change his fortunes.

"Your place is cosy," Maneka said, looking around.

The rooftop apartment was small, but it had everything he needed. The yellow walls were adorned with prints and posters of movies. He refused to display his photographs here like Jessica had once suggested. He did not need reminders of his professional life around him. Tonight, he was especially glad he had made that decision.

He walked across the room and flung open the door to the roof. Instantly, a moist breeze blew in towards them.

Maneka flipped through a pile of gramophone records on the hand-painted side table he had found in a used-furniture bazaar. "I didn't know people still had these. My grandparents had a gramophone, I've been told. Never saw it. Never saw the pure silver water pistols with which my mother and her cousins played Holi, the classic cars my grandfather once collected, or the organ my grandmother played." She gazed wistfully at the records, then began reciting the names of the artists. "Miles Davis Quintet, Billie Holiday, Ray Charles, Al Jarreau. You like jazz," she said.

He couldn't tell if she approved. "Mike listens to classical music."

Ashok wasn't surprised by this taste. He imagined Mike also liked Renaissance art, the opera, and Shakespeare.

"Can we?" She held out the Norah Jones.

Ashok was disappointed. That was the only sort of jazz most people in Hrishipur could appreciate, but Maneka, he had hoped, was different. Still, he wordlessly pulled the record from its sleeve and slipped it on. As the slow crooning filled the room, he brought out the bottles of fruit wine he had collected from his last trip to the mountains. Again, Maneka had to make a selection. Pear, peach, rhododendron, apple, plum.

"Pear," she said, tapping the bottle.

Ashok poured it out into a pair of glasses, hoping she wouldn't mind the dust. She didn't seem to notice. The wine was warm and sweet, and they drank it like juice. The bottle soon emptied, and they moved on to apple. He felt drowsy, and the world began to fade away.

When she excused herself to go to the bathroom, Ashok finally fished out his cell phone from his pocket and glanced at the eleven missed calls and numerous texts he had ignored throughout the day. He then scrolled through the photos he had taken that afternoon with Maneka. Most of them were failed attempts to catch the lightning. He thought of how the two of them had run about in the damp air with open mouths, waiting to drink the rain. The room filled up with the remembered fragrance of wet earth. Ashok knew there was only one thing to do. He returned to the texts, deleted them, and blocked the sender's number.

When Maneka opened the door of the bathroom, she was holding her bra in her left hand. She dropped it on the floor as she climbed on to the divan next to him. He put his arms under her shirt and pulled it off as gently as possible. If he was slow and tender, he thought he just might be able to atone for everything he had ever done or been asked to do.

She clung to him in the hungry kind of way people did when they had spent the entire day building up to something. The flickering lights from the candles threw shadows on her face so that sometimes he saw her and sometimes he didn't. She closed her eyes and straddled him, moaning as they rocked back and forth. He opened his eyes and looked at her face but was frightened to see he couldn't recognize her. She looked like a stranger.

He felt a great sleepiness wash over him like it used to when his mother sang her lullabies. He clutched Maneka as if she were a doll he could protect. They moved quicker now, more urgently, and he held on because he wanted her to go back to the town full of wildflowers and remember this on the loneliest of nights. He once again smelt the earth from that afternoon on her skin, and he thought maybe paradise just meant being safe.

She started to speak even as he was sliding out. "I miss my mother."

He lit a cigarette and watched the smoke drift up towards the ceiling fan, which revolved overhead with a steady hum. When he was a little boy, Ashok used to be so terrified of the fan falling on him at night that he refused to fall asleep, staying awake with eyes wide open as long as he possibly could. Now, he gazed up at the blur of the blades as they spun, and felt a familiar dread. He stretched out his arm to turn up the volume on the record player, hoping to drown out the murmur of the fan and Maneka's voice next to him before she could begin telling him her mother's story. Norah Jones crooned the lyrics from 'Long Way Home', her voice rising and falling in the darkness, asking someone for forgiveness.

"This one is my favourite," he said.

She did not return to her mother. The moment passed. Ashok let out a little breath of relief.

Instead, Maneka brought up Michael.

"He didn't sound surprised at all when I called him. It was almost as if he were waiting for me to tell him. Maybe he's relieved. Maybe he's also met someone. I hope we can stay friends. His office is down the hall from mine. It will be awkward if we don't talk to each other."

"Have you always been attracted to older men?"

"Clearly."

He smiled in the dark even though she couldn't see his face, and wound an arm around her. She folded her body into his and spoke into his skin.

"It's this time in India," she said. "Just being here, after so long, loosens something inside you. You think you don't belong here, that you've grown out of this land, the heat, the chaos. Then a few weeks immersed in it, and it's like you never left. Except you did, and you will again. Because there's no turning around for us any more."

She turned on her side until he felt her breasts press against him. She continued speaking, and he wondered if she even cared whether or not he was listening.

"Mike tried his best. He's a decent person. Almost too decent. Midwestern liberal. It's all relative, isn't it? Compared to the people I meet at conferences and artists' residencies, the Jewish writers from Brooklyn, or the academics and activists from either coast, Mike is actually a little conservative. He tries so hard though. He even said he would like to visit India someday. He doesn't know it, but if he came to Hrishipur I think he would die."

"How long was he married?"

"Twenty years."

Ashok whistled.

She laughed. "I know. A lot of baggage. Unlike you, who have no baggage tying you down."

"You sometimes seem very certain about everything. And about people."

"I have gut feelings. And one of them is that you like to be wild and free. No committed job, family, or girlfriend. You're lucky. You can get away from it. At least for now. But things change. Everyone is forced to grow up one day."

"What about you? When did you grow up?"

"I am doing it right now. Or maybe I'm not. I won't know until later, will I? The night my parents first told me that they might not get the flat they had booked and they had no more money left with which to buy another one, I realized as I was sitting in my little apartment in Heathersfield that I had no roots. No permanent address or family home. But as long as I had them both to fuss over me, I still had an anchor. Now, with her gone so suddenly, I feel like even the ground I am standing on is unsteady." She paused. "I am rambling. Sorry."

When he didn't respond, she began to hum a tune.

"*Ramona rare, Ramona fair. Ramona of the ethereal hair. Ramona will you let me through? Ramona will you love me true?*"

"Why are we singing about your friend?" he asked.

"That was the song we used to sing for her back when we listened to Air Supply and Richard Marx. We had songs for everyone. But she was the princess, the chosen one. Beautiful, rich, stylish, influential parents, a flat in a mansion in the right neighbourhood, multiple drivers for multiple cars, membership at all the colonial clubs, vacations in London every summer. And the worst part was that she never got into any trouble. She sat in the middle of class, didn't fail exams, never got punished, always just sat there with a faraway look on her face and those beautiful long fingers with which she played the piano at home. I yearned for lessons when I was a child, but my parents couldn't afford a piano. My grandparents were once the only people in their neighbourhood who had an organ, and my parents, a generation later, couldn't afford a piano." She spat out the last word as if it embodied all the ills of the world.

"But was she ever mean to you?" Ashok asked quietly.

"My grandmother?"

"Ramona."

"No. How could she be mean to me? She didn't even know I was there. She never talked to me."

"Was she mean to anyone else?"

Maneka thought about it for a second. "I don't remember."

"You do remember. You remember too much. It was high school. So long ago. Why are you unable to forget? You have to forget things that don't make you feel good. You have to keep moving away from the darkness until you find the light." His arm was beginning to tingle under her weight, but he wrapped it around her body, which still smelt of him.

Maneka grasped his hand.

"You know, Ashok, you're right. All summer, I have been wondering why I like hanging out with her now. Why I keep saying yes when she invites me somewhere. At first, I thought I was jealous. I wanted to live through them, experience their lives, the lives I had envied since I was a teen. But it's not just that. I have never ever heard her say anything negative about someone she knows well. She always finds something good to say about them. Unlike you and me, the cynics of the world." She peered at his face. "Do you mind that I included you?"

Ashok laughed. It was, he realized, a cynical laugh. "I've never said I'm a good person."

She traced his cheek with a finger before taking the cigarette from his lips. He watched her take a puff and cough.

"You didn't even inhale. What good is an American who can't smoke?"

"No one in Heathersfield smokes, dude. They eat kale and run fifteen miles a day in freezing temperatures and go to the ER every time their stomach rumbles. I had forgotten what a cigarette smells like. It's good. I will miss this too."

In the dark, he couldn't see the expression on her face and he was glad she couldn't see his. This was the most vulnerable he had been in a long while. The air around them felt rarified, as if they were cocooned inside a bubble, delicate and trembling like the ones he used to love blowing into the air when he was a child. If someone saw them now, from the outside, they would shine in iridescent colours like a rainbow.

"I saw a bruise on Ramona's arm the other night. Does Salil hit her? He's so sleazy, I wouldn't be surprised. Just the sort of patriarchal thing you would expect here."

Ashok felt the bubble stretch thin, as if it might collapse at any second. He held her tighter.

"What was your song?" he whispered.

"What?"

"The song they sang about you? You said there was one for everyone."

"It's a Russian folk song, not one they had to make up. 'Minka.' *From the Volga was he riding, On his horse so quickly striding, When he saw in ambush hiding, Who but pretty Minka. Minka, Minka, go not from me, Do not in the forest hide thee, Come and tell me if you love me, Pretty little Minka.* Do you know it?"

He groped for his phone on the floor next to him and typed *Russian song Minka.* Together they watched a choir of schoolgirls sing it. When it ended, the audience broke into applause until the screen went black. Maneka buried her face in his armpit.

"Everything has been coming back to me these past few months. Not just here but when I was there too. Mike was not able to understand it. He would look at me with this confused expression on his face, unable to comprehend my memories of Russian songs, Bengali movies, Camay soap, and the tins of Kraft cheese that my dad brought back from his trips to Nepal. When the only cheese available in shops here was Amul. You remember those cubes? The foreign cheese was a treasure." When Ashok didn't reply, she continued as he had known she would. "And yet this summer, these nights, I have been thinking of other things. Sunsets over the Great Lakes, the silence of snowfalls, the laughter of English professors in a crowded bar, the wide expanse of freeways stretching endlessly on. It's like having two lovers. Which one will prevail?"

She touched his hand in the darkness, and he thought how torn they all were, like patches of a quilt.

"Everyone has baggage," he whispered. "From the perspective of this guy you're complaining about, you are carrying baggage too. The baggage of never having married, the baggage of not having children, the baggage of being an immigrant."

For a minute she was silent.

"I never thought of it like that. You keep making me think of new things. I know Mike gets lonely over there. Even they get lonely. They are just better at dealing with it than we are." She peered at her watch and slid off the bed with a groan. "It's so late. I have to go home. Baba has been alone all day. I'm living with one of my parents again, like a teenager. Will you drive me?"

"Of course."

He got up and turned on the lamp. Maneka looked a bit drunk in the sudden onslaught of light. She stood there naked, blinking furiously to steady herself.

He could see her reflection in the window as she began to get dressed. Only her face and arms were visible as she pulled her bra around her breasts and began to fasten the clasp. It was a very thick bra that expanded her bosom by a few inches. She didn't need that, he thought.

"You're beautiful, Maneka. And intelligent. You don't need to be like anyone else."

When she didn't answer, he felt shy. This was a new side of him, being sweet and kind to a woman in his room. Maybe it wasn't what she liked about him. His sarcasm and wisecracks and occasional meanness were probably a whole lot sexier.

But she wasn't even listening. In the reflection, he saw she had frozen, her top half on and half off, bunched around her boobs.

She wasn't pulling it all the way down.

He turned around to see what she was looking at.

She picked up a lacy handkerchief in her fingers from a crevice in the bed and held it away from her body as if it might be contaminated. He didn't have to peer at it to know what it looked like. The pretty, girly frill at its edge. The curly letter *R* embroidered in green.

He might have said he had borrowed it once and forgotten to return it. Or that he had had a party on his terrace one night and they had all come and had a great time and then left together. He might have acted puzzled or said, What the fuck is that doing here? He might have even said, Is that yours? Who is *R*?

Ashok didn't say any of those things. He realized he had been waiting for this moment all day. An enormous pressure lifted off his chest.

She looked at him.

"Did you leave this here so I would find it?"

He knew then why she had looked so unfamiliar to him when they were making love. She was, after all, a stranger. She would judge him, was judging him even now, but she would not understand him any more than her American lover had understood her.

"You don't know anything about me," he said quietly. "About any of us. This is your summer break, your *break* from your real life. You don't have to live here or deal with anything."

"And you don't know anything about me," she said, as she picked up her handbag. "You men are all the same. Across races and generations. The same."

"Let me take you home."

"I can call an Ola."

"It is not safe for women here late at night. This is not the village in your Hallmark movie." He couldn't help himself.

Her body was completely still as she ordered the Ola on her phone. Her eyes held a steely hardness that he had not seen until now. Somehow, it reassured him. It would help her. It would see her through.

He followed her downstairs, with a finger on his lips to remind her not to wake up his elderly landlady. They waited together by the gate, next to the tree with which he shared a name. Crickets chirped into the night. In the distance, someone yelled and a bottle crashed. This wasn't one of the fashionable parts of Hrishipur but it was all he could afford.

"You know, Ashok, you were right about Ramona never being mean to anyone. I'll give you that. But then she's always had everything. Why would someone like that need to be unpleasant?"

"No one has everything," he said. "You are an essayist. Surely you know that." The last person he wanted to talk about right now was

Ramona, but he felt an inexplicable need to defend her. "She likes you a lot. At first, I wasn't sure why. You two seem so different. But now I can see why. You and Ramona have more in common than you may realize."

"Do you love her?" she asked, looking away as if she didn't really want to hear the answer.

He laughed. "It's not like that with us. Not like this afternoon. Nothing like that."

They stood in silence, listening to the croaking of frogs in the gutter. When Maneka suddenly turned to him, he wished she hadn't. He was tired of words.

"There is one thing that has been bothering me from the day I first met you."

He waited. Perhaps she was perplexed by the casual way he insisted on dressing, no matter how formal the occasion or venue.

Or perhaps she didn't see what someone like Ramona could possibly want from him.

"How come you get all weird and distant whenever I talk about my mother?"

"Huh?"

"Every time I mention her or the fact that she died, she fucking *died*, which is why I'm here and which is impacting everything I say or do, you turn away or pretend not to hear or change the subject or turn the music up. As if you couldn't care less. You ask me questions about every other part of my life and are so kind and sensitive and yet, when I bring up this one topic, you stare off into the distance as if you're a thousand miles away. I simply can't understand it, but I can tell you that every time you've done it, my heart has broken a little. Yes, even more than tonight, more than any handkerchief can break it. Because my mother? She was everything to me."

He moved backwards until his body suddenly rested against the old tree under which autorickshaw drivers played cards during the day. He leant against it for support.

"Yes," he said, forcing himself to look straight at her this time. "Yes, I know. That's how mothers are."

The cab rolled up next to them. Ashok opened the door for her and held it open until she was seated.

"Maneka, I'm really sorry," he said. "My life's been complicated for a while. I never meant—I wasn't—" He couldn't think of any words that might sound sincere or not clichéd. "I didn't plan any of this."

He closed the door and stepped back as the car sped off into the night. A stray dog ran behind it barking, followed quickly by other dogs. He looked apprehensively at the window where his landlady slept. But the window remained dark and curtained, her old-woman's evening sheltered from this world that had changed so drastically while she aged.

Back upstairs, the light hurt his eyes. He turned it off with a snap. The gesture made him feel more in control. Out on the terrace, he lit another cigarette and watched the smoke curl away into the silvery night. Alexander the Great sat next to him with his tail between his paws. He looked sad, as if he too missed Maneka's presence.

Ashok had begun smoking when he was only a boy. At first it was an act of secret rebellion, but then it became a source of comfort during his mother's illness. He would smoke out on the roof with his hands pressed to his ears. Still, sometimes her stifled cries would float up alongside the howling of the street dogs and the strains of Hindi film music on a distant loudspeaker. Ashok could not remember his father's presence by her side, not even at the very end when her body, ravaged by cancer, had lain alone in bed night after night, calling out her son's name. If Ashok closed his eyes now, he could still hear her voice, screaming in pain, begging him for help.

Did he really give her the extra dose of morphine, so easily purchased with a false prescription in the Seth's shop?

Most of the time, he could barely remember, but tonight it had all come back, clear as glass. He looked up at the sky and laughed. His life resembled the plot of a bad novel, the type Maneka would never read. He searched the hazy sky until he found a star, faint and glimmering like a firefly. His mother was a ghost now. He had been only sixteen. He had done what he had had to do.

Just then, his phone flashed a text. He grabbed it, hoping it was Maneka. But it was not. He wondered if it was Ramona, but he remembered he had blocked her number. He should have been more careful. The last time, she had wanted him to hit her, harder and harder, without leaving marks. But he had made a mistake. That was the bruise Maneka had seen. Ashok felt nauseated. He was a nobody in Hrishipur. Salil knew people in the city, men who would not hesitate to make you disappear, men who were capable of anything

And he should have been more careful tonight about the kerchief. Why had he not checked the sheets when they got home? Maneka had asked if he had left it there deliberately for her to discover. Maybe she was right. Wasn't that just one way of saying goodbye?

He thought again of how they had run around that afternoon like idiots, trying in vain to photograph a flash of lightning. Two streaks that flashed in the sky. That was what they were. Like a red kite fluttering in the breeze, some things were meant to be fleeting, *images à la sauvette,* captured for eternity on film and then released gently into the ether.

RAJESH

RAJESH LOOKED UP LONGINGLY AT THE CEILING, ABOVE WHICH the rowdy gathering was taking place on the roof. He stood on the narrow balcony of the chawl he shared with other drivers, plumbers, rickshaw-wallahs, and night watchmen, dressed in an old grey shirt and pajamas. Even out here on the verandah, there was no breeze.

He had located himself at the far end of the balcony so he wasn't too close to his apartment. It was really only a single room. But since he had married and brought Swapna home from the village, it had distinguished itself from the other rooms in his eyes. It was wonderful what a woman's touch could do to a home. Now, when he awoke at the crack of dawn, tea was already brewing on the stove in a corner. His shirts lay folded and clean on the mattress. The sheet that covered it smelt of washing detergent. He liked opening the door at the end of the evening to be greeted by the scent of boiled rice and the sound of Hindi soaps on the LG TV that Salil saab had gifted him for his wedding. But most of all, he liked having her around.

He had discovered the extent to which his happiness depended on his wife's presence only when she had left for a few months, not long after the wedding. It had not been easy to cajole her back to him, but he had worked at it and finally succeeded. And now, with a baby on the way, she was unlikely to ever try that again. But one never knew.

Raucous laughter burst forth from the roof. He glanced nervously at the door to his apartment, which remained shut. His wife disapproved of the goings-on overhead. She disliked langda Gopal, who was responsible for tonight's bawaal, as she called it. "They will get drunk and cause commotion," she had warned him.

Rajesh had tried to reassure her that he was not going to participate in any commotion. He was just going to step outside for a little bit to see what was up. She had not opposed him. The baby growing inside her had made her more pliant than before. Besides, even she was curious about Gopal, who appeared to be in unusually good spirits recently. The rumour was that he had come into a sum of money, and Swapna was convinced that nothing honourable could be the cause of this sudden good fortune.

"It is those folks from Amreeka," she had declared. "They must have given him a contract to do all the electrical work for the new building."

It was not impossible. Everyone knew that Trump Towers was going to have millions of lights inside. It was going to look like an enchanted fairyland once they had all been lit.

"The lighting companies that do these contracts are very big and famous," he had explained to Swapna, stretching his arms wide to demonstrate the extent of their power. "Maybe he got a job with one of them."

Swapna had sighed loudly into the embers of the stove. "He must be getting a larger salary than all of the other idiots in this town," she had said without looking at him. But he had detected the reproach in her voice.

Footsteps clamoured directly over him. It sounded like hooves galloping. He glanced up at the ceiling again. Gopal did not even live here any longer. He had limped away to a tenement building on a different street where there were more gated high-rise communities and therefore more broken appliances to fix. But like a dependable cockroach, he had returned tonight to celebrate with his old friends. And ready for any excuse to drink, the men had poured out of their rooms to climb up to the roof. Their whoops of delight mingled with the new film songs blaring from a portable music system. Percussion beats and electronic music provided the backdrop to the bawdy lyrics about kissing someone's moist lips all night long.

Rajesh's feet, restless and with a will of their own, led him to the winding iron stairs that curled towards the roof. He hauled himself up, one step at a time. As he emerged on the rooftop, he felt energy course through his veins like liquor. The roof was a flat rectangle that covered the rooms and shared bathrooms below. A low wall ran around its periphery. If he reached out and stretched, Rajesh would have been able to brush the tops of the trees.

On hot nights, the men came up here to sleep. Their charpoys now stood on the floor of the roof. One of them was covered with a sheet to serve as a table. Bottles of liquor stood on it along with glasses and a plate full of samosas. Next to them, in an empty bottle, someone had placed a sprig of champak flowers. Something about the frail white petals moved Rajesh. He wondered if it was Ahmad, the guy who had been kicked out of the Mughlai restaurant on Sigma Road a few months ago for making that stupid mistake.

Here was the electrician approaching him with his familiar gait, one leg dragging behind the other. Gopal was dressed more smartly tonight than usual, in a dark shirt and a pair of white pants. For some strange reason, in this heat, he wore a hat. He looked a bit silly. But when he drew closer, Rajesh smelt on him not the usual stench of country liquor but the strong odour of cologne.

"Wearing a scent?" he asked, sniffing his shirt.

The electrician slapped him on the back. "Rajesh, imported scent."

"From Amreeka?' Rajesh asked, eager to confirm his wife's suspicions so he might have some information for her when he went back.

"From my new boss," said Gopal. He offered no further explanation. "Have a drink. We have whisky and rum. And eat samosas. I bought them for everyone." His chest seemed to expand quite literally with satisfaction.

Was it the American president? Rajesh wanted to ask. He knew that was not possible, not really. Still, there might be an indirect link, some thread that tied him to the distant power.

After all, everyone in Hrishipur was connected these days to that power by the very presence of Trump Towers.

Someone shoved the plate of samosas at him. He touched one and felt the corners of the crust, sharp like tiny hills. They were cold. The rum in the glass someone handed him was warm.

Nothing here was as it should be.

He took a generous bite of the samosa and savoured the potato and pea filling. It was his favourite part. He didn't care much about the crust. Then he remembered Swapna. She had been craving anything spicy.

"Can I take one for my wife?" he asked shyly, self-conscious about the fact that none of the other residents of the chawl had a wife living with them.

But tonight, he need not have worried, for Gopal's magnanimity was boundless.

"Of course. Here, take two. One for her and one for the one inside. Nanha munna." He cradled his arms and sang to the unborn baby, as the others burst into laughter and slapped their thighs.

It was Gopal who had suggested, back then when he still lived here, that Swapna must have run away with a lover. Rajesh had returned home from work one night and found her gone. No letter, nothing.

She had taken her clothes and the small box of gold jewellery gifted to her by her parents at the wedding as security. Rajesh realized she had left when he saw that her petticoats and bras were missing from the clothesline on the common balcony. "That look in her eyes," Gopal had said knowingly. "She flirted with me too. If I had been a weaker man. . ." His voice had trailed off as he took a swig from the bottle of whisky.

But there was no man. A note was delivered to him a couple of days later from his father-in-law, stating that she was at home with her parents. She had left because she was miserable with him.

"Why?" Rajesh asked the messenger from the village. "I treated her like a queen."

"You said you had two rooms, but you have only one. There is a common balcony where there's no privacy. You don't take her to the movies. You don't buy her saris."

"She has so many saris she got at the wedding," he said, confused.

"But you don't buy her anything. You are her husband. She wants to feel loved."

Now he brushed the top of the wall next to him and placed the two samosas there. They looked like rocks. Heated up on the stove, they would taste just fine. He would not tell Swapna they were a gift from Gopal.

The men danced around the charpoy, singing tunelessly. Their happiness was contagious. Rajesh leant against the wall and took slow sips of the rum, with half-closed eyes, feeling almost at one with the night, when suddenly a quiet voice interrupted the calm.

"Rajesh bhai, beedi?"

Rajesh opened his eyes to see the familiar pale face of Jeevan holding up an unfiltered lit beedi for him to share. Rajesh took it gratefully. Jeevan's soft-spoken ways were a respite in this town where rough voices and coarse language were all you heard from dawn to dusk. The two of them stood side by side, passing the beedi back and forth in a gesture of comradeship. Rajesh listened to the beats of the music, feeling almost festive. He was glad to be here. Sometimes a man just had to relax with other men.

A tall, lanky figure left the group of dancers and walked towards them. In a few seconds, Ahmad's gaunt face came into focus even as he pointed at what Rajesh had forgotten about, the samosas resting on the wall.

"Samosas. I am saving them for Swapna, Ahmad mian," he said.

"Here, don't keep them on that dirty wall." Ahmad shook out a paper napkin from his pocket and slipped it under the samosas.

He did it slowly and gently, as if the samosas might crumble under pressure. His fingers were long and shapely, not just like a woman's but like a fashionable woman's. They reminded Rajesh of Ramona madam. He wondered if Ahmad missed waiting on rich and beautiful people.

"Did you get another job?" he asked finally.

Ahmad did not reply right away. Instead, he leant on the wall and stared out at the street below where a dog was scavenging for scraps in a rubbish heap.

"Who will give me a job?" he asked. "Everyone knows what happened."

It had been a couple of months since he had been let go by the restaurant for his 'mistake'. The neighbours had crowded around him that evening, slapping him on the back and applauding him for doing the right thing. But no one among them had been able to give him a job. One concerned journalist had written an article about him in the papers. The piece had been accompanied by a photo of Ahmad taken by Madam's friend on Delta Road. How had Ahmad paid the bills these past two months?

"Gopal is helping me a little bit," Ahmad muttered into the night air.

"With money?" Rajesh asked, surprised.

"I will pay him back," Ahmad looked at him defiantly.

"Of course you will," Rajesh said. "He will make sure that you do. Just be grateful that you don't have any sisters here."

"It is not just the job," Ahmad whispered. "They don't want us to live here any longer. They only want vegetarians."

"Shall we all live on samosas then?" Rajesh laughed, fingering the soft shapes on the napkin. He licked the crumbs off his fingers.

Ahmad did not laugh.

Rajesh regretted his joke. The landlords had sent forth an official-looking paper that banned meat. No one who ate any would be allowed to live there. Alcohol was fine. Even bhang was all right. No meat. No kababs. No biryani.

"They want to make this a Hindu town, Rajesh. Maybe it is best that I lost my job. Now I can go somewhere else to try my luck. Like Mumbai."

"I heard of someone who went to Qatar," said Rajesh. "They make lots of money there."

"Maybe they will send us all to Qatar."

"Ahmad mian does not have to leave his own country." Jeevan's voice cut through the air. "There are many cities for him right here."

Shame ripped through Rajesh. "I did not mean that, Ahmad mian," he cried out. "I want you to live here in this chawl, with us."

In the dark, he thought he saw the man smile, but he couldn't be sure.

"And you?" Rajesh said, turning to Jeevan. "How is your family doing?"

Jeevan said nothing.

"He is coming with me to Mumbai," Ahmad said. "Aren't you, Jeevan?"

"Really?" Rajesh asked. He had recently heard a little gossip about Jeevan and a maid in one of the high-rises near Eternity Mall. "Do you think you too will make more money elsewhere?

What about your parents? Won't they miss you?"

Jeevan let out a little laugh. "My parents are sitting at home. One is drunk and swearing at my sisters. The other is crying all day into the boiled rice and watery dal we eat for every meal. My mother's shoulder is ruined from years of massaging the backs of rich women. My father's back is sprained from digging a heated swimming pool for the people who will live in Trump Towers. If I leave, the only thing they will notice is that there is one less person waiting to eat."

Rajesh didn't know what to say. He had already left his village and his old parents and relatives, as had most people on this roof. The irony was that Jeevan was thinking of leaving the city they had come to in hopes of a better life. It puzzled him, but something about the way the young man held his body, stiff and guarded as if it were tightly wound up, made him afraid for him. He hoped he was planning on taking this girl with him so he wouldn't be all alone.

"One last hustle before I leave," Jeevan whispered. He looked up at the clouds. "I need the money." Then he turned to Rajesh again. "Don't hate me."

"What do you mean?"

Just then, something cold and damp touched Rajesh's shoulder. It felt like the muzzle of a pistol, the type he had seen in movies. But it turned out to be only the whisky bottle from which Gopal was drinking. When he grinned, his teeth shone in the darkness in two straight even lines.

"Jeevan, not telling him our secrets, are you?" Gopal slapped Jeevan on his arm. "Arre, don't worry Rajesh. He is too innocent, lives in his own world of dreams with his wife and now will be a father soon."

Rajesh's sense of unease grew. Were they planning to bump someone off? Who? Was it someone he knew? In the centre of the roof, the men were still dancing and singing. Next to him, Jeevan climbed on to the wall and sat on his haunches, balancing on the ledge.

"Be careful," Rajesh said, alarmed. "You might fall."

"Yes, better not have any accidents now, Jeevan," Gopal added. "I need you." Then, unexpectedly, his voice softened. "And I don't want you to get hurt. It's those chutiyas out there who should pay for their ways. Their greed and selfishness. How callously they deal with us. Look what they did to Ahmad mian here."

His voice was raised now. The singing and dancing had ceased.

The men crowded around.

"Fired him for what reason? Because he got hungry. Because he got tired of serving overpriced food to fat people who eat and drink all day. Because he took a few bites out of their precious korma. If he had enough money to keep his stomach full, would he have done it? If they offered him a meal once in a while, would he have done it? And now?" He gestured wildly as if he were a politician giving a speech. "And now they want him to leave because he is Muslim. They don't even want him to live here in this building. Where will he go?"

The men roared their approval. Rajesh wasn't sure which side they were on. They all laughed at Gopal behind his back. But lately, he had been commanding more respect than usual. He wondered again what he was up to.

"Are you working for the Amreekans?" he asked. "For the new building?"

Gopal bent over backwards and laughed like a madman. As if someone had fed him laughing gas. He thumped Rajesh on the back, then ruffled his hair as if he were a child.

"That building?" he sneered. "Those losers." He emptied the contents of his bottle into his mouth and let out a loud burp.

The crowd broke into applause. Even Ahmad clapped. The only person who didn't was Jeevan, who still crouched on the wall next to Rajesh. He stared at the men, and in the faint light of the moon, Rajesh saw the fear in his eyes. It made him wish he were down in the safety of his room, holding the soft body of his pregnant wife.

He left the roof carrying the samosas nestled in a napkin. Behind him the radio was still playing lurid songs. And Jeevan remained a statue on the ledge with his legs crossed, looking like a penitent sadhu. Rajesh paused at the top of the winding stairs to glance at him, hoping he wouldn't fall. It was just three floors. If he slipped, he would probably only break a leg. But Rajesh didn't think Gopal would have much use for another fellow with a limp. As he climbed down to the balcony and made his way to his apartment, the sound of tuneless singing and laughter followed him, making him feel like he was missing out on something.

Rajesh stared at the fifty-rupee note in disbelief. The businessman from Bengaluru who had summarily handed it to him just before climbing out of the car was supposed to be a rich man. He looked prosperous enough with his curling, oiled moustache and ample belly protruding underneath his purple shirt. He had, with an air of accustomed generosity acquired no doubt from issuing orders to people, given Rajesh the money with what had sounded like a command.

"Eat your dinner."

What food could he get for that amount?

Rajesh glanced up at the house in the South Delhi neighbourhood. Its balconies were lined with potted plants. The party seemed to be on the second floor. All the lights were on behind the french doors that had been shut to keep the temperature-controlled rooms cool. Now and then, a shout of laughter floated downstairs. Sweat trickled down his back. He had started to roll down the windows even as the man was climbing out. Gupta had strict orders for his drivers. Air-conditioning was only for the passengers. Rajesh didn't mind as much as some of the other drivers did. He'd never been able to grow accustomed to the stale, cold air. It stuffed up his nose and gave him headaches. The air outside was muggy. Delhi always felt even hotter to him than Hrishipur. Rajesh endured these brief trips to the capital with strangers sitting in the back only because Narendra Gupta paid him five hundred rupees each time.

He started the car back up and drove slowly along the treelined lane towards the gate. In the dark all the South Delhi neighbourhoods looked the same. Narrow streets flanked by two- and three-storied houses with rows of cars parked outside, gated colonies, small parks, and canopies of trees.

His stomach groaned, reminding him that he had not eaten since early that morning just before leaving home. Breakfast had consisted of a stale chapati from the previous night and a cup of tea. Swapna had nagged at him to eat a banana, but he'd waved her off. "You eat it," he'd said. "You need it now more than I do."

He glanced at the Motorola lying next to him on the passenger seat. Three missed calls from his wife. He hadn't dared speak on the phone while driving. The cops had become quite strict of late, and Rajesh simply could not afford to have to pay an extra rupee on anything tonight. That morning, he had been late and forced to take an Ola to Gupta's office. Of the five hundred he would get paid that night he had already spent a hundred. The thought made him shake his head in regret.

He pulled up at the gate where the watchman sat on a stool by his post, scrolling through his cell phone.

"Where will I get some food?" he asked.

The watchman gave him directions to a shack on the main road just outside the colony. Rajesh couldn't help but think of the food his mother used to make for him and his five sisters back in their village in Bihar when he was a child. He was the youngest of the lot, naturally, since his parents had no further need to keep conceiving once a son was finally born. There was never enough food at home, it seemed. The didis were always crying for more.

Sometimes they got just a handful of rice with salt, or a wheat chapati rolled up. But Rajesh, the boy, ate first and ate enough.

Now he remembered his favourite treat. Hot chapatis slathered in ghee and sugar. Seated behind the wheel of Gupta's green Toyota Etios, Rajesh thought he smelt warm ghee and tasted the crunch of sugar until his mouth filled up with saliva. He thought of Ahmad mian, who had been so hungry one night, and so tempted by the smells of the food he was serving, that he had snuck into the hallway and swallowed a few spoonfuls of biryani and korma. Who could blame him?

The shop had a shutter pulled over it. A sign on top spelled out *Bhaiya's Chai*, a mockery of his anticipation. A young man smoked a beedi against the wall next to the shop. Rajesh beckoned to him, but the boy stayed where he was, blowing smoke rings in the air. Rajesh wondered if he was hungry too.

"Why is it closed?" he yelled out. His voice sounded loud on the quiet street.

"Bhaiya died," the boy replied and continued to stand there without a care in the world.

Rajesh recognized that look. He had seen it in his village among the young men who failed to find jobs and gave up looking.

They wandered around listlessly, high on ganja or drunk on paddy liquor. He glanced again at the closed shop and wondered what had killed Bhaiya.

He drove around the quiet streets lit by halogen lamps for a while, looking for a convenience store that sold bread or a roadside stall that might have tea and biscuits. Nothing. The market was shut because it was Sunday. This was the type of residential neighbourhood where small, inexpensive shops were deemed unnecessary. Even the help were well fed and comfortably ensconced inside their servants' quarters.

The main road was busy with traffic even at this time of night. Rajesh remembered seeing a dhaba on his way in. It had looked a little too nice for him, but now he decided to try it anyway.

As soon as he stepped inside, he regretted it. It was a rustic looking place all right, with plastic tables and chairs, no AC, and that ubiquitous sign of humility, white tube lights. But the people sitting at the tables were not drivers. They were the kids who had rejected their parents' drivers and made it a habit to eat with their hands at simple places like this so they could post photos of the "authentic" food on the internet later. Rajesh went up to the counter and stared at the menu. He skipped the biryanis, tandoori chicken and haleem, and even the vegetarian dishes. He scanned the right side quickly. The cheapest item on the menu was a plain chapati, for thirty rupees. He could afford one. Nothing to go with it. Just one chapati. No ghee, no sugar. He debated going somewhere else, but the saliva in his mouth had turned sour. A chapati would tide him over until he got home, where Swapna would have kept food aside for him. He suddenly felt a wave of gratitude for her.

"Thirty-five," the cashier said.

"What? But this says thirty."

"Eighteen per cent tax," the man replied grimly. He didn't bother looking up at Rajesh, who could sense his disapproval. Who ordered one chapati? A bloody villager who had no business coming to this place full of pampered kids playing at being down to earth.

Without a word, Rajesh walked out, slamming the door behind him. He half hoped they would come after him. Maybe he should have broken something. He strode to the car. Once inside, he revved the engine a bit, as if he were going to race someone. For a foolish minute or two, he fantasized about driving off at maximum speed, leaving behind a cloud of dust and a roar of the engine that would force all the rich brats inside the dhaba to look up from their plates. The thing about being behind a steering wheel was the sense of power. You could turn the wheel this way and that, or accelerate, or slam the brakes. You were in charge. He imagined the Etios speeding through the unlit roads of Delhi as if it were being chased by police.

When he finally took his foot off the pedal, the noise both in the car and in his head subsided. He was spent. He turned the car around and drove slowly back towards the houses inside the colony.

When the phone rang again, Rajesh answered it reluctantly. He wished Swapna would not call him when he was driving. It always reminded him of the baby and the expenses looming.

"Hello?" he said, in a gruff voice.

"Rajesh?"

He glanced at the number just to make sure. It was indeed Ramona madam.

"Yes, Madam," he said, modulating his voice to make it sound more respectful. He hoped nothing was wrong. Saab was travelling again, and every now and then she wanted something done.

A quick errand, a delivery. But then he remembered it was Sunday. That was why he was here. They were not supposed to need him on a Sunday.

"Please, Rajesh, can you drive me to Delta Road? I will come back on my own. Just need to get there."

"But, Madam, I am in Delhi," he said. What he really wanted to say was, But, Madam, it is Sunday. My only day off from being at the whims of you and your husband.

She didn't need to go until later. Maybe around midnight? "If I am back by then, Madam," he said.

"Please, Rajesh." Her voice shook as if she was about to cry. Rajesh sighed. Madam had always looked as fragile as a sweet-smelling snow-white champak flower. But lately, she had seemed even more disturbed. He imagined her green eyes filling up with tears. Sometimes he glanced at her face in the rearview mirror as he was driving her to the spa or the mall, and caught her lips quivering or her eyes glistening. But if she ever sensed that he was noticing her, she would stiffen up instantly. Controlled, silent, expressionless. Sometimes Rajesh imagined that she was made of glass, that if he touched her, all he would feel was the cold surface of some immovable thing.

He did not really enjoy being around her. She made him uncomfortable. It wasn't that she yelled at him or anything like that—in fact, Rajesh couldn't imagine her yelling at anyone. Except that one night when Salil saab and Ramona madam had just come out of a loud rooftop bar. She had cried and screamed and accused her husband of flirting with all the women and of having a mistress who had apparently been present at the bar. Salil saab had sat impassive and silent throughout the drive. But when he took the keys from Rajesh later that night and thanked him, his voice was taut with a quiet anger, as if he was trying to hold everything in.

But apart from that one time, Madam rarely raised her voice. No, it was worse than that. She simply ignored Rajesh. She issued instructions as soon as she climbed into the car. *Diva. Atmos. Come back by three. Pick me up after the errand. Drop my friend off.* Then she retreated into her cell phone or stared out of the window or turned to whoever was with her and forgot Rajesh was there, absorbed in her own mysterious world of which he was not a part.

But what was he to do now? He wasn't *supposed* to be hustling in his free time. He was a full-time employee of the Singhs. They paid him slightly more than the going rate for drivers. If they learnt what he did on Sundays, they might dismiss him and hire someone else. There were plenty of drivers around. He didn't want to go back to driving someone's Ola. Gupta wouldn't hire him full-time and even if he did, his salary would be lower than what it currently was.

The moonlighting had seemed like a crime to him at first. Rajesh had been reluctant. The other drivers in Magnolia Gardens had laughed at his hesitation. *How are you going to support your young wife*, one of them had asked in an exaggeratedly nasal voice, making the shape of a curvy woman with his cupped hands as he spoke.

They all did it. In fact, most of them used their employers' own cars to run random errands for other people or even occasionally to drive a stranded passenger around. The owners did not notice, or if they did, they turned a blind eye. The drivers ended up earning a few thousand extra rupees every month and everyone was content.

Still, Rajesh had resisted. He liked Salil saab, who always asked about his family. He knew he wouldn't want him having a part-time gig. Especially since he had told Rajesh once to be prepared to come in on Sundays "for emergencies," when he wasn't in town, in case his wife needed something.

When Swapna had left him, Rajesh had been at work even earlier than usual. Salil saab had noticed. He seemed very interested in the details of Rajesh's matrimonial life. *Kya hua?* he had asked him one morning as he scrolled through his cell phone.

She just left, Saab. When I got home, she was gone, with all her things. When I went to the village, she sat there without speaking while her father told me I needed to take better care of her.

He had secretly hoped that pouring his heart out to Salil would result in a raise. But his employer's generosity extended only to chatting with him. And when Rajesh realized no actual assistance was forthcoming, he clammed up. They were all the same. Some a little nicer than others, but none on his side. He had called Gupta that afternoon.

With the businessman safely ensconced in the back once more, Rajesh drove away from the residential streets of the capital towards the Golden Expressway that connected Delhi and Hrishipur. As they left Delhi behind, and the neon signs of Google, ESPN, AmEx, and the rest came into view, the futile pursuit of a meal lifted from his shoulders. If he drove quickly, just over the speed limit, and they made it back to the hotel in less than thirty minutes, he could give Ramona the ride she wanted, and then he would go home to his wife.

The businessman tapped him on the shoulder. "Radio?" he asked.

Rajesh tuned the radio, wondering where to stop. "I want to hear old songs. Kishore, Lata, Rafi."

Rajesh smiled. Maybe this guy wasn't such a bad fellow after all. He found the golden oldies station and leant back against his seat.

His passenger hummed behind him. Kishore Kumar's mellow voice crooned one of Rajesh's favourite songs, 'Ruk Jana Nahin'. His father used to sing that to him a long time ago, when Rajesh was just a boy growing up without a care in the world in their little village. When the voice on the radio reminded him to keep going no matter what, Rajesh imagined his father patting his head with the words of encouragement from the song. He admonished himself for his earlier anger at the world, for his lack of gratitude. Was it really that bad? Yes, money was tight, but he was better off than many.

He thought of the shapes of men he often saw on the sidewalks when he rode his bicycle home late at night after driving

Salil saab back to Magnolia Gardens. The shapes who had no home, not even a tiny room in a slum, and who had to find a spot on the road on freezing winter nights. He thought of his best friend from the village, Bachchu, who had gone soft in the head a few years ago and had to be sent away to the lunatic asylum.

He turned up the radio slightly. Behind him, the businessman grunted. Rajesh stole a look in the rearview mirror. The man had dozed off with his mouth slightly open. His large head, from which tufts of hair grew in all directions, rested against the window. He exhaled with little grunts as he slept.

A rumble overhead made Rajesh look up. The silhouette of a plane emerged from behind the high-rises to the left and glided across the sky until it disappeared somewhere to the right where the airport lay. He loved seeing the aeroplanes high above the traffic on the road. He imagined entire lives being conducted inside, for not one or two but hundreds of people all at once, and he wondered what it must feel like to be up in the sky looking down. He wondered what it must be like to leave this vast country and go someplace foreign.

Rajesh knew he would never see any other country. Such adventures were not for the likes of him. It was for people like Salil saab who travelled all over the world. Rajesh was the one who had to ferry him to and from the airport. In the early days, he would ask him where he was going. *Now where, Saab?* used to be the default question. Salil would respond absent-mindedly as he checked the messages on his phone. *Australia, Singapore, Dubai.* Rajesh fantasized about those places. He had heard that Dubai had the tallest building. Was it true? He had heard that Singapore was very clean. Was it true? Those short trips to the airport with his employer had offered a window to the world. Unlike his wife, Saab was easy to talk to. Rajesh didn't feel quite as intimidated with him. But Madam was a different story.

He clicked his tongue when he thought of her request tonight. He knew where she wanted to go. He knew what was going on. When Saab went out of town, she seldom stayed home alone. Sometimes she went to Atmos, although of late she would emerge from its interiors without shopping bags. Sometimes she went to someone's house for a private gathering. But usually, he had to drive her to Delta Road, where he dropped her off a couple of blocks from the building. He pretended not to know where she was headed. He came back when summoned by text, and picked her up from the same spot, the intersection next to an ashoka tree whose red flowers carpeted the sidewalk in the winter. He didn't care. None of the drivers did. Their job was not to care. But if it had been *his* wife, he would have killed her.

He thought of Swapna, a wife so lovely and clever that all his friends envied him. He had a baby on the way. He had a steady job with an employer who treated him with respect. He even had this additional Sunday gig that enabled him to supplement his income, however meagerly. He allowed himself to feel contented. Life was going to be better. The baby would be a girl. He knew it in his heart. Everyone wanted a son who would grow up to help earn money and take care of the parents and maybe bring some dowry. His parents' house had been a hub of gloom until his arrival, he had been told. It was he who had brought light to the home. For him, though, his daughter would do the same. A little baby girl, the incarnation of

Lakshmi, the goddess of good fortune. Daughters did more for their parents these days anyway. Look at Madam's friend from America. Unlike Madam, she always smiled at him and asked how he was. And her tips had grown in amount since the first time. They had gone from fifty rupees to two hundred, almost as if she had looked around Hrishipur and realized how much everything cost. She was more generous than this fat businessman who was paying thousands for a single night at the fancy hotel.

As the car neared the end of the expressway, Rajesh rolled the window down slightly to let in a little fresh air. He emerged on the other side of the tollbooth into Hrishipur, where he saw Atmos glowing like a lighthouse, heralding those who entered the city as if they were sailing across a dark ocean.

The mall was fully lit up all night. Rajesh had been inside only once. The security guards who frisked visitors to weed out possible terrorists waved them off if they tried to enter. However, one of the night guards owed him a favour, and had let him sneak in late, after the mall had closed. Rajesh had walked around with the guard as if he were in a trance. The granite floors were so slippery he had had to make his muscles taut and walk carefully to avoid falling on his face. The shops were closed, obviously, but their lights were still on and their windows dressed with mannequins who looked like memsaabs from Amreeka. In the middle of the lobby stood the most beautiful car he had ever seen. Electric blue and low on the ground like a sleeping animal waiting to pounce. It was an odd shape. *What is that?* he had asked the guard escorting him proudly like a tour guide. *Lambooji*, the guard had replied. Or so Rajesh remembered. It didn't matter. The car had only two doors and they opened upwards like the wings of a bird.

How does anyone drive it? he had asked. *How can you sit? It must be like sitting on the floor? How much does it cost?*

Five crores, the guard had said, puffing up his chest like a pigeon. As if the car belonged to him. As if he could drive one.

The car cost more than a flat at Trump Towers. It was officially the most expensive single item Rajesh had ever seen in person.

But the mall had been cold. An empty place with no heart. No bustling crowds, no smell of cooked food, no shouts from shopkeepers trying to persuade customers to buy something, no young children running about. Rajesh could not understand how anyone would actually enjoy the experience of shopping there.

He had wished he had not entered the mall. His fantasy of it had been more interesting.

He turned the corner on to Sigma Road. To his left were the lights of Leisure Valley. Watching over the nightlife in the square, like a big brother, was the lavish Monsoon Palace, the seven-star deluxe hotel. Before he came to this part of the country, Rajesh had had no idea that a hotel could have more than five stars.

How do you get the extra two stars? he had asked, open-mouthed, his first week here.

Swimming pool, market, haircut salon, golf course, five restaurants—Chinese restaurant, American restaurant, rooftop restaurant, drinks restaurant, all-night restaurant—cinema hall. Bhallu had counted each one off on his fingers.

Rajesh had gazed at the long, curved exterior of the building, trying to imagine men in suits playing golf inside. That was eight years ago. Since then, he had grown more jaded. But he still felt on some nights that Hrishipur was the closest he would ever get to a foreign country.

The streets were uncharacteristically quiet tonight. Swami Vivekananda Road, one of the main thoroughfares in the city that had been renamed by The Party after freedom fighters and Hindu leaders, was dark. It was an important road, but the lights on either side were frequently out. Like on this night. The highrises were dark, the shops were dark.

It was peaceful here. He couldn't see very far but there was not much to see. If a car or truck appeared, he would see its lights. The businessman's snores sputtered at periodic intervals like a scooter trying to start its engine. Lata Mangeshkar was singing on the radio now in her high-pitched voice. It reminded him of the religious bhajans his mother used to sing when she was doing her chores at home.

Rajesh resolved to take Swapna to the Kali temple outside the city soon. She wanted to offer prayers for the well-being of the child that was coming, but he had not had the time to take her yet. He felt remorse. They ought to pray for the baby's future. Rajesh was determined to work hard, even harder than he had so far, to ensure the baby's life would be a lot better than his own had been. She would go to school, maybe even college. Perhaps she would become a doctor. Rajesh hummed along with the crooner on the radio, cruising along, until he turned on to Omega Road and glimpsed, somewhere to his right, the silhouette of Trump Towers.

The property had grown rapidly, almost by magic. Only a year ago there was a square plot of land here, and now its towers shot up to kiss the sky. By day it looked severe, and by night, eerie, a cluster of silhouettes stretching skyward.

Rajesh craned his neck to look up at the building. One day soon, the windows would burn with light from all the bulbs and lamps and chandeliers within. He imagined this golden light shining from a thousand spaces. He imagined the fashionable flats inside, decorated with fine things and inhabited by beautiful people who would throw lavish parties. Perhaps Jessica madam would cater one of them for Ramona madam and Salil saab. Madam's boyfriend would be taking photos for the papers. Some of Gupta's drivers would wait in the parking lot for their clients to return with full stomachs. And what would they serve for dinner? Reshmi kabab? Shahi korma? He conjured up visions of food, a sumptuous feast laid out on a long table covered with silk cloth embroidered with zaris. Even grander than the sarpanch's son's wedding back in his village. His mouth watered and tasted sour. Acid was climbing up his throat. He swallowed and imagined juicy gulab jamuns and creamy kheer filled with raisins. His fingers trembled a little on the steering wheel, and without thinking he pressed his foot on the accelerator.

Out of the corner of his eye, he sensed something move. A silhouette, nearly imperceptible in the darkness. He jerked upright in an instant. All thoughts of the property just behind him vanished from his mind as he tried to focus. No traffic. No speeding car or lurching truck. Nothing but the hulking shape. He tried to slow down, slammed the brakes, but it was too late. The car crashed into the massive body of a cow, throwing it into the air with a horrid wrenching sound, and then kept going, veering to the right and left, choking on its own rage. In the back seat, the man screamed. Rajesh swung the wheel this way and that to steady the car until it was moving in a straight line again, just managing to avoid the divider that kept him from oncoming traffic.

"What happened?" the businessman asked, clutching Rajesh's shoulder from behind.

"Cow, Saab," he responded calmly because nothing had really registered yet.

"Idiot. You didn't see it?"

"It was black or brown. No light, Saab. How to see it in the dark?"

"Is it dead?"

Rajesh slowed down, instantly provoking another onslaught of abuse from the back seat.

"Arre, don't stop. Mad or what? Why are you stopping?"

All Rajesh could think of were the animals that roamed freely in the meadows behind their mud hut when he was a child. The large, placid cows that were so stupid they couldn't move unless pushed. All they did was stand around and chew all day long. But they were gentle creatures that never hurt anyone. Rajesh dared not turn around to look back in case he hit something else, but he wanted desperately to make a U-turn to see if it was all right. If it had died or, worse, was lying maimed in the middle of the street, or if it had in fact been thrown somewhere far.

"I want to see if it's okay, Saab," he said.

"You are going to go back for the cow?" The man's voice now sounded shrill. "Are you insane? In this city full of crazy Hindu bhakts? Where beef is banned? With all the Kanwariyas on their way to Haridwar? Do you realize what they will do to you if they learn you hurt a precious cow?"

Rajesh wanted to point out that there was no one around. But he let out a breath and kept driving. A part of him knew the man was probably right. You never knew who was lurking in the alleyways. Someone or other was always related to a local politician. Everyone here carried guns.

The man continued talking. He was also mopping his large brow with a handkerchief. It did not seem equal to the task.

"Bloody cows roaming around the roads. Why can't the owners keep them tied up? Hope when it's found someone has the sense to kill it and put it out of its misery. At least tonight someone can eat some good meat." He suddenly laughed at his own joke. Then he leant forward and slapped Rajesh on the back. "Yaar, your car. You think it got a big dent?"

Even though he had nothing in his stomach, Rajesh felt it all try to pour out of him. He had been so preoccupied with thoughts of the poor cow that he had forgotten about the car. Gupta's newest Japanese car, the one he reserved for the most important customers. He kept driving through the unlit streets, past skeletons of half-formed buildings on either side and banyan trees with dangling roots, trying not to visualize the damage the vehicle must have suffered.

Rajesh's phone began to vibrate as the businessman made his way out of the car. It was Madam. He ignored it.

The businessman slammed the door behind him, walked around it once, shook his head ominously, and gave Rajesh a thumbs down before receding into the glittering lobby of the Hyatt. Rajesh stalled the engine for a while, until one of the valets came over and knocked on his window.

"What happened?" he asked, gesturing towards the hood.

"Motherfucker left his cow on the street in the middle of the night," Rajesh replied.

The valet nodded wisely. "Government has banned all cow slaughter, so now when they get old and no longer produce milk the owners just let them roam freely on the roads."

Encouraged by the valet's sympathetic tone, Rajesh got out of the car to look. He felt numb as he stared at it.

The passenger side had caved inward. The left headlight was smashed. The bumper hung on precariously like a broken limb.

The valet came around to stand next to him and scratched his head.

"It's not that bad. At least you did not die."

"You go tell that to Gupta," said Rajesh.

"Your employer?"

Rajesh shook his head. It was too complicated to explain. Magnolia Gardens was on the way to Gupta's garage. Rajesh took the lift to the fourteenth floor. An hour ago, he had been unsure of whether he should give in so easily to her demands. But now, he felt like he had no choice. If Gupta fired him from his weekend gig, Rajesh would have only the Singhs to rely on. And there was another reason. In his current state of mind, which was churning much like his stomach, he imagined the look of concern on Ramona madam's unblemished face as she heard about the accident. He would tell her how sorry he was about not being able to drive her tonight, and maybe, just maybe, she would give him a little cash to help with the repairs for Gupta's car.

But the instant Madam opened the door, he regretted his decision to come and apologize personally. It was like looking at the car all over again. The day before she had appeared as pristine as the Etios. Now her kajal was smudged, which accentuated the pallor of her complexion and made her look like a ghost. She stood in the doorway in a sleeveless black dress and high-heeled black shoes with pointy toes. Her hair was tied tightly at her neck, making her face slightly pinched as if she was in pain.

"Sorry, Madam, I had an accident," he said, looking at the money plant next to the door instead of her face.

"Can you just give me a lift? Please? I am already late. People are waiting for me."

Even in his current state of mind, Rajesh wondered who the people were. As far as he knew there was just one person. He had never liked him. He was always trying to be clever, and he never looked at anyone when he spoke. Shifty. Unlike Salil saab, who was straightforward. There was a sincerity about his employer that the other fellow lacked.

"Madam, I was driving a friend's car. It is damaged. I have to take it to the garage."

Ramona's eyes filled with tears.

"I have to go tonight," she whispered. "It's important. Maybe I will not ask you again."

If she was ending things with that chap, Rajesh was glad of it. He had never been comfortable driving her there. He felt some sort of loyalty towards her husband, which he had always tried to ignore. Now, confronted with this pleading, he had no idea what to do. Perhaps it served him right. For lying to Saab about where he took his wife when he was travelling and about working for someone else on Sundays. For lying to Swapna and her family about what life he could afford when he first went to see her.

"I will call you an Ola. I know the driver. You will be safe, Madam."

She stepped out of the doorway and clutched Rajesh's arm. Her eyes had a frantic look in them. It was the first time she had touched him. Her grip was surprisingly strong for someone who seemed so frail. Rajesh glanced at her hand around his upper arm. Her nails were long and painted white.

"But I don't want a stranger driving me there. I want you."

Rajesh stood still, looking at her fingers encircling his arm. Not once had she asked him if he was all right after the accident. He needn't have worried about whether she would ask him too many questions about whose car he had been driving. She was concerned only about herself.

"Sorry, Madam," he said, looking straight at her for the first time in the eight years he had worked for her.

She withdrew her hand from his arm and took a step back. Tears brimmed in her large, frightened eyes.

"Even you won't do anything I ask. No one ever does." She stared into the distance with glassy eyes as she spoke.

He bowed his head and walked towards the service lift. Ramona remained standing there in the doorway, looking out of the window where she could probably see nothing other than a reflection of her own face, a face split in two by the sharp crack that ran along the glass. He pulled shut the collapsible iron gates of the lift. Through the bars, he saw her standing perfectly still like the sculpture of some sacrificial goddess. Something about her frightened him, and he found himself wishing he would never have to see her again. Then the lift began to move, and he was on his way down, away from the spectral figure of Ramona madam, descending to ground level and a broken Japanese car and the prospect of facing a furious Gupta. He leant against the wall of the lift, shut his eyes, and pressed a hand to his stomach. He was so hungry he could eat anything at all. Maybe even that most impure thing, the meat of a cow.

GOPAL

HE HAD BEEN NAMED AFTER KRISHNA, THE BLUE GOD WITH A flute perpetually stuck between his lips so he could play tunes to woo women. The god who pranced about the fields on his two strong legs, offered martial advice to great warriors when needed, and climbed up high to steal freshly churned butter. The naughty, impish, beautiful god who was the favourite deity of millions of Hindus, as well as a brother or son to those who lived in the village of Sital, located deep in the heart of the country where it always smelt like rain.

Gopal's name had proved to be a mockery of his parents' divine aspirations for him. He had been only a young boy when they discovered that, unlike the god, their son had one leg slightly twisted and longer than another, a condition that no quantity of herbs boiled in water or slokas chanted by holy men could cure. There he was, an ugly, deformed boy, dragging one leg clumsily after another wherever he went. Disappointed, they left him to his own devices and focused their attention on their other three children.

Forgotten creatures sometimes find an unlikely saviour. For little Gopal, it was his father's mother, a woman with rough skin and hollow cheeks, who chewed paan all day as she did her chores, who saw him playing in the dirt in his parents' courtyard one morning and scooped him up as if he were her own. Even now, when he thought of home, it was his dadi's weathered face, brown as the bark of a tree, lined with age for as long as he could remember, that he saw, as if she were right next to him, about to place a cool hand on his brow when it was burning with fever.

Sometimes Gopal felt that fever take a hold of him with a viselike grip that was hard to shake off. It wasn't just in his body. It was a fever in his mind. Even these days, when he was often in a good mood, he was aware that it could turn all of a sudden. All it took was a nervous glance from someone, or a whispered remark, or, worst of all, the sight of someone moving away from him in disgust.

That morning, he had called the village like he did every couple of months. The neighbour's son had run off to fetch Dadi, whose grumbling he could hear on the phone even before she picked up the receiver. Gopal had tried to convince her to use a cell phone. Had promised to send her one the next time a friend of his from the village went home. But she had cackled at his suggestion. That day, she panted for a full minute before finally speaking the same words she always asked him. *When are you coming home, Gopu?*

Her heavy breaths had pressed deep into his heart. Guilt did not come easily to Gopal, but as he had listened to her wheezing on the neighbour's phone, he had berated himself for not calling her enough. And for not seeing her in nearly two years. No one, including Dadi, knew how old she really was, but it was clear that she was moving closer to the end. At this stage of life, she should get to see her grandchildren more, especially the favourite one who used to hide in the folds of her sari before he became brave enough to take on the world.

He walked without looking to his left or right, his eyes fixated on the ground to make sure he didn't stumble on a loose stone. He muttered to himself as he walked. In one hand he tightly clutched a coarse jute bag and in the other he still felt the warmth of the cell phone that he had just slipped into his pocket.

The text from Ahmad had cut into him like a dagger. Not one to get sentimental about things, he gnashed his teeth and kept on walking towards his destination. He did not need the two of them. Hell, he didn't even need one of them. He could take this on and any other task entrusted to him by Tripathy and his men or indeed anyone in the world—why, the president of America himself, if necessary—without any assistance. He had only been trying to help Ahmad. That ungrateful fellow. That idiot. No, he would be fine without him, without his long, girlish fingers and sharp nose and large eyes that made him look away every time they met his. He didn't need the heat of his body next to his, making him want things that made him even more disgusting and sick than people already thought he was.

He kicked a stone in his path and sent it scattering into the open ditch. The splash of water and the motion of his foot calmed him a little. There was still Jeevan. It was not the same as having Ahmad there, but it was in many ways much better. With him, Gopal would be able to concentrate on the job. His facial muscles relaxed as he turned into the alley where the young man lived.

Jeevan was a good boy. When he had first met him a year ago, at a Holi celebration in Tehri village a few miles west of Hrishipur, Gopal had laughed. He was so proper with his manners, standing until someone asked him to sit down, refusing the glass of bhang with a polite shake of his head. *Arre, drink it, it will make you laugh. Why so serious?* Gopal had said. Jeevan had kept his eyes lowered to the ground and then said the words that had set them all off into an explosion of laughter. The words mixed with the sweet bhang. *My mother does not like me to drink.*

Arre, it's not drink, Gopal had said, snorting and rolling on the floor. *It's mithai mixed with heaven.* The neon colours of gulal powder had formed clouds in the air. Through the red, green, and yellow haze, Gopal had seen Jeevan lift his brown eyes and look at him with a mix of awe and curiosity, almost like a shy bride. His skin had been so pale, the colour of date palm jaggery, a contrast to the darker faces around him. Then he had opened his mouth and smiled with those chipped teeth of his and Gopal had caught a glimpse of something else. A hint of resentment against the world that had wronged him. It bubbled under the surface, waiting for a spark to ignite it. He had after all grown up in Hrishipur. How could he not harbour in his heart the bitterness that set them apart from those who had more than them, more than they could ever need? Gopal had recognized in him that quiet seething anger against the world that could turn men mad.

Now he shuffled towards the chawl where Jeevan lived, holding the bag with *Kohinoor Rice* scrawled across it in faded green letters. It was a nondescript bag that had once held long-grain basmati rice from the Himalayan foothills at Dehradun. It was supposed to be top-quality rice, the kind people used to cook biryani for feasts. Not that Gopal knew what it tasted like. He had never eaten basmati and he had no idea why rich people were so fascinated with it. For him, the thick boiled rice he had eaten all his life was a feast. It filled him up for hours and it smelt like home.

Lately, he had been thinking of home more and more. Of the rice-paddy fields that lay submerged in water for months, the huts with cow-dung cakes plastered to the walls, the cries of foxes in the night. And of course, of his dadi squatting outside her house, a house that needed repairs every monsoon. What she really needed was a new house, built with cement and proper windows and doors.

He tightened his grip around the bag's neck and crossed the narrow street to arrive at the block of flats. Gopal paused at the bottom of the damp, dark stairs that led to the second floor, where

Jeevan lived with his parents and younger sisters. He remembered the look in Jeevan's mother's eyes the last time they had crossed paths. She had been working in the spa then, doing beauty treatments for rich women. She had come across him and Jeevan unexpectedly in a bazaar, where she had looked Gopal up and down with narrowed eyes before finally resting them on his face. They had asked a silent, simple question. *What do you want with my son?* Gopal, who sneered at everyone who dared to make fun of him or treat him with disrespect, had looked away, ashamed.

He ascended the stairs with one hand on the railing for support. He did not like stairs. They took him too long to climb and more importantly, they produced a slight sound in his footsteps, an almost imperceptible snap of the left foot when it landed that might be mistaken for the flap of a bat's wings. Still, it was a sound that might just attract a little attention on a very quiet afternoon. It was one of the main reasons he had approached Jeevan for assistance. That and the despair he had glimpsed on the boy's face in the last few months.

Jeevan opened the door himself. He had clearly been sitting right by it, waiting. His face, unsmiling these days even when he received a guest at home, looked questioningly at Gopal, who nodded in response.

"Come inside, Gopal bhai," he said. "Have a glass of water." Gopal stepped into the cramped apartment just like he stepped inside so many other homes all day when summoned to fix a fuse or repair a snapped wire that would instantly restore the air-conditioning or washing machine or microwave oven for the residents. But none of them ever offered him a glass of water, not even on the most scorching of days. They barely glanced at him.

To them he was less than a servant, perhaps a stray animal or an object that had somehow acquired the useful skill of restoring their power.

Except that elderly Bengali man whose daughter was visiting from Amreeka. The few times that Gopal had limped into their flat, the Bengali babu had asked the maid to give him water to drink. The maid had been terrified of him at first but then had slowly begun to relax every time he whispered into her ear before stepping out. Her expression had softened when she realized he was not just an electrician but also a messenger for his friends.

He glanced now at Jeevan's freshly scrubbed face and neatly ironed T-shirt. The boy had begun to look a lot more respectable in the last few weeks, and Gopal knew it was not because of him. "Jeevan?" he said in a teasing voice, slapping him on the back. "How's it going?" He shot him a knowing, leery smile and a quick wink.

"Gopal, please," Jeevan whispered with a blush that instantly made him look even younger than his twenty-four years, almost like a schoolboy. "Not now. My mother and younger sister are here."

As if on cue, the mother appeared behind him with a glass of water and held it out. Gopal drank the whole glass in a gulp. He had not realized how thirsty he was.

"Want more?" she asked.

He shook his head. But her tone had caught him by surprise.

Her voice was full of kindness. He dared to look directly at her now, and saw that her eyes too had changed. They were no longer narrowed in suspicion. She regarded him with a mix of weariness and gratitude.

The room was small but cluttered with things that made it look like a home. An embroidered tablecloth, pillow covers with hand-painted designs, little statues of gods on the shelf, a jug of water on the dining table, a tulsi plant on top of the refrigerator that filled up the room with its scent. Books wrapped in brown paper lay in a heap along with a colourful bunch of what looked like comics. In the corner the TV stood draped in a green fabric covered with appliquéd flowers.

"My younger daughter, Namita, likes to make things with her hands," the mother explained as she saw him looking around. "She likes to sew and embroider and do fabric painting. Maybe . . ." Her voice trailed off and she looked away.

But Gopal knew what she had been about to say. Maybe she could find a job in a tailoring shop. Maybe he, who knew so many people in town, could find her something.

"Namu," she called out.

The girl emerged from the room inside and immediately went and stood next to her brother. Jeevan put a long arm around her shoulder.

"My younger sister, Gopal. The one who sews."

"Did you make the dress?" he said as kindly as he could muster. It was not easy. His voice had acquired an edge over the years that had become part of his persona. He kept his eyes down when he spoke to Namita, hoping he didn't seem lecherous.

"Tell him, Namu," her mother coaxed when the daughter refused to answer.

"Don't be afraid, Namu," Jeevan added. "Gopal is my friend."

Namu nodded shyly.

Gopal felt something in his throat. It had been a long time since someone had called him a friend. To everyone he knew, he was a fixer or a goonda, but never a friend.

"We are going to eat lunch soon. Not much. Dal and rice. But you can eat with us. Why don't you stay and then you can both go out later?" the mother said. "Or, come back for dinner. I am making chicken curry. Jeevan's father will come home early. It is a very important day." Her face erupted in a smile that crinkled up her eyes. "Tell him, Jeevan." She giggled.

"My other sister, Smriti, has passed her accounting exams. She got a diploma." Jeevan smiled too.

Next to him, Namita looked up at her brother and grinned.

"Arre wah, this is wonderful news," Gopal said. "Where is she?"

"Celebrating with her friends," her mother laughed. "But she will be here for lunch soon. You two should stay."

The thick curtains at the windows kept out the harsh sunlight. The vision of this family sitting around the dining table and eating a simple meal made Gopal want to sit down too. All he wanted was to lower his legs on to the divan with the colourful pillows. To spend a few hours in this home full of smiling faces would be like living in a dream.

He glanced at Jeevan. The boy had taken his arm off his sister's frail body and was frowning at his mother. Gopal remembered what he had said to him not very long ago. If he could leave and go somewhere else and fend for himself, there would be one less mouth to feed.

"No, Amma," he said, using the same term he had heard Jeevan use to address his mother. "I am not hungry now. And I already have an invitation for dinner. Maybe some other day." He turned to Jeevan. "We should go now."

His mother and sister watched them slip on their shoes, still smiling. The other sister's brand-new diploma had brightened the home like a bouquet of fresh flowers. And that too, a girl.

Gopal marvelled at how the drunk father had allowed his daughter to study accounting. From all his years in and out of people's homes, he had come to understand one truth. Everyone was a bundle of contradictions.

He wondered if Jeevan's mother knew that too. After all, her job at the spa had in some ways been like his. One of them crept in and out of people's flats all day, tinkering with their various appliances, while the other spent hours alone with her clients.

They both knew people's secrets. He was sure of it. But there was one difference between them. Her clients probably confided in her willingly. As for him, he only saw and heard things he wasn't supposed to. Wives did not plan for power cuts when they were having weekday trysts with their lovers. Husbands did not expect their washing machines to flood the living room floor when they were in the middle of screwing their maids. They all tried to cover their tracks but Gopal knew more about the sordid, sorry lives of the rich people in Hrishipur than anyone else. Except perhaps Jeevan's mother. He wished she would ask him one more time to stay for lunch, but that moment had passed. Jeevan was holding the door open.

"Jeevan beta?" his mother said as they were about to pull the door shut behind them. "Will you bring back a small box of sweets for this evening? For celebrating?"

Jeevan nodded, though he didn't look too happy about it. He shot a glance at the jute bag Gopal had not set down for even a single second.

"And Gopal?"

"Yes, Amma?"

"Come again. Next time, have food."

Again, the catch in his throat. She knew he was a well-wisher.

She understood now that whatever shady business he might involve her son in, he would take care of him. Of them. He hesitated in front of the door, even as Jeevan climbed noisily down two stairs at a time. He wanted to say something, but what if it was not the right thing?

"Yes, Amma," he said, raising his right hand in a salute to assure her of his intentions. Then he turned and began to go downstairs, one stair at a time, slowly, laboriously, aware that a mother's eyes rested on him.

~

Trump Towers was a flurry of activity on weekdays. Gopal and Jeevan stood with their arms resting side by side on the low wall near the rear entrance, away from the main thoroughfare. Intermittent sounds of afternoon traffic floated in and out just as they did all day and night inside their homes. The reassuring background score to their lives.

Plumbers were installing pipes in the ground while labourers carried large bags on their turbaned heads from one end of the property to another. A few men in orange helmets and yellow vests walked around with clipboards in their hands, barking orders at the workers. They were the engineers from the big firm that had been hired to oversee various aspects of construction.

"So many people here, Gopal bhai," Jeevan muttered next to him.

"Not on Sunday," Gopal replied swiftly, to quell any doubts that might be passing through the younger man's mind. "You already know that. Remember how silent and deserted it was all the Sundays we came here?"

"I still think nighttime would be better."

"It's what Tripathy wants," said Gopal. "That is what the extra money is for." He put an arm around Jeevan's shoulders and was surprised to find how narrow they were. "Don't worry, we have it all planned; no one will know it was us, and before they even realize what's happened, we will be far away."

Gopal half expected Jeevan to pull himself free of his clutch. But he stayed where he was and gradually, his shoulders began to relax. It was only then that Gopal removed his arm.

"This place reminds me of the old forts in movies, where communities live contented, sheltered lives. Until someone new comes and disrupts them. An outsider, someone strange and maybe a little twisted."

Gopal was irritated with this sort of speech. He thought he had already spent hours explaining to Jeevan that what they were doing would disrupt people's bank balances but not anyone's life. It would be a rude shock, a lesson to those who deserved it.

"If this were a movie, Gopal bhai, we would be the villains." Jeevan's voice shook.

Gopal pointed upwards, and the younger man's eyes followed. There, high against one of the towers, half concealed inside the scaffolding, was a man painting a wall. The very top of the building was no longer the naked shade of plaster as the rest. It was in fact a brilliant blue. Gopal could recall no other blue buildings in Hrishipur.

"They are turning the building into sky," cried Jeevan.

"No," said Gopal. "They have named the seven towers after rivers. In this desert, they want to bring the illusion of water. Maya, Jeevan. This is not even real. It is just maya. What is real is that man's life up there."

He told Jeevan the story of a fellow electrician a few years younger than himself, a kind man who sang bhajans every morning and went to the temple frequently to pray. One day he climbed up an electric pole using just his bare hands and feet to repair a snapped wire. It was something he did effortlessly day after day, shimmying up that pole like an acrobat in the circus. Gopal had often watched him in envy, wishing he too could climb like that.

"But that day the bastard was thinking of his old father who had fallen ill in the village and his younger sister who needed a dowry to get married. The momentary lapse in concentration was enough to cause a sudden fall that none of the horrified onlookers could stop. It resulted in the loss of both his legs. It was worse than any limp. It was the end of his livelihood. The man now lives under the expressway where he rolls about on his wooden platform with wheels, begging for alms at traffic lights.

"What he needed was a harness to tie himself to the pole. And rubber gloves. And shoes. If he had been working for a big company, they would have put him on a platform with a crane. He had nothing. Just a pole, his arms and his legs. Did anyone care that he fell? That he is now a homeless beggar? Not the people whose homes were flooded with light after he managed to fix the wire right before losing his balance. Not the gods he used to pray to."

Jeevan was quiet.

"These people don't care. They have many investments, many homes, and many lovers." Gopal cackled, pleased at his joke.

They were standing to the right of a semicircle of towers covered in scaffolding from top to bottom, which stood in the shape of a crescent moon, curving away from them. The semicircle faced a low, flat building with only three floors. Until the residents moved in, which was still some ways away, that horizontal block, labelled Main Building on Tripathy's map, was the most important part of the property. It housed the office and various other rooms that would one day provide amenities and recreational facilities to those who made their home high up in the towers.

"Do you know what all is being built inside?" Gopal asked, ready to launch into an impressive list.

"Clubhouse, gym, restaurants."

"That's everywhere," Gopal said dismissively.

"Indoor swimming pool. My father was helping to dig it."

Jeevan's face darkened.

"Shopping arcade just like in the five-star hotels."

"I have heard there will be a cinema hall inside."

Gopal tried to recall something that Jeevan couldn't possibly have heard of.

"Skating rink," he finally said, stroking his chin.

"What?"

"Arre, it is a big room." Gopal stretched his arms out wide to indicate the magnitude. "With a wooden floor, where people walk around on shoes with wheels."

"Wheels?"

Gopal fished out his cell phone and scrolled down WhatsApp to find the video someone had sent him. There it was, the room with the skaters, mostly children, going this way and that on their high strapped shoes. The movement of all the wheels together made a roaring sound. Jeevan brought his head towards Gopal's to watch the video, which froze, then resumed, then froze again. But it was enough for them to understand what people did in rooms like that. Glided rather than walked, with no apparent purpose, round and round the enclosed space.

"Why do they do that?" Jeevan asked under his breath.

"Time pass," Gopal said, putting his phone back in his pocket.

No one took any notice of them. The labourers were too exhausted to care about onlookers, and the engineers were too absorbed in their own sense of importance. They had managed to get the plum job on the right construction site. Gopal and Jeevan might have been two curious kids who had wandered over or two out-of-work men looking for something to do or passersby who had stopped to stare at the impressive project. In this particular part of town, few knew Gopal. Due to his disability, he rarely strayed too far from the familiar neighbourhoods where he could shuffle along at his own pace. The relative anonymity in this area had frustrated him in the past, but these days it was proving to be an advantage.

The only one who knew him was one of the watchmen who stood guard at the side entrance on afternoon duty. Like most other people who knew Gopal, he too owed him a favour. It wouldn't take much, a leisurely stroll away from the gate at the right moment, a tap-tap-tap signal with his stick if needed. There he was now, glancing over at them. Gopal raised his hand to scratch his head and the watchman did the same before turning away.

The thick, coarse fabric of the jute bag was uncomfortable in this heat, but Gopal dared not put it down. Instead, he plunged his right fist into the pocket of his worn trousers and fished out a wad of paper that had been folded numerous times.

"Open," he commanded, holding it out. Dutifully, Jeevan unfurled it to reveal a map.

"OK, now, let's go over everything one more time."

Jeevan was a few inches taller than him, as most people were. But still they stood so close that Gopal could smell the faint scent of hair oil on his head. He wished it was Ahmad next to him instead. Ahmad who always smelt of the ittar he bought from the by-lanes of old Delhi next to the Jama Masjid. The memory of that smell now made Gopal's eyes water with disappointment.

"Circumcised coward," he growled without thinking.

"Ahmad mian?" asked Jeevan instantly.

Gopal said nothing. Had he given anything away? But how could he? Gopal, with his drunken lecherous behaviour with all the girls he came across, his groping hands in Jeevan's auto that night, his lewd whistling and catcalling any time a girl walked by. How could anyone know that the limp was not the only dark thing in his life? His hands, holding the map of the property's basement trembled. He remembered the affection in Jeevan's mother's eyes on him an hour ago. What would she think of him if she knew everything?

"He changed his mind," he said, and spat on the ground next to them to indicate his disgust. "Didn't have enough balls to keep his word. No wonder they threw him out of the restaurant."

"That is a bit harsh, Gopal bhai. Don't be angry with him. He is more sensitive than us, not as tough. He probably felt it was not the right thing to do."

"Yes, like a woman," Gopal slapped the map. "Look here. Let us focus. We cannot afford to make a mistake."

They talked in low voices. They barely noticed the midday sun that beat down on their heads or the sweat trickling down their backs. Gopal pointed to the map and to the buildings, muttering all the time. Jeevan listened and occasionally asked a question. "Here?" "What about those?"

They had gone through it countless times already. Gopal had it memorized. Wires, circuit breakers, outlets. They had been his loyal companions for years. They would not let him down now.

It was only the look of uncertainty on Jeevan's face that worried him. He was such a mama's boy. For a few months when he was growing the beard and moustache, he had begun to look like someone who could be taken seriously. But now that he was mixed up with the girl, he had shaved it all off and looked like a chikna.

And still, Gopal did not feel the mix of nervousness and longing he had when he was with Ahmad. Instead, he was reminded of his younger brother, the spoilt baby, the healthy one, but his brother nonetheless. The one who had made Gopal's mother forget all about him the second she saw his scrunched-up little face. The one who had been named this time after Lord Vishnu himself and not after one of his avatars. Gopal still remembered the sound of his howls that night he was born. He had been so excited about having a baby in the house, a brother he could play with and also boss around. But baby Vishnu had run away every time Gopal went near him. Finally, one day, Gopal had stopped going near him at all. Just like he had stopped going near the other children in the village.

But now here was Jeevan, leaning close, nodding at everything he said. He had taken him to his home. He had called him a friend.

"Are you afraid?" Gopal asked gently.

Jeevan shook his head.

"In a little over a week we will be gone."

Jeevan sighed.

"What? You are not going to Mumbai or what? Where you said your friend will give you a job. Arre, in Mumbai you can do anything. You can work for the underworld. After all, you have been trained well, hahahaha." Gopal slapped him on the back.

"I need some time. I am not ready to run away." Gopal stared at him.

"Gopal, I have to sort out my matters here. My family needs me. I want to make sure they are okay. Then, there's Chaya."

"Take her with you," Gopal said. "Get married. You will have enough money now." He lifted the bag. "Take," he said. "Even Ahmad's share. You take it."

"No, no, I don't want that. We will split it like you said."

"Go away from here, Jeevan." Gopal let out a sigh of frustration.

What was wrong with these young men? With their strong bodies they could do whatever they wanted. And yet, they allowed the world to drag them down. If Jeevan stayed behind after they had brought their plan to fruition, what if someone recognized him? What if he blurted out something in a moment of guilt? What if the cops showed up at his parents' home? What if they traced him back to Gopal? It was folly, utter folly.

"Look, Jeevan, first go and find a job, a respectable one, and then come back for Chaya," he said. "If you continue here, it will not be safe. Not only for you but also for your family. For your sisters."

Jeevan stared at the labourers as if he would prefer to be one of them.

"There is a whole world out there for you. You know how many film stars live there? With your chikna face, you might get a role. First an extra, then hero. Today you are a villain, tomorrow, who knows. It will be a new life, Jeevan."

"And you, Gopal? Where will you go? Back to your village?" he asked.

"Who knows where I will go," Gopal grinned.

He liked Jeevan but there was no way he was going to disclose his plans to him. These soft boys, you never knew what they would do or say when pressed by police and their goondas in jail. No, their paths would diverge the following Sunday, and then they need never see one another again. There was that ache in his throat again, welling up inside him, rising to his eyes. Gopal rubbed a sleeve over them quickly.

"Chal," he said, "it's very hot. Want ice cream?" He pointed at the Walls ice-cream cart in the corner of the street.

Jeevan's face broke into that toothy grin of his. Gopal walked up to the man dozing by the cart. "Two chocobars," he said.

They walked slowly down the street, holding their ice creams like little boys. The thick coat of chocolate cracked in Gopal's mouth, giving way to the milky coolness underneath. He could not remember the last time he had eaten ice cream.

"When I was a child, my mother would buy me ice cream," Jeevan said. His lips were coated in milk. "I used to love the frozen lollies. They made my lips turn orange." He smiled shyly at some secret memory. "All the girls liked to eat it because it made them look like they were wearing lipstick."

Gopal nodded. Those lollies were the cheapest ones. It's what he had planned on buying, but when he got to the cart and saw the coloured images of the various bars on the menu, he had decided on a special treat. After all, they were already richer than either of them had ever been. He stroked the jute bag fondly.

"You are right, Gopal. I will marry her," Jeevan said suddenly. He stared at the ice-cream stick in his hand as if he might will it to grow more ice cream. Then he turned to look at Gopal with serious eyes. "Thanks to you. Thanks to your help. On the first Sunday of next month itself, I will go to her after all this is over." He waved at the building that now lay behind them. "It will make the day worthwhile if I do something good. I will remember it all my life as the day I told Chaya we must get married—not as anything else."

"Wah beta, that is a good decision." Gopal saw Jeevan smile. "I think she will be very happy. Every time I have given her one of your messages, she has smiled at me, a man she thought was no better than a rat."

They had paused next to a wall painted with chalk graffiti that included The Party's logo, a garland of saffron marigolds around a light bulb, right next to a clumsy drawing of a bird with a big tail.

"Look, a peacock," said Jeevan. "It's a good sign, isn't it?"

"This does not even look like a peacock. Which bastard made this drawing? In our village, we had giant ones." Gopal spread his hands to show the span of a tail fanned out. "They always appeared in the summer to let us know that rain was coming."

"I have not seen a single one dancing this year, Gopal. It means there will be no rain. The gods are not going to be so kind to us," Jeevan said. "So many dying here of famine and Chaya said to me the other day that in Dhaka, where some of her friends are from, the floods are killing the poor people, washing away their villages. What kind of world is this, Gopal?"

A world where happiness only lasted three minutes while you licked a cold ice-cream bar. And the second it was gone, all that remained was the little stick between your fingers.

When someone had lived with a condition all their life, that was all they knew. For instance, when Gopal watched rich people go about their days, there were those among them who he was sure had been born into money. They were not aware of any other kind of life. The same with beautiful women who had been pretty and slim and light-skinned as little girls. And the successful ones, the ones who had stood first in every class, and got the top ranks in all-India exams before going on to become doctors, lawyers, or engineers. In the same way, someone who had always been fat or pockmarked or, heaven forbid, lame, from the beginning, could not recall or imagine a life where things might be different. A life where people did not look at you before hastily turning away, or exchange glances with others as if you couldn't see them do it. A life where you were the same as everyone else. A life of happiness.

Gopal flung his ice-cream stick in the rubbish heap next to the wall, where a lone fat pig was grazing desperately for some scraps. He looked around to make sure they were alone before thrusting his hand inside the bag to bring out a slim wad of notes tied with a rubber band. He slipped it into his shirt pocket with the sort of sleight of hand a magician might use on a stage, and handed the bag to Jeevan.

"Your share and half of Ahmad's. You can count it," he said. Jeevan took the bag without looking at it.

"No need to count, Gopal," he said. His eyes were wet. "This will help my family," he said. "Are you sure you don't want to come back with me and eat dinner with us? You can meet Smriti too."

Gopal shook his head.

"No, but I want to send a present for her and for your mother. Let us go to Karamchand Sweets."

The shop's name was deceptive, for there was a lot else you could find there besides sweets. As soon as Gopal and Jeevan walked in the front door, the air-conditioning revived their spirits. "Can you smell all the food?" Jeevan whispered. "My mother used to buy samosas for us on her way back on the first day of each month, after she got her salary."

"Jeevan, what are a few samosas? Today we will buy for your family whatever your heart desires." Gopal slapped his companion on the back.

"No, no, Gopal," Jeevan said, frowning. "Only a small box of sweets for Smriti's results. But let us take a look around."

They took a casual stroll through the interior. At four in the afternoon on a weekday, it was mostly packed with mothers who had brought their children in for a snack. Men in light-green uniforms stood behind glass windows and tossed up various kinds of chaat, all of which were doused in generous portions of yoghurt and sprinkled with different chutneys. Piles of hot samosas stood on one counter, and fluffy yellow dhoklas on another. The customers were walking from one station to the next with their tickets, trying to figure out who was making what.

"Such a complicated system, no?" Jeevan muttered into his neck. "Why not just take orders and bring everything to the table? Wouldn't that be faster and easier?"

"This is called self-service," Gopal explained. "No waiters needed. More profit for the shop."

"But the people are lost, Gopal bhai. Look at that woman. She can't find what she wants." He pointed to a young woman with a bewildered expression on her face as she stared at the tickets in her hand.

"It's part of the plan. Make them hungrier. They will eat more." Gopal nudged Jeevan in the chest.

The sweets section was its own room, separate from all the greasy, savoury food. It smelt of ghee. Behind the windows stood rows of sweets in different shapes and colours. Orange motichoor laddoos, clay pots of yellow saffron rabri and creamy ras malai, reddish-brown gulab jamuns that glistened with syrup, translucent pethas, fried gram-flour sweets studded with dried fruit, cham chams stuffed with kheer and nuts, flaky golden soan papdi, fluffy white rasgullas, soft and firm varieties of sandesh, and barfis. Piles and piles of diamond-shaped barfis in every possible colour and flavour. Pistachio, chocolate, rose, almond, cashew, coconut, mango, carrot, pineapple. Barfis made from urad dal, barfis made from cream, barfis made from burnt sugar.

Gopal gazed at them so long that the man behind the counter came over to hurry him along. When he was a child, his dadi would make sweets out of khoya or kheer from rice and milk. She would spend hours squatting over the pot on the kerosene stove, stirring the milk and sugar. His dadi's sweets were renowned. Nowadays, her fingers were too gnarled and painful from the arthritis. Besides, she had told him pointedly, who was there to make sweets for?

There was one colour that was prominently missing. "Have you ever seen a blue barfi, Jeevan?" Gopal asked.

"No," said Jeevan, looking thoughtful. "What would they make it with?"

"With pieces of the sky. Or the oceans and rivers. Or, a piece of—" He leant in to whisper in Jeevan's ear. "Trump Towers." He shrieked with laughter.

Jeevan did not laugh. He frowned, looking around as if the mention of that name might arouse suspicion. Gopal felt reckless. In the bag Jeevan held, they had enough money to buy all the sweets in this shop right now if they wanted.

"What should we buy for your home, Jeevan?" He held up a hand before Jeevan could protest. "It's my treat. I want to buy the celebration sweets for Smriti behn."

They bought cashew and almond barfis, moong dal laddoos, a pot of ras malai, a box of soan papdi, and some gulab jamuns as large as tennis balls.

"It's too much," Jeevan protested. But his eyes gleamed with pleasure.

"Is it every day that your sister gets a diploma in accounting? Is it every day you eat chicken curry for dinner? Is it every day that you and I go to a mithai shop together?" Gopal turned to the man behind the counter. "Pack it all up nicely in gift boxes and tie them with gold ribbons."

The man began to do his bidding mechanically. He did not look the least bit sceptical about Gopal's order. Many saabs sent their drivers or office peons to the shop all through the day to order large quantities of sweets to gift to people for every possible occasion.

Armed with the Karamchand Sweets bags, they paused on the sidewalk under the awning.

"Are you sure you won't come home with me for dinner?" Gopal waved Jeevan off and looked into the distance.

"No, no, I have a lot of things to do. I am a busy man as you know. Have to meet some people now, promised to help someone from Nathu's village, supposed to go to Belvedere House for electric work. No time to waste for me, Jeevan. You go home and enjoy your dinner with your family. Don't forget to tell your mother that the sweets are my gift."

"Of course, I will tell them. We will think of you, Gopal, when we eat them." Jeevan looked like he might cry.

"Arre beta, go home. And I will see you in ten days. Between now and then, remember, no contact. Not even one phone call or message."

He watched Jeevan mount his bicycle and ride away with a wave of the hand. He would see him one more time, but something about him pedalling furiously across the busy street, dodging the unruly traffic that came at him from all directions, made Gopal wait on that road. He looked so small against the buildings and rush of vehicles. So small against this monster of a city that swallowed up people like them every day. Sometimes you got crushed under a mammoth wave of traffic, and sometimes you fell from the sky like a dead bird and smashed your legs. It didn't even kill you. It just disabled you so that you were condemned to living each day watching other, luckier people walk past.

At least he was helping improve the fortunes of one young man and his entire family. They deserved it. Gopal thought of the rows and rows of sweets in that shop and felt proud of himself for having brought some joy into the world.

When the speck that was Jeevan disappeared in the haze of dust and sunlight, Gopal turned to walk towards his home. He had said he had numerous things to do but for once he couldn't think of a single one.

~

The park at the corner of Sunder Bagh was surrounded by houses in pale colours. Occasionally, a car crept up the narrow lanes that crisscrossed the neighbourhood. But the people around were mainly domestic helpers. Maids walked between homes to complete their afternoon chores, ayahs accompanied children to the park, drivers wiped down the cars left in their charge, and a lone sweeper stood gathering litter into big heaps. There was no sign of their employers or the children's parents. They were either at work, or inside their air-conditioned houses, or tucked away behind the tinted windows of their cars. It was a sleepy neighbourhood, a little oasis in the concrete jungle of Hrishipur.

Gopal strolled along, listening to the cries of children in the playground. He watched the small bodies dart in and out of the monkey bars, back and forth on the swings, up and down on the slide. As he walked, he made sure his figure was hidden behind the bougainvillaea shrubs, until he eventually found a spot of shade under a peepul tree. He sat down cross-legged, like the wise sages used to do thousands of years ago.

From where he sat, he could still see the children. To his right a group of women lounged under the shade of another tree. They were the ayahs who had escorted the children to the park. The women were of different ages and shapes, but they were all uniformly thin, as if they did not get enough to eat. Some wore salwar kameezes, others wore saris. Some wore their hair in ribboned braids, while others had theirs rolled up into buns. Some sat on the bench, while others squatted on the ground. One of them was lying propped up on the grass on her elbow as if she didn't have a care in the world. They were all talking loudly to each other in Hindi or Bengali. Most of them were undocumented migrants from Bangladesh. They had travelled a long way to work here.

Their faces were vaguely familiar to him. He had encountered the women when he had been summoned to their employers' homes for electrical work. One of them glanced at him before leaning forward to whisper to the group. Gopal clenched his fists. There was no peace for him anywhere.

He leant back against the bark of the tree and found his eyes closing. The afternoon air and the rustle of leaves transported him somewhere. He was at a funeral pyre. The flames leapt into the air, which crackled and hissed. The sound of sobs came to him from a great distance. Then a man's hands yanked his ear and dragged him away. He wasn't supposed to be there. He wasn't supposed to watch the cremation of his brother, the love of his mother's life, the nanha munna little one who had won the hearts of everyone who had ever laid eyes on him. When Vishnu had fallen into the well and drowned, Gopal had been blamed for it, not because he had pushed him in but because he had been born to bring his family and everyone who knew him ill luck.

What he remembered about the fire was how beautiful it was. How the glow from the flames had turned the twilight sky red. How the sound had carried in the wind even when he was back home wrapped up in the starched white cotton of his dadi's sari as she rocked him and made comforting noises.

Gopal's eyes flew open. He stared wildly about him, trying to locate the source of the sound he had just heard. Perhaps it had been a dream. The sleep cleared from his eyes, and in an instant, he was on all fours, crawling into the scrubby overgrowth off the walking trail. He heard the cry again, plaintive and mewling, and called out in a voice he reserved only for nonhumans.

"Aaja, aaja," he whispered. "Come here. Don't be scared."

A pair of eyes peered out from among the bushes. Gopal carefully parted the branches and scooped up the little brown creature.

It wriggled in his hands, unsure of whether to trust him. Gopal spoke to it softly, making encouraging sounds, until it calmed down. He wished he had kept some of the mithai for himself from the sweet shop, just so he could feed this one. Then he remembered the leftover keema at home and grinned at the pup. "We will go home and eat, don't worry. Your belly will be full, little one."

A couple of nights a week, Gopal went to the butcher's shop to get the leftover pieces of meat no one wanted to buy. Then he went to the dhabas where drivers and watchmen ate for the remnants of the day's meals that would get tossed in the trash. The people he had helped were pleased to be able to give him the entrails if that meant they no longer owed him anything. Being indebted to Gopal was not a state they wanted to be in for long. On those days, Gopal went home and ground and cooked everything into a mushy meal. Every night, he poured the concoction of minced meat into bowls to feed to the stray dogs in the neighbourhood. Apparently, word had spread, for their number had grown in size.

That was how he had met Ahmad.

Can you bring me the meat they will throw away at the restaurant, Ahmad mian? he had asked his former neighbor.

Ahmad had nodded quietly. Then one day, while Gopal was surrounded by the wagging tails, Ahmad had folded his delicate arms across his chest and laughed quietly. *You like dogs more than humans.*

They like me more than any humans do, Ahmad mian, he had responded.

Now he nestled the squirming puppy in his arms and wondered who might have a home for it. A few weeks ago, he had given one to the photographer who had loaned him some money.

He had said he didn't want a dog, but Gopal knew he was lonely.

He had heard the rumours and seen the women with him. Every time a different one. Ashok strutted about in that sneering way of his, much like Gopal did, but Gopal had detected in his eyes that haunted look, like Ashok didn't belong here but didn't know where else to go. He had slipped the dog into his arms, using money as an excuse, and hoped that on the lonely nights when the women he bedded didn't come over, the dog would offer some comfort.

Suddenly, there was a cry of excitement as someone appeared inside the park pushing a cart. It was Ahmad's brother, Kasim the fruitwallah. His cart was heaped with fruit. Bunches of bananas, ripe papaya, green guavas, fat mangoes, pomegranates, and chikoos. Within seconds, the cart was surrounded by children. Gopal watched, amused. He would wrangle a little fruit from him later for the puppy. He would ask him about Ahmad very casually. Swear at him a bit for being such an idiot. Even though Ahmad was nowhere near, the thought of talking to his brother made him shiver.

"Want one?" the fruit seller asked, holding up a custard apple at the children. Unlike Ahmad, who had a deep, clear voice, Kasim spoke with a lisp. "They've just started coming in," he said. "Very sweet sharifah like kheer."

A little girl who had stood behind the cart, watching, now reached out her arm to take the fruit. Kasim retracted his.

"Ten rupees," he said.

"Zohra Bibi," she cried out, running towards the group of ayahs. "Can I have ten rupees for a sharifah?"

"Arre, Titli, come here." One of the other ayahs swooped her up. "Zohra, give her some money," she said.

Titli's ayah looked worried.

"She has been naughty today," she said. "Her mother won't like it."

"Did she give you money or not?"

"Yes, but for emergencies."

"What emergency at the park other than hunger or thirst? See how hot it is. One fruit, come on. She's just a child."

The little girl stood watching as her fate was decided. The expression on the ayah's face shifted from doubt to pity. Then she pursed her lips as if she were making her mind up.

"Zohra Bibi," one of the women nudged her. "Give her the money and then let us all go and get some fruit. The first sharifah of the season." She dug her fingers into her ribs. "Her mother won't even notice. She is making lots of money these days." The women exploded into giggles, nudging and poking one another.

Gopal knew then why the girl looked so familiar. She was the child Tripathy's woman had adopted. Her mother was another case. Like the photographer. He watched as the little girl ran back to the cart where Kasim was deftly slicing bananas and guavas and sprinkling salt on them to make fruit chaat. He ladled it into small bowls woven from dried sal leaves, and handed them to some of the children, then tossed a chikoo to one boy and a mango to another.

Titli flung the ten-rupee note on the cart in front of Kasim and grabbed a custard apple.

"Arre, let me cut it for you," Kasim said, brandishing his knife.

She ignored him and sniffed the fruit. Then, she dug her teeth into it and ripped off the skin. It came off easily, a sliver of green peel hanging from her lips like a leaf. She spat it on the ground, scooped out some of the flesh-covered seeds with her fingers, and crammed them into her mouth. Gopal hoped she would not accidentally swallow some of the seeds like he had done once back in his village. But she was smarter than that. He watched her spit them out with the expertise of a child who had spent the first few years of her life on the streets.

"Junglee," someone yelled out. It was another little girl, but this one wore a frilly pink dress and ribbons in her hair.

One of the boys threw a stick at Titli.

"How she eats, like an animal. Look at her."

A chorus of jeers filled the park. Titli looked down at her hands and appeared to notice the mess she had made for the first time. Sticky white flesh from the fruit clung to her fingers as if she really had been eating a bowl of rice kheer. Her chin was wet.

The remains of the fruit had dropped on the ground, collecting dirt. Titli glanced up slowly, blinking. She stood still and listened to the jeers and boos for a moment. Then she gathered up the peels in her fist and hurled them in the direction of the girl who had called her a wild creature.

There was a gasp. The debris of fruit had landed successfully on her lacy dress. The girl, whose frock did not look like it was made for an afternoon in the playground, started to cry, her wails resonating through the park. The other children surrounded her, shutting Titli out. Just like the group of boys who had played kabaddi all afternoon when Gopal was ten. They had not stopped playing, not even for water or a piss, because they knew kabaddi was a game he could not participate in. He had stood on the sidelines, waiting for them to finish and start another game that did not involve so much running. Finally, only after hours spent standing in the sun, had the realization dawned on him that they were waiting for him to tire and slink away.

Gopal clapped his hands.

"Baby, come here," he yelled out to Titli. "Look what I have here."

She turned and ran towards him. Her face, he noticed when she came closer, was streaked with tears. He held out the puppy.

"This is Bittu. Want to touch him?" he said.

Titli hesitated. The newly christened Bittu's little pink tongue darted out.

Gopal started to walk towards her, slowly, so that he wouldn't scare her. He was very conscious of his limp. It was children he hated to frighten. He had never meant to do that, not even when he was a child himself, back in the village. And yet, even here in the city, where children watched all sorts of violent movies about monsters, they usually scattered when they saw Gopal coming.

But Titli was not looking at his foot. She was fixated on the puppy.

"Touch, touch. See how slippery," Gopal said.

Titli reached out and ran a finger along the dog's body. She giggled.

"Want to hold him? But he's very wicked. Will try to lick you," Gopal warned as he handed the puppy over.

Before Titli could grab a hold of him, however, there was a shriek, and the ayah was upon them. Her hair had come undone from its bun and was escaping down her back in loose strands.

She looked a little insane as she appeared in view, wringing her hands.

"Titli," she screamed and ran up to her. "You wicked, wicked child." She clasped her to her bosom. "Gopal, what are you doing? Are you trying to steal the child? You evil langda."

Gopal's vision clouded. His ears burnt. It was upon him before he could do anything to stop it. It was the fever.

"Steal this child?" he sneered. "I can find any number of these in the slum behind Chikki Bazaar. You crazy bitch, don't blame other people for neglecting your duties. You don't even belong here. If the government finds out you have no Aadhar card, you will be packed off to the village in Bangladesh that you ran away from. You think they want anyone here apart from us Hindus?"

The mood in the park had changed. The ayah's bosom was heaving like the slide, up and down, up and down. Kasim was staring at them. Gopal wondered what he'd heard and what he would report back to Ahmad. The other children were standing still and watching the scene. It would be replayed, with suitable embellishments, when they returned to their beautiful homes. And Gopal's legend as the evil langda would continue to grow.

He shook his fist at them all.

"Acting all uppity with me, as if you're any better. A servant to a woman who is—" He spat on the ground without finishing the sentence. "And the child." He pointed at Titli, who shrank back into the folds of the ayah's sari and turned her face away. "Her mother named her after a butterfly? When she really is a wild rat. She was born to someone like us. Someone who had no money to feed her and was probably not even married. Look at her, look how dark she is, look how she eats when she is hungry as if she has never been fed. Yes, yes, now she has money pouring in from rich men in the city, she dresses up fine and goes to a fancy school and is learning to speak English and eating cakes with a spoon. Does not change where she came from."

The child began to whimper. The children stood in a huddle on one side and the ayahs on the other. Zohra Bibi held Titli close, as if she were afraid that Gopal might try to take off with her.

"Don't cry, Baby," she said in a soothing voice. "I will tell your mummy, and she will make sure that this park is safe. It is so close to Trump Towers," she muttered as she walked away with the child. "How can they let such ruffians here? Where are the police?"

The child looked over the ayah's shoulder at Gopal and the dog. Her eyes were large and puzzled, the eyes of a world that did not understand him and wished he would disappear. Well, he would disappear. They need not worry about that. No one was going to find him in the heartland. This was why he had not told Jeevan where he was going. There would be no trace of him after the following Sunday. Where he was going, the people would never know about his life in Hrishipur. And the people here?

Why, they would only talk about him in hushed whispers as that strange crippled electrician who had changed their city. For the city would change. Yes, he would make sure of that.

He straightened his back to try and look more confident and intimidating. But those in the park had turned their backs to him.

Children were easily distracted. Their ayahs shot him a look of disgust and moved away to where they could no longer see him.

Gopal cradled the pup in his arms and shuffled out of the park. His heartbeat was still accelerated from his own rant.

The sounds of traffic were only white noise now. His mind was a hum of activity like the streets around him. In the next ten days he had left here, what else could he accomplish? He tried to think of people he knew who seemed happy. Like that young plumber who had recently moved to his chawl. He had seen the wife with her plump hips and soft, dimpled face. She had turned away from him of course, but he had noticed her glancing shyly at the watchman who lived next door.

Gopal grinned to himself as he thought of the cloud that would pass over the plumber's face when he heard the gossip about his wife. He quickened his pace, his mind now racing with ideas about how to disrupt some lives. His time in Hrishipur was coming to an end. There was not a moment to waste. His parents had thought him capable of nothing. But they had after all named him after a god. The people of this town would never forget him. Long after the name Trump was obliterated from their minds, they would continue to remember his. *Gopal.*

SALIL

WHAT DID YOU DO WHEN YOU HAD SEVERAL HOURS TO KILL IN AN airport that you'd once found deeply fascinating, but was now just a place in which to wait with nothing to look forward to, a place of transit between cities you didn't belong to?

On this particular morning, the probability that he might never belong struck Salil with some force as he walked briskly down the carpeted hallway of Terminal Two, the domestic departure area in Mumbai's Chhatrapati Shivaji Maharaj International Airport. His flight had been further delayed due to fog over Delhi. Not fog, call it what it is, fucking pollution, he wanted to yell out. If he did, of course, he would startle all the passengers who were walking past him in an endless stream. He would draw attention. Salil paused to visualize the scene: him frozen in place, them gawking. To stop the world in its tracks. That had been the dream that sunlit morning twenty-two years ago when he had climbed down from the Rajdhani Express to attend college in Delhi. But today, that dream felt like it was slipping away rather quickly.

The past three days in Mumbai had been a whirlwind as usual. Meetings over breakfast, lunch, cocktails, dinner, and nightcaps.

Unlike earlier visits, however, the mood at these meetings had been sombre and devoid of the usual liquor-induced show of bravado. That very morning, Jayant Dubey, his business school friend and now the CEO of Black Diamond, had ominously pointed a finger skyward as they were having breakfast at the Oberoi Hotel, where Salil always stayed when he visited Mumbai. Dubey had said he had come to say goodbye but really, Salil suspected, also to caution him against incurring unnecessary expenses for the company. *Be prepared*, he'd said. *For the inevitable.*

There was no point in denying it any longer. Salil had fought both the financiers as well as Harry, who wanted to fold their share of the company and start looking for a proper job, for over a year now. There had been no bonuses for the employees in two years. He, Harry, Dubey, and the other two partners had not taken a raise in three. Morale was low. Now he would have to go home and fire at least one guy in marketing. And, of course, he would have to try to explain the situation to Ramona again. The memory of his last night with her still sent an icy finger down his back.

What he really wanted to do at the moment was run down the hallway. If only he could break into a sprint and let these shops and restaurants go by in a blur, he might feel like he could accomplish something. His body was tense from lack of exercise. In Hrishipur, he worked so hard at the gym every evening that Ramona was convinced he was trying to be in good shape so he could screw other women. What she didn't understand was how the workouts themselves made him feel. The roll of the treadmill, the groan of the pulleys and bars, the lift and pull of the weights. Some nights he thought they were the only things he could be in sync with after long hours spent arguing with people and crunching numbers on a computer screen. In the gym, he could focus all his attention on various parts of his body, flex and heave and push until his mind drew a blank over the anxieties that seemed to multiply by the day. In the gym at least, he was in control.

An airport gym would have provided the perfect way to pass the time before his flight. His arms felt flabby and he wanted to arrive at the office in Hrishipur the next day armoured with toned biceps. Besides, the Polar watch on his wrist was sending him beeping signals, accusing him of neglecting his fitness regime. His love of gadgets was a blessing and a curse.

But there was no gym at this airport. Salil found that strange considering how important it was for people in this city to look their best. What did all the movie stars do when their flights were delayed and their pecs felt soft?

Well, at least there was a spa. He stopped by its entrance to glance at the life-size poster on which a man lay in a field like a corpse, his body covered from the waist down by a black satin sheet. A pair of feminine, manicured hands hovered over his bare chest, poised to begin the massage. It was tempting. Just thinking about it loosened Salil's muscles.

He grunted and turned away, willing his mind from the vision he had had of himself lying supine and looking up at a strange woman's face. First of all, Ramona would get hysterical if she learnt of a massage. Also, the massage would cost a bomb. Ten thousand at least. It seemed like a waste of money right now, with what lay ahead.

He could go to his gate and wait there, but he knew he would just get up again in a few minutes. Sitting still at noon made him feel like an old man. Yes, he had turned forty a few months ago and yes, his hair was greying at the temples at an alarming rate. But he could still lift with the best of them and he could still beat the boys at the office at squash. One of whom he would have to let go of the next day. Yuvraj. A man with a wife and two teenage daughters at home. Yuvraj didn't have family money and his wife, like Ramona, didn't work. Except she was nothing like Ramona. She was friendly and sweet and reminded Salil of the girls back in Gwalior, the city where he had grown up. He imagined Yuvraj's face, his mouth slightly open and his eyes boring into his own when he gave him the bad news. *Sorry. Inevitable.*

When Salil saw the spotless corner on the carpet, with its orange-and-grey pattern, an impulse took over. It was a quiet, secluded nook. He flung his duffel bag on one of the seats and lowered himself to the ground, inches away from a leathery fake plant. It was easy. Even with the shirt tucked in and the belt and the tight black boots, it felt right. One, two, three, he counted as he did the push-ups. He focused until everything around him disappeared. The purring of luggage wheels on the conveyor belt, the smothered coughs of passengers walking by, the periodic announcements for boarding. Everything except the count in his head and the weight of his own arms, up, down, up, down.

"Salil? Is that you?"

He leant on his elbows and looked up, confused. He had not done the push-ups for attention, but only to make his body move and his brain stop thinking about impending disasters.

It was Priyanka, the young advertising executive whose agency did PR for them. Over the last few years, she had helped turn their brand into a liquor for hip yuppies. She was always flying in and out, like him, to meet various clients, fledgling entrepreneurs with stars in their roving eyes. She was used to attention from men and also to start-ups folding like tents, their magic gone just as swiftly as it had once appeared.

"Are you doing push-ups? Here?"

She sounded incredulous. It embarrassed him, as if he were gauche again, a lanky teenager trying not to stare at the stylish Delhi girls on campus.

"Gotta flex the biceps," he grinned as he sprang up.

His body felt like it had been tightly coiled. Energy coursed through him. He couldn't tell if it was the push-ups—he had gotten to eighty-six—or the presence of a woman looking at him adoringly.

It was even better than a gym. It was an audience. Talking made everything better. Talking about nothing of consequence drowned out the voices in his head.

"Where are you off to? When is your flight?" he asked. "Do you have time for a quick drink?"

She flipped her hair back and smiled so the dimples deepened in her cheeks. Girls with dimples were all the same, shamelessly displaying them whenever they could.

"Off to Hyderabad to meet a client, and then home for a weekend trip." She glanced at her watch. "I have about an hour before boarding. How can I refuse a drink with a client who sells drinks?" She laughed.

He led the way to Eclipse, the swank pub filled with black leather couches and glass tables. It almost felt like another meeting. Salil was glad he had run into Priyanka. Now he could put both their drinks on the company tab. A perk that like all the others was now in jeopardy. After they were seated in their plush leather seats, he ordered a Black Diamond lager. She asked for an Alphonso mojito.

"Make sure the rum is Black Diamond," she told the waiter as she flashed a coy smile at Salil.

The waiter gave them both a strange look before walking away. Salil wondered if he was rolling his eyes at what he regarded as a pathetic attempt at flirting. In this city of performances where the act of flirting had been perfected to a high art, the waiters must think them novices.

When the drinks arrived, Salil caressed the label on the bottle of beer. He felt emotional looking at it. They had started the company together, the five of them, and split up between Mumbai, Hrishipur, and Bengaluru to take care of regional sales and marketing. It had been eight years since that fateful day when he quit his job and embarked on this adventure, but right now, it seemed like an eternity ago.

He watched Priyanka make a great show of stirring her mojito without drinking it. It made him wonder if she enjoyed drinking at all. Her long fuchsia nails fiddled with the cocktail stirrer. He noticed her clothes now too, letting his eyes casually run over them. She wore a low-cut forest-green blouse with flouncy sleeves. A star-shaped pendant studded with tiny crystals sat steadily without moving right where her cleavage began.

Salil had a simple motto: *Look, don't touch.* Anything might happen in his mind. It was necessary to enjoy some relief from the drudgery. He allowed himself the occasional fantasy about women he encountered, and he had his fair share of porn stashed away on the office computer just like Harry did. In real life, though, nothing happened. No trespasses. But he no longer knew how to convince Ramona of the truth.

Finally, after having stirred the drink until it frothed, Priyanka opened her glistening mouth and sucked the straw intently. In the past, he would have found it alluring, but today, he got the distinct impression that she was putting on an act. That this was all a game of charades and neither of them had any choice but to keep playing.

"This is very refreshing." There was that dimpled smile again. She knew he had been watching her.

He took a gulp of beer, even though it gave him little pleasure. The sight of empty glasses lying around his home late at night over the past year made him want to drink less and less. He liked keeping his head clear and his vision unclouded. But the drink would help him think of clever things to say.

There was a reason he chatted about whatever he could with everyone he met. He showered his driver Rajesh with questions. He talked to the guy who came to clean his office late at night when he was still there working at his desk. He joked with the trainer at the gym. He knew all their stories. They liked him for it. But what they didn't know was that without those conversations that meant so little to him, Salil would have to rest quietly and think. About his marriage, his investments, his career, his elderly mother living alone in Gwalior.

He pointed at Priyanka's glass.

"Do you know this mango was named after the Portuguese general Afonso de Albuquerque, considered a military genius in the sixteenth century? He led the first voyage by a European fleet into the Red Sea and initiated the war against the Ottoman Empire. Basically, he was the one responsible for building the global Portuguese Empire. Which involved, of course, the conquest of Goa."

"Fascinating," said Priyanka, looking at him with complete concentration as if they were the only two people in the room. "I had never eaten an Alphonso until I moved to Mumbai. Now it's my favourite. I love this city," she said dreamily. "Love the energy. Even in this lounge in the airport." She waved her hand around as if to embrace the ambience in the room.

Salil glanced at the massage chairs, buffet table, and the guy deftly mixing cocktails at the bar. This pub served as a pit stop for businessmen, movie stars, cricketers, and others who also had mysterious connections with the Mumbai mafia, as they waited for flights that seemed to be perpetually delayed. At the far end of the room, a familiar-looking gentleman lowered himself into one of the massage chairs. A waiter jogged up to him with a glass of what looked like Scotch on a tray. The man leant back as the chair began to vibrate gently. His hair was slightly long and swept back from a broad forehead.

"There's Saif Ali Khan," said Salil, trying to keep his voice casual.

Priyanka shrugged. She had clearly grown accustomed to sighting Bollywood stars everywhere she went. But despite all his travels and lounging, Salil had never quite grown used to it. The sight of a familiar face he had seen often on TV still made him a little excited and a little nervous, as if he were about to perform for someone and was destined to fail.

When he had first arrived in Delhi as an eighteen-year-old, Salil had worn his small-town insecurities like a blanket. They had comforted him like an old friend. The first boys he had found on campus were like him. New to Delhi, lacking the easy gloss of their local counterparts who did not need to live in the hostel. The day scholars went back every afternoon to their villas in tree-lined neighbourhoods, leaving behind the students who had travelled from all over India with higher grades and vernacular accents. Among them, Salil had quickly become a leader. But it had offered him little satisfaction. It was just an extension of his old life in Gwalior.

On humid nights, as he lay under the slow-whirring fan, his soul had hungered for more. Outside the confines of that hostel lay the vast capital of India. Somewhere to the south were the wide roads and canopies of the architect Lutyens' Delhi. On Sundays, he took the bus to Connaught Place and walked around the circular streets, weaving in and out of the columns on the sidewalks, staring up at the historic restaurants and bars. He did not have enough money to actually go inside and order anything, but he figured that if he walked around long enough he might begin to belong. And then, when he met Ramona, the dream started to crystallize.

"Speaking of mangoes," he resumed, leaning forward. "How many varieties can you name?"

"Let's see, Alphonso, Dasheri, Kesar, and Chausa, which we used to eat back home, Himsagar, Gulab Khas from Lucknow." Priyanka counted them off on her fingers. She paused and looked at him expectantly.

"Badami, Totapuri, Raspuri, Amrapali, Langra, Mallika, Imam Pasand."

"What beautiful names."

"You've probably only tasted a handful of varieties. But there are over a hundred kinds in the state of Kerala alone. Have you heard of the Kilichundan?" he asked.

Priyanka shook her head.

"It means bird in Malayali. The mango looks like a bird's beak."

He turned the beer bottle around out of habit. It used to be important to display the Black Diamond label on the table.

Maybe Saif would notice it on his way out.

Priyanka sighed.

"This topic brings back such memories. My nani used to make mango pickles when we were children growing up in Ranchi. Slices of mango would be laid out to dry on sheets on our roof all winter."

Like him, she had moved from a crowded city with limited opportunities to metropolitan India. Like him, she dressed stylishly and smelt of expensive perfumes to fit in. Salil debated for a manic second if he should confide in her about his troubles.

Perhaps Priyanka, who was whip smart underneath the fluttering eyelashes and tight cleavage, would understand. He wanted very much to confide in someone.

The previous three days had been sombre ones, and not only because the monsoon had brought a dark curtain down across Mumbai. The competition had increased in the last decade, with global distilleries, breweries, and even wineries all wanting to capitalize on the growing thirst of young Indians with new money. With so many competitors, you had to stay on top of the game all the time. There was also the fact that the Hindutva brigade disapproved of alcohol consumption. The prime minister was rumoured to be a teetotaler. Six months ago, the central government had raised tariffs on alcohol. Last week, a twelfth state had been declared dry, which meant bootleggers would thrive but small companies like Black Diamond would be pushed out.

The irony was that the urban youth drank more and more. Every week in Hrishipur, a new bar seemed to sprout up somewhere. But the hedonism wasn't going unnoticed. It was, those close to the prime minister whispered, beginning to irritate him. They were not his vote bank after all. In the hinterland, those who had voted for him and who garlanded his life-size deities and prayed to both gods and cows for his good health fumed at the thought of the spoiled brats in places like Hrishipur who were out getting wasted in plush hotels and rooftop lounges. The worst culprit of all was the expensive spirits. If the villagers could get drunk on country liquor, then why not the rest of them?

Salil had never been overly political. He had naively imagined that the corporate world would protect him from the vagaries of national elections and so on. He smirked at the thought.

"What's so funny?" Priyanka demanded.

"It's that man in the black shirt over there," he riffed. "He's been staring at you for the past twenty minutes, since we sat down." It was, in fact, true. Out of the corner of his eye, Salil had caught the man ogling.

"Well at least someone's paying attention," she said with a wry smile.

"Sorry," he said.

"What were you thinking about? What's up?"

He shook his head.

"Nothing major. Just the plans we made on this trip and all that I have to implement when I get home. There's going to be a lot of bad news."

She opened her mouth to speak, aware no doubt of her client's misfortunes, but Salil raised his hand to stop her. Talking about his troubles would make him grow close to her, develop a bond that felt more complicated to him than a torrid fling.

"No shoptalk now. Let's relax. Are you looking forward to going home?"

Once she began to talk about home and parents and all that, he knew she might go on for a while, making it easy for him to tune out. He only needed to nod and interject occasionally as he contemplated how he would approach Yuvraj in his office the next day. "My therapist says I need to go home more often. That I need to get away from all this." She waved her arm around at the lounge.

The utterly casual way in which she said the word *therapist* irritated him. What was it with all these young people nowadays and their obsession with *mental health*? Of course everyone felt depressed or frustrated or anxious when they participated in this rat race, and all their relationships were fragile. Who could stay unperturbed when surrounded by corruption and nepotism? But what would talking to a stranger about your troubles resolve? He was convinced it was a scam. All those people who had gone and acquired degrees in psychology or social welfare or whatever it was they studied now needed customers and were in cahoots with the drug companies who made antidepressants and anti-anxiety pills. It was all addictive, a Western influence that he did not, for a change, buy into.

Ramona had suggested it to him a few times that summer.

She had expressed interest in seeing a person who had returned from Harvard with a list of diplomas and a licence to practice counselling. Even Jessica had mentioned therapy, as had Harry's wife. They all thought something was ailing Ramona. What was wrong with these women? Of course she was sad, after what she had gone through. It would take a little time, and then she would be fine. He had told her to go to the gym like he did. Or dancing. Loud music would help. Or soft music. Whatever.

"Why would someone like you, young, successful, living the good life, need therapy? It's a Western import."

"And you don't like things from the West?" Priyanka tapped his watch with one fluorescent nail.

"It's a waste of money. How much does this person charge you anyway?"

The moment the words were out he regretted them. Talking about money was tacky. Ramona used to reprimand him for it in the early years every time he did it, until gradually, he had overcome the habit.

"She charges a lot. Five thousand for an hour-long session."

"That's absurd. You can talk to your friends for free. You see, people in countries like America and England have no friends. They have no one to talk to. They are not close to their families. Their parents kick them out the moment they turn eighteen. So, who can they go to? They need this shit. We don't. You should ask your nani what to do when you are sad. I'm sure she would not suggest therapy. I'm sure she talked to her siblings, neighbours, and cousins. I'm sure she would be able to give you better advice, filled with wisdom, than any stranger who's read Freud."

"Therapists don't talk about Freud. Not unless they're hypnotists or psychoanalysts. As for my nani, she has cancer in her throat and can't even talk any more. That's why I am going home and that's why I need the therapy."

Priyanka downed her drink. Her dimples remained hidden. Salil realized she had bleached the skin on her face or done something else to it that made it look taut and smooth like a mask. It was unnatural. He fought the urge to reach out and touch it, to stroke her blemish-free cheek and say it was all right. He wished she would go back to flirting with him.

Over by the window, Saif now sat on a sofa with his arm resting casually along the back. He occupied the entire seat with the nonchalant yet proprietorial air of one who owned the city. Which he kind of did. A waiter came up to him, leant down like someone about to serve a prince, which he was, and nodded obsequiously at whatever he was told.

"People in this country are so condescending to waiters," Salil remarked, stroking his goatee. "In America, you know the waiters are not from a different class. They are people like you and me. Young students trying to make some extra cash. Can you imagine us working as waiters when we were in college? We are too class conscious." The beer had loosened him. He felt like he could talk about anything. The global economy, the American education system, the political situation in the Middle East.

"And it is this that is going to destroy us. The class divisions. Yesterday we were on top, but today we are on the way down. Already, as a revolt, the people have voted for this government. It was an anti-elite vote. They hate us. The voters want to burn down the bars and hotels and malls. They want to riot in the streets because they are tired. And the prime minister hates us. He hates our brands, our clothes, our booze. We have the degrees and the breeding and our fancy country clubs and spas and golf courses, but we couldn't even return our own party to Parliament. The power is about to go out. Wait and see."

He was almost panting by the time he stopped. His little speech had excited him more than his defensive presentation to the company's financiers two days ago.

Priyanka was looking at him, confused. "Whose side are you on?" she asked.

Salil paused. It was the sort of question he didn't like to consider deeply.

"You know, I don't know. The older I get, the less certain I am that the things I wanted once are the things worth fighting for." Just then the announcement came that his flight was delayed by another hour.

"Disappointed? That you can't go home just yet?" Priyanka had reverted to her teasing voice.

Salil shrugged. In truth, he was glad about the delay. For it meant he wouldn't get to Hrishipur until five in the evening, and Ramona would have to go to the Malhotras' housewarming thing alone. If she stayed there long enough, he might even fall asleep by the time she returned. He might not have to talk to her about his trip until the following morning.

The night before leaving, they had eaten a rare dinner together at home. She had seemed unusually chatty. In fact, she had talked incessantly through the meal about how Maneka had grown too busy to see her after Ramona had introduced her to everyone and taken her to all the parties. She had said she was planning to organize a reunion for their friends from high school. One final flamboyant gesture for Maneka and the other girls. Something they would never forget. She had shared her ideas for the venue, catering and theme, none of which Salil could now remember. He had pretended to listen, with his mind on weightier matters as usual.

But then her manic chatter had led to him blurting out the truth about the impending layoffs and the dismal sales. There would be no bonuses again this year. He had started talking to headhunters for other prospects. Ramona had dismissed his fears at first.

"Everyone goes through these bad patches. It's the corporate world. I saw my dad do it too. You're so good at your job. You will be able to fix everything," she had said, while ladling more soup into his bowl. "I feel like this flat is unlucky," she had added. "Once we move into Trump Towers, things will change. I can feel it."

Salil had pushed his bowl away and grabbed her hands across the dining table. She didn't understand. They were paying tens of thousands of rupees each month for a home they had not yet moved into. In addition to their rent at Magnolia Gardens, which was already more than most people could afford. He had been thinking seriously about selling the flat at Trump Towers and maybe booking a smaller, cheaper one. After all, it was just the two of them. What did they need such a lavish residence for?

Ramona had sat quietly in her upholstered chair for a few minutes, with her eyes focused not on him but on his hands gripping her wrists. Then she had spoken in her cool voice, with that polished accent of hers that could sometimes send a chill down his body.

"You are useless, Salil. There is no hope with you."

If only she had shrieked or thrown something at him. If only she had brought down the tablecloth along with the plates and cutlery. If only she had caused a scene that made the servants come running. Anything but that icy calm, that cold disdain. She had moved her hands away. His own, curled into fists, had rested next to the granite coasters from Turkey and the vase full of lilies.

He unclenched his fists now. It was his fault. He should never have married her. They were from different worlds. He had only made her unhappy.

In front of him, Priyanka was talking about her grandmother again.

"Nani never wanted me to come to this city. She thought it would ruin me. Like in the movies. I remember saying, *But Nani, people also go there to find success and prosperity and of course love. Not women*, she said at once. *Only the men do that*." The light in her eyes dimmed for a second. Then she recovered, quickly, and spoke again in that overly peppy voice that sounded both nervous and euphoric. Not for the first time, Salil wondered if she used something. He had heard that a lot of the folks in advertising did drugs. Just like the movie stars.

"I better go to my gate. Can't miss the flight." She waved at the waiter to get the bill. "So, what about you?" she said, while they waited for him. "How did all this start? I just realized I've never asked you. In fact, I've never had a chance to talk to you alone. What made you quit your job with a big global brand and take a chance with a start-up?"

Normally, any interest in his ambitions would have excited Salil. But not today. He would rather talk about anything but that. Heck, he would rather talk about his marriage.

"You know. Everyone wanted a piece of the consumer pie. The economy was booming, the middle class had more money to spend, and everyone wanted to drink. It felt like one long happy hour." He laughed carelessly.

Priyanka nodded and waited for him to say more. Her eyes were filled with sympathy. Or pity. What was the difference anyway? They were dangerously close to telling each other their stories. It was what Salil wanted most of all. It was what frightened him above all else. Sex, one could forget. But the intimacy of shared confidences? He was the type of person who would not be able to forget that.

When the waiter arrived with the bill, Priyanka dropped two five-hundred rupee notes.

"No, no, the company can cover it," Salil protested, shoving them back into her hand.

She didn't resist, and he was relieved. Money in this city was always tight. The thought of her paying for her own drink in this overpriced airport bar filled Salil with compassion for her. In some ways, she was not unlike him. He clasped her hand.

"It was nice to see you," he said. He felt a little regret at not listening to her more closely. Priyanka and the other women. He could have listened to them all a little more when they talked to him. "I hope your nani recovers."

This time when she smiled, despite the dimples, he saw the worry in her eyes.

"Until next time." She leant over to give him a dainty peck on the cheek before leaving.

Salil hoped she hadn't left any trace of her perfume on him. If he entered his flat smelling of a woman's scent, God help him.

Outside the pub, the crowd had thickened. He stood in the middle of the throng for a few moments, wondering what to do. He had reports to write, phone calls to make. But his body still felt flabby, and now also lethargic. Maybe it was the too-early beer. Maybe that's why their sales were down. People needed to stay awake these days. You couldn't slack off for a few minutes without something going up in flames.

He walked without purpose towards his gate, past the American fast-food restaurants, the Indian ones with more elaborate menus and indoor seating, the gift stores, and the celebrated designer's boutique.

Salil glanced at the crimson-and-gold ensemble hanging in the window. Who would buy an expensive lehenga choli at an airport? Why, someone who was on her way to a wedding and had not had time to shop. A couple of uniformed salesmen loitered at the back of the store. There were no customers. Was this designer as worried about sales as he was, he wondered.

Airports had never quite lost their fascination for him. He still remembered the first time he had flown abroad. At the layover in Muscat, he had stood mesmerized in front of the rows of monitors displaying flight schedules. Arrivals and departures from across the globe. But it was so much more than just the airport. The new job with Seagram's, the crisp pastel shirt that had been ironed at the hotel and delivered to his room, the black Merc that had been waiting to pick him up outside the lobby, and the business-class lounge where he had pretended to settle in like everyone else. Salil had grown up in a strict Hindu household where his mother performed daily pujas in a flat that smelt perpetually of incense. In that airport, at the age of twenty-three, surrounded by strangers from all over the world who walked by him in jet-lagged silence, he had discovered a new religion. He became a believer. He liked to share with strangers at parties this insight: Where else in the universe did people pray as much as they did at an airport?

It occurred to him as he walked past the Swarovski store with a sparkling display in the window that this place was not very different from a mall. Maybe Ramona found the same sort of bland solace from shopping at Atmos as he did walking around airport terminals. Maybe he ought not to be so hard on her.

The last shop along the hallway before the gates was the bookstore. It looked friendlier and more cheerful than all the other places he'd just passed. The colourful paperbacks on the shelves drew him inside.

Salil had never been a literary guy. When he was a kid, he couldn't wait to go outside in their colony and play cricket or football with his friends. He had been good at English, but not exemplary. He had been captain of the quiz club and knew the first lines of all the famous old classics. But he never could finish one of them.

Now he ran a finger along the spines on the new Indian fiction shelf. They sounded stupid. *The Instagram Affair*, *Call Centre Rendezvous*, *WhatsApp Women*. What shit was this?

Harry's wife loved to read these books. He and Ramona had exchanged looks the first time they had gone to Harry's place for dinner and seen the bookshelf. Salil was glad he was married to someone who leafed through glossy magazines like *Vogue* and *Vanity Fair* rather than waste her time and his money on books like these. In the bookstore, he started to walk away, when suddenly a sunny yellow cover caught his eye. Turquoise lettering announced the title. *Your Best Life*. But it was the author's name that had drawn his attention.

He pried the book loose from the shelf to look at it closely. Rahul Sanghvi. He knew that name. He flipped to the back to see the author photo. Yes, it was him all right. The skinny, nerdy guy who used to sit in the middle of the class throughout high school. The good students sat at the front while the naughty ones sat at the back. Salil confounded teachers and students alike by sitting at the back where he could play the clown, but then going and acing all the exams. Salil had been one of the outgoing boys; a born leader, they called him. The aura he had built around him had carried him through college. It had helped him win Ramona over. He had convinced her as well as himself that he was one of them. Salil was the one who went to an elite college in Delhi. Rahul had gone to some second-rate college in the heartland and then disappeared. He wasn't even in their high school WhatsApp group now, where they all swapped lewd jokes about women.

And now here was this familiar headshot staring up at him. It was the same round, chubby face with the pointy ears and shock of curly hair that looked jet black in the photo. Did he use hair dye? The bugger had written a self-help book. Salil snorted. The cover showed the silhouette of a man seated behind the wheel of a red sports car with the top down, the type of car he had never seen on the streets of India, poised precariously on the edge of a cliff. *Your best life*. Yeah, right.

He glanced at the blurb. Why, it was not a self-help book at all but a novel. About a man who had broken free from his stifling marriage and now lived alone, travelling to wildlife parks and mountains solo. The brief author's bio stated that he had decided to 'convert his personal therapeutic experiences into an inspirational story'.

A pang of envy stabbed at Salil. Maybe all his decisions had been stupid. Maybe he should sell his share of the company after all, and instead of looking for another corporate job, perhaps he could go somewhere new and start over. He could do something with his hands like grow vegetables. Be a gentleman farmer. Start a bed-and-breakfast place in the hills. Ramona would like that, surely. She could decorate it. Maybe if he wrote a book or recorded a song or made a movie or did some other utterly pointless but romantic thing, then she would like him more.

He stared at the cover again. It resembled a poster of an old Hollywood movie. Curiosity got the better of him. He knew he would have to read the damn thing, even though it was probably a terrible book. They published all sorts of crap these days. At least that was what Ramona's pretentious friends had been talking about at their last party. That condescending friend from America and that fake Jessica, who placed books strategically all over her house to cover up her nefarious activities. And Ashok. That slimy bastard.

Salil's distaste for Ashok gave him renewed purpose. When was the last time he had purchased a sweet and foolish gift for his wife, one that did not cost a bomb and served no practical purpose whatsoever? If he ever bought her something from an airport, it would likely be a Swarovski choker or maybe even that ostentatious lehenga choli from Ritu Kumar's boutique. He would not consider buying Ramona a cheap gift like this one. Still, it might make her laugh. It might be a fun change. He slipped the book into his leather briefcase, clasped it shut, and walked out.

"Sir?"

Salil looked around.

"Sir?" the voice yelled again.

It was the guy from the bookstore.

Salil wondered if he'd left something behind. His phone? He patted his shirt pocket briskly. There it was.

The man was pointing at him and talking angrily to the people who'd stopped to watch the unfolding scene.

Salil's facial muscles slackened as realization dawned on him.

Oh, fuck.

"Here," he yelled back, quickly unfastening his briefcase as he walked forward. In his hasty effort to retrieve the book, he dropped the now-open bag to the floor. Out tumbled a sheaf of papers, a folder, pens, his iPad, and the photograph of Ramona and him from their honeymoon that he always carried with him. Shit, he muttered, crouching down to clear up the mess.

A small crowd had gathered into a circle outside the store. The bookseller was gesticulating wildly.

A man in a suit walked up to Salil with a walkie-talkie in his hand.

"Excuse me, Sir, did you take a book from this shop?"

"Yes, of course I did, I forgot to pay him."

"Forgot?" The man sneered.

"Do I—?" Salil tried to articulate his thoughts but the words wouldn't come out right. "Do I seem to you—? Do you know anything about me? I am not a fucking thief."

The man stared at him stonily.

"Here, take the book back," Salil held it out. "I don't even read this shit."

The bookseller, who had walked out of the shop, wagged a finger at him.

"You took it out of the shop, you pay for it."

"Okay fine, I'll pay. How much?"

"One hundred rupees."

Salil stared at the guy, who looked self-righteously past him.

Behind him people were snickering. One of them was a little boy. He hid behind his mother's long red skirt and covered his mouth to laugh.

All this drama for a hundred rupees. Rahul's books cost a hundred rupees. How much money was he going to make from his literary career? Then he remembered what else those asses had been saying at the party. Of course it was a hundred rupees. These were called the hundred-rupee paperbacks. They were aimed at the masses, who could read them when they were riding the local train to work, or in bed at the end of a long day. They were not going to teach these books at any American university. Nor would they discuss them at housewarming parties across Hrishipur. Jessica wasn't going to place one on her end table every time she had company. It was a book that a lot of people would read, perhaps even secretly, simply because it gave them pleasure.

Salil took out his wallet and two hundred-rupee notes.

"Here, take both. One for the book, and the other one for my mistake. Sorry, Bhai," he said. "You can tell that I am no thief."

The bookseller shook his head.

"One hundred only. You keep all your extra cash."

Salil gave him the money, and the others scattered in different directions. In a city where film shoots happened all over the place, this real-life drama would soon be forgotten. Heck, if he were lucky, some might even think this was part of a movie.

But the kid behind the red skirt had emerged now and was still giggling. Salil attempted a brave smile, then gave up and walked slowly towards gate five. The energy that had rushed through him just a couple of hours ago seemed to have oozed out, leaving him deflated.

At the gate he learnt that the aircraft would be ready to board in about forty-five minutes. He went to stand by the window. His ears still burnt from what had just happened. He looked around quickly to see if anyone was staring at him, but no one was. People appeared to have moved on to their own lives. He felt a little indignant. He wasn't even a spectacle long enough. He clutched his briefcase for support and stared out through the glass.

The tarmac outside looked indigo from that morning's downpour. While the north remained parched, the monsoon had swept the western states. As always, Mumbai was underwater. For the past few days, Salil had sat in the rented Audi as he was chauffeured around the flooded streets, and watched pedestrians wade through them. The city had never failed to amaze him, no matter how many times he visited, with its spectrum of people from dirt poor to filthy rich. He used to think Hrishipur was like Mumbai, all bright lights and dizzying buildings, corporate deals and a partially visible underbelly. But after twelve years of travelling there, he knew better. Mumbai, for all its contradictions had the old art deco architecture, the art galleries, the Irani cafés, the jazz bars. It had the ocean, however dirty that was too. And it had the rain. It was what Hrishipur aspired to be. The adolescent city, clamouring for attention, building higher and higher. Until all that was left was a cluster of unfinished buildings at various stages of construction, standing like scarecrows with empty arms and vacant gazes.

The day before, on his way from yet another meeting, Salil had asked his chauffeur to pull over on Marine Drive so he could catch a glimpse of the sunset over the Arabian Sea. Couples of all ages sat on the low wall that separated the street from the rocks on the beach. The women wore saris or salwar kameezes, while the men wore trousers or jeans and shirts that hung over their bellies. These were the hoi polloi, the middle-class residents of Mumbai who lived in the suburbs and travelled by train every day to the city to their jobs. Now they sat watching the sun set over the sludgy grey ocean without speaking. Some of them held hands.

Salil had spent three days wandering in and out of five-star hotels and the Gymkhana Club and brushed shoulders, quite literally, with people in lifts who were dressed to the nines and reeked of perfume. None of them had moved him the way these men and women did, touching one another in a world where touch was forbidden, washed out by the end of the day, sitting in silence against a backdrop of crashing waves and drifting seagulls. His cell phone had beeped, reminding him of his dinner appointment with Dubey, and he had urged the driver on with a lump in his throat he couldn't have explained to anyone he knew.

Now he stood in front of the window and watched the attendants wash one of the aircraft. Every few seconds he glanced at his phone. Ramona had not replied to any of his texts since the morning. *The flight will be late. I should be there by four. Now five. Go to the Malhotras' without me.* He typed out another one. *Guess what just happened. I almost got arrested for stealing a book.* He just wanted her to respond. He was exhausted with their quarrels.

In the last couple of weeks, Ramona had grown even broodier. Sometimes when he came home late at night, hoping she had already gone to bed, he found her sitting in the dark. When he flicked on the lamp, there she was, all dressed up, her hair in an updo, her lips painted as if she were about to step out for one of her fashionable parties. What Salil found most disturbing was the perfume. That signature Christian Dior fragrance that floated around his home. He had locked the liquor cabinet but he knew she had been drinking, more and more, because her eyes held a listless gaze as if she were looking at him but thinking of something or someone else. Instead of going to her or trying to begin a conversation, Salil had wanted to avoid her even more. He knew she needed something. Validation or reassurance that the world was still a normal place where she was a princess. Something he could no longer conjure up. Something she sought, perhaps, in losers like Ashok. In the airport lounge, Salil bit his lower lip so hard he tasted blood. When had it become like this? When had it started? When had he grown so dizzy with work and worry that he had stopped noticing what she did?

He could still summon up her face from that college fest. Not one to compete onstage, she was merely accompanying her friends. He on the other hand was on the quiz team, representing the business school. He had spotted her in the audience. It was difficult not to. He remembered her narrow cat's eyes, so strikingly light against all the black ones, and her long, slim neck.

Ramona's cold beauty had arrested Salil like it did everyone who encountered it. But few got past the reserve and the haughty smiles. Somehow, he had. And having conquered it, he had found he didn't know what to do with it. The elegance and sophistication had grown to be monotonous. The quiet underlying snobbery extended itself to her entire clan and circle of friends. He recalled the image of her father smoking his pipe on the patio of the Tolly Club in Kolkata, and of her mother snapping her fingers at the uniformed waiters to bring another gin and tonic. The clipped accents, the gold-rimmed glasses, the silk fabrics, the black-and-white photographs in silver frames. Their temperature-controlled, scented lives had both fascinated and repelled Salil. When amid them, Salil found himself yearning for his childhood friends more than ever, that gang of loud, crude Punjabi men singing and laughing over stupid jokes.

Be careful, his own father had warned when he told him of his intention to marry Ramona. *You can make a lot of money, but you will never be one of them. They are hi-fi people, not like us.* Hi-fi. Salil smiled at his reflection in the window. He had come so close to believing that he could be like that too, fit into a class of people that sounded like a sophisticated stereo.

For some reason he was reminded of Maneka. She was an odd one. Like him, she was between places, neither here nor there. Despite her occasional smirks and her intellectual snobbery, she did not quite fit in with Ramona's crowd. He had wanted very much to have a proper conversation with her at his party back in May when she had first arrived from the States. He had caught a glimpse of her standing alone, forlorn. Something about her loneliness had struck a chord in him. He knew of her recent bereavement and understood something of what she felt. He had worried so much about his mother since his father's death a few years ago. He had recognized the same look of worry in Maneka's eyes and knew she was thinking of her one surviving parent whom she would leave behind when she returned to America.

Salil had been curious about her life. She was the only person he knew who actually lived in the heartland of America, the interior region that one did not see in Hollywood movies and celebrity magazines, at least not here in India. The region that had voted for America's right-wing government. What was it like living there as an immigrant? What was it like living there after Trump became president? Of course, he had resisted the urge to ask her anything. Even so, Ramona had accused him of being interested in her when she found him looking up Heathersfield. Besides, Salil had seen Ashok sidle up to Maneka at the party and he had turned away, irritated. He had wondered if Maneka would fall for Ashok's charming socialist act. Looking at them out on the terrace that night, he had concluded that she would. All women were fools, then, no matter how many books they read.

A hand tapped him on his arm. He turned, puzzled, then looked down. It was the kid. He was standing there looking up at Salil. When their eyes met, his face broke into a grin.

"Where's the book?" the kid asked. Salil's face felt flushed again.

"You look like an uncle, not a chor," the kid said. "Ronny!" someone yelled.

Before Salil could say anything, the kid's mother rushed up, her red skirt ballooning behind her. She didn't look at Salil, but instead grabbed the boy's arm and pulled him away. As they walked, the boy turned to look at Salil again, still unable to comprehend what someone dressed like Salil, with a gold-embossed briefcase, was stealing books for.

"Hey," Salil called after him. "I'm like Robin Hood. I steal books from all over so that I can donate them to poor children in the villages." It was a good thing the boy had not seen the actual book. *Your Best Life*. And that ridiculous cover. A little nudge was all the car needed to plummet over the cliff's edge and take that prick with him.

The mother and son were greeted a few feet away by a man, husband and father no doubt, who held a baby girl. She stretched her arm out to her mother and let out a wail. The man transferred the baby to the woman, who began to slap her bottom loudly and make cooing noises.

Salil turned back to the window and pressed his face to the glass so no one would be able to see it. His shoulders heaved. He didn't know how to stop it. It was all too much. The late nights, the pressure at work, the numbers in red, the stale, freezing air of the airport, the pathetic flirting with a young girl who was as bewildered and lost in the city as he was. But none of that really mattered. What mattered was that a few months ago he was going to be a father.

His vision blurred. He had wanted a girl but he would have taken a boy too. Any child that could have belonged not just to Ramona but also to him. He would have funnelled all his hopes and dreams into the son or daughter just like his parents had done with him. Together they would have meant something.

He had wanted to tell Ramona many times since the miscarriage how he felt. His heart had broken too, not just when she collapsed on the floor in pain with blood trickling down her legs, but over and over in the days and weeks that followed. Every time Harry's kids came to the office. Every time he heard Ramona cry in the shower. Every time someone on his WhatsApp group announced the birth of another baby. He had even felt the stab of pain when the driver had told him his wife was pregnant. He had been jealous of the damn driver.

But he had said nothing to Ramona. He had not even extended his arms to try and hold her. If he had, she would have pushed him away. He had been afraid to be vulnerable. He thought of her green eyes and said softly to the window, *I'm so sorry*.

Just before he had left home for the airport on Tuesday morning, Ramona had come to the door. He thought she wanted to say goodbye. But a glance at the circles under her eyes had indicated another sleepless night. She had looked at him with such sorrow. He had thought she was sad about their marriage. But then she had spoken.

"Really? You really want to sell the flat at Trump Towers?" He had shaken his head.

"Not if you don't want me to, Ramona. You know that. If it means so much to you, we will keep it and move in there one day and make it our beautiful home. Or, if we can't afford it, someday maybe we will sell it. It will be an investment. Whatever will make you happy."

"Don't you see?" she had said. "It's the only thing to look forward to."

He had debated whether to respond or to touch her delicate, sad face. He thought it might feel like touching a flower, soft and fragile. He imagined her tears turning into petals as they reached the floor. He had decided he was losing his mind, turned around and left. He had resolved to sit down and have a proper conversation with her when he returned and had more answers from the headquarters.

Now that time had come. He would be home soon. Ramona was still his wife. Some shabbily dressed good-for-nothing lafanga wasn't the answer to her problems. He would take care of Ashok. He would go to his barsati, wherever it was, and talk to him firmly, man to man. Rajesh would show him where it was. He had seen the guilty look in the driver's eyes many a time. He would know exactly what to do.

Salil let out a slow breath. He was beginning to see again. The tears had dried on his cheeks. He wiped the trails with his sleeve. They didn't have to live in any fancy building. Moving into Trump Towers was not going to help them or anyone else feel fulfilled. Everyone knew that. It was in all the books, even the ones for children. Even Rahul Sanghvi knew that. He would tell Ramona what he should have told her while he stood in that doorway three days ago, that there was a lot to look forward to. They could go to Goa and buy a small place by the sea. Or he could look for jobs in Australia or Canada. A lot of people were moving there now. They could start over. They would try again. They would have a child. Maybe even two. Life was all about giving it a go. That was all he had ever tried to do. *Your best life*. It was not too late.

HRISHIPUR

On the morning of August 8, the residents of Hrishipur woke up and proceeded to do the same things they did every Sunday. They ordered their maids to cook a big, late breakfast of parathas stuffed with radish or cauliflower, or pooris and sabzi, or pancakes and masala omelettes. As the smells of cooking filled up their homes, they lounged in their dressing gowns and watched cricket on TV, called their parents and grandparents in other cities, and checked out the afternoon movie listings at the malls. It was the only day of leisure for many of them, for even on Saturdays most of the adults went to work while the children went to private tutoring classes or painting or guitar lessons. Today, however, the flats bustled with all family members home at the same time, all gadgets murmuring simultaneously, all cell phones beeping with texts and WhatsApp messages. It was, in short, a Sunday just like any other.

When a reporter on Prime TV declared it officially the hottest day of the year by early afternoon, people shrugged. Forty-three degrees or forty-four. It was just a number. What mattered was how they felt when they went to their windows and looked up at the sky, which was white with sunlight and smog, or down at the streets that trembled like water.

On those same streets, the invisible people of the city continued their lives without even noticing that it was a Sunday. Sweepers swept dust away from guests outside five-star hotels. Autowallahs ferried passengers to their destinations. Coconut sellers lopped off the tops of coconuts for customers driving by. Florists stood under the shade of large trees and watched their bunches of carnations, asters, dahlias, and tuberoses wilt in the heat.

By three in the afternoon, families inside their homes remembered that all their air-conditioning window units had been on without a second's pause. The electricity bills were not going to pay themselves. So they left their flats and did what any sensible person in Hrishipur would do on a Sunday afternoon in August. They went to the malls. Soon, the city's forty-five malls were all packed with bodies. There, the air changed, first from chilled to cool, and then to *at least not as hot as outside.*

It was between afternoon and evening that the city seemed to awaken suddenly from its siesta with a second wind. People poured out of movie theatres to crowd the malls' food courts. Those still at home sat on their balconies with a cup of tea and chocolate cream biscuits to watch the children play downstairs in the playgrounds. Even the maids were released to go for a stroll with their friends and catch up on the neighbors' gossip. No matter where they were that afternoon, most found it difficult to look up at the sky with their naked eyes. The surfaces of buildings shimmered in the sunlight. The entire world had turned yellow with heat. On days like these, where two million people went about their lives in a sun-induced stupor, it was natural that nobody would initially notice the sparks that flew into the air at a quiet intersection.

On the city's eastern outskirts, on the porch of a fourteen-thousand-square-foot farmhouse, the traffic and crowds felt distant. Ashok set his camera down and exhaled. From where he stood, he could see inside the floor of the hall, covered in rich, dark carpets, where the mehendi ceremony had ended a short while ago. Ladies in silk lehengas lounged on the velvet couches, their hands held out to dry the intricate patterns of henna recently painted on them. Ashok had wanted a few closeups but he was only the second shooter for the day, summoned to assist his former colleague Randeep, the wedding photographer. Randeep would take care of the artistic shots. All Ashok needed to do was follow the guests around for candid photos.

He walked down the steps and on to the gravelled driveway, away from the house. His feet hurt. He had arrived early that morning in his nice white shirt, black trousers, and Reeboks. Randeep had scowled and run to his car to fetch a pair of brown leather boots for him. *Idiot, you can't wear sneakers to a wedding,* he'd said.

Now Ashok limped in the too-tight shoes past the dramatic orange canopy of marigolds strung up across the massive lawn. For some reason, his feet reminded him of Gopal the electrician. He wondered what it must be like to go everywhere limping like this, in a city full of strong, swift-footed men.

The farmhouse stood on a wide street flanked by other such properties. Each was over ten thousand square feet and separated from the world outside by high walls. To get to Hrishipur from Delhi, you could either take the expressway out on the other side, or this quiet road where wealthy Delhiites spent their weekends tucked away with friends. And during the wedding season, when the stars aligned on the horoscopes of brides and grooms, they rented their sprawling homes out for lavish festivities that continued for days on end.

At the gate at the bottom of the long, winding driveway, a couple of armed guards lounged casually outside their post. They sprang to attention when they saw Ashok. But once he stood next to them and slouched against the wall, their bodies relaxed as they realized he was not really a member of the club inside.

"Chai, Saab?" the taller of them asked, a bit tentatively, testing the waters.

He looked like a bodybuilder. Ashok wondered if his job involved throwing unwanted visitors out of the property. He eyed the thermos flask on the stool and shook his head. It was too damn hot for tea.

"Beedi hai?" he asked instead.

The man fished out a pack of Winston Golds.

"Where did you get these?" Ashok asked.

"They bring them, Saab," the darwan said, nodding towards the house. "From duty-free."

The two of them stood in peaceful silence for a while, smoking their cigarettes. The second darwan twirled his moustache and drank his cup of tea.

"You don't feel hot drinking that in this weather?" Ashok asked.

"Helps me stay awake," he said.

"You have something else in there?" Ashok held an imaginary glass in his hand and tipped it into his mouth.

The darwans laughed together.

"Only the wedding guests can get drunk during a wedding, Saab. We have to remain alert."

Ashok kicked his boots off and stood on the scalding hot driveway in his socks, jumping from foot to foot.

"Bloody shoes," he said.

"Here, take this," the darwan offered his wooden stool.

Ashok shook his head. He wouldn't sit while they were standing. He was one of them for now. Couldn't ruin that. He would get used to the hot surface. He curled his toes and stood on the balls of his feet, which were thicker. The penance felt fair to him for the firmness with which he had broken things off with Ramona the night before. He thought of her face now, narrow and pale in the gentle light of his barsati.

She was not in love with him. Of that Ashok had no doubt. She had clung to him on the nights they had spent together as if she were drowning and he were a raft floating by. Later, if you asked her for its colour, she would be unable to recall it. She had even called him Salil once or twice, and he had felt strange. Not jealous, but as if he were inhabiting someone else's body.

The previous night, she had told him someone knew about them. Someone who wanted money from her in exchange for keeping her—their—secret. *All the more reason to end things, Ramona,* he had said as gently as he could. She had cried and begged, but he had turned away from her. And after she left, he had gone to his cupboard and taken out some of the things she'd bought for him. He had worn the Versace shorts and the Movado watch, sprayed Armani cologne on himself, and gone out to his terrace like that, smelling like an asshole, and stood there blowing smoke rings into the night air as if he could purge himself of her, of all of them. Just like he was doing now, allowing the ground to burn his feet.

They had grown numb. He could hardly feel them. He hoped she was all right. She was rich; at least richer than him. Surely, she would be fine. She had a husband in whose eyes the fire of jealousy burnt every time he looked at Ashok. Yes, she would be fine. Her feathers were a little bruised, that was all. He had told her that when he had taken her hand in his. She had always reminded him of a beautiful little bird, he had said, trying to make her smile.

The darwan was asking him something about the wedding inside. Oh, yes, he would soon have to return, before his boss noticed his absence. He didn't want to antagonize Randeep. Despite all the sneering about these ridiculous weddings, the truth was they provided a steady source of income for several weeks. You followed the bride and groom around, took pictures from every possible angle of all their costume changes, partook of the delicious catered food, and received several lakhs in exchange for the effort. It was something Ashok was thinking about pursuing more seriously, which was one of the reasons that, when a couple of women at the ceremony inside had flirted with him, he had smiled politely and walked away, pretending to adjust his lens.

In the horizon, to their right, stood the towering statue of Hanuman. The pink sculpture of the monkey god stared down at them with his eyes shut and his hand raised to bestow a blessing. How ironic, Ashok thought, that he was looking down protectively on these cloistered country villas, with his back turned to the other side where workers slept in chawls at night. He took the last puff of the cigarette before flinging it to the ground and turned to go.

That was when he noticed above Hanuman's head, directly behind him, the cloud slowly growing larger like a balloon. For a second, foolishly, he thought it was rain.

But the men chattering excitedly next to him confirmed it was not a cloud at all. It was smoke, billowing out like a giant wave.

"Something's happened," said the darwan. "Something's burning."

The sky darkened until he could see nothing else but the monstrous shape of the smoke cloud climbing higher and higher like a rapidly growing high-rise. The smoke loomed in the distance, comfortably far from these beautiful houses designed by the best architects in India. They would not burn today. No, the smoke was blowing outwards from the other side, the side that, he realized just now with a pang, had become his city, his home.

"Hrishipur," he whispered.

Inside the narrow hallway between Mrs Doshi's beautifully furnished living room and the front door, Pinky sat on the edge of a high-backed chair upholstered in pink and cream and waited for the lady to return with her money. It was hard-earned money, not something she had procured through questionable means. She deserved to get her cash after spending ninety minutes caressing Mrs Doshi's oily skin. Still, she hovered on the edge of the chair, ready to fly out any moment like a criminal.

Even though the clients invited her to sit on their furniture, Pinky found it hard to get accustomed to doing so. When she had mentioned this to Smriti, her daughter had reminded her that she was not a servant. Her children were not happy about their mother going from home to home to ply her trade. They would have been even less pleased if they knew about the envelope of cash fattening slowly inside her Godrej almirah. The extra income she was accumulating for a very rainy day. She considered that hard earned too, but her children would not understand.

In the living room, Mrs Doshi's husband and sons, all dressed identically in shorts and T-shirts, had gathered to watch TV. Pinky caught snatches of their conversations and the voices on-screen as she sat near the front door next to a bronze elephant, waiting, just like she did inside the bedroom when Mrs Doshi took a nap.

A woman of few unnecessary words, Mrs. Doshi always fell asleep after Pinky applied the mask. While Pinky waited for it to harden, she sat on a chair next to the bed, listening to her client's snores and looking idly at the objects around her. The photos on the nightstand, the clothes flung carelessly on the back of a chair, the magazines on the table, the bottle of pills next to the pillow. Pinky took it all in, searching for clues that might come in useful sooner or later. Even though Mrs Doshi was not a candidate. Not yet.

The figurine on the cabinet next to her was a glass ballerina. One leg raised up in the air, chiselled features, slender frame. She reminded Pinky of Ramona and their last encounter two days ago. She shook her head at the memory. How that pretty face had hardened as she had listened to Pinky. How her lips had pressed into a thin line as she had spoken in a hoarse whisper. *Surely you would not continue to do such a thing to me. I trusted you.* How her hands had trembled as she had fished out an envelope full of money and handed it to her. *This cannot go on.*

The maid interrupted her reverie with a glass of nimbu paani. She glanced at it and then at the maid, who smiled reassuringly. Convinced that the glass was one the maid used herself and not the Doshis, Pinky drank the sweet and tart lemonade in a single gulp.

From inside the living room, the men all yelled simultaneously. "Oh my God," one of Mrs Doshis's sons shouted out.

Pinky assumed they were watching a cricket match or a movie with a lot of fighting. Their excitement reminded her of Dilip and her son. She stifled a giggle at the thought of Jeevan and herself standing on their tiny balcony early that morning, whispering so the others would not hear them. He had shaken her awake and pressed a finger to his lips. Still drunk from sleep, she had followed him outside, where he had disclosed to her the big secret that she wasn't supposed to share with anyone yet. Not until that night when he returned with plenty of sweets for everyone. He had sought her blessings for what he was planning to do that evening.

Pinky had given him those along with a simple gold chain she had inherited from her mother on the day of her wedding. *Are you sure, Amma?* Jeevan had asked. She had nodded, unable to speak. It was time he settled down. Time he found someone who would help calm the restlessness in his breast. Even if it meant he had to move away to a bigger, more chaotic world like Mumbai, where he could earn a proper living and look after his family. His new family. She had wiped her eyes as he had slipped the chain in his pocket, and asked just one question. When would she meet the girl? *Soon*, he had promised. *Thank you, Amma. I will take care of you all now, don't worry.*

Jeevan had asked her repeatedly in the past few weeks not to continue with her home facials. *Amma, there is no need to go to people's flats. It may not be safe. You have worked for years. You can take a break now. Let Smriti and me do the work.* The arguments usually ended with him storming out of the flat, a space he seemed to enjoy less and less.

He simply didn't understand. It wasn't just about the money. Pinky didn't know what to do with herself at home when no one else was around. She felt useless and extraneous, as if she had lost her footing in society. She needed to go out and talk to people who were not related to her and who did not care about her. She needed to do things with her hands. She needed to make people feel beautiful.

Mrs Doshi returned with an envelope. Pinky sprang up from the pretty chair, feeling guilty, as if she had been caught stealing.

"Count it once," Mrs Doshi said.

"No, no, it's okay," Pinky said, putting it in her handbag and clasping it shut as if it didn't matter to her at all.

Even though Mrs Doshi always looked bored and disinterested, she had informed her WhatsApp group about Pinky's *special facials* and had even persuaded the caretaker of the building to let her post a flyer on their bulletin board. Without the clients who let her into their homes for facials that cost a third of the price at the salons, Pinky would have had no work. If they discovered her other 'job', no one would let her inside their homes. But Pinky was careful. She had selected only Ramona for now, to see how it went. It was an experiment. Ramona was not part of this circle. She lived at the other end of the city. She was too much of a snob and too worried about her reputation to share her problems with strangers. She was the perfect victim to start off with.

"Papa," one of the boys shouted from the other side of the drapes "Does Karan uncle know? He has two flats there."

"I have to call him," replied Mrs Doshi's husband. "Where's my phone? Antara, come here. You won't believe what's happened." Mrs Doshi hurried Pinky out of the door. Just before she shut it behind her, she called out.

"Oh, and remember not to eat garlic next time."

"Yes, Ma'am, no problem."

Pinky closed her eyes as she entered the lift. She had not added extra garlic to the previous night's okra sabzi, just the same as usual. Had she sighed when standing next to Mrs Doshi's bed? Was that when she had blown garlic breath into her face?

She would have to be careful.

It was only when she emerged from the lift downstairs that she switched on her cell phone. She never turned it on while in her clients' homes, not even when they dozed off, in case the light or vibrations woke them. Smriti had explained to her that nowadays customers left reviews on the internet for people to find, and Pinky didn't want to take any chances.

When her phone flickered on, she discovered numerous missed calls. *Mummy, call soon. Urgent.* They were all growing up so fast, and yet their need for her care and attention didn't seem to wane. Pinky smiled at the screen and slipped the phone inside her purse. They would have to wait, for today she wasn't going home without a treat to celebrate Jeevan's good news.

Her steps quickened with the adrenaline that always rushed through her when she left the clients' homes. The venues had changed but not the satisfaction she felt at a job performed to the best of her abilities. Perhaps one day Pinky would be popular enough to start her own little salon. Then, it would all have been worth it. Even Ramona would understand. Why, Pinky would invite her personally and give her free facials for the rest of her life. She laughed at the thought, suddenly giddy, and headed towards Metro Plaza, where you could buy everything from cell phones to homoeopathy medicine. She would get chicken rolls for that night's celebration. They were celebrating a lot these days. It felt like a new beginning.

When she got to the middle of the plaza, she paused.

People stood on top of each other's shoulders to stare at something on the horizon. More climbed up until a few men were perched precariously on each other, forming human towers.

"What's happening, what's happening?" she asked a young man next to her.

"Something happened. Don't know what. There is some smoke blowing."

Was it a bomb explosion, someone asked?

Pinky wanted very much to climb on the men's shoulders as well to see what was up. She wanted a view of something strange or interesting that she could share with her family over the special dinner that night, right after Jeevan had shared his own good news. She craned her neck, trying to look past the taller figures in front of her, until she finally caught a glimpse of the smoke that was coiling across the sky like a dark, angry snake. She shuddered.

It was an ill omen. And it seemed to be heading straight for her.

As she looked up at the desolate reddening sky, Pinky knew intuitively that this was her punishment. Her world had already begun to collapse and there was nothing she could do about it.

~

Jessica guided Titli's little hand slowly over the fortress as the two of them watched the cheerful yellow frosting curl around its perimeter. It was going to be the wall that would keep the enemies out. Titli insisted the enemies were animals, but Jessica said they were people.

"Why, Mamma?" she asked when they put the decorating tip down on the large wooden table in what they called the Cake Room. "Why not wild animals?"

"Because they are not really scary, just wild. People on the other hand can do terrible things to you."

Titli stared up at her mother with big round eyes, just as Jessica had hoped. Jessica enjoyed grabbing her attention. She enjoyed startling her. It was good to get started early. The fewer surprises later, the better.

But from the corner of the room, she felt the disapproving gaze of Zohra, the ayah, who thought, just like Jessica's mother did, that children should be protected as long as possible from the realities of the world.

"Okay, forget the creatures outside the house. They won't appear on the cake anyway. You can imagine whatever monsters you like. Now, we need to make the garden."

Titli clapped her hands in delight as Jessica brought the bowl of shredded coconut dyed green out of the refrigerator. She had kept it inside where it could retain its moisture and look like it was slick with dew. Or rain. It was, after all, a dream house.

"Can I do it, Mamma, please?" Titli asked, jumping up and down.

Jessica held the bowl for her, while Titli scooped out spoonfuls of grass and scattered them carefully on the layer of cake that lay flat in front of the house. Strands of green coconut flew across the table. Mother and daughter were making a delicious mess.

Titli had chosen the cake for her ninth birthday party to be held the very next afternoon. They had handed out flower-shaped invitations to the kids at the new school, the park, and her roller-skating class. From the Cake Room, nestled between the kitchen and dining room, if they turned around they could see the pink and purple streamers they had hung up across the front porch.

The cake looked like an English cottage, with pink fondant roses creeping over yellow walls, red doors and windows, navyblue roof, and now a grass lawn in front. Too much colour, too much joy, Jessica thought. But when Titli turned to her mother with dabs of green and yellow frosting pasted to her face and wrapped her skinny bark-brown arms around her waist, Jessica felt something move inside her.

It was the same emotion she had felt when she was coming home with her five years ago, sitting in the back seat of Sandeep's car—the first of the men from whom she'd asked a favour—the little girl clutching her hand tightly as she stared out of the car window at the magical world outside the orphanage.

And what had she, Jessica, done to this world? What would her daughter think of her when she grew up and discovered the truth their lives were built on?

She glanced over at the dining room where on the table lay the birthday present Tripathy had sent for the child from Mumbai a week ago. She wondered again where he was and why he hadn't answered her thank-you texts. It was as if he had suddenly disappeared from the face of the earth. Jessica was torn between relief and concern.

Zohra had begun to sing. She sang a folk song in her native language, Bangaal, the dialect of Bengali from across the country's eastern border that even Maneka claimed not to understand fully. The song reminded Jessica of everything she had ever lost. Her father when she was just a child, only a little older than Titli; her brother, who was here but not quite here; and her mother, whose spirit seemed to be dimming by the day. Jessica wanted Zohra to keep singing even though the sound made her heart ache.

If she had nothing else, at least she would have this. This child of her own, the cake they once baked together, the quiet humming of an old folk song from Bangladesh.

Titli was still holding on to her but her face was turned slightly. She was looking at something behind Jessica. Her mouth formed an O, the same expression she had when she saw a sparkling dress in a shop window at the mall.

"What are you looking at, Titli?" Jessica asked without turning around, reluctant to have this moment of contact cease.

"Look, Mamma. So beautiful." Jessica turned.

There, in the distance, beyond the streamers crisscrossing the porch ceiling, beyond the magenta flowers in the garden, beyond the roofs of the other houses, somewhere in the direction of the park, rose dark-orange flames.

"Oh," said Jessica. "Oh, no."

"Mamma, is that the new building?"

The most innocent of questions. Jessica stood rooted to the spot. There would be time later to think about it all. Even though her brain, forever alert, was already starting to make connections, like wires that when joined together could make sparks. A sense of dread began to creep over her entire being. She held on to Titli tightly and gazed at the flames that looked like a painting in the evening light, while Zohra's song grew louder and louder in the background, a haunting soundtrack to the scene in front of them. This moment. She felt like she was melting in the fire before them. She wanted to confess every sin she had ever committed, she wanted to say to her daughter and to her mother that she was sorry, that she wanted nothing more than to start over.

~

Only a few weeks ago, Chaya would have hated being left alone in the flat. The silence of the still afternoon would have sent her to the balcony where, despite the heat, she would have waited for Uncle and Didi to return.

But now, she stood in front of the mirror in Didi's bathroom, the one that was the most flattering of all the mirrors, leant forward, and stuck the green bindi on her forehead. She shook her braid but dared not untie it to comb it out. It was almost six. She didn't have time to sweep the floor, and it wouldn't do to have strands of hair all over Didi's bathroom. Hopefully, the bindi would distract him from the hair. The bindi and the scent.

She opened the door of the cabinet and took out the tall plastic bottle covered with pink flowers. Chaya had already sniffed it a few times on mornings when she cleaned the bathroom right after Didi's shower. It smelt sweet and fresh. A little would go a long way. And no one would miss it.

In the past, she would have felt guilty. But these days, things were different. A recklessness had come upon her recently that made her hum as she dusted the furniture every day, and now it made her pick up the bottle and spray a few drops on her green dupatta. Before Uncle and Didi returned, she would rush back to the flat to chop some onions and grind some spices, and go back to smelling like her usual self. No one would know except the two of them. She giggled with a hand over her mouth. She smelt like a flower. A flower ready to sit on the grass moist with evening dew right behind their building. She wanted to be a little late but not too much. To make him wait just a few minutes, enough to make him pace down in their special place by the gulmohar tree.

She took a last look around the flat. The laundry had been ironed and put away, the kitchen sink and counter sparkled, the dining table was covered with a fresh cloth. She couldn't cook because she didn't know what they wanted to eat. It was likely they would eat somewhere outside. Didi's remaining days here with her father were numbered, and Chaya knew he wanted to make the most of them. She closed her eyes. She would not think of sad things tonight.

She went to her room to slip off the rubber chappals she wore at home and replaced them with a pair of sandals in red and white, reserved for occasions when she would neither be working nor walking. She had a feeling her life was about to be transformed. That morning, before she began her household chores, she had received a hurried phone call from him and instructions to meet at the plot at six, for he had something important to tell her.

Chaya knew what it was. She would come back tonight and break the news to Didi and Uncle and hope they could be happy for her even if it meant she would leave them. Uncle would find someone else in Kolkata, a Bengali-speaking girl who would be able to cook all his favourite fish dishes. She imagined the look on Uncle's face when she told him, a little sad but also pleased for her. If Aunty had been here, she would have cried with joy. She had teased her about getting married for so long and threatened to find her a boy.

"I found him myself, Aunty," she whispered.

Then she flew down the stairs and along the pathways, past a blur of stones, trash cans, children, cars, and maids like herself. She thought she heard someone call her name. She thought she saw their eyes upon her. But she didn't stop to talk to them for she didn't want to deal with their affectionate teasing just now. She only wanted to see him and his crooked teeth when he smiled. All the way to the back she went, through the little gate to the adjoining plot of land that was supposed to become a gated community like this one but so far had remained just a square where cows grazed and the young maids met their lovers when they had a moment between chores. She went to their tree and stopped and looked around in every direction.

But he was not there.

She was a full fifteen minutes late. Was it too much? Had she gone too far? She looked at her cell phone and called him, but there was no response. That was unlike him.

Chaya sat down on the ground underneath the tree that had provided such ample shade on many sweltering afternoons. The air smelt of smoke. She wrapped the scented dupatta around her shoulders even though it was too warm. She noticed only now that the communal lawn of the property next door where she lived was not the same as on every other evening. Children huddled together in the middle of the lawn but they were not playing badminton. Maids whispered to each other but they were not laughing. Watchmen gathered by the gate but they were not patrolling the grounds. How could she have missed this stillness, this calm? It frightened her. Why did they keep looking at her? Where was he?

She felt let down. If he had wanted to marry her but had changed his mind, he should have told her. If he had fallen in love with another girl, he should have told her. She would have tried to understand. Indignation bubbled up inside her.

Chaya was debating whether to go or stay when she saw someone walk towards her. At first she thought it was him, but a wave of disappointment washed over her when she realized it was just Sunil, the watchman. He was walking slowly as if he was in pain. Like Gopal, he too had been commissioned to pass messages between the two of them. Chaya decided she would not accept any today, just to demonstrate her indignation.

"I have some news," he mumbled, looking at the ground.

She hugged the dupatta tighter around her and looked away in disdain.

"Very bad news. There was a fire."

"No."

Her first thought was of Uncle and Didi. Why would Sunil tell her this? What further mishap could have befallen them?

"At Trump Towers. It burnt down."

"Why are you telling me?" she cried.

"One person died." He sat down on the ground, crossed his legs like a sadhu, and looked out into the distance.

Only one of them, either Didi or Uncle. The other was alive. How would she deal with this new crisis? How would she take care of one of them? How would they go back home together to the empty flat?

"Oh, Aunty," she cried instinctively as if Maneka's mother were right next to her. Then she remembered the guard's presence. "What were they doing inside Trump Towers? I thought they went to the mall."

The guard looked confused. "Who?"

"Uncle and Maneka didi."

He shook his head. "Not them." He said a name, but Chaya clapped her hands on her ears to shut it out.

"No one knows what he was doing there, but the police will find out. They found his body. It was charred. They had to call the father to identify him."

Sunil reached out an arm and gently touched her. His face was so full of sorrow she couldn't be afraid any more. She allowed him to draw her close and rested her head on his shoulder. Around them, a sea of strange faces had gathered to whisper and point. She stuffed the dupatta into her mouth. It smelt of some unfamiliar flower. A foreign flower that did not grow here.

Chaya heard moans coming from somewhere. It sounded like a little animal in pain. She screamed, again and again, the name that had for a brief spell meant life, living, being alive. *Jeevan. Jeevan. Jeevan.*

All day father and daughter had run errands. First, they went to the local branch of the Cottage Emporium to buy last-minute gifts for her friends. Then they went to Croma Electronics despite his protests to the contrary. He didn't need a bigger TV, for heaven's sake. She had insisted that he could not continue to watch an old tube TV. *Especially since that's all you do now,* she had pointed out. They had argued about the size. She thought he needed fifty inches. He didn't see the point. *I may as well live in a movie theatre,* he had said. Finally, they had settled on a compromise and purchased a thirty-two-inch Sony, which the salesman had assured them would be delivered that evening. Just in time for them to watch *The 39 Steps*.

Now they walked across the smooth lobby of Atmos, flanked by the stores. Burberry, Fendi, Dior. In the centre of the lobby stood a red Ferrari with a bow wrapped around it. At the far end, the glass elevator glided up and down soundlessly. Sunlight streamed in through the glass roof.

"The mall is full of people and yet no one is inside the shops," Maneka said.

"No one who is here today can afford to actually buy anything from these stores. They have only come to eat at the food court, watch movies, and get away from the heat."

Samiran had a distaste for this particular mall. It was a microcosm of this city itself, which, thankfully, he would soon leave.

They managed to find footholds on the packed escalators that carried them to the top floor. It was filled with people—young couples, families, children. Among the attractions was the reason they had come: a brand new Häagen-Dazs whose window advertised a variety of specials and flavours. Tiramisu, dulce de leche, Black Forest bomb, strawberry cheesecake sundae.

Customers of all ages scrambled in front of the counter. The kids pointed and smacked the glass with their little fists. There were no empty seats inside, so Samiran and Maneka took their waffle cones out into the lobby. They sat at a table as soon as it was emptied, ignored the trash left behind on its surface, and tried to eat their ice creams before they melted. Through the window beside them the sunlight looked diluted. If they stood up, they would be able to see the buildings in the distance.

"It's good," Samiran said of his caramel biscuit ice cream.

"Ma would have liked it," Maneka added, inexplicably, flinging them both into melancholy silence.

The mall was filling up even more rapidly now. Back in Heathersfield, when Maneka went to the one mall on the edge of town, it was usually for a movie or to buy something she couldn't get online. Her colleagues never went with her. They were opposed to malls, zoos, chain restaurants, and fireworks. All the things her mother would have loved about America. Sometimes, when Maneka was feeling defiant, she would drive to McDonald's in the middle of the night to order a Big Mac and a large Coke. Sometimes she would head to the mall. There, even more than anywhere else, she felt invisible. The salespeople helped everyone but her. People looked through her as if she were transparent. Here, in Atmos, no one looked at her either, but the reasons were not the same. There she looked like no one else. Here she looked like everyone else.

"Did you buy something for Mike?" her father asked casually. He thought it important to gain some sense of what she was doing with her life, and her plans for the future, before she took off.

"I bought tea."

"Is that enough?"

"Yes, Baba. It's enough."

That was it then. A silk sachet of Darjeeling tea. A year ago, Samiran would have been relieved. The idea of this strange middle-aged man who had already been married once was not one that had appealed to him. But now, it occurred to him that the alternatives might be even worse. She could be alone over there, where he knew no one and could send no help.

"This friend of yours, Ramona? Won't you invite her for dinner once before you leave?"

"No need." What would Ramona do in their rented flat, Maneka thought. Would she speak to Chaya? Would she eat Bengali food with her hands? Would she think the bathrooms were not nice enough without tubs?

"But you have been to her place. Isn't that rude?"

He sounded just like her mother, who had forever been concerned with what other people thought. No, Maneka realized almost instantly, it was not her father. It was she herself who was worried about what people like Ramona might think. Her father was trying to be kind. Kind like Ramona.

The first time she had come to Atmos had been with Ramona. They had sipped tall glasses of iced coffee that cost more than entire meals she used to eat in restaurants with her parents back in Kolkata. She and Ramona had talked about the old times. About boys they remembered from high school, and the teachers who made them laugh and the bakery where they would eat chocolate pyramids and chicken envelopes. And at the end of it, when Maneka was quite bored and tuning out, Ramona had leant forward and asked when they would hang out again. All through this long and lonely summer, Ramona had seen her. She had noticed her, wanted to talk to her, asked for her company.

"Baba? Do you really think I should invite her?"

"Why not?" he said gently. "If she is your friend, wouldn't she want to come over?

Samiran glanced at the top of her head, bent down as she looked at her cone. Near the parting, he spotted a strand of grey hair. He inhaled sharply. Where had the years gone? What would he do when she left? Would his friends and relatives be enough?

He finished his ice cream and stared out the window at the orange light cast by the setting sun. His life had been full but it was like that sun now, on its way down, with only the cold night to look forward to.

Maneka too was looking at the orange sky. The sunsets in Heathersfield were stunning. The thought of returning to its rolling hills, wooded trails, and placid lakes in a little over a week felt surreal to her as she listened to the children yelling all around them. Some of them were pressed against the window now, looking out as if they saw something glorious there.

"You know, in Heathersfield, the entire sky turns different colours. First red, then pink, and finally violet. But I've noticed the sunset here too. Against the gritty skyline, above the city, it's not bad. Not bad at all. Look at that. Baba, look at that." She nodded towards the glass.

Something told Samiran to stand. He rose, slowly, on his achy knees.

"Mishti, that's not a sunset."

"What do you mean? That colour in the sky. It's so pretty."

He beckoned to her to join him. Together they stood with their faces pressed to the glass, like spectators watching a movie outside on a very large screen. Others watched alongside them, and Maneka felt she was part of something important. She had missed so many events in India over the years. World Cup victories, cyclones, eclipses, Diwali. Now she was in the middle of things like she belonged somewhere.

Someone in the crowd screamed. A woman had fainted.

"Everyone is screwed," said Samiran, shaking his head. "All the investors, the couples, families, everyone. Just like us."

He hoped that no one had died. If they had, it would not be an investor. It would probably be some unfortunate worker, a poor man, or woman, bound to be forgotten by next week. It was the dispensable poor who perished in such disasters.

A sadness rose from deep within him somewhere. It shocked him. When he had realized the dream of Jannat was dead, he had fantasized about something bad happening to these towers. The fantasies had involved assassinations of the American president, riots on the streets of Hrishipur by all the betrayed investors, and, yes, he swallowed at the memory, even arson. Yet now, watching the flames dance, he felt grief. It was as if the city were losing something precious.

Next to him, Maneka thought of a face turned towards the night nearly three months ago when she had first arrived here. A face that looked like it belonged to another world, a world of dreams, a world they had once shared. The face of a friend who had made her summer less long and less lonely.

"Oh, Baba," she cried. "Oh, no. Poor Ramona."

~

Gopal watched the world recede behind him. The train sped through the heartland, leaving behind a blur of mustard fields, little ponds that had dried up and turned into craters, huts with cow-dung cakes plastered on the walls, and placid grazing cows among the unkempt grass. The wind rushed in through the open windows, making his eyes burn. Or maybe they felt like that from earlier in the afternoon. An afternoon that seemed to have been years ago, in a world that seemed so distant he could barely remember it.

He had intentionally selected a compartment on this train that was mostly empty, but now it was filling up. Men and women moved about the train with their belongings tied in bundles. Children wailed. An old man with close-cropped white hair and gnarly hands lay curled up to sleep on the bunk across from him, oblivious to the sounds. From time to time, a vendor walked by, clattering his pots and pans and yelling, "Chai, chai."

For the first half hour or so, Gopal had stiffened up every time someone new passed through or stuck their head in. Every time the train stopped at a station, he gripped the seat with his hands and pressed his feet down firmly on the suitcase that lay underneath the bunk. But gradually, as the afternoon turned to evening and the sunlight became less harsh, his body loosened. Now, a couple of hours later, Gopal inhaled the scent of manure that floated in from the fields, and let his head rest against the steel bars in the window. His heartbeat had calmed down. Slowly, the realization dawned on him that no one knew him on this train. Fellow passengers and porters paid him no heed. He did not have to converse with anyone. None asked for his help. No shouts of *Gopal bhai*, *Gopal bhai*, rang out.

For the first time in over twenty years, Gopal understood that he was a free man.

Where was the city with its tall buildings rising into the sky like monsters? Where was the rush of traffic that roared night and day in the background? Images of Hrishipur were fading now. Already, that life seemed like it had belonged to someone else, to a cursed man, a man under an evil spell. Here, there was only the slight breeze and the rhythmic rocking of the train. The wide expanse of the sky called out to him. He thought he saw someone there, but was it his brother or someone else?

Gopal's left foot nudged the suitcase underneath. Everything he owned was in that case, including his share of the cash he had received from Tripathy. Its solid shape reassured him.

Always a practical man, Gopal was not given to wondering about people or things he could not see or touch or hear. It was difficult for him to imagine what Tripathy was doing right now. Perhaps he was celebrating in some five-star hotel's bar with his chamchas around him. Was he pleased with the job they had done?

They.

Gopal clutched the steel bar with his fist. A vision of Jeevan's spectral figure floated up and sat down next to him on the train.

Gopal, are you sure we will be all right?

Through the open window he got a whiff of firewood and burning flesh, that same smell he had first smelt when he was a ten-year-old boy standing in front of his brother's funeral pyre.

The odour had clung to his clothes, his hair, his skin. He knew now that this odour would never leave him. He would smell it everywhere he went, for the rest of his life, until the very day he himself lay on a pyre somewhere, burning his way to hell.

He had done his job well. Tripathy could not complain. The old, faulty wires that would short-circuit when all the lights were turned on in the main building, the damaged outlets, the malfunctioning circuit breakers, the piles of discarded newspapers in the vacant air-conditioning ducts. He had studied it all for months and executed the plan to perfection. The only thing he had failed to take into account was his accomplice's inexperience, not with electrical wiring, on which subject he had been trained for weeks, but with a life of subterfuge and crime.

His screams had made Gopal turn around, but he knew there was nothing to be done. If he had stayed to help, they would have both turned to ashes. For all the troubles he had faced his entire life, Gopal knew one thing: he didn't want to die. The world was a terrible place. But it was still better to be alive. Living meant another day when you could find a way to fight. He had limped away, his vision blurred from the smoke, the cries ringing in his ears. He had climbed over walls and slunk into the crowd and slipped into its midst. In the mayhem that followed, no one had noticed him shuffling away towards the edge of town.

Only once had he turned around to look. He was not interested in the property. He knew what fires looked like. No, what he had wanted to see was the people. Gaping, screaming, pointing. The people of Hrishipur, rich and poor, men and women, united at last. They had come together after all. This was his doing. A moment of unity. Jeevan's sacrifice was not in vain.

Next to him a woman whose head was modestly covered in her sari's pallu opened a steel tiffin carrier. Three infants gathered around her, and one climbed on to the bunk next to Gopal with snot running down his nose. The smell of aloo sabzi and fried puris filled the compartment. Gopal stared at the food, wishing he had something to eat too. He had enough cash to buy a plate of pakoras at a station. But he had dared not walk in case someone recognized his infamous gait.

He remembered how Jeevan's amma had invited him to eat with them. He resolved that one day he would return to Hrishipur to find her and ask for her forgiveness. He would return to the crowds and noise and greet them like an old friend. Who knew if the city would recognize him then? Who knew if it would even be there?

It was not his fault. He was neither a god nor a villain. He was simply a man trying to survive like everyone else. They had their skills and he had his. Someone had employed him to do a job and he had done it. That was all. In his entire life, Gopal had never intended to harm anyone physically. He had misbehaved with the women but that was only to save himself. He had never raped anyone or killed anyone. No, he had not. The entire village apart from his dadi had looked at him with fear because they thought he brought ill luck to baby Vishnu. But he had not pushed him into the well. His only crime was to exist on this earth. By his mere presence on it he had caused someone's death. Again.

The lights came on inside the train. The old man across from him stood up and yawned. He had no teeth, just like Gopal's dadi.

He would send her some more money in a few days, when he had arrived at his new destination.

In the dying light of the day, as the train sped away from the life he had known since he left his village and family at the age of seventeen, a strange calm began to overtake Gopal. The children had settled on the floor with a pack of cards. The woman was sitting at the far end of his bunk, the pallu pulled halfway down over her face, rocking slowly with the train.

Someday, the fever would return. But for now, it had been quelled. He felt no desire for acclaim or recognition. He simply wanted to blend into the night. He simply wanted to go somewhere new where no one would know him at all. Wherever he was going, there he would begin again.

Outside the train, the sky grew purple. He kept his eyes on the darkening landscape. Cities crumbled in the end. They were made by people after all, and people did not live forever. No matter how much wealth they managed to accumulate, their power was finite. Buildings would melt. Malls would sink. Rupee notes would fly away in the wind. What would remain was this. The vast sky and the earth beneath it. They belonged to no one. No builders or politicians or businessmen or even electricians could destroy the land itself. In the end, they would perish and it would outlive them all.

~

Ramona shook the remaining drops from the Smirnoff bottle into her glass and surveyed the liquor cabinet to her right, but as had been the case in the past few months, Salil had locked it and taken the key. She glared at the bottles of Black Diamond—blended whisky, rum, and vodka—behind the glass door with a sense of both longing and despair. The bottles were like her, shiny and trapped. She imagined herself picking up the crystal vase on the dining table behind her and slamming it with all her force into the glass.

Then she turned and went into the master bedroom, where she mostly slept alone now. From underneath the bed, she dragged out the suitcase Salil never opened. He had reprimanded her for that sort of sentimental crap. *You have to stop wallowing*, he had said.

Ramona pushed aside the soft baby clothes, the baby books, rattles, and other toys, and the stuffed elephant from Maneka that had recently been relegated to this jumbled mess. She dug with her fingers until they touched the bottles that lay at the bottom of the luggage. The gin was too mild. She needed something stronger today. She took out the tequila and wondered what it would be like to drink it straight from the bottle. But that was not her style any more than smashing things.

She poured herself a glass and carried it back to the living room, where she sat on the white leather couch with her legs crossed as if she were entertaining someone. That was, after all, one of the reasons they had chosen to rent this place out of all the ones they had looked at. So they could entertain and network. Magnolia Gardens was within walking distance of Atmos and the Monsoon Palace. You could see the expressway from the windows, but the immediate surroundings were quiet and residential. It was near the entrance to Hrishipur, which made it easier for people from Delhi to visit them.

Ramona looked around the living room to try and find something she could hold on to, something that would give her hope. But on this afternoon, all she could see was the black and white furniture she had so carefully selected for an understated classic look. The other things—the pink throw, the oil painting above the sofa, the yellow cushions, every object chosen deliberately to set off the contrast against the backdrop—seemed like pathetic attempts to infuse colour into an essentially bland existence.

The tequila burnt her throat and, somewhere inside her body, it mingled with the vodka she had already drunk a little earlier. In front of her lay a few coffee-table books. Ramona leant forward and fondled the newest addition, a collection of photographs by Annie

Leibovitz. She had read all about her and purchased the book for Ashok's birthday. She liked to give him beautiful gifts. *Had* liked. She stood up and walked across the room, back and forth, barefoot. The marble floor felt cool. She shivered and turned the AC off. The room was chilly, like a refrigerator preserving everything from the oppressive heat outside. The velvet curtains were drawn, shutting out the harsh light. It was too dark here, too cold. Like winter in some European country. Or Heathersfield. Ramona wondered again if Ashok was sleeping with Maneka. But Maneka was so serious. Could she be as passionate, as fiery, as Ramona? But maybe she had learnt things with the white men.

If she could have blamed Ashok for ending things, it might have been more bearable. Anger, an emotion that did not come easily to her, would have given her strength. But she knew that he was right. Especially now, with that slithering woman from the spa who had the audacity to threaten her with exposure. The very idea of Pinky standing there, not even looking her in the eye, and *threatening* her. Threatening *her*, Ramona. She had trusted Pinky. It had never occurred to her that someone like that could exert any power over her. Her mother had been right all along. You could not trust the servants.

Ramona did not care as much as Pinky imagined about blackmail. Things were already pretty bad between her and Salil. Heck, he might even be pleased that she had found someone, leaving him free to do whatever he wanted with whomever he wanted. Except she had not found anyone. Even Ashok had left her. Even Ashok. A man, a boy, she had not even been able to love. But the humiliation of being spurned by a boy, likely for her friend, no, not even a friend, an acquaintance, a girl whom no boy would have looked at a second time when Ramona was in the room. Back when they were sixteen.

The flat was too spacious for just two people. There should have been more of them. There should have been children. How could a couple who never touched each other any more possibly live in this flat that resembled a chessboard for the next God-knew-how-many years?

Then she remembered that they wouldn't live here for much longer.

Ramona put on her pumps, slid the french door aside, and walked out on to the terrace, where she always felt better. One of the advantages of living on the fourteenth floor was that they were sheltered from the sounds and smells on the ground. It was always peaceful up here.

The instant she emerged out in the open today, she was struck by a blast of hot air. It was nearly six in the evening and the light had paled, but it was still warm. And there was something else. The smell of a bonfire like the ones they used to light on the lawns of their old school in the winter.

She looked over at the city skyline that had so charmed her when they first moved here. Even though she would have preferred to live in Mumbai or New York, there had been something about Hrishipur. *Potential*, her father had said, after he first met Salil, trying to placate her sceptical mother. *He has potential.* And so did this city with its rapidly expanding skyline, its steel and glass buildings that aspired to be a hub of modernity in an ancient country. Ramona had been in love with Salil then, and he with her, and the future was theirs.

Now the buildings looked hard and unfeeling. They reminded her of Salil's face every time she talked about the baby. How he set his features tightly to act tough. He thought she didn't know how he grieved. All she wanted was to touch him but he wouldn't let her. She had gone to Ashok because she wanted to hold someone, to feel like she was mothering someone. He allowed her to feel like she was, for the first time in her life, in charge.

But he too had tired of her. What had he said? She was like a bird. He had talked about feathers and wings. If she were a bird, she would fly right off this terrace. Ramona placed the empty glass in her hand on the wall, where it balanced precariously. With one flick of her fingers, she could knock it over and send it crashing down fourteen floors below. But she knew she wouldn't do that. She was too weak to make a noise. She was a perfect little lady, just like her mother had been, sitting daintily on that swing in their verandah, and just like her snooty sister in Singapore with her chichi ways and her fake British accent. They were all like the figurines her mother liked to collect. If Ramona was a bird, why, then, Ashok was right. Her feathers were bruised and her wings were broken.

Down below, figures of men and women ran to the gates. Something was happening. She heard a faint cry from where she stood. She longed suddenly to know what it was. FOMO. That's what it was, the term all the young people were using nowadays. She was afraid of missing out. She had felt like that for years. She wanted to yell to them and ask what was going on. Why were they running?

She ran in the same direction as they did, to the west of the terrace where the sun had nearly set. There, every night since the miscarriage, even before they made the investment, Ramona had gazed out at the flickering gold sign. But tonight, when she looked, the familiar letters did not look back at her. Instead, what she saw was a magnificent sight.

Seven towers named after seven rivers were now engulfed in flames. That morning, they had all been freshly painted, a beautiful shade of aquamarine, the colour of water in this dry land. In one of those towers, Danube, the beautiful blue Danube, was the imaginary flat in which Ramona and Salil were going to begin their new life.

Her head spun from the heat and the tequila. She leant forward just a little bit more and then a little bit more. She hugged the wall in front of her that came up to her waist, and felt the leaves of the plant perched on it brush against her skin. She thought she heard someone call her name. Was it Ashok, who had so callously cast her aside? Was it her parents, who had transferred all their snobbish expectations to her? Was it Salil, who had warned her that Trump

Towers was not where their happiness lay? Had he known something she hadn't? Had he set fire to her dreams?

She heard the voice again. It belonged to an unborn child, a baby whose sex was unknown. Their little androgynous baby. Mamma, mamma, it cried. In the distance, high above the fire, she saw a gold sign once again, teasing her, calling out to her. And she heard the beautiful girls sitting in a circle around her, chanting her name. You can do it, Ramona, they cried out. You can do anything you want.

She closed her eyes and saw the gold sign again, a flash of light in the western sky that burnt burnt burnt as she leant over the wall and released herself into the air like a strong, fabulous bird that could fly anywhere it pleased.

Salil leant back in the soft leather seat of the car. The pollution was already making his throat scratch. He missed Mumbai's humid air. The traffic had slowed to a snail's pace. Rush hour in Hrishipur continued until eight or nine as folks made their way home after another long day. The odour of smoke intensified.

In the front seat, Rajesh, who seemed more sullen today than usual, coughed. Salil hoped he did not have tuberculosis. In the villages, nearly everyone had a trace of TB in their lungs, lying dormant for years until it met a city person like Salil.

The sky looked strange. It was redder now than it had been even a few minutes ago. He felt a growing sense of unease. They had sat there in the traffic jam for nearly forty minutes, with very little movement. People were now getting out of their vehicles and walking about. There was a kind of restless impatience in the air.

Suddenly, Rajesh sprang up. Other drivers also rushed out of their vehicles and yelled to one another in a unique show of solidarity.

"Saab, dekho," Rajesh pointed to the horizon.

Black smoke blew across the sky like a veil. When it lifted, Salil saw the sky was crimson. Flames leapt out from behind buildings.

Salil climbed out of the car into a world that had turned blazing hot and allowed himself to be pushed along with the human traffic, farther and farther, until they reached a clearing in the road. All of Hrishipur seemed to be crammed into the small square space. Young boys climbed on to each other's shoulders. One young man climbed on to the roof of his silver Honda Jazz. The flames were now leaping higher and higher. As Salil watched, a slab of stone slipped and fell to the ground, and suddenly there it was, the property engulfed in flames now in full sight. A collective gasp went up.

Salil stood mesmerized, staring at the sight in front of him, even as the story began to circulate like the smoke through the air. It had all started sometime that afternoon with an electrical short circuit in the basement parking lot. The fire had spread rapidly, aided by the soaring temperature outside and the arid conditions. The site had been nearly deserted thanks to it being a Sunday. Only a couple of darwans had been at their post. One had been napping in the shade, while the other rose periodically to do his rounds, which was when he discovered the smoke.

Some were saying the electrician, Gopal, had come in that morning to leave some wiring supplies. The first darwan had been surprised to see him on a weekend, but he was a jovial chap who got on well with everyone. They had exchanged a little banter before he let Gopal and his assistant in. But they had not seen either of them exit through the front gate. Someone said he must have climbed over the back wall. But then he had that limp. Someone else said he might be dead. No, it was not he who was dead. It was the assistant. One person had burnt to a crisp. The father had been summoned to identify him. People guessed he was a Muslim chap. You could never trust those guys.

Anyhow, there had been a fire. It was now leaping over the city. The most prestigious property in Hrishipur was swiftly getting gutted.

The sun had set behind the buildings, where it could no longer be seen but where it still left enough daylight to make everything visible. But the glow from the fire made the sky seem bright, almost phosphorescent. Swirls of black smoke flew through the air, which now smelt of burning paper.

Then someone cheered. Others followed. A loud, collective roar of approval went up. The fire trucks had apparently arrived on the scene. They were out of the line of vision but their presence was signalled by the spray of water that rose up through the smoke. It looked pitiable against that blaze.

Salil sat down in the middle of the road. All around him were pairs of shoes and sandals and chappals on people's feet. The asphalt was still hot to the touch. He was not thinking of the money. Or of the floor plans or the company or the loans. There was only one thing on his mind.

His hand went to his shirt pocket of its own accord, took out his phone, and texted Ramona. *Home soon. Stuck in traffic on Gandhi Marg. Massive fire. Do not worry. We will figure it out together. We will be fine.*

As if on cue, a shattering sound pierced the air. Then, a chorus of cheers. He looked up. The giant black sign with the gold letters had come unhinged and was dangling precariously from the side of the building. *Trump Towers*, it screamed sideways and swayed in the breeze generated by the hoses that were now spraying water on the walls. Salil gazed at the sign, unable to look away, as it swung like a slice of the property itself that had come undone.

How many times had he looked up to see that sign loom high above in the sky?

They always said in the movies that your life flashed before your eyes when you lay dying. Now, the life of this construction flashed before Salil's eyes. The initial advertisement in the papers, the excitement generated among developers and investors in the city, the launch at the Monsoon Palace, the visit by the American tycoon's son to promote the property, the gradual rise of the buildings, inch by inch. All of this had happened against a backdrop of stalemate among the Indian developers. Other constructions had stalled, while this one had simply kept going. In a city of broken dreams, this sign had been steadfast. A promise that would not be broken, because it was American. And now, here it was, a smouldering chunk of metal with the letters melting into oblivion one by one. *Rump Towers. Rum Towers. Rum Owers. Um Owes. U O.*

He glanced around at the crowd that had now begun to disperse quietly as if they were leaving an open-air concert. A surreal silence had descended upon the scene. This was not normal for a place where a slight delay at a traffic light led someone to draw out a gun and shoot people dead.

The air was thick with smoke. The lights on either side of the street had begun to come on. In the pink glow of dusk, Salil saw the faces of the residents of Hrishipur. The entitled sons of businessmen, their drivers, the rickshaw-wallahs, shopkeepers who had rushed out of their stores, vendors from the bazaar nearby, janitors and maids who cleaned the malls and office buildings, managers and executives who were headed home, young kids on their way back from coaching classes. Irrespective of age, gender, or class, their bodies drooped and their faces were bent to the ground. All around him Salil felt the pall of gloom. He glanced back at his phone, expecting a flurry of texts from Ramona. But there were none.

Salil yearned to be home in a way he had not for a long time. But Ramona had not replied. He tried to rationalize. Maybe she hadn't yet heard about the fire. Maybe she was still angry with him. A little bile crept up his throat. What if she were off with Ashok?

He was in shock, he told himself. He just needed to go home and take a shower and then sit down with his wife and talk to Harry. *It's just money, man, come on*, he told himself. *Just like everyone else in this city who never got the flat that was promised to them. Now you know what that feels like, you bastard.*

When he climbed back into the car, Rajesh was already waiting to drive him home. His face was even more glum than before. He was probably wondering if Salil would fire him that same night. How could he possibly afford a driver now?

By the time they got out of the main thoroughfare and on to the side streets, it was completely dark. It took them over an hour to leave the offices and malls behind and turn into the residential part of town. The commotion seemed almost forgotten here, as if the middle-aged man walking his dog or the two women in track pants taking a leisurely stroll down the road were unaware of what had just occurred in the other part of town. Salil picked up his phone to call Harry, but the black screen stared back at him impassively. The phone had died, and who could blame it?

"Charger hai?" he asked Rajesh.

The driver shook his head. Goddammit, where was the car charger when you needed it? He leant back and rubbed his forehead to try and ease away some of the tension. On the front passenger seat, Rajesh's phone buzzed, but the driver made no attempt to answer it.

"You don't want to see who is calling?" Salil inquired.

"Better not talk on the phone while driving, Saab," Rajesh replied. It was the first time he had ever given Salil advice.

Salil patted him on the shoulder.

"You are right, Rajesh. Better not."

They exchanged a glance in the rearview mirror. The cops were getting stricter now. Gone were the days when you could slip them a couple of hundred-rupee notes and keep talking on your phone. Now they wanted thousands. Rajesh understood that Salil did not want to pay anyone anything if he could help it, that he didn't want to spend one more rupee on anything he didn't need. Salil was comforted by his driver's presence inside the car, and grateful not to be alone tonight.

"Wait, stop," he said suddenly.

The car screeched to a halt. On the sidewalk stood a florist with a few buckets of flowers. Salil stepped out of the car.

The darkness smelt sweet. Faint lamplight fell on the sidewalk from a lantern that hung from a branch overhead. It had been a very long time since Salil had bought flowers for anyone. He peered at the buckets. There were roses and carnations, and tall lilies. Ramona loved lilies. Salil had told her once, many years ago, when she stood sniffing them after he had bought her a bunch, that she looked like a lily herself.

"How much are the lilies?" he asked the young man, who stood watching him with great interest.

"Fifty rupees, Saab."

"One dozen?"

"No, Saab, one."

Salil stared at him. The boy stared back.

"Fifty rupees for one lily?" he asked.

"Yes. Half dozen for three hundred."

"And the roses?"

"Thirty for one."

"Carnations?"

"Twenty for one."

"But carnations don't even have any smell."

The boy shrugged. No doubt he thought Salil a fool, standing there in his polyester shirt that now clung to his back, his silk tie, and his polished brown leather shoes by Salvatore Ferragamo that he had purchased on his last business trip to Paris. If only he knew just what a great fool he had turned out to be.

It occurred to Salil that his driver couldn't afford to buy flowers for his wife. What did he do when he needed to give her a present, he wondered. On her birthday, for instance. Or when a tragedy struck and he needed to comfort her?

Salil examined the flowers again. They didn't look very fresh, which was not surprising, considering they had been standing out in record heat all day. The petals of the roses looked withered at the ends. The stems of the white rajnigandhas drooped. The flowers seemed to be apologizing for the state of the world.

"Two dozen roses. And give me the tiger lilies too."

"How many, Saab?"

"All of them."

The boy ran off to count them.

That was when Salil noticed the prearranged bouquets. An assortment of particularly colourful flowers, red roses, yellow sunflowers, pink gerberas, tied together with a purple ribbon and packed into cellophane. He couldn't imagine the look on Ramona's face if he gave her these.

"Give me one of those too," Salil said to the boy.

Back inside the car, he handed the colourful bouquet to Rajesh.

"Give this to your wife," he said.

Rajesh placed it on the seat next to him without saying a word. Not even thank you. Salil didn't mind. He guessed the driver was in shock too. He had heard him boast to other drivers that Salil saab had booked a flat *there*.

They heard sirens as they turned on to their street. Salil's first thought was of another fire. He hoped it was not in his building.

They couldn't lose their rented flat too.

They were just outside the formidable iron gates of Magnolia Gardens when they saw the crowd. Whatever had happened inside the gates had spilt out to the streets. At first Salil thought it was a delayed reaction to the fire, but all the other complexes on the street were quiet and undisturbed. Something was very odd about the crowd. No one was yelling or speaking loudly. It was silent.

Someone in the crowd noticed the BMW and whispered to the man next to him. The crowd parted for Rajesh and Salil so they could drive into the building. The darwans were absent from their posts. For some reason, this annoyed Salil. Whatever had happened, the situation would be easier to control if the men stayed at the gate. Anyone in this crazy crowd could barge inside and make their way up to the flats. It was not safe to leave the gate unmanned. He wanted to get out and complain to someone about this. He recognized a few neighbours. They saw him inside the car and stopped their conversation. Salil waved to them but they did not respond. Instead, they just stared at the car as if they had never seen anything like it before.

The door opened and arms reached out to him. Strangers were speaking, all at once, and trying to surround him. He felt as if he were inside a riot. He felt suffocated. It was hard to breathe. It was hot too. Hotter even than it had seemed when he was looking at the fire. He saw it once again in his mind's eye, leaping hot and red towards the top of the building. He thought he saw it reach the wide terrace outside his flat, ready to engulf those inside. He wanted to scream out a warning to Ramona so she would manage to escape. He did scream out her name, and then his legs gave way. Someone propped him up. But Salil barely knew the neighbour. He needed a friend.

"Rajesh," he cried out.

The driver put an arm around his shoulder. He walked like that, on shaky legs, towards the police who were waiting for him with clipboards and pencils.

MANEKA

In the middle of the night, when everyone else was asleep, Maneka sat cross-legged in front of the moss-green steel trunk, its lid propped open against the wall and its contents spilt out all around her. This trunk had rested under her parents' bed until she arrived, as if her father had felt the need to guard it with his body as he slept. But Maneka remembered the trunk from Kolkata, where it would lie in a closet, packed with their woollens, emerging annually for the mild, fleeting winters of the east. It still smelt of mothballs.

She had sifted through the contents all summer with the wonder of someone browsing treasures in an antique store. The black-and-white photographs from the years preceding her that stuck together and had to be prized apart. The colour photos from her childhood that lay inside tacky albums with pictures of flowers on the covers. The loose pages from a grandaunt's diaries that had recorded the events of her parents' wedding. A hardbound copy of *Mrs. Beeton's Book of Household Management* whose pages had yellowed with time. Old tapes with recordings of her grandmother's voice singing the songs of Rabindranath Tagore as she played the organ. Recipes torn from women's magazines. A crocheted tablecloth. These were the relics of a traditional Bengali family and the life of a woman who had married young and dedicated herself to the well-being of her husband and child. Of someone who had followed, unquestioning, the path laid out for her.

And then there were the other objects, souvenirs of a life that Maneka had not known.

She skimmed through the French certificates her mother had received for each level she passed at the Alliance Française, back when Maneka was in high school. She had a vague memory of her mother sitting hunched over the dining table to study for tests, with books spread out around her. Were they the same as the ones lying around her now? Or were they more advanced?

Were they textbooks like this one that conjugated verbs with colourful illustrations, or were these for much younger learners? Was one of them this dusty copy of the collected poems of Baudelaire? Or this illustrated edition of *Le Petit Prince*? Maneka had loved literature all her life, ever since she was a little girl sneaking away on hot, sunny afternoons to the window seat to read storybooks when she was supposed to be napping. Why then had she never talked about these books with her mother? Her mother, who did not after all have a secret life. She was right there, living in the same home, doing her homework in the next room. And yet she could not recall offering her mother any words of encouragement on the day of her oral exam. She could not remember a single conversation about the other students in her mother's classes or the names of any of her teachers.

What she did remember was the beautiful girls stretching out on the dew-slick grass of the school lawn, their laughter floating in the breeze as she walked past. She remembered Ashish, the boy with whom she had exchanged her first kiss one afternoon in the middle of a school dance, and how dark it was under the stairs.

She remembered the things her mother would cook for her when she herself had to stay up all night to study. Aloo parathas, fish sandwiches, dahi vada, chow mein. She remembered the fuss her mother made over what Maneka ate during her school exams, year after year, half-yearlies followed by finals, each one a stepping stone to her future, glittering and without limits.

She opened the notebooks filled with French words in her mother's neat, elegant handwriting. Maneka had resisted learning this language because she knew the arguments would shatter any peace between them. Her mother would have corrected her pronunciation or offered advice, clicking her tongue in impatience. Sooner or later, a door would have slammed or a book would have been flung across the room. It had not seemed worth the inevitable friction. And, if she was being honest, the disappointment on her mother's face every time Maneka told her she wasn't interested in learning French had offered her a perverse satisfaction.

She thumbed through the pages now, unable to read or decipher the text. Her mother's life had turned into a foreign language.

The mess of papers included flyers and brochures for events, a school diary, and cards from students. She opened one, a typical Hallmark greeting card with a bouquet of flowers on the cover. Inside, it said, in a messy scrawl, *Dear Roy Ma'am, you have been my favourite teacher. Thank you for everything. Love, Sonal.* It was the type of message Maneka herself had given to her teachers before leaving her old school. She wondered if Sonal said the same thing to all her teachers or if she had sincerely liked her mother the best. And if so, why? Didn't her mother ever scream or break anything at school? Didn't she call the students monkeys or, even worse, slum children? Didn't she ever gather up all her belongings and leave the room in the middle of a lesson, slamming the door behind her so the sound reverberated throughout the building?

Roy Ma'am. What a strange way to address your teachers. They never did that back in Kolkata. There they said Mrs Mazumdar,

Mrs Soni, Mrs Mehta. And the handful of pitiable unmarried ones were Miss D'Souza and Miss Banerjee. This must be a North Indian thing. Roy Ma'am. French teacher at Royal Valley School, founded less than a decade ago, in a city that Maneka had not even heard of when she was in school herself. An avatar of a person she used to know so well.

She picked up a photo of Roy Ma'am in a classroom. In the photo, the teacher stood in the middle of the room, wearing a white sari with a red border and a scarlet bindi on her forehead. Roy Ma'am beamed at the camera, her face alight with joy. Her arms stretched wide to encompass the group around her, young boys and girls in their white uniforms all standing around their French teacher. On the wall behind them was a sign that read *Standard Nine*. The students were about fourteen then—as old as the beautiful girls had once been. But for all their Halloween parties and foreign trips, the expression on the faces of these kids was not one of entitlement or disdain. It was nothing like what Maneka had remembered all these years. The teenagers looked innocent and hopeful. As if everything would work out in the end. It was faith in a world that for them had always been, more or less, benign.

Everyone looked at the camera except this one boy in the back, who gazed at Roy Ma'am. Perhaps he was about to ask her a question. Perhaps he was in awe of this Bengali lady who was older than all the other teachers, who wore saris unlike the others, and who had suddenly started teaching in her fifties, at a time when everyone else was preparing for mandatory retirement. Or perhaps he was simply having a rough day and wanted to give her a hug and bury his head in the folds of her sari because she looked like someone's mother.

The memory of an evening from Maneka's childhood emerged like a cold blast from the air-conditioning vent, slowly at first, then gradually taking over the room. She is little that evening, seven or eight years old, and she is hungry. She wails for a snack, prompting her father, a typically taciturn presence on weeknights before dinner as he tries to recover from the day's corporate dealings, to lift his face from between the folds of the newspaper. *Why don't you give the child something to eat when she's hungry?* The living room's pale yellow walls close in, and the sound of the news anchor's clipped accent on the black-and-white TV in the corner grows louder. Her mother gets out of her chair without looking at anyone, slips on her sandals, opens the door, and does something she has never done before and will never do again. She leaves.

Hours later, long after her father had gone to bed, Maneka listened to the key turn in the lock and sobbed with relief into her pillow. The next morning, no one spoke of the temporary disappearance. The days and months passed and turned into years, and her mother never went out alone again except to run an errand. Not until she moved to Hrishipur.

Maneka had called her mother one night after she first moved to Heathersfield. She had only just begun to discover the winter that poets in the West had always written about. She spent the season by herself indoors, too afraid of the weather to venture out. That night on the phone, she told her mother that perhaps she had made a bad decision. Perhaps she should never have left her own country or embarked on this wild adventure. Perhaps she ought not to have broken up with her first boyfriend. Or the second one or the third. She had listed all the mistakes she had made.

Mishti, you cannot look back, her mother had said. *You can only look forward. You can only move in one direction.* Then, after a long pause, she had added, *You are very fortunate, Mishti. I would have done anything to have your life. That was why I was able to let you go even though it felt like one of my limbs was being torn from me when you left. So that you might experience all the things I could not.*

Maneka had finally asked her then the question that had haunted her for years. *Where did you go, Ma? That night when Baba got mad at you for not having the dinner ready for me? Do you remember that night?*

Of course I remember. I just walked around, one street after another, along the sidewalks. I wanted to go away for a while but I had nowhere to go.

There was one thing her mother had not been right about. You *could* look back, even as you kept travelling forward.

Maneka would never understand everything about her mother or even about herself. That was what essays were for. In French, the language her mother grew to love late in her life, the word *essay* meant to try. For months she had resisted this. The book she needed to write. Not about a country at all, but about a person who was no longer there but who might live on through her and her words. Her mother would continue through her, for that's what mothers did. If they stopped, the daughters carried on. But if the daughters stopped? Why, then the world would have to come to a standstill. "Oh, Ramona," Maneka whispered. "If only we had talked more."

She placed the materials back into the trunk. The flat was quiet, the air still. Her fingers were coated in dust. She shut the lid and rested her face on its surface. The scent of mothballs enveloped her, and for a moment, she was a child again.

Her father went everywhere with her that week. His eagerness to drive Maneka to shops, help with packing, and provide food she may have forgotten to eat in the last three months drove her a little crazy, but that week she refrained from complaining or criticizing. That week, her thoughts were blurred, the contours of their shapes indistinct.

They bought things that might sustain her on the long winter nights that lay ahead. Boxes of flaky, sweet soan papdi, a jar of fiery red chilli pickle, packets of sweet and sour churan candy. They ordered her favourite foods, thus ensuring a nonstop feast. Idli and dosa, kababs and kormas, jalebis and kulfi. By this time, Maneka had grown weary of the spices and grease. What she craved now was a salad, made from homegrown lettuce and cherry tomatoes, mint from a pot on the windowsill and fresh mozzarella. But she didn't have the heart to disappoint her father and so she ate it all, stocking up like a camel, aware that in a couple of months, she would miss these same foods.

She went to Diva for one last facial and upgraded it from fruit to floral. One final indulgence with crushed rose petals and jasmine-scented creams. She inhaled the fragrances as she lay alone in the cold, still beauty room, left to her own devices with a mask on her face applied by the unfamiliar facialist, Rosie. Rosie was polite and full of questions about America. But she never talked about her own life and didn't like the smell of fish. On her way out, Maneka stopped to say goodbye to Mrs Khanna, who fawned over her like an affectionate aunty.

"Do you know where Pinky is these days? Is she all right?" Maneka asked.

Mrs Khanna's smile deepened.

"We don't really pry into our employees' lives once they leave here. Pinky and Diva have terminated their arrangement. I do hope you will come back and see us the next time you're in India. Perhaps you can try one of our gold packages then."

Throughout her last week in Hrishipur, Maneka saw the colours of the Indian flag everywhere she went. Independence Day decorations were scattered across the city like confetti as if to help cover up something. Plazas were festooned with ribbons in saffron, green, and white. Tiny flags hung in a canopy over the streets like paper boats, and larger ones fluttered on the branches of trees like lanterns.

Underneath those decorations, the city looked just like it had back in May when she had first arrived. The residents went about their lives as if nothing had happened. Cars still blared their horns at each other to get out of the way, swerving across the white lines that were supposed to signify lanes. Fat hogs still grazed at the heaps of rubbish piled up in street corners. Billboards still crowded the facades of every mall. Concrete and steel buildings still rose into the sky in clusters, allies looking to each other for comfort.

But just because the city looked the same as before did not mean it was unchanged.

The smell of smoke lingered in the air like it did in Heathersfield the day after a barbecue. Maneka could not tell if the smell was real or imagined like the shadow pain of an amputated limb.

On the way back from one final shopping trip, her father stalled the car on Omega Road, where, cordoned-off from the rest of the world with yellow tape, lay the charred remains of Trump Towers. It felt strange to call it by that name now that the sign was nowhere to be seen. Maneka wondered if it had melted. There was an empty space where it used to hang day and night, radiating with such bravado. She rolled the window down to let the odour of burning leaves crawl into the car.

"Nothing left. They did a good job. All that investment now gone." Her father stroked his chin thoughtfully. "It was coming up too fast. Everything good is worth waiting for."

Maneka had a vision of Halvard Solness climbing to the top of his steeple. There stood the master builder, atop the sign, wrapping his arms around the gold letters, suspended in time before the fall to his death. *But he mounted right to the top. And I heard harps in the air.*

There were already talks among the developers of starting over. They had reassured the investors they would get their flats, if only they were willing to exercise a little patience. In the meantime, they would all receive some compensation.

Maneka couldn't remember the name of the person who had died in the fire. It had appeared in the news for exactly one day before being replaced by other casualties elsewhere in the country. She hoped his family would be compensated too, but so far it seemed unlikely since he was a suspect in the arson case.

"Who do you think that chap was who died?" she asked her father. "And why would he do such a terrible thing?"

Before her father could answer, the chanting reached their ears. It took her a second to recognize the sound. *Bam Bol. Bam Bam Bol.* Then she saw the men, some alone and others in pairs. Their poles slung across their shoulders, heavier this time, for they carried pots full of holy water. Their mission had been accomplished, but they still needed to make their long way home to their villages in Bihar. The Kanwariyas kept their eyes on the road as they walked, either accustomed to the heat or determined to ignore it. Their saffron clothes a ribbon of fire down the street. As they passed directly across from them, Maneka thought she saw one of them glance up at the remnants of Trump Towers.

"Roll up the window," ordered her father from the driver's seat on the right, wiping the sweat from his brow. "It's not safe." He waited for the men's voices to die in the distance before starting the car again.

"It's very humid this week," he continued. "The dry heat was better."

"It's to help you get acclimatized back to the clammy nights of eastern India. You should get ready for coastal weather," Maneka teased.

His laughter sounded carefree to her ears. She had missed the sound. It sprang from so simple a source, somewhere deep inside her father. It sounded like relief. The thought of going back home. "The next time you visit, you can experience the monsoon," her father said as he drove away from the cordoned off property, past patriotic balloons strung across the facades of Subway, Chili's, and KFC.

"Baba?" she asked as a last-minute whim took hold of her. "Can we stop at McDonald's?"

"If that's what you want," he said.

They split a spicy McPaneer burger and a green chilli kabab burger. She would never be able to admit this to her friends back in America, but they were both delicious.

Over mouthfuls of french fries, her father told her about his plans.

"Ashish Jethu has looked at some flats for me. He will send me a list tomorrow. Most of them are in South Kolkata. There are a lot of new properties there now, where the old houses have been torn down. But I asked him to try to find me something like our old home. Not too new. Not in a neighbourhood full of upstart non-Bengalis. Then I may as well just stay here."

"People are looking for flats for you?" she asked.

"Yes, all of them. Bikram knows someone who is looking for a reliable tenant. His flat has a nice terrace attached to it. But it does not have a room for Chaya and also it is near Park Street, hence out of my budget. Munai said she will check with her neighbour in Topaz City to see if there's an empty flat there. Topaz is the new complex in front of Galleria Mall. They even have an artificial lake."

"It does not sound quite like the Kolkata you miss," Maneka said quietly, hoping he was prepared to see the ways in which his hometown too must have changed since he had left. Places had a way of doing that.

Her father focused on his burger, eating messily as usual. A strand of lettuce stuck to his chin. Maneka suspected that he had heard her, but had chosen not to respond. She missed the cheerful mood he had been in a minute ago.

"Everyone seems quite involved," she added. "Everyone likes to get involved in Kolkata."

"Yes, exactly. There will be plenty of company. Not like here where there is no one to share a drink with."

At least he would not be alone. He would have all the pishis and mashis, kakus and jethus, as well as his old colleagues and friends from college. He even had friends from elementary school. Unlike her, he had stayed in touch with many of them, and they didn't even need Facebook to do it. Maneka saw him sitting on a verandah somewhere, drinking Scotch with his friends, attending religious rituals all year long in Topaz City or wherever he moved to, enjoying the veneration reserved for seniors there. Unlike her own life in Heathersfield, where she could hear a snowflake drop to the ground, his would be full of sounds.

"And Chaya will be with you," she said.

He nodded. They were both quiet, thinking about the girl who had stopped smiling this past week. She had stopped going downstairs to chat with her girlfriends. When Maneka looked at her, she quickly averted her face. Once, when Maneka suddenly walked into the kitchen, she saw Chaya wiping her eyes with her turmeric-stained sleeve. She had asked her what was wrong, but Chaya only shook her head and mumbled something about a friend not being well. She had gone to Maneka's father one morning when Maneka was still asleep, and asked if she could move with him after all.

"She will make new friends there," her father said to Maneka.

"Everyone needs friends." He looked at his daughter, his brows furrowed in concern.

"I have friends too," she protested.

"You need good friends, Mishti. Not crazy people like that girl in Magnolia Gardens."

"It was an accident," she whispered.

She tried to conjure up Ramona's face, serene and ethereal like she had appeared at Magnolia Gardens three months ago when Maneka had had a proper conversation with her for the first time. She remembered a maroon dress and a profile, the mist of a floral fragrance, an air of watchfulness. But she could not, for the life of her, recall her face. Instead, what she saw, again and again, was Ramona as a teenager, standing in front of the school gate in Kolkata, whispering to the other beautiful girls while the boys across the street watched them. She remembered her vision of Ramona and what she had stood for. Everything beautiful and unattainable, everything worth aspiring to.

"Maybe someday you can buy a flat again in Kolkata," she said to her father. "I could help when I've earned tenure."

"Mishti, does it really matter?" he asked. "Whether I own the flat I live in? So long as I can go to Lake Market to buy fresh fish on Sundays, and have my friends over for a drink and a nice dinner once in a while, and so long as you are married and happy and we are both healthy. If Ma had worried less about such things . . ." He left the thought unfinished.

If her mother had been there with them now, she would have enjoyed this meal very much. They would have reminisced about relatives and made plans for the following summer. They would have slept under the same roof, a roof they owned or not, what difference did it make? Maneka missed home. She had been missing home all summer. She had missed it, in fact, since the day she left India for the first time, long before their flat was sold. Because home was wherever her mother was, wherever her parents had left traces of their lives. And what had Ramona missed so deeply that she couldn't live without it? Why had Maneka never asked her? Why had she never paid attention?

She turned to the one who was left.

"Will you be all right, Baba? Are you sure you don't want me to come back during the winter break and go with you?"

"Rubbish. Why will you come all the way again in a few months? I moved here before; I can move back."

He wasn't alone then, she wanted to remind him. But he held his hand up to stop her because he did not need reminding.

"Will someone come to the airport to pick you up?" he asked, pivoting the concern back to her.

He knew the answer to that too. She shook her head anyway.

Mike had offered. She had declined.

"I am used to this, Baba."

"What movie will we watch tonight?" her father asked quickly, perhaps to change the subject. He seemed so determined to be cheerful these last few days.

"*Rebecca*," she replied. "I want to watch Manderlay burn down."

Three days before her departure, it could not be put off any longer. Jessica and Maneka made their way up the lift at Magnolia Gardens, past the nonexistent thirteenth floor, to the fourteenth, where Maneka found herself once again in front of the window with the crack running through it.

It reminded her of the first time she had come here three months ago. How envious she had been of the Singhs. She wanted someone new to envy now. Envy felt like hope. If there was someone out there who was completely happy or fulfilled or beautiful, that meant there was something to aspire to, long for, dream of. If everyone was broken, then who would pick up the pieces of them?

Maneka traced her finger along the crack caked with dust. It looked like the bolt of lightning she had wanted so desperately to catch on film that afternoon with Ashok on those barren grounds of what could have been Jannat. Heaven.

The interior of Ramona's flat was as spotless as ever. Maneka almost expected to find Ramona's beautiful, untouched figure lying on the marble tiles like a sculpture. She searched for her presence in the flat but failed to find it. The living room was impersonal, like the lobby of an expensive hotel. People could come and go and leave no trace of themselves behind.

The servants brought them glasses of iced tea, a departure from the past that signalled the presence of the aunties. Sure enough, they were informed that the parents were all there too.

"Let's not stay long," Maneka muttered to Jessica, who was looking around at the splashes of colour as if she couldn't recognize them from before.

Jessica's hands trembled as she picked up her glass and swallowed hard.

The burgundy velvet drapes at the french doors were pulled across, leaving no inch of open space for the sunlight to enter. It was as if there were nothing beyond, no terrace, no flowerpots, no skyline. Maneka glanced at it from time to time, but Jessica kept her gaze firmly away.

When Salil came out to greet them, Maneka heard Jessica draw her breath. His beard was gone, along with its salt-and-pepper traces. He looked younger and his face was scrubbed and blank as if he had been washed of memories. He held out his hands to Maneka, looked her straight in the eyes, and spoke in a voice she had not heard before. Gone was that affected breezy tone in which he used to dismiss everything. He sounded almost normal.

He told them that he and his partner Harry had decided to sell their shares of the company. He hoped to get a job in Mumbai now and, later, farther, perhaps Singapore or Melbourne.

"Maybe, someday, America?" Maneka asked.

"Never say never," he said.

He thanked them for coming and said other friends from their school had been trickling in that week as well. Maneka had seen the Facebook posts and WhatsApp group messages with shared memories of adolescent parties and snatches of conversations over the years. She had heard some of the theories being volleyed back and forth. Someone had suggested that Ramona had been pushed by that upstart husband of hers. *But he had not been at home*, Maneka had typed in his defence.

When Ramona's mother emerged from one of the inner rooms, Maneka expected to feel tongue-tied and shy just as she used to back in school when the fashionable mothers came to collect their daughters. But instead, she felt pity. Mrs Kaul, dressed in black slacks and a grey-and-white pinstriped shirt, was as elegant as she remembered. Her face was made up to look like it was not and her hair was perfectly coiffed, glossy and smooth, almost as if it were a wig. The only difference was the colour. It was more auburn than all those years ago, the result of too many henna treatments. But it was her eyes Maneka was drawn to. Eyes swollen and shadowed with grief.

She looked Maneka up and down as if she could find answers in her appearance. Perhaps she would always look at everything now in this searching way, willing answers to appear like invisible ink on every surface.

"Are you a friend of Salil's?" she asked finally. Maneka detected the hint of suspicion in her voice.

"No, Aunty, I'm a friend of Ramona's. Was," she added. "From school."

"Burton House?" she asked, raising her eyebrows. Maneka nodded.

"I don't believe I remember ever meeting you back then," Ramona's mother said slowly, trying to recall. "I think I met all of Ramona's friends."

"No, Aunty, we never met," Maneka said, and the expression of doubt on the lady's face shifted into one of smug satisfaction. Her memory had not failed her. This was not a friend, after all.

No one cried during the visit. Not Ramona's impeccably dressed parents. Not Salil's mother, who waddled on her short, chubby frame from room to room, trying to pick up things and issue orders to the servants as if she needed to take control of her son's residence. Not Jessica, who talked too much, as if it was her sole responsibility to fill the silence. And certainly not Salil. He simply sat there with a slightly stunned look on his face, alone and out of place in his own home. But something told Maneka they all cried when no one was looking, which was more than she had done for either Ramona or her mother.

When they arrived downstairs, they discovered Ashok, pacing up and down with a cigarette dangling from his mouth. It seemed inevitable, like the final scene of a romantic comedy, that he and Maneka would meet here again, like this. He had not shaved in a few days. The thick stubble made him look even sexier than he had on that first night out on Ramona's terrace.

"Are you on your way up?" Jessica asked. He shook his head. "I can't," he said.

Can't what, Maneka wondered. Can't enter the flat that might still smell of her? Or can't look at Salil? Or can't meet the parents? Or all of the above?

"Why not? We were there. It wasn't so bad," said Jessica. Ashok looked at Maneka but she quickly looked away, at the tops of buildings in the distance. Most of them were still there. She felt his eyes on her back as they all walked down the driveway together to wait for the Ola. There was no BMW to chauffeur them this time. It had not occurred to Salil that they might appreciate a ride.

"Do you think she was trying to hurt Salil? Or her parents?" Jessica asked. "Was she trying to make a statement, do you think?" Maneka was angry with her for implying that it was a deliberate act. She hated the thought that this would grow into a scandal in the months and years to come. The beautiful girls would pass the story on to their children, who would talk about it at their reunions. *Remember Ramona?*

"It was an accident," Maneka said with her teeth clenched. Anyone could topple over the wall of a fourteenth-floor terrace.

But Jessica had already climbed into the cab.

Maneka heard Ashok call her name as she was about to follow.

She turned around and looked past him at the waterfall cascading down the wall.

"The last time I saw her, an evening I replay in my mind like a loop, she said she was sad you were leaving. She said that spending time with you was like going back home. She asked me if we had, you know . . ." His voice trailed off but he kept his eyes on her. "I said no. So, I just wanted you to know that she didn't know."

Maneka closed her eyes in relief. When she opened them, she saw him, more clearly than before.

"Thanks, Ashok."

He held the door open for her.

"Will you be all right?" She looked at him.

He nodded, but as he did so, he focused on some distant spot behind her as if looking at her directly might blind him. His eyes were narrowed slightly, in search of something. When the car reached the gate and she turned around to look back one last time, he was still there, a forlorn, solitary figure staring into the distance.

Maneka turned her gaze upwards at the tall cluster of pastel-pink buildings. One of those flats had been Ramona's home. One of those terraces was where she had stood every night and gazed out at a skyline both real and imaginary. Maneka imagined a willowy figure rising up in the air above the buildings, where it floated like a cloud, looking down on the city, waving, waving, waving, until the car turned the corner and all that remained was the blinding white sky.

The morning of her departure, Maneka was woken at the crack of dawn by music blaring on loudspeakers. She lay in bed for a while, listening to patriotic songs, before making her way to the balcony. Her father sat in a wicker chair, watching the sky lighten and sipping his morning tea. At this time, the air was almost cool and the balcony lay in shade.

As soon as Maneka sat down, Chaya brought her a cup of milky sweet ginger-flecked tea, just the way she liked it, and a plate of biscuits. Chaya had not said much the last few days. But she made her special french toast with tomatoes and cheese and extra green chillies for breakfast one morning without waiting to be asked. She changed the bedsheets every day and dusted all the books on the nightstand even though they didn't need dusting.

"Chaya," Maneka called after her. "Give me your hand." Chaya did it reluctantly, aware of what was coming. Maneka curled the wad of notes in her fist.

"Na, Didi," she said. "I don't need money."

"But you must keep it," she said. For washing all her bras by hand and not ruining them in the washer like she did back in Heathersfield, she wanted to say. "It's a bribe so you take care of my baba. And yourself."

The tears in Chaya's eyes made Maneka jealous. It was so easy for them to cry.

The building next to theirs, right outside the complex, was only five floors tall, which allowed an unobstructed view of the flat roof. Occasionally Maneka had sighted young boys, maybe the sons of domestic helpers or daily-wage earners who lived in the chawls nearby, playing cricket on that roof. Her attention was always drawn to them by the loud cheers. Today, however, the roof was empty. She wished she had woken up early enough on other days. She felt like she had missed out on an important part of the city's life.

Down below, maids began to trickle in one by one. One of the darwans washed a car by hosing it first and then wiping it down. An old man with a head of white hair stretched slowly in white pajamas and a kurta. In the middle of the communal lawn, preparations had been made for a flag-hoisting ceremony later in the day. Like the rest of the city that week, their residence was festooned in little replicas of the Tricolour. It had been many years since Maneka had been in the country on this day.

Suddenly, a harsh cry pierced the early-morning silence. It was a cry Maneka had occasionally heard at daybreak when she was still half asleep. But today, her father rose to his feet and yelled.

"Look at that. Mishti, you have to see this. Chaya, Chaya, come look."

She and Chaya followed him to the other end of the balcony and peered at the next-door roof to see what he was pointing at. A peacock was slowly unfurling its feathers. They spread out behind it in a circle of green. The bird's neck was an electric blue. It danced for a few minutes while a low, rumbling sound, almost like thunder, reverberated in the air. It was the first time that Maneka had seen a peacock's tail open like that. It looked like the creature was fanning the world, trying to help it cool down.

~

From a distance the airport looked like an aquarium. All those people trapped like fish behind the glass doors. Their families thronging outside, unable to go beyond the roped-off areas to say a proper goodbye or give a last hug. Those leaving and those left behind.

Maneka had done this before, but never from this bustling, important airport. And never on Independence Day when the capital was on red alert for potential acts of terrorism. But still, the sequence of steps returned to her like the instinctive moves of a lover. She went through the motions with practised efficiency, ensuring that the physical actions pushed any emotions below the surface. She pulled a cart, hoisted her heavy bags on to it, wrapped her cardigan around her waist, turned to her father to say goodbye. He wore a gaudy yellow T-shirt and smelt faintly of Old Spice.

"Do you have everything?" he asked.

The grey car stood like an open-mouthed whale, its trunk gaping wide. The car that had taken her parents across the country to a new life and then on little road trips to forests, hill stations, and historic cities across North India for five years. The car was better acquainted with the last years of their lives together than she would ever be.

"Take care of yourself," he said, hugging her with only one arm like he always did, too shy for a more overt gesture of affection.

She wanted to return the advice, but it would only sound inane.

The line of passengers in front of her was growing by the minute.

"You should go home. It's late."

"Certainly not. I will park and then come back and wait here until the aeroplane has taken off. In case there is any problem with your bags or anything else."

After she had checked in, she returned to the entrance, where a surly guard sat on a stool and twirled his moustache. No amount of pleading would move him. She was not permitted to step out with her boarding pass.

"No, Madam," he said without even glancing at her.

"I just want to say bye to my father once. Look, there he is."

She pressed her face to the glass. Behind the tape, her father waved and summoned a smile. Then, suddenly, he came forward, crossed the barrier with his rickety knees, and was at the entrance.

"Did you have to pay for excess baggage?" he asked.

"Of course. But it was only a hundred dollars." She knew he would not feel as bad about the sum if she didn't convert it for him.

He touched her face with his calloused hands.

"Try to sleep a little on the flight and send me a message when you arrive."

"It will be very late for you. I can call when you wake up."

"No, send me a message. I will be awake, waiting to hear from you."

"Okay, Baba. Don't worry."

A wooden stick appeared between them.

"Saab, back, back, you cannot come inside without a plane ticket." The guard shot them a look of reproach.

Maneka looked back once to wave cheerily at her father, whose yellow T-shirt looked too loud against the night. Then she remembered that he had chosen to wear it so he would stand out, in case she needed to spot him in the crowd. She saw the yellow in her mind all the way through the endless walk on the patterned carpet to the very last gate. It burnt like the sun had all summer.

While she waited for the flight to board, Maneka watched the people around her and recalled that first time she had left her country twelve years ago. For that departure, she'd had both parents next to her and a few friends too. She was in her early twenties, on her way to graduate school in a big city full of Indians. The departure for the West that had been recorded in so many postcolonial novels that it was hard to remember what was real and what was literary. The first time flying overseas, the first goodbye, the first customs check, the first stroll through duty-free. How alone she had been, how terrified. How young she had been then, when everything had seemed possible.

Unlike many others, she had not left for a better life or material comforts or to follow a husband. All of those would have perhaps been more easily attainable right here in her own country. No, she had left for adventure. To explore the unknown. A journey that would never end. Not as long as you kept moving.

Out of nowhere came the vision again of the beautiful girls seated on the green lawn of their colonial high school. The girls threw their heads back and laughed carelessly. Their joy was infectious. In the centre of the circle sat Ramona, smiling in contentment like the Buddha, assured that her life would always turn out the way she wanted it to. This time, instead of the familiar resentment bubbling up inside, Maneka felt pity. For Ramona, for her mother, for the foolish, delusional people who had invested in Trump Towers and other properties in Hrishipur, for the stranger who had perished in the fire, for Chaya with her secret longings and heartbreaks, for all those she would never meet in her lifetime who were condemned to the cycle of hope and disappointment. Yes, even for the beautiful girls.

For even when she was in a different country, Maneka had carried them with her. It had never really been about them after all. It had been about her childhood. The years lost, consigned now to sudden flashbacks in unexpected places.

When everyone was settled in their seats and the lights dimmed for takeoff, Maneka leant back. Somewhere in the aisle, flight attendants were demonstrating security precautions. Out in the white lights of the tarmac, men in orange vests were carrying stairs away, walking around, inspecting. The minutes seemed endless. The world outside was washed in a late-night blue tint from all the pollution.

She knew her father was still outside the airport, standing quietly in his garish yellow T-shirt, looking up at the sky, wondering which of the aeroplane taking off carried his daughter. He would lie awake until she texted him from Heathersfield. In a couple of months, he would pack and move once more and head back to the city where he had been born. A year later, Maneka would visit him there. In a lifetime of fresh starts it would be just one more.

Before switching off her cell phone, she sent her father a final text. *See you in Kolkata.*

She turned off the phone and slipped the SIM card out, thus cutting herself off from everyone in India once more. In a total of twenty hours, she would be in Heathersfield.

Her mother would have loved the town. She would have marvelled at the cherry blossoms that drifted to the ground in the spring, the silver lakes and white beaches in the summer, the splendour of fall colours along winding trails in the autumn, and of course the snow. She had always wanted to see snow. Snow that blanketed the ground and branches of trees and rooftops and windowsills until everything was buried underneath. Snow that fell so quietly you didn't realize it was coming until you woke up and went to the window and saw the world had turned as white as it did in the American comic books of your childhood. Snow that was both beautiful and treacherous, tearing your heart in two. Snow that washed everything clean so that life could begin anew.

Maneka pressed her face against the glass of the window as the aeroplane skidded down the runway. Her shoulders shook with her sobs. She could not remember the last time she had cried. It felt like she was finally being released from some invisible creature's grip.

As the plane rose in the air, the specks of light scattered across Hrishipur, with pockets of black woven in here and there, became smaller and smaller. Then, the clouds swept below the Boeing 777 like a curtain across a stage. In an instant, the city, with its individual and collective stories, had disappeared from view. And all that was left was the dark, deep unknown and a window streaked with her tears. Several minutes after she had stopped crying, the glass continued to streak. She wiped the surface with her palm but it misted over instantly. She squinted to look more closely. There was no mistaking it. It lashed the window and ran down the glass in sheets. The night was wet with rain.

ACKNOWLEDGMENTS

IT TAKES MANY PEOPLE TO HELP BUILD A DREAM, MORE THAN I could possibly list here.

I feel fortunate to be part of the Tin House family and shall be forever indebted to them for opening their submissions to unagented authors for two days and thereby changing my life. Thanks to their entire talented and dedicated team. Special thanks to Diane Chonette for designing the stunning cover. And, of course, my eternal gratitude to editor extraordinaire Elizabeth DeMeo for championing *The Dream Builders* and for helping me make it the best novel it can be.

This book has gone through many revisions, and I owe much to its early readers. Thanks to Chitra Banerjee Divakaruni and the others in my writers' group—Keya Mitra Lloyd, Irene Keliher, Zack Bean, Nick Brown, Will Donnelly—who provided honest and thoughtful feedback, without which my novel would never have seen the light of day. Thanks to Samrat Upadhyay for his faith in this book when I was on the verge of giving up. And thanks to Paromita Chatterjee for taking on the role of unofficial fact checker in India.

A very early version of the first chapter was workshopped at the 2016 Sewanee Writers' Conference, where Jill McCorkle and Steve Yarbrough's words of encouragement helped lay the foundation for the novel. And it was in the serene surroundings of the Virginia Center for the Creative Arts three years later that I began revising the first complete draft of the manuscript.

Grand Valley State University has been my home for over a decade. Thanks to GVSU's Center for Scholarly and Creative Excellence for awarding me several grants that allowed me to travel to India for the immersive research this book needed. I am especially grateful to my colleagues in the Department of Writing for their support and friendship.

Thanks to the editors who published my work in their journals; those publications kept me going. A modified version of Pinky's chapter, published in *Ecotone* and beautifully edited by Anna Lena, set the standard for the rest of the book.

Many thanks to Renée Zuckerbrot, Angie Cruz, Caitlin Horrocks, Keith Lee Morris, and everyone else who shared their valuable insights with me, especially when I didn't have an agent.

I would like to thank everyone at the University of Florida's MFA program who made me feel welcome when I first arrived in America twenty years ago, and especially David Leavitt for his wisdom through the years. Thanks to the University of Houston's graduate creative writing program for providing the best community a writer could ever hope for, and to Inprint Houston for supporting my work with awards and fellowships. And thanks, also, to Emory University for the two-year Creative Writing Fellowship during which I learnt how to write (and how not to write) a novel.

The friends who have accompanied me on this journey all these years, and especially during the lonely months of the pandemic when I was trying to finish *The Dream Builders*, have my love and gratitude. You know who you are. Kakoli Roy deserves a special mention for being more excited than anyone else about this book. My parents, Aloke and Sukla Mukherjee, who ignited the flame and kept it alive—Thank You for Everything.

Finally, my brilliant agent Jessica Friedman, who puts up with my endless questions, I am grateful to have you in my corner. Thank You for believing in this book and the stories I am yet to tell.

ABOUT THE AUTHOR

Oindrila Mukherjee grew up in Kolkata, India, and now resides in Grand Rapids, Michigan, where she teaches creative writing at Grand Valley State University.

30 Years *of*

HarperCollins *Publishers* India

At HarperCollins, we believe in telling the best stories and finding the widest possible readership for our books in every format possible. We started publishing 30 years ago; a great deal has changed since then, but what has remained constant is the passion with which our authors write their books, the love with which readers receive them, and the sheer joy and excitement that we as publishers feel in being a part of the publishing process.

Over the years, we've had the pleasure of publishing some of the finest writing from the subcontinent and around the world, and some of the biggest bestsellers in India's publishing history. Our books and authors have won a phenomenal range of awards, and we ourselves have been named Publisher of the Year the greatest number of times. But nothing has meant more to us than the fact that millions of people have read the books we published, and somewhere, a book of ours might have made a difference.

As we step into our fourth decade, we go back to that one word – a word which has been a driving force for us all these years.

Read.

Harper Collins · 4th · HARPER PERENNIAL · HARPER BUSINESS · HARPER BLACK · हार्पर हिन्दी

HarperCollins *Children's Books* · HARPER DESIGN · HARPER VANTAGE · Harper Sport